The Complete]
Brief (
Books 1 - 8
by
Andrea Frazer

The Complete Falconer Files Brief Cases
Books 1 - 8
Andrea Frazer
This edition published by JDI Publications 2023
Copyright 2013 by Andrea Frazer
The right of Andrea Frazer to be identified as the Author of the
Work has been asserted by her in accordance with the Copyright,
Designs and Patents Act, 1988

Other books by Andrea Frazer
The Belchester Chronicles
Strangeways to Oldham
White Christmas with a Wobbly Knee
Snowballs and Scotch Mist
Old Moorhen's Shredded Sporran
Caribbean Sunset with a Yellow Parrot
God Rob Ye Merry Gentlemen
The Falconer Files
Death of an Old Git
Choked Off
Inkier than the Sword
Pascal Passion
Murder at the Manse
Music to Die For
Strict and Peculiar
Christmas Mourning
Grave Stones
Death in High Circles
Glass House
Bells and Smells
Shadows and Sins
Nuptial Sacrifice
The Fine Line
High Wired
Tightrope
Holmes and Garden
The Curious Case of the Black Swansong
The Bookcase of Sherman Holmes
Other Titles
Choral Mayhem
Down and Dirty in the Dordogne

A Fresh of Breath Air

Author's note

Brief Cases is an occasional series of short stories, used as a device to record the times between the full-length works of The Falconer Files. They confirm that life does go on in the meantime, between big cases, and that not everything they work on together is of the highest priority. I hope you enjoy reading them as much as I have enjoyed writing them.

The books in this collection

Book 1. Love Me To Death

On Christmas Day the two detectives are summoned to a block of apartments in Market Darley, to investigate the unexplained death of a young woman whose fiancé was due to move in with her on New Year's Day.

At first, her death seems a complete mystery, then, something that Dr Christmas discovers on the internet indicates that her death could just have been a tragic accident, or was it?

Book 2. A Sidecar Named Expire

A young man and his girlfriend decide to celebrate their first St Valentine's Day together, with a cosy evening of cocktails at her house. But as the evening progresses, events don't go quite as Malcolm Standing planned.

The next morning, DI Falconer and DS Carmichael are called in to try to sort out what really happened.

Book 3. Battered To Death

DI Falconer and DS Carmichael are both enjoying a well-earned rest day, when they are summoned to a most distressing incident that has occurred at a chip shop on the parade of shops in Upper Darley.

It was obviously murder, but was it something to do with the robust behaviour of some of the more aggressive customers from the night before or was it closer to home?

Book 4. Toxic Gossip

DI Falconer becomes involved in a gossip-fuelled hate crime, only to find himself questioning his own judgement when it comes to protecting Miriam Darling from her anonymous persecutors...

Book 5. Driven To It

Abigail Wentworth is looking forward to her reunion lunch with Alison Fairweather. They are old schoolfriends who met twice a year, usually for Alison to dish the dirt on the others they had known when they were younger - and for Abigail to gloat over their 'inferior' circumstances, in comparison to her own respectable existence.

During lunch, though, Abigail recognizes a face from the past - and from that moment onward, her life skids completely out of control...

Book 6. All Hallows

Harry Falconer is summoned to an address in Carsfold on the evening of 31st October when a man is found dead in his garden, a hollowed-out pumpkin jammed over his head, and his garden shed blown-up and fire-damaged.

Carmichael is immediately summoned to join him and, together, they interrogate the victim's neighbours, uncovering a plethora of damaged and broken relationships, in their search for his killer.

Book 7. Written Out

A regional television programme, Get One Over, where amateurs search for and discover antiques and valuable objects in junk shops, has captured the nation's zeitgeist and gone nationwide.

The Christmas episode is to be filmed in Market Darley, and being antiques fans, Miss Emily Jarvis, and DI Falconer and DS Carmichael plan to be in town to bump into the stars of the programme.

But on a crispy cold December morning, as the chase around the town to find the TV stars continues, it proves to be a terminal performance for one of their number.

Book 8. Death of a Pantomime Cow

DI Harry Falconer has managed to duck two days spent over the festive season in the Carmichael household by pleading other commitments, but treating the whole family, himself included, to tickets to the first performance, on Boxing Day.

But he seems to be able to do nothing straight forward, and when tragedy strikes in the very first Act, he is catapulted back into his professional role with a vengeance: and on a Bank Holiday, too.

Love Me To Death

On Christmas Day the two detectives are summoned to a block of apartments in Market Darley, to investigate the unexplained death of a young woman whose fiancé was due to move in with her on New Year's Day.

At first, her death seems a complete mystery, then, something that Dr Christmas discovers on the internet indicates that her death could just have been a tragic accident, or was it?

CHRISTMAS 2009

<u>STAVE ONE</u>

Death's Shade

25th December, 2009

Harry Falconer spread garlic and tarragon butter evenly over the skin of the guinea fowl, wrapped it with fragrant whispers of Parma ham, and placed it lovingly in his cast-iron casserole dish, over a bed of sliced potatoes, julienne carrots, celery sticks, bay leaves and thinly sliced onion. This he placed in a wall cupboard, to keep it at room temperature and away from his Siamese's alter-ego, Mycroft, and his two more recently acquired cats, Tar Baby and Ruby, until it was time to pop it into the oven.

Returning to his sitting room, he surveyed with satisfaction the perfectly trimmed tree in the window, its fibre optics twinkling and reflecting in the copper and gold-coloured glass baubles that had complied with this year's colour co-ordinated design. Only gold lametta hung from its branches and, at its apex, he could almost hear the singing of the pure white plaster bird with its delicate touches of gold leaf, its tail and wings like gatherings of delicate glass threads; a bird of peace and glad tidings, rather like an avian angel.

No cards crowded his mantel; rather did they hang suspended on golden ribbons from the picture rail, even spaced around the room. The mantelpiece did, however, contain some gesture to the traditions of the season, in that it was draped in ivy, freshly bought the day before, and holly and mistletoe sat atop this where it topped the fireplace.

The radio was tuned to a Christmas morning Eucharist broadcast, and the blood-stirring harmonies of Tavener's 'The Lamb' floated through the air, dramatic, simple, yet complex at the same time, and inviting nostalgia and wonder anew at the Christmas story and its implications for mankind, but this latter meant little to Falconer. He was listening to this, as he had the Carols from King's, broadcast the day before.

His parents had never bothered about the religious aspects of Christmas, being too busy swilling champagne and cocktails, and entertaining, to let that sort of thing bother them. The real reason he turned on such broadcasts was because the army padre always insisted that, at Christmas, if at no other time in the church calendar, his 'lads' would get a bit of BBC church, whether they liked it or not (even if the men did sing alternative words to the carols, to bait their spiritual adviser, and draw his ire). Listening to these broadcasts, now that he had left the army, flooded Falconer with a warm glow of nostalgia.

Falconer's eyes swept over to the area below the tree, where a pile of small wrapped offerings had been meticulously arranged, and he smiled as he remembered what he had chosen for Mycroft, and the other two cats, and would present them with, after they had partaken of their meal. Then, of course, there would be the Queen's speech to attend to, something that had been part of his Christmas Day since as long as he could remember, and which he had never missed, no matter where in the world he had been.

He smiled contentedly, as he realised how right he had been to decline (impeccably politely) his family's invitations – exhortations, even – to spend Christmas with them, their gaudy decorations, cocktail parties and false gaiety. For he had not grown to their pattern – he was not the social animal manqué; did not share their vast spider's web of friends, associates and acquaintances. Of course, their joint profession had fashioned their form, but he was different: he had not carried on the family tradition of the call of the Bar and had, as a result, become a more introspective person, who was happy both in his own skin, and company. He was self-sufficient, and at Christmas, as a rule, he was not a social animal.

As The Lamb gave way to a reading – And there were shepherds in the fields abiding – his contented reverie was shattered by the brash ringing of the telephone. He rolled his eyes, knowing it wasn't

Aunt Ursula to wish him the compliments of the season, nor his mother Hermione with a last minute plea for him to join them and 'have some fun' for once in his life.

No, it would be work that was causing this untimely intrusion into the privacy of his celebrations, as it so often had in the past. Christmas was not a time of peace and goodwill, and of quiet contemplation, when you were a policeman. Picking up the telephone, he turned his steps back to the kitchen, to place his delectable but still raw game bird in the refrigerator.

It had been Superintendent 'Jelly' Chivers himself, who had summoned him, in tones both abrupt and imperious. Chivers never minced his words and, given the chance, called a spade a bloody shovel. He had risen to his present position through the ranks, with no buffer of a degree to set him on the road for fast-track promotion. It was said of him that, beneath his carapace of steel, lay a heart of pure flint. His diplomatic skills could be scored with a minus number, and it was rumoured in the staff canteen that he was an alien, originating from the planet 'Bastard'.

On the phone, Falconer was being told, and told good and proper. Chivers expected this whole mess to be cleared up today, and would accept no excuses for failure; failure, for him, being a dereliction of duty. As Falconer hung up, he thought, with a rueful smile, that old 'Jelly' would no doubt have a luxurious and happy day, celebrating in his own inimitable way, with his friends and family. What a pity the superintendent could not have left him alone, to celebrate Christmas in his own fashion.

Outside, the air was as sharp and biting as ice, a frost still underfoot. Overhead, thick banks of clouds were rolling in, to encase the day, as if under a Victorian glass dome – a December tableau to be picked up and shaken, to let loose the snowflakes for some giant child's amusement.

Pulling his cashmere scarf a little more securely over the shocked skin of his lower face, he headed towards his car, and the inevitability of what lay ahead of him. For one person at least, there was to be no Merry Christmas, no Happy New Year: just a pit of despair, loneliness, grief, and 'what ifs.' Life would go on, but not for one soul in the vicinity today, and for another it will be perceived as time standing still, as death mocks from the side-lines.

Shaking such sombre wraiths of thought from his mind, he started the engine of his car, and pondered on what he had learned from the telephone call. There had been a death in a block of apartments near the town centre. Not unusual at this time of year, for someone to depart this life, if only to avoid yet another Merry Christmas of jolly family arguments and seasonal acrimony, but it was usually an elderly or very sick person that chose this season of the year to shake off his or her mortal coil.

But this had been the death of a healthy young woman; in her prime, not at death's door. According to her fiancé, he had left her safe and well the previous evening, had let himself in with his own key this morning, for they had planned for him to move in with her on New Year's Day, only to find her dead, in the bed that was to have been theirs, in just a week's time.

There were no signs of a break-in, nothing was apparently missing, and there were no signs of violence on her body. It was her enjoyed youth and health that had flagged this as an unexplained death that would bear just the ghost of an investigation. A post mortem would probably provide a perfectly reasonable but unexpected cause but, for now, all avenues had to be explored, and this must be treated as it was being treated, as an unexplained death, with the police in attendance, in case there arose any hint of suspicion that this was an intended death, at the hands of another.

Superintendent Chivers had been more than forceful in his opinion of the rightness of their course of action, on today of all days. He had been insistent. He had a horror of unpleasantness in the press, and anti-police opinion, and was even prepared to interrupt the celebrations of the newly-appointed police surgeon to investigate the possibilities of a physical cause for her demise.

Acting DS 'Davey' Carmichael met him just outside the entrance lobby to the block of apartments, as unmoved by the slicing inclemency of the temperature as a giant would be by the passage of an ant. "Merry Christmas, sir," he boomed into the frozen void, his breath the phantom of a past bonfire, issuing from his lips in smoky clouds.

"Merry Christmas to you and yours, Carmichael," the inspector replied, and added, "and now we'd better get on with whatever awaits us here, for that'll be no merry Christmas. Why are such things sent at this time of year? Why does fate play games with the date for misfortune, ensuring there will be no other memories than this, on this day, every year, for the rest of people's lives?"

"Dunno, sir," mumbled Carmichael, almost looking upwards, as his superior's words shot over his head, to see if he could detect their flight-path. "Boyfriend's still up there, but the SOCO team's done its work, and they're just about to move the body. Better get up there, I suppose."

"You suppose right. It's really a public relations exercise for the old man, and his obsession with our relationship with the media, so the sooner we put our noses in, and declare everything clean and above board, the sooner we can get back to our respective households and recommence Christmas."

"Yes please, sir." Really, Carmichael was like a child – an exceedingly large child, notwithstanding – in his enthusiasm for this season of the year, and had been straining at the leash (more like a huge puppy now) since the first of December, eager for all the joys of Christmas shopping, Advent calendars, pine trees, paper streamers, cards, wrapping paper and carols. So intoxicated had the acting sergeant been by his seasonal love affair, that he had made Falconer seem like a re-incarnation of Ebenezer Scrooge himself.

Their office was hung with an abundance of paper chains and tinsel, a bunch of plastic mistletoe hung in the doorway, and a small silver tree stood on Carmichael's desk, hung with bright-coloured baubles, its lights winking on and off in an irritating way that drove Falconer nearly to distraction, and he couldn't wait for the New Year, so that his workspace could be returned to its normal, stark self.

This implied comparison to Scrooge, thought Falconer, wasn't really fair, as he had sent at least a dozen cards, bought gifts for the favoured few, decorated his home (according to his own lights – fibre-optic ones), and attended Midnight Mass the evening before. *So* he had no guests joining him today? *So* he was not spending the day with relatives or friends? Let Carmichael keep Christmas in *his* own way, and let him leave *him* alone, to celebrate it in *his*.

In the lobby of the building, they stopped to share what information they had gathered, from the phone calls that had separately summoned them to this address. Carmichael's call – lucky lad! – had originated from Bob Bryant, who was duty desk sergeant today. "Surely he's not on duty on Christmas Day? Does the man actually have no home to go to?" Falconer queried. The man was never off duty!

"He said the 999 call came through on the boyfriend's mobile. Apparently he just kept saying, "She's dead! She's dead! She's dead!" When Sergeant Bryant had managed to interrupt this three word obligato, he had been informed that the boyfriend and Miss Cater had spent the previous evening together, but he had returned to his own flat, so that he could wrap a very special present, which he planned to bring round this morning. He had already brought her other presents round to her apartment, but this had been something out of the ordinary, which she was not expecting."

"Lot of detail!" Falconer had commented.

"Seems that once Bob had got him going, he couldn't shut him up. 'Spose it must have been the shock. It gets some of them like that, doesn't it, sir? Anyway, he came round here, yesterday, late afternoon, they put up the tree – very last minute, because both of them had been so busy at work – then they had a meal and a quiet evening in. He left about midnight, he thinks, to go and wrap up this secret present, and not be too late to bed so that he could be round here first thing."

"Surely he could have wrapped her present at the office?"

Falconer's gaze moved slowly round the lobby in which they stood. The mansion block had been built in the thirties; outside, a tall, decorated pine tree stood to attention on each side of the double doors, each a fairy-land of white lights and silver stars. In here the lobby had been restored to its original character, obviously at some expense to the residents, and another large tree adorned this space: conveniently placed in a corner, beside the elevator doors. Its decorations were either original period pieces, or carefully copied reproductions.

The inspector's gaze, initially approving, shifted minimally to allow a shadow of uncertainty to enter his expression. One whole wall was taken up with burr walnut glass-fronted display cabinets, gleaming with the regular loving attention of beeswax. There were three of these, perfectly abutted, and all internally illuminated. The one on the left displayed a fine collection of Art Deco figurines in bronze, the one on the right, a similarly fine collection of elegant ladies, this time in impeccably painted porcelain.

It was the display cabinet in the middle that had given Falconer pause for thought. It boasted a proliferation of Clarice Cliff pieces, brazen in their gaudy rainbow hues and, although they were period-perfect to be included in this fine horde of objets d'art, he found their inclusion puzzling. The figurines, he could accept, but

Clarice Cliff had originally been offered for sale in, of all places, Woolworth's.

In his opinion, the interior designer responsible for this ostentatious display of thirties finery, should have played the snob – so unacceptable in the twenty-first century – and realised, that, though the period was correct, the class was just *so* wrong. Becoming aware of Carmichael's voice, he shook his head to free his mind from such unworthy thoughts, and returned, reluctantly, to the here and now.

"What do we know about the deceased, Carmichael?"

"Twenty-three years old. Single. Angela Cater. Clerical officer for the local authority. No brothers or sisters, no pets, no children. Doesn't smoke, doesn't drink, doesn't take drugs."

"Golly, Bob must've got a right earful! Do we know if she rents, or owns the property?"

"Not yet, sir, but the bereaved gentleman will, no doubt, provide you with the information, if he's in the same loquacious state he was in when he phoned Bob."

"No doubt. Press the button for the lift. I'm beginning to suffer from era confusion, standing here."

<u>STAVE TWO</u>

The First Spirit – The Ghost of Christmas Ruined

25th December, 2009 – a little later

The flat, when they entered it, was immaculately tidy, decorated, and dressed in the manner of its era. There was a proliferation of art deco furniture and knick-knacks, and the wallpaper and flooring were also in sympathy with this shift in time. Appropriate paper chains hung from the ceiling of the living room, which also housed a magnificent decorated fir tree, its presence made possible by the elegant proportions of the rooms of the apartment. At its foot were several brightly wrapped parcels, their wrapping paper blowing a raspberry to the art deco period and gaudily boasting their twenty-first century origins.

"Where was she found? In the bedroom? Which door do we need?" From their position just inside the front door they could see into the sitting room, but from the grand hall there were six other doors, all firmly closed to them.

At the sound of Falconer's voice, a door opened on the left-hand side of the hall, to reveal PC Green, Dr Christmas, and a white-faced young man, his head in his hands, seated at the stool in front of the dressing table. His position hid any view of the all too overwhelming presence of his girlfriend's body on the bed, eiderdown and bedclothes now flung aside, her nakedness barely concealed by a skimpy nightgown, incongruous in such dignified and respectable surroundings.

Seeing them at the door, Dr Christmas made to leave the room, leaving PC Green to guard the couple who had planned to spend the rest of their lives together, now irrevocably separated by the great black void of death.

"It's a bit of a stumper," commented Doc Christmas, scratching his head. "She was in perfect health before, but there are signs that she might have had some sort of severe allergic shock. Either that, or she's been poisoned. I won't have any firm idea, until I've sliced her open and done the business."

Falconer shuddered at the matter-of-fact way Christmas referred to the slicing and dicing of a post mortem, and hoped he'd never find himself under such off-hand hands (sic). "What I need to know is whether or not you suspect foul play?" stated the inspector.

"At this point, I've no idea. There was a Medic-Alert bracelet on the bedside table, indicating that she had an intolerance to peanuts, but the boyfriends said they were both vigilant, in ensuring that nothing that contained nuts ever entered the house.

"Apparently, if she travelled anywhere by plane, she would request that peanuts were not served to the other passengers, because of the re-circulated air – we really were better off when they stuck the smokers at the back of the plane, and pumped through fresh air, but that's an entirely different subject."

"I'll go and have a word with him myself," Falconer declared. "But, before I go in there, what's his name?"

"Dominic Cutler."

"Change the name and not the letter; change for worse, and not for better," piped up Carmichael, then subsided in a glowing blush, as the other two men shot him disapproving stares. "Sorry. I suppose it's the date they were going to move in together, that's unsettled me. That's the date that Kerry and I are going to get married."

"I know, Carmichael, I know. I'm going to be your best man, for my sins – may God have mercy on my soul – so I can hardly forget, can I?" said Falconer, with the look of a condemned man on his face.

"Oh, congratulations, Davey," added Dr Christmas, holding out a hand to shake the sergeant's.

"Thank you very much. I'm sorry about that comment just now. It just slipped out."

"Already forgotten, my boy. You've got work to do here, with old Harry, before you can kneel before the altar and plight your troth."

"I don't know what that means," said Carmichael, "referring to a church and all, but I hope it's not rude. And anyway, we're not having a big church 'do'. Remember Kerry's been married before, and she just wants something quiet and dignified."

"And a little less of the 'old', if you don't mind. You're a few years my senior, I know for a fact. Now, let's get back to the matter in hand," declared Falconer, firmly stamping on the tangent that had led them astray so effortlessly. "I need to speak to that chap in there, see what he has to say about last night, and that young lady's allergy."

He spoke to Dominic Cutler in the sitting room, just a few feet from the Christmas tree, and felt a heel for so doing, but he had little choice in the matter, not wanting to have to take the young man to the police station, on today of all days, for questioning.

"Tell me about yesterday, Mr Cutler; from the moment you left work, to the moment you arrived here this morning. I know how painful this must be for you, but we must get this matter cleared up. For all we know, someone with a key may have entered the premises during the night and murdered Miss Cater, so we need to know everything that we can about what happened in those hours. I'm sure you understand the necessity."

Dominic Cutler shook his head, as a dog does when getting out of water, maybe to clear his thoughts, so that he could converse in a rational manner.

"Let's start with where Miss Cater worked, and whether she owned this flat, or rented it," suggested Falconer, desperate to get the young man to tell him something – anything – to get him started.

"She worked for the local authority as a clerical officer, but she had no need to work: she did it because she needed something to occupy her time. Her parents are very wealthy – my God! This will destroy them – and actually own this apartment block, and this particular one's been signed over to her. That's why she lived here: so that she could have her independence, and still be under her father's care, if you see what I mean. If there had been any high jinks, it would have been reported to him by the concierge – complaints about noise, and that sort of thing."

"I completely understand, Mr Cutler. And what about you? Do you come from wealthy stock as well?" Falconer asked, hoping for an answer in the negative.

"As a matter of fact, I do," admitted Dominic. My parents have a huge house out in the countryside – quite isolated really – and it was them I went to see, after I'd wrapped Angela's tree presents yesterday, before I came here."

"Carry on," Falconer nudged him verbally, as he fell silent, and gazed off into the middle distance, maybe assessing the future life that would not now be his. Carmichael had tucked himself into a wooden-backed chair in a corner, folding himself on to its seat like a human ironing board, due to his height, and was busily taking notes, well-trained and needing no prompting, now that he was under Falconer's tutelage. Carmichael made a lot of furniture look as if it belonged in Lilliput, and not in people's everyday homes at all.

"We had originally planned to get married this Christmas, you see, but my father is very ill, and would not have been able to make the ceremony – that's why we postponed it, and I was just going to move in with her.

"I knew it would be the last Christmas Eve I would be able to do things the way that I had done them as a child. Father always used to read ghost stories, to everyone who was there for the celebrations, in front of a roaring fire, and crack nuts as he did so, for anyone who cared to have a munch on them. He wasn't fond of them himself, but he liked to crack them, and see others enjoying the 'nuts' of his labour. God! How can I make a pun when this has happened?" he asked, of no one in particular, except, maybe, himself.

"It was something my grandfather used to do," he continued, now recovered from the shock at his own unintentional words, "and he just carried on the tradition, as I had hoped to do, when Angela and I had a family to spend Christmas with." This last statement reduced the young man to tears again, and Falconer called in Dr Christmas, to see if he would give him a sedative, or something to make him sleep, then asked PC Green to run the bereaved man home, so that he could get some rest.

Unconscious was the best state for him, at the moment: a chance to let his mind work on all that had happened, and start to sort it out for him, so that he had everything in order, to deal with when he had had a little time for his subconscious to digest what had happened, and all the implications thereof. They could speak to him the next day, when maybe he'd be able to talk more coherently.

"Can you do something about opening her up?" Carmichael asked the doctor, a little stunned by the callous wording of his request.

"Nothing much on at the moment that can't wait," replied Christmas. "I can get on to it right away, if you want me to."

"Please. This peanut thing is nagging at me, and I need to know if she had any in her system that may have caused such a reaction. It would be a weird way to murder someone, giving them peanuts, disguised as something else, but nonetheless possibly effective. I just can't see a motive, though, can you, Carmichael?"

"What?" asked the big, friendly giant. "Oh, no, sir. Can't think of a thing." Carmichael had been gazing lovingly at the Christmas tree, with all the presents below it, no doubt imagining the fun and excitement going on in Jasmine Cottage, in Castle Farthing, where his fiancée Kerry lived, with her two sons from her previous marriage.

He could almost see them ripping off gay wrapping paper, and exclaiming in delight at what had been bought for them; almost smell the turkey, cooking slowly in the oven, and all the other trimmings as well; not forgetting the Christmas pudding. Kerry had made this one, and he was anxious to try it.

He had eaten there many times during their engagement, but this was their first Christmas together, and he hoped against hope, that her pudding was a suitable rival to his ma's, but maybe that was hoping for too much. Kerry was so perfect in every other way, in his opinion, that he could forgive her the Christmas pudding, if that proved necessary.

"Come on you, Davey Daydream! Let's get you back to the bosom of your family-to-be. There's nothing more here for us to do, today. But, I'd have thought you'd have been up to your eyes in wedding preparations, instead of having enough time to celebrate Christmas."

"No, that's all done and dusted, sir. Both families have been a real help in the arrangements, leaving me enough time to enjoy our first Christmas together."

"Oh, thank you very much, Carmichael. I never knew you cared," Falconer answered, smothering a smile. He had intentionally misinterpreted Carmichael's 'our first Christmas together', just to see how he reacted.

"Don't be silly, sir. Me, Kerry and the boys, I meant."

"I know you did. I was only pulling your leg. You get off and have a super day with them, and we'll carry on with this business, the day after tomorrow, if nothing urgent shows up. It's just bad luck, for everyone involved, that it's Christmas, but the day after Boxing Day's not quite so bad for being interrupted. Most people have had enough by then, and just want the whole business to be over and done with."

"You've no heart, sir. Where's your Christmas spirit?" asked Carmichael, bemused by the inspector's attitude to the season of goodwill.

"In my Christmas drinks' cupboard, where it belongs," answered Falconer, walking away from the day's unpleasant interruption, and thinking only of his own Christmas meal.

STAVE THREE

The Second Spirit – The Ghost of Christmas Restored

25th December, 2009 – a little later

When Carmichael returned to Castle Farthing where his fiancée lived (but where he would not reside until after their marriage, due to his old-fashioned moral principles), he found that Kerry had halted proceedings where they had left off, when he had so unexpectedly been called out.

The stocking presents had been opened, as they had been when he received the telephone call from Bob Bryant, but she had delayed the opening of the presents from under the Christmas tree, in the hope that Carmichael would not be gone all day, and she realised she had been right in her instincts, when he walked through the door, barely two hours after he had left.

"Daddy Davey!" the two boys, Kyle and Dean shouted, in their pleasure and excitement at his return. Not only was he back, to continue sharing Christmas Day with them, but now they could get at all the brightly wrapped packages and parcels nestling in a huge pile under the tree.

Ten minutes later, Carmichael was settled with his huge mug, filled with hot, very sweet tea (for he was no drinker), and the room was filled with the joyous shouts of children, ecstatic not only with what they had unwrapped, but with the sheer magical atmosphere of the day.

Back home, Falconer removed his guinea fowl from its temporary resting place, and popped it into the oven, which had only taken a few minutes to heat, and dealt with the rest of the trimmings that would accompany it for his, not quite solitary, Christmas meal, for he fully intended to share it with the cats, putting their bowls on the floor by the dining table, right next to his own place.

He hadn't quite worked out how he and Mycroft would pull a Christmas cracker together, nor how any of the cats would cope with being required to wear a paper hat, but these were mere details, and could wait until after they had finished eating, before he had to address them.

Finished in the kitchen, he removed the apron, which he had worn to protect his clothes, (he was very fastidious about his appearance), and removed three small parcels from under the tree, its fibre-optic lights with their ever-changing colours adding some seasonal cheer to the rather sparsely adorned room.

'Here you are, little friend,' he said, calling Mycroft over to him. "'This is for you, from me,' and he proceeded to remove the wrapping paper for his pet. Inside was a small felt mouse, filled with 'cat-nip', which Mycroft immediately accepted delicately with his mouth, put down on to the floor, in order to give it a good sniff, then started to throw it up into the air and catch it, occasionally running across the room with it, to kill it to his complete satisfaction. Tar Baby and Ruby were just as pleased with their gifts, too.

There were several more little parcels in a similar vein, waiting for the already delighted animals, for the feline trio could smell the cooking, too, but Falconer would save those for later, when his pets tired of this first offering.

The smell of food floated enticingly on the air from the kitchen, making Falconer aware of its presence anew, and he sniffed, and sighed with anticipation at the gastronomic pleasures to come, in total agreement with his furry companions on this subject.

STAVE FOUR

A Seasonal Confection of Misdirection and Deceit

27th December, 2009 – morning

Carmichael called for Falconer in his old Skoda, seasonally trimmed with tinsel on its old-fashioned radio aerial and round the door handles, a tiny Christmas tree affixed to its parcel shelf.

"Did you have a nice Christmas, sir?" the sergeant asked, as soon as the inspector had taken his uncomfortable place in the clapped-out passenger seat, having had to brush aside empty crisp packets and chocolate bar wrappers so to do.

"I certainly had a nice peaceful time, and Mycroft, Tar Baby, Ruby and I listened to the Queen's speech together, as is our habit. What about you? How was your first Christmas with your family-to-be?"

"Absolutely fantastic, sir!" Carmichael declared, delight and happiness writ all over his face in large letters. "I can't believe my luck, when I remember what I was doing this time last year. I must be the luckiest man in the world, I reckon."

"I think that applies to all four of you, considering the circumstances under which you and Kerry met," replied Falconer, squirming and removing a now somewhat squashed tube of Smarties from underneath him. "We'll go to Cutler's apartment first, then on to his parents' house, then, finally on to Miss Cater's parents' place. PC Green and WPC Starr did the honours, with the distressing job of informing her parents of their daughter's death. Damned charitable of them to volunteer. I must say, I didn't fancy doing it myself; not on Christmas Day, anyway."

"Me neither, sir. I think we owe them both a drink, to say thank you. Any news from Doc Christmas yet?" asked Carmichael, receiving an answer in the negative, which wasn't surprising really, considering the time of year. He'd no doubt be in touch, as soon as he had anything for them.

Dominic Cutler's address turned out to be in an apartment block, of a similar housing class to that of his late fiancée, and he answered their ring at the external intercom with surprising promptness, almost as if he had been waiting for them, which, of course, he had. He had hardly slept since Christmas Day morning, despite being given something to aid him in that respect, and was desperate to know what they had discovered about Angela's death.

Inside, the flat was luxuriously appointed, but without overwhelming the visitor with its occupier's obvious wealth. Everything was discreet, the colours muted, the atmosphere airy and relaxing. Dominic begged them to be seated and make themselves comfortable – his manners impeccable now the first shock had worn off.

"I wonder if you can tell me about your movements, in detail, from when you went to your parents' house on Christmas Eve, to when you found Miss Cater's body on Christmas morning?" asked Falconer. Carmichael was seated slightly out of sight-line, so that his note-taking should remain discreet, and not unnerve the bereaved young man.

"I know we went over this on Christmas Day, but I'd just like to recap, in case you've remembered something you forgot to tell me before, in your distress."

"No problem!" answered Cutler. "I just called round to see them, knowing it would be the last Christmas my father saw. He's suffering from cancer, and is in the latter stages now. It won't be long, for him, now – Last Chance Saloon, as it were. As I told you on Christmas Day, we just did the ordinary traditional things that we always did on Christmas Eve: the telling of ghost stories, and the cracking of nuts.

"My mother gave me a rather valuable necklace for Angela, as a Christmas present. It was one of the pieces of family jewellery, that she wanted her to have, now that she was going to be a member of our family. I concealed it in my wallet, when I went round to Angela's, because I wanted to go home and wrap it, as a surprise for Christmas Day.

"When I got to her flat, everything was just as normal, or as normal as it can be at this time of year. We were to spend the next day together, and she was already fussing about the ingredients for the Christmas meal. You know how women are!

"She put a CD of carols on while she buzzed about in the kitchen, and I looked on, not daring to try to get involved, in case I made her lose concentration. Then we went into the living room, and she put on a DVD of Dickens' *Christmas Carol* – the one with Alec Guinness. 1954, I think it was made, but it's the absolute best one, and we put up the tree, which was a bit of a monster, but suited her place perfectly well.

"After that, we ... we ... er ... went to bed for a while." Revealing such an intimate detail had obviously embarrassed Dominic, and his narrative ground to a halt.

"Thank you very much for being so frank with us, Mr Cutler. Dr Christmas said there was evidence of sexual activity, and you have just given us a rational explanation for that. Please carry on," Falconer encouraged him.

"Then I came back here, wrapped the necklace for the next day, and went to bed. There's nothing else to tell, except for me going round to Angela's apartment, the next morning, letting myself in, a little bit pleased that she had not yet woken, so that I could play Father Christmas with the necklace from my mother. I knew she'd love it, and would probably wear it on our wedding day."

"Do you have a date for that, Mr Cutler?"

"No, we hadn't got round to that yet. We wanted it to be Christmas Eve, but, with my father being so ill, we decided that I'd move in here on January the first, and we'd set a date ... afterwards – you know. When my father had ... gone."

"You have a lot to cope with, emotionally, at the moment, but I must press you to tell us of your discovery of Miss Cater's body," said Falconer, feeling like a louse. The young man had postponed his wedding, and lost his fiancée, and all the while, his father was dying a slow and painful death. Life could be a fair cow at times, he thought.

"I went into the flat, and stopped and listened. There was only silence, which I thought confirmed my first idea, that she was still asleep in bed, and that mine would be the first face she saw on Christmas Day, and I put my hand into my overcoat pocket, just to check that I hadn't forgotten the necklace in my hurry to get over there.

"I went into the bedroom, and she had her back to me, the covers all over the place, as usual. She was a very restless sleeper. That made me smile; how I would surprise her by waking her ..." Again his voice trailed off, and he put his head in his hands. "I'm sorry, but this is really difficult," he mumbled, rubbing at his eyes, as if there were grit in them.

"I crept over to the bed, and put my hand on her shoulder, but it was unnaturally cold. That made me feel a bit anxious, so I gave a little pull at her, to make her turn over, and then I saw ..."

"That's all right, Mr Cutler. We know what you saw. And you're perfectly sure that there weren't any peanuts in her apartment, in any shape or form, when you left it on Christmas Eve?"

"I'm positive. Angela was paranoid about the things. Shopping with her was a nightmare. She had to read every label, to see what was in everything, and if it even said 'may contain traces of nuts' she avoided the product, even if it hadn't specified 'peanuts', saying that she couldn't be too careful, given the severity of her allergy.

"She was due to have more hospital tests in the New Year, to ascertain whether her allergy also included other nuts, so she was extra vigilant in everything she bought, and we never ate out, just in case. In fact, we hardly went anywhere. She couldn't go to pubs or bars because of other people eating peanuts, and she couldn't trust the recipes in restaurants. In fact, the only places we've ever been together are the cinema and the theatre.

"I think that's all we need to know, for now, except, do you know if anyone else had a key to Miss Cater's apartment?"

"Except for me, only her parents, in case of emergency," he answered, looking a little calmer.

"And how long had you known Miss Cater?"

"Only about three months. It was love at first sight, followed by a whirlwind romance – all those terrible clichés were true, for us."

"Oh, and would it be possible to speak to your parents, just to confirm the events on Christmas Eve?" Falconer slipped in at the last minute.

"I'd rather you didn't go to the house. My father's in a bad way at the moment: in a lot of pain, and heavily sedated, but if you'd like to call back here tomorrow, about five o'clock, my mother is going to come over to see me, to discuss ... arrangements. She doesn't like to do that where Daddy or the nurse might possibly overhear – not even on the telephone – so she'll be visiting me in the afternoon, and I can give her back the necklace, at the same time. There's no use me hanging on to it, now that Angela's dead," Dominic explained.

"That seems perfectly acceptable," replied Falconer. "We just need corroboration of your story, for our records. I wonder if you'd let us have a look at the necklace, before we go."

"Of course. Here it is," Cutler replied, pulling it out of a small drawer in a desk just behind him.

It was a real beauty! Light sparked from it, in myriad rainbows of colour, which reflected on the walls and ceiling, and made moving patterns of light as Falconer turned it this way and that. "Thank you very much, sir," he commented, handing it back. "It's a lovely old piece. I'm sure Miss Cater would have loved and cherished it."

"So am I," replied Cater, in a faltering voice. "I'll just show you out."

STAVE FIVE

A Christmas Gift of Pertinent Information

27th December, 2009 – afternoon

As they now had no need to visit Dominic Cutler's parents, Falconer and Carmichael shared a companionable lunch in 'The Shoulder of Mutton and Gherkins'. This was the first suspicious death that they had worked on that had actually taken place in Market Darley, and, for once, they had no need to dash about the countryside to some far-flung village. It all seemed terribly civilised.

"I'm sorry I haven't had the opportunity to ask you yet, but are you having a nice Christmas, Carmichael?" Falconer asked his sergeant, and was suddenly flooded with a perfect cataract of a narrative, about this 'first of many' Christmas and Boxing Days.

"They'd waited for me, when I got back on Christmas morning. The boys hadn't opened any of the presents from under the tree. They'd put it off until I got back, so that I could share in their excitement. Wasn't that thoughtful of them all?

"And Kerry's Christmas dinner was easily as good as anything my ma's ever cooked. We listened to the Queen, then the boys played with all their new toys. Oh, and the Christmas pud! It was the most delicious I've ever tasted – absolutely first rate, and made to one of Kerry's godmother's family recipes. You remember Alan and Marian Warren-Browne from the post office in Castle Farthing, don't you?" he asked.

Falconer was given only enough time to agree that he did, indeed, remember them, before the momentum of Carmichael's narrative resumed. "We had a cracking tea, with fruit, jelly and ice-cream, Christmas cake, and mince pies and sausage rolls. It was all top-notch scoff." Carmichael needed to consume a lot, to fuel a frame as large as his, so his mind was frequently preoccupied with food – what he had already eaten, and when and what he would eat in the future, given the opportunity.

"The next day we did something that is a tradition in my family, and Kerry had never heard of before. My ma realised, a long time ago, how children ache for just one more present, on Boxing Day, after all the excitement of the day before, so she always used to wrap a little something for everyone, and hang the parcels from the Christmas tree. Then, when we came down on Boxing Day, after breakfast, we used to get to open what she referred to as 'the tree presents', and it was just a lovely little extra, to all the presents from the day before.

"Anyway, we did this after breakfast on Boxing Day, and the boys loved it. Then, after lunch – oh, the lunch! Tons of cold meats, oodles of pickles, and the most buttery mashed potatoes you could imagine, sir. Kerry and the boys had a load of salad stuff, as well, but I couldn't be bothered with that – there was too much other lovely stuff to get through.

"Anyway, after that lot, I went up to get what I had hidden in Kerry's wardrobe, when I originally arrived, and came downstairs with a little sack of presents, with numbers stuck on them – it's another tradition in the Carmichael family, that there is a 'lucky dip', and I'd kept this as a surprise.

"Everyone pulls a number out of a hat (ready and waiting, of course), and chooses the present with the matching number. There should be loads of little gifts: tiny, inexpensive things, like a comb or a lollipop, so that it doesn't get too costly. It can, in fact it did, last all the afternoon.

"We had an absolutely smashing time. What about you, sir?"

The tirade suddenly stopped. The whirlwind ceased, and left Carmichael staring in enquiry at the inspector.

"Very nice, thank you, Carmichael," Falconer replied.

Mr and Mrs Cater lived in a very large detached house, about a mile outside Market Darley, with about five acres of garden – or grounds. Falconer couldn't decide exactly how he would describe the land they had.

The door was opened by a housekeeper, who bade them enter, and showed them into the morning room, where they awaited the bereaved parents. Alan and Edith Cater joined them, a few minutes later, grief still marking their faces, their footsteps slow, as if nothing were of any importance any more.

After the usual introductions, and expressions of sympathy for their loss, Falconer apologised for bothering them, and said he would keep their visit as short as possible, so that they could be left in peace, to come to terms with what had happened.

"I'd like to ask you how well you knew your daughter's fiancé. Did he come here a lot? Did you ever go to his home, or meet his parents?" Falconer began his questioning, as Carmichael, inevitably, prepared to do his version of shorthand.

"He came here once, very briefly, just so that we could meet him, but they had to rush off somewhere – I can't remember where, now – the theatre, or a cinema, or some such place. He seemed a nice enough young man, but we were a little concerned, at the speed at which their relationship was developing," Alan Cater informed them.

"Why was that?"

"Because of the amount of money that Angela would in– would have inherited, should anything happen to us. We didn't want her to get involved with a gold-digger. But he seemed a nice enough young man. We went to his apartment, once, for a drink before a function we were attending in Market Darley, and he seemed to be very comfortably off, so it set our minds at rest," Edith Cater continued, on her husband's behalf.

"I suppose, with the tests she had booked for the New Year, they would have discovered something else she was allergic to, if she died of an allergic reaction." Mrs Cater couldn't go on, and her husband took over.

"I presume that Cutler knew all about the peanut thing, and didn't just make a mistake, did he?"

"He certainly explained her condition to us, in some detail, and said that he always avoided peanuts, or anything that had them in it, for her sake," Falconer informed them.

"Well, I suppose the proof of that will be in what the post mortem discovers, won't it?" Mr Cater asked, his face a white mask of disbelief and disgust. "Children aren't supposed to die before their parents. It's an obscenity, if you think about it. No one should ever be asked to bury their child," he added, visibly trying to pull himself together.

"We'll leave you in peace now," Falconer said, having decided that they'd got the information they'd come for, and would burden the bereaved parents no longer with their company.

Back at the office, Dr Christmas rang Falconer, with some preliminary findings from the post mortem. "It was definitely a severe allergic reaction that killed her, Harry, but I can't seem to determine what triggered it. I've been through the stomach contents with a fine-tooth comb – if you'll pardon the ghastly phrasing – and I can't find any trace of peanuts. In fact, I can't find traces of any other sort of nut, either, in there. Her stomach was definitely a nut-free organ, and I don't know what to make of that.

"I'm going to have a look through some learned journals now, and then look on the internet, and consult a couple of colleagues, to see if I can come up with anything, but, frankly, I hardly know what to look for, let alone ask about," he concluded, his voice sounding as puzzled as he felt.

"The reaction must have been triggered by something, and I expect you to work your clinical little socks off, to find out what it was. We must know the reason for that reaction having been triggered. Anything less will leave the lot of us looking like a bunch of rank amateurs," was Falconer's reply.

"I'll carry on for now, and give you a ring in the morning. I hope I'll know more by then. Bye for now." And the doctor was gone, no doubt, back to his own detective work, to explain the demise of his current 'customer'.

STAVE SIX

The Third of the Spirits – The Spirit of Justice

28th December, 2009 – morning

About ten o'clock on the morning of the twenty-eighth, Falconer received another phone call from Dr Christmas, this time with some very interesting information, which he promised to e-mail to CID, so that it could be recorded in the official file, and which confirmed that Angela Cater did have a nut allergy that was more far-ranging than just peanuts. One final quirky fact made up Falconer's mind for him.

Doc Christmas had located the site of the allergen, and declared he had never come across anything like it in his whole professional life, before. The inspector would be going to see that young man again, this afternoon, but he'd go prepared for what he intended to do, and he'd face Cutler with what he'd just been told.

Carmichael's mouth dropped open in disbelief, when Falconer related the contents of the call from Dr Christmas to him, and it took some while for him to believe that Falconer wasn't just pulling his leg, to see how gullible he was.

"I promise you, Carmichael, that's the God's honest truth. I've checked it out myself, for much the same reason as you suspected me of: of having you on, but it's true. I'd never have guessed it was possible, but apparently it is, and we've just got to accept it, and what it implies."

"But she hadn't eaten any nuts?"

"None whatsoever, Carmichael. Her stomach was as clean as the proverbial whistle of traces of any nuts of any sort."

"I've done a couple of other checks on various things that we've been told, and I think I'm as prepared as I can be for this afternoon's visit."

28th December, 2009 – afternoon

When they reached the apartment block that Cutler had given as his address, Falconer noticed for the first time that the name in the little holder by the intercom was written on a tatty piece of paper, by hand, and not printed on card, like the others above and below it.

Why had he not noticed that before? Probably because he couldn't have imagined the bizarre turn that events were about to take, and had accepted everything at face value – a very dangerous and unprofessional thing for a detective to do.

A resident on the way out passed the open door to them so there was no need to ring the doorbell. This was just as well, as it would give their arrival the element of surprise that having to ring would not have done.

The door was opened, with only a wait of thirty seconds or so, during which, voices could be heard from within, and then Mr Cutler was there, in the doorway, inviting them inside, to meet his mother. There was definitely a familial resemblance between him and the woman who rose from a sofa to greet them, but, with the information he now possessed, Falconer was able to discern easily that there was something not quite right about the way she was dressed.

"Your arrival has just reminded me that I promised to return that necklace to my mother today," commented Cutler, moving to the desk, whence he had extracted it previously to show to Falconer.

"I'd be grateful if you'd pass that to me, if you don't mind, sir," Falconer requested, noting a little frown of anxiety cross Cutler's face.

"Of course. No problem. Is there something wrong, Inspector?"

"There most definitely is, Mr Cutler, but fortunately I've been able to put the pieces of the jigsaw puzzle together, and see the whole picture, and not just the part of it that you wanted me to see."

"What are you talking about? I don't understand what's going on here."

"Oh, I think you do, sir, as does your mother. I am arresting you for the wilful murder of Angela Rebecca Cater on 24th December, 2009 ..." the official caution followed, then Falconer turned his attention to Mrs Cutler.

"Mrs Rita Lesley Cutler, I am arresting you, for withholding of evidence, in a case of murder – oh, and probably some other things as well, when I can get round to working out what they are. You don't live in some big house in the country with a dying husband, do you? You live in a council house on the Wild Birds Estate, on the outskirts of Market Darley, and your husband did a runner, years ago. I've got a patrol car, which should now be waiting outside for us, so I'm asking you to come quietly, or I'll have to call the occupants of said patrol car up here, to help you to cooperate."

"I told her I'd love her to death, Inspector," Cutler shouted, as he was escorted out of the flat. "After a while, she used to beg me, when we were having sex 'Oh, love me to death, Dom. Love me to death,' she'd moan, so on Christmas Eve, I did."

"Come on, sir, give! There're lots of pieces to this particular jigsaw puzzle that I don't know about, so spill the beans, or I'll have to get PC Green to frighten the truth out of you."

They were back in the office now, and Carmichael, who had not been party to much of the digging that Falconer had done, was waiting with baited breath to hear the whole story.

"Apparently it had all started when Dominic, in his usual guise of an habitual layabout, in scruffy clothes and with wild, unkempt hair, had gone into the council offices to report a blocked drain. He was living at home with his mother, both of them on benefits, in one of the local authority houses out in 'the wilds' of the Wild Birds Estate, and on that particular visit to the local authority, it was Angela who took the details from him.

"I don't know how he found out things about her, but he obviously did, and became obsessed with her, as well as her wealth, and he thought he could do himself a bit of good, if he got to know her. Anyway, he spruced himself up a bit and got a decent haircut, then he had a stroke of luck that he could not have foreseen.

"An old school-friend of his, who had prospered, was going away, on a six-month contract, to Dubai. They had always been particular friends at school. This friend knew how Dominic was fixed, still living at home with his mother, and, very generously in my opinion, asked him if he'd like to move into his apartment while he was away, to keep an eye on it, otherwise it would be standing empty – a magnet for anyone with evil intentions, who could manage to get inside it.

"Of course, Cutler jumped at the chance. Now, he could engineer a meeting with Angela Cater, and not only look the part, but have the right address, to go with the manufactured background he was going to feed to her.

"He was the one who really made the running in the relationship, Angela just getting carried away with the romance, probably, and swept off her feet, with the speed with which things happened. He never let her visit his family, because the family he'd told her about simply didn't exist. But he did get her to make a will, in his favour, when they'd talked about marriage, explaining that it was best to do it straight away, even if their marriage nullified it, as anything could happen to anyone, in the blink of an eye, and he would do the same for her.

"He took a bit of a risk with his plan to kill her, but it obviously paid off, as we all found out only three days ago. His friend had left behind a diamond necklace that belonged to his grandmother, and had asked Cutler to get it cleaned, before leaving for Dubai – this was a vital piece of evidence, should his plan come off. If it didn't, he just wouldn't mention it, and would have returned it to his friend on his return to this country. It was really the only thing he had with which to fool us about his wealth, but it was a risk he was willing to take.

"He knew that any nuts found in Angela's stomach at the post mortem, might point the finger directly at him, so he couldn't risk that happening. But he did stumble across a little known fact about Brazil nuts that suited his purposes perfectly."

"And that was what Dr Christmas rang up and told you about?" asked Carmichael, sitting with his chin resting in his hands, as attentive as a child being read a particularly enjoyable story.

"That's right, Carmichael. Cutler had found out that eating Brazil nuts would cause traces of them to be passed on through sexual contact"

"So his nuts contained traces of nuts?" asked Carmichael, with a wide grin at his witticism.

"Don't be coarse, Sergeant!" replied Falconer, and then dissolved into mirthful laughter, not just at the witticism, but at Carmichael's crestfallen face at this rebuke. "Anyway, to continue, he then stuffed himself with them all day on Christmas Eve, hoping that he'd eaten enough, and given them enough time to get through his system. Then, as we know, he made love to Miss Cater, just before he left her apartment on Christmas Eve."

"Bastard!" commented Carmichael casually, hoping not to interrupt the inspector's flow.

He didn't, as Falconer continued, "She was probably already showing signs of her allergic reaction before he left, but he stayed on to make sure that she was in no condition to phone for help, or leave the apartment, to seek it elsewhere.

"The next day, he knew exactly what he would find, when he turned up at her door, and, I must say, in my opinion he turned out to be a pretty good actor."

"But how did you suss out all that other stuff, sir?" Carmichael asked, with a face that indicated that he regarded all the other facts garnered as nothing short of magic.

"Simple, and all of it readily available to be found. I thought it was a bit iffy, that Cutler had never taken her to his family home to meet his parents, and then he didn't want me to visit them either. Was that because they didn't exist, or because there was something very wrong about his background?

"I contacted the concierge of the block that he's been living in, confirmed that the apartment had been sub-let to him, with the permission of the lease-holder, and got said lease-holder's contact number, should anyone need to be contacted in an emergency. I also got a contact number for the real tenant, in Dubai.

"A quick phone call to Dubai confirmed that Dominic Cutler was no more the affluent young man about town than Bob Bryant is, and that he was only living there, to give him a break from living with his mother in a council house, to try to sort himself out, find himself a job, and gain a little more self-respect.

"Well, he'd done more than that. He'd found himself a wealthy young woman. All he had to do was, literally, love her to death, as he told us so callously."

"God, that's evil, sir," Carmichael commented, sitting up straight, as he realised that Falconer had reached the 'and they lived unhappily ever after' point of his story.

"He'll get his comeuppance, and he won't get a penny from that will, either," stated Falconer. It might just have worked, however, with less diligent officers, too bound up in their own families, at this particular time of year, to do much digging.

"He was prepared for us to come round and give him the tragic news, that Brazil nuts are something that can be transmitted from one body to another during sexual intercourse, and would have played the broken-hearted fiancé who had lost his beloved, because he had accidentally and unknowingly killed her, by making love to her – loved her to death, in fact.

"How that phrase makes me shudder, when I think about it! Instead, he got the spirit of justice, rather than the spirit of Christmas, and the next season of goodwill he sees will be from the inside of a prison cell. And that's just how it should be.

"What an audacious plan, and to think that he thought he could fool the police like that! Well, I suppose we'd better be getting off home."

"Would you like to come to ours for your tea, sir? Kerry's promised that she's got the most delicious recipe in the world, for cold curried turkey, and there are loads of mince pies, and a whole hunk of Christmas ham left."

"I don't know, Carmichael. I'd planned on a quiet night in."

"On your own again, I suppose," declared the sergeant, with both disapproval, and concern.

"With my pets, Carmichael."

"Well, I won't hear of it! Those cats can stay on their own, for one evening. You're coming home with me, and having some proper seasonal company, for a change, you miserable old Scrooge, and I'll not take 'no' for an answer," the sergeant stated with vehemence.

"That's very hospitable of you, Carmichael, but are you sure Kerry won't mind?"

"Mind? She'll be over the moon! She's been dying for you to visit: she's heard so much about you."

"From you, Carmichael?" asked Falconer, apprehensively.

"Of course from me, sir."

"Oh, dear!" said Falconer, following, Carmichael out of the room, to his uncertain fate, that evening.

STAVE SEVEN

The Fourth Spirit – The Spirit of Christmas Yet to Come

28th December, 2009 – evening

Falconer was surprised and secretly delighted to be welcomed, as an honoured guest, at the cottage in Castle Farthing where Carmichael would live after his marriage, in just a few days' time. Kerry was obviously delighted to welcome such an important figure into her home, and the two boys, who treated Carmichael's position as a detective sergeant with casual contempt, were thrilled to have a real detective inspector visit their home.

The cottage was decorated in a suitably over-the-top festive manner, and some work had been done to connect the rooms with the cottage next door. A much too tall fir tree dominated the front room, drowning under its own weight of baubles, tinsel, and other seasonal ornamentation. In the grate, a wood fire was burning, and the whole atmosphere was redolent of the sort of Christmas that Falconer had never experience before, and it filled him with an unexpected joy.

Carmichael was a very luck young man, to be moving into this home, with its convivial and welcoming occupants, devoid of any of the airs and graces that would have been present at one of his parents' Christmases.

Flopping down into an armchair by the fire, indicated to him by Kerry, he accepted the half pint of beer that Carmichael thrust into his hand, and prepared to enjoy himself, with not even a hint of the 'keeping up appearances' attitude that had , and probably still did, prevail in his family home, for the first time in years.

The End of it

"Why don't you come for Christmas Day, next year, sir?" asked Carmichael, seeing Falconer relaxed and perfectly at ease at the fireside.

"I might just take you up on that offer, Carmichael," Falconer mumbled, feeling his eyes droop, in the warm and welcoming atmosphere of the little home. "I might just do that!"

Maybe Christmas wasn't so bad after all!

THE END. . . . . until the next time!

A Sidecar Named Expire

A young man and his girlfriend decide to celebrate their first St Valentine's Day together, with a cosy evening of cocktails at her house. But as the evening progresses, events don't go quite as Malcolm Standing planned.

The next morning, DI Falconer and DS Carmichael are called in to try to sort out what really happened.

Chapter One

14th February

'Now, my cocktail starts with one-and-a-half measures of gin.' There was a short glugging sound from round the angle of the L-shaped room, as Chelsea Fairfield began to mix the drinks with which they were going to celebrate their first St Valentine's Day together.

They had only been an item for three weeks or so, but Malcolm Standing had been captivated by her since their first meeting, and had gladly accepted her invitation to spend this evening at her house, drinking cocktails together. He had high hopes of not going home at all tonight, and sprawled on the sofa in an ecstasy of expectation. Tonight would probably be the night!

'One-and-a-half measures of Cointreau,' her voice purred on, 'and one-and-a-half measures of lemon juice. Shake,' he discerned the quiet sloshing of the cocktail shaker being agitated, 'and strain into a frosted glass, over ice. There! That's my White Lady sorted. Now for your Sidecar.'

'How come I don't get to choose my own cocktail?' he called out to her.

'You can after the first one. I just thought a Sidecar was rather appropriate, as you ride a motorbike,' she called in answer, and Malcolm could feel his whole body tingling in anticipation of the evening to come.

'Right! A Sidecar. Bit of information for you here, my dear. This cocktail was originally created after the First World War, in 'Harry's Bar' – the one in Paris, not the one in Venice, and was named after an officer who used to go there by chauffeur-ridden motorcycle sidecar. See what I mean?

'And now for the ingredients. One measure of cognac, one measure of Cointreau, and one measure of lemon juice.' As she shook the cocktail, he raised his voice to give his opinion of the two recipes.

'Yours seems to be half as strong again as mine. Why's that? It doesn't seem fair to me.'

'Just think about it, sweetie,' she answered, and he heard her speaking in a slightly quieter voice. 'There we go! And strain, garnish with a slice of lemon, over crushed ice. I'm on my way.'

In less than a minute, she came round the 'L', carrying a small silver tray with the two glasses on it.

'Hand it over, then,' Malcolm said, holding out his hand.

'Not just yet, big boy. I want the occasion to be just right, so, just before we drink our cocktails, I want us to enjoy a black Russian cigarette.'

'But I don't smoke!' he protested.

'Neither do I,' she replied, 'but trust me, this is definitely the best way to enjoy these cocktails,' and in so saying, she removed a small black box from a drawer in a wall unit, opened it, and held it out for him to take a cigarette, took one herself, and produced a lighter to light them. 'Now,' she ordered, 'a couple of puffs on that, and we can have our glasses. Happy Valentine's Day, darling.'

'And the same to you ... darling.' He hesitated over the last word, as this was the first time that they had used it, but he got over his surprise by gazing at the huge bouquet of flowers that he had brought with him, and thought that they had been worth the money, if this was the effect they had on her.

While all this was going through his mind, he was having difficulty not to succumb to a fit of coughing from the cigarette smoke. He had tried smoking when he was about nine or ten, but it had made him throw up, and he just hoped that this unfortunate consequence did not recur this evening. How that would ruin things for him!

Asking for an ashtray, he took a token puff on the cigarette and put it down in the corner of the receptacle, looking pleadingly towards the two glasses on the tray.

'You can have your drink, now,' Chelsea purred, and placed the tray under his nose with a flourish. 'Enjoy!' she said, taking her own glass, and setting the tray down on the wall unit where it had sat in the meantime.

Only a few minutes later, Chelsea stood up and announced that she was going to mix them another drink. 'What, already?' he asked.

'Yes! Come along, slow coach. Get that down your neck, and we can have another one before seeing how events develop.' Eager at the promise in her words, he downed the last of the liquid in the cocktail glass and watched as she disappeared behind the 'L' again.

'That seemed awfully strong,' he said, raising his voice a little so that she could hear him, and realised that his head was beginning to spin.

'I'll cut down on the measures this time, if it's a problem for you,' she called back. 'And don't forget to have a couple of puffs on your cigarette. They're dead expensive, they are, and if I don't see you smoking it when I get back round there, I'm going to be very cross with you.'

'But I don't like 'em,' he replied, realising that his voice was beginning to slur.

'I don't care! I'm educating you in the finer things in life, and you'll do as I say, or else!'

When she came back to him this time, she put down the tray, extracted two more cigarettes from the box, and lit them both, handing one to him, but when he reached for it reluctantly, he seemed to have two hands on the end of his arm. 'Blimey!' he thought. 'The things that blokes do, just to get a leg-over.'

Putting the slightly smoked cigarette down in the ashtray, he held his hand out for his glass containing his second Sidecar of the night.

As he supped the cold liquid, he took a moment to protest. 'I thought you 'ere goin' to le' me cock my own choose-tail, af'er the firs' one,' he complained, listening to the deterioration in his speech with puzzlement.

'You can choose the next one, my darling,' she soothed him, holding up her glass in salutation to encourage him to drink more of his.

Malcolm had no idea of the time, but it seemed to be a lot later, and he was incapable of moving, and barely capable of thinking. Chelsea was telling him something, but he couldn't understand what she was saying. It seemed to be in a foreign language; one that he had never heard before.

He was aware of her tucking his feet up on the sofa, and removing his shoes and the cocktail glass, which his right hand had still been clutching. How many had he had? He had no idea. His memory was a blank. Slowly his eyelids closed over his reluctant eyes, and he slept.

Chapter Two

15th February

The voice on the phone was breathless with urgency. 'But he's dead, and he's on my sofa, and I don't know what to do about it. Please send someone as quick as you can. It's so horrible, looking at him just lolling there and ... well, being dead, I suppose.

'I've given you the address, but I can't bear to sit here looking at him any longer, so I'm going round to my next door neighbour's. I'll watch for the car from there. Please be quick. This is doing my head in. Oh, I know that sounds awful, but it's just not *him* anymore, it's an 'it', and it's really giving me the willies.

'God knows what happened. He must have had a weak heart, or something. All I know, as I told you, is that he's dead, and in my house, and I simply can't cope with that a moment longer than I have to. Goodbye.'

Desk Sergeant Bob Bryant put down the telephone receiver and made a quick decision to alert Detective Inspector Harry Falconer and his partner, Detective Sergeant Davey Carmichael. This one sounded right up their street, and shouldn't take too long to wrap up once Dr Christmas had got the poor gentleman on the table and opened him up.

Using the internal phone service, he rang through to Falconer to send him and his sergeant on their way, then went back to an external line to contact Dr Philip Christmas to attend the scene as well. As it was an unexpected death, he decided to send a small SOCO team as well. It was better to be safe than sorry, he'd always found, and if things didn't turn out as simply, as he was almost sure they would, it would be in his favour if he had dotted all the i's and crossed all the t's.

Following that flurry of activity, he called one of the uniformed PCs, who had just wandered in, to take over at the desk for ten minutes while he went for a cup of coffee. It was thirsty work, holding the fort at Market Darley Police Station, and he needed a break after that sudden burst of activity.

'It's not far, so we'll take my car,' DI Falconer decided as he and DS Carmichael exited the station, noticing that Bob Bryant was no longer on the desk. 'What was that address again, Carmichael?'

'Twelve Coronation Terrace – built just after the coronation of our present Queen,' he observed, displaying, as usual, more local knowledge than Falconer would have believed could exist in the young man's head. He had recently got married, and seemed, if possible, even happier than he had been when he was first partnered with Falconer the previous summer.

In fact, it was during the previous summer, on their first case together, that Carmichael had met the young woman who had recently become his wife, and he lived with her and her two sons from a previous marriage in the village of Castle Farthing, the locus for said first case.

It only took ten minutes to reach Coronation Terrace, and as they slowed to read the numbers of the houses, a woman came out of one of them stepped over the low dividing front garden wall to the house next door and beckoned to them to stop.

'I've got 'er in 'ere,' she informed them, indicating her own house by the bending of her head in the direction of her front door. 'She's in a terrible state, poor little thing. Such a dreadful thing to 'appen, when you're as young as she is. She can 'ardly take it in, nor neither can I. I'm Ida Jenkins – Mrs – by the way.'

The woman was in her late sixties, and had a motherly look about her. A comfortably round figure with an apron tied over the front of it was presented between sensible carpet slippers and wrinkled stockings at the bottom, and a mop of greying curls and a sympathetic face at the top. She looked kind; just the sort of neighbour one would want to have in an emergency.

'You come on in,' she exhorted them, stepping back over the wall on to her own path. 'She's inside, with a small glass of brandy to perk 'er up. You go in an' see 'er, and I'll make us all a nice cup of tea. I reckon I've got an unopened packet of chocolate digestives in my kitchen cupboard as well. Nothin' like tea to raise the spirits, my old ma used to say, and she was right, too.'

She led them into her living room, which had not been knocked through in the way that many of the houses had, and they found a young woman sitting on the only sofa, quietly crying into a handful of tissues. 'Chelsea Fairfield?' enquired Falconer.

At the sound of his voice she looked up, displaying red eyes and a face made puffy by weeping. Unable to manage a spoken answer, she just nodded her head in acknowledgement of her identity.

'I'm Detective Inspector Falconer from Market Darley CID, and this is my partner, Detective Sergeant Carmichael,' the inspector said by way of introduction. 'We've come in response to your 999 call.'

Miss Fairfield began to cry again, her body wracked by great hiccoughing sobs, as she remembered afresh what had happened. 'I-I'm s-so s-sorry. I just d-don't seem t-to be able t-to t-take it in,' she stuttered, between waves of tears. 'It all s-seems s-so unreal – like a d-dream – a n-nightmare.'

Carmichael immediately sat down beside her on the sofa, his giant frame dwarfing hers, and put a hand round her shoulders. 'Just let it all out,' he advised her, 'and then you'll feel a little better, and we can talk to you, and start to investigate what took place.'

At that juncture, Mrs Jenkins re-entered the room carrying a large, old-fashioned tray, and set it down on a low table that sat so conveniently for the sofa, and the two armchairs that comprised Mrs Jenkins' three-piece-suite, a dazzling affair in red, orange, and yellow velour.

As Mrs Jenkins poured tea for everyone, solicitously asking whether they took milk and sugar, Falconer gazed around him at the room in which they sat. Mrs Jenkins was evidently fond of bright colours, her three-piece-suite being a sufficient example of this to confirm such a belief. Just to add even more evidence to his surmise, the walls were hung with bright prints, and the two rugs on the floor also glowed with jewel-bright colours.

'Very nice, bright room,' he complimented her. Although he preferred more muted shades himself, he needed her on his side if he were to question Miss Fairfield without undue interruption and opposition. She must become an ally, not an enemy.

With the chocolate biscuits being handed round on a pretty porcelain plate, Carmichael removed himself from the sofa, Mrs Jenkins sat down comfortably beside Chelsea Fairfield, and Falconer took the spare armchair. There! That was them all settled now. He'd give it a couple more minutes for the tea and biscuits to do their job of soothing, then the questioning could begin.

Miss Fairfield was calmer now, and had accepted a cup of tea and a couple of biscuits with admirable dignity. Carmichael, without a shred of dignity at all, shoved a chocolate biscuit, whole, into his mouth, to free his hands to extract his notebook from his jacket pocket. To see his sergeant's mouth dealing with such a large offering was an experience Falconer rather wished he had not been witness to. The faces he was making made him look totally alien, and not a little half-witted.

Fortunately, neither of the women noticed, and Falconer only stared because he could not avert his fascinated eyes. They were glued to the spectacle, and there was not a thing he could do about it. Swallowing mightily, Carmichael smiled across at the inspector, and helped himself to another biscuit.

As the whole of it disappeared into his mouth again, Falconer pretended to be interested in the knick-knacks on the mantelpiece, to save himself a repeat of what he had witnessed before.

Chelsea Fairfield finally put down her cup and saucer, blew her nose quietly into the bundle of tissues she still had in her hand, and pulled herself into a bolt-upright sitting position, thus indicating that she was composed now and ready to talk.

Carmichael jammed a final biscuit into his gaping maw and sat with notepad and pen at the ready, but turned slightly away from the group, so that his activity would not be too intrusive and interrupt the natural flow of questioning.

Falconer opened the proceedings. 'Mr Standing – I believe that's the name you gave the desk sergeant? – Mr Malcolm Standing was your boyfriend?' he asked gently, starting with the easier-to-ask questions so as not to upset her too early in the process.

'Yes,' she whispered.

'And you had been going out with him for how long?'

'About three weeks.'

'And what were your plans for last night?' Falconer was gently approaching the nub of the matter.

'It was our first Valentine's Day together, and I wanted to make it really special.'

'In what way?' he probed, but he had obviously touched a sensitive spot, because her face crumpled into a grimace of misery.

'I was going to let him spend the night with me.' She spoke so quietly that he could hardly discern the words.

'And that would have been the first time that he had been invited to do so?' Falconer felt like a rat, poking and prying into this very private part of her life, but it was part of the job and had to be carried out and accepted for what it was.

'That's right,' Chelsea confirmed with a small nod of her head.

'So, what had you planned for the evening?'

'We were going to have some cocktails. They're not something I've ever really drunk before, but a couple of weeks ago I went out with a bunch of girls and we went to a club that specialised in them, and I thought it would be really romantic if we had some, to celebrate being together.'

'You're doing very well, Miss Fairfield,' Falconer praised her, then had his attention distracted by Carmichael, who was doubled over in his chair, coughing, biscuit crumbs flying everywhere.

'Sorry, guv,' he said, between coughs. 'Crumbs went down the wrong way.' Honestly, you could only ever take Carmichael anywhere twice; the second time to apologise.

Trying to recreate the intimate atmosphere that Carmichael had so thoroughly shattered, Falconer continued, 'And what cocktails did you drink?' This might have seemed a pointless question to some, but it could produce the key to the young man's death in that he may prove to have had a severe allergy to one of the ingredients.

'I had a White Lady, and he had a Sidecar.'

'And was it just the one drink?'

'Oh, no. We had more than one. It was such a special night, you see,' she explained. 'And we smoked Russian cigarettes. I wanted it to be so exotic and romantic, and as far away as it was possible to get from a night down at the pub.'

'I understand,' Falconer assured her. 'And who mixed the cocktails?'

'I did. I bought a book, so that I could get the recipes right. I even bought a cocktail shaker. No one in my family's ever had one of those before.' So, she was breaking new ground, socially.

'What happened, when you'd had your cocktails?' This was the difficult bit – finding out about how the young man had become ill, deteriorated, and finally lost his life.

'He said he felt funny, but I just thought it was the exotic drinks that he wasn't used to. Then he got sort of dizzy and unwell; said he felt awful, so I thought the best thing to do would be to settle him down on my sofa for the night, and see how he was in the morning.

Of course, it ruined our romantic Valentine's night in, but that didn't matter.

'I got a blanket, and made him as comfortable as I could, then I – I went to bed. That sounds terribly callous, but I didn't think there was that much wrong with him. I thought it was just the strength of the cocktails. If I'd have known how serious it was, I'd have called a doctor. I'm so sorry. This is all my fault!'

'Of course it's not, Miss Fairfield. You're not medically trained. How on earth could you have known what the consequences would be?'

'I should have played safe and called for help,' she stated, tears now coursing down her cheeks. 'But I was woozy too. Cocktails seem to be much stronger than you think they're going to be. I just thought he was a bit more of a lightweight than me where alcohol was concerned, and staggered up to bed because my own head was spinning so much. So much for a romantic evening in! 'Oh, why didn't I call a bloody doctor'?' she wailed in despair, and Mrs Jenkins took her in her arms and rocked her like a baby.

'There, there, lovey. Don't take on so. There's no way anyone can turn back the clock, now is there? We just has to put up with what life dishes out to us, and make the best of it, don't we? Come on, lovey, pull yourself together. You were doin' marvellous there, givin' all that information to the nice inspector.

'Get a hold of yourself, now, and just answer the rest of his questions, then I'll put you upstairs in my own spare room, what used to be my Sharon's, and you can have a nice nap while everyone else gets on with finding out what happened to your poor old boyfriend.' Mrs Jenkins patted Chelsea on the back in a maternal fashion, and gently returned her to her upright position. 'There you are, my duck. Won't be long now, and I'll make you a nice cup of cocoa afore you goes up.'

Falconer had judged this neighbour well, for she was proving a tower of strength now, dealing with Chelsea Fairfield's explosions of emotion, and he was grateful to have been spared the job of doing it himself. Of course, Carmichael would have been better at it than he, he acknowledged, and, in reality, he would probably have left it to his sergeant to restore a calm atmosphere.

<u>Chapter Three</u>

15th February, – –later

The two detectives left Chelsea Fairfield in Mrs Jenkins' tender care and went round to take a look inside number twelve. Red and white crime tape sealed off the house at the path, and they ducked under it to approach the policeman on duty at the door, who had stood stoically silent as Mrs Jenkins had hopped, slightly arthritically, back and forth across the adjoining wall when they arrived.

'Good day to you, PC Proudfoot,' Falconer greeted him. 'Dr Christmas showed up yet?'

'Arrived just after you went in next door, sir,' answered PC John Proudfoot, drawing up his somewhat portly body into the best imitation of 'attention' he could manage. 'Photographer's been, and so has the fingerprint jonnie, sir. There're a couple of SOCOs waiting to see what you'd like them to do with regards to searching.'

Duty done, the constable lost his grip on his strenuously maintained upright position and slumped into a version of 'at ease'. His protruding belly just could not cope with being held in restraint for longer than a couple of minutes, and he thought he'd really have to cut down on the pork pies and Mars bars that he usually had about his person for emergency snacks.

Falconer and Carmichael entered the house, and Falconer couldn't help but notice the complete contrast in decor between this house and the neighbouring property. Where Mrs Jenkins filled her house with chaotic and eye-catching colour, this house was presented in muted shades, highlighted here and there with the addition of a couple of bright cushions or a single picture on a wall.

No bric-a-brac crowded shelves or mantelpiece, and the whole place, knocked through as it was into one large living, dining, and cooking space, was airy, light, and contemporary.

Mrs Jenkins' house looked like it had been furnished by someone who habituated market stalls and went on holiday to the more English resorts in Spain every year. Chelsea Fairfield's home, in contrast, looked as if its interior design had been culled from up-market magazines and such like. Falconer favoured neither look, but was nonetheless impressed with how very different two neighbouring homes with identical floor plans could look.

Fingerprints having been taken, they found Dr Christmas round the other side of the 'L' shape, washing his hands at the kitchen sink. 'Sorry about this,' he apologised, apropos of nothing. 'It's those damned gloves I have to wear. They leave an awful smell on my hands, and I can't wait to wash them as soon as I've taken the damned things off.'

'Hi there, Philip,' Falconer greeted him, having worked with the doctor a few times now, and managed to establish a congenial working relationship with him. 'Anything to tell us?'

'Apart from the fact that you've got a dead 'un, not really. To all intents and purposes, it would appear that he ingested something that disagreed with him, to the point of fatality. What that substance was I can't tell you at the moment.'

'Stomach contents?' queried the inspector.

'You've got it in one. Also, the fingerprints guy waltzed off with a couple of cocktail glasses and a cocktail shaker. I've rung for the meat wagon, to take the body to the mortuary, and I'll get him opened up as soon as I can. Do you want to sit in on this one?' he asked.

'Why not?' Falconer replied. 'We'll both keep you company,' he volunteered, pretending not to notice the greenish tinge that was colouring Carmichael's face at the very thought of attending a post mortem. 'I haven't attended one for ages – must be getting squeamish in my old age. What about you, Carmichael? When did you last attend an autopsy?'

Carmichael had to suppress the impulse to gag, before he managed to squeak, 'Just the once.'

'Well, it's time you widened your experience, my lad,' Dr Christmas commented hard-heartedly, totally unaware that Carmichael had a weak stomach and was liable to lose the contents of his own insides with remarkably little provocation. 'I'll get on with it first thing tomorrow morning, Harry. See you both at the mortuary at nine o'clock, sharp!'

As the doctor made his exit, the two remaining police personnel approached Falconer to receive instructions as to what they should be looking for. One of them took it upon himself, to be the first to speak. 'By the way, sir,' he began, addressing Falconer, 'we found the back door unlocked this morning. Maybe the young lady forgot to lock it, given the circumstances of her boyfriend being unwell, and feeling a little drunk herself.'

'Gadzooks!' Falconer exclaimed. 'The jungle drums round here are damned efficient. I've only just learnt all that myself, but thanks for the information. If it was unlocked all evening, it might not preclude the possibility that someone entered that way and put something in the cocktail shaker, or one of the bottles, because if Miss Fairfield and Mr Standing were round here, drinking, they wouldn't have been able to see the back door. The bottles will all have to go away for testing as well.'

'You don't think this could have been the work of the young lady then, sir?' asked the other officer.

'From what I've seen of her, I don't think so, but we must investigate all possibilities. When we've finished here and got everything nicely recorded at the station, Carmichael and I will go back next door and dig a little deeper into her background, and that of her boyfriend.

'I shall need a fingertip search done of the garden and any pathways. If anything was introduced into something that young man drank, then it had to be contained in something, so you'll be looking for a small discarded container of some kind. If it was glass, then maybe it was even ground underfoot. Pull out all the stops on this one, and don't forget the wheelie-bin's contents. Many a vital clue has been lost because no one fancied scrabbling through the contents of a refuse container. As it is, the local paper will probably lead tomorrow with the story, with a ghastly headline like "St Valentine's Day Massacre".'

With a duet of 'yes, sirs', the two SOCOs went about their business, and the two detectives headed back to the police station to consolidate what they had learnt so far.

Having stopped for a drink, with a cup of coffee for Falconer and a huge mug of tea (with six sugars) for Carmichael, they chatted about matters unrelated to crime to give themselves a proper break.

'How are you finding married life, then, Carmichael?' Falconer asked, for Carmichael had married his sweetheart at New Year. 'I believe I've actually recovered from the wedding hangover now, but it's taken a long while.'

'You're pulling my leg, sir,' retorted Carmichael, more at ease with the inspector now than he had been when they had first been partnered together. 'And it's grand. I felt like I'd won the jackpot before when we were engaged, and I went over to spend the evenings with Kerry and the boys. Sometimes the Warren-Brownes would babysit, and we'd go out on a proper date. But being married? It's absolutely fantastic, sir. I'd recommend it to anyone.'

'So you quite like it, then?'

'Ha ha, sir. Very funny!'

'Any plans to add to the family?'

'!' Carmichael gave the inspector a very old-fashioned look, which was immediately understood.

'Of course, it's none of my business. I apologise for prying, Carmichael.'

'That's all right, sir, but you know how I feel about discussing anything ... like that.'

'I should have remembered.'

'How are your three cats getting on, sir? All well?'

'Very well, thank you. And all eating me out of house and home. Their latest little stunt must have been a joint effort, considering the strength needed to accomplish it. I got home one night a couple of weeks ago, and they'd managed to deposit the back half of a dead rabbit in the middle of the kitchen floor.'

'Half a rabbit?' Carmichael was dumbfounded.

'That's what I thought, until I realised it was probably one that had been run over on the main road, and they'd found it, just grabbed the best bit of booty on offer, and brought it home to me as a little present.'

'Makes a lovely stew or a pie,' said Carmichael, a faraway look in his eyes. 'One of my ma's treats for us when I was a nipper was a rabbit pie. One of my uncles used to go out lamping, and bring her back a brace now and again.'

'I don't think we want to pursue that line any further, Carmichael. I'd hate to have to arrest a member of your family for poaching.'

'Much appreciated, sir,' replied the sergeant, only now aware of what he had let slip.

'Well, better get our noses back to the grindstone. We've got to go back to Coronation Terrace before we're finished for the day, and I want to go to see someone from Standing's family too.'

Bob Bryant had managed to trace Malcolm Standing's next-of-kin, and PC Green had been dispatched to break the news of his death, a job Falconer had hated doing in the past, when it had fallen to his lot. It was the worst news you could bring to anyone, and it always made him feel like an absolute heel having to be the one to break it. He and Carmichael therefore had the address of Mr and Mrs David Standing with them, so that they could pay a visit after returning to Coronation Terrace to continue their questioning of Chelsea Fairfield.

She was up and about, having woken about a quarter of an hour before they arrived, and was now having a cup of tea at Mrs Jenkins' kitchen table. She looked less panic-stricken and upset than she had before when she turned to greet them, and Falconer considered that she had only been going out with the young man for three weeks, and they had not yet instigated a physical relationship. Maybe she'd get over it quicker than he'd thought when he saw her earlier.

At their arrival, Ida Jenkins hurriedly produced two more cups and saucers and poured tea for her two new visitors. As Carmichael ladled sugar into his, she remarked, 'I've never seen anyone take his tea that sweet before, Sergeant Carmichael. But then, you do have a big frame to maintain, so I expects you needs it.' Carmichael just smiled at her, and continued to spoon a little more sugar into his already sticky brew.

Falconer courteously finished his cup of tea before announcing that it was time they resumed questioning. 'I need to know a little more about you and the deceased,' (he winced at the harsh reality of the word) 'Miss Fairfield. I know this is painful for you, so soon after the event, but it is necessary, I assure you.'

'I do understand, and once I've told you, it's done, so fire away, Inspector.' replied Chelsea.

'I need to know, and this may seem a little odd, where you work, and where Mr Standing worked. I would also like you to tell me how and where you met, and anything you know about his life before he met you.'

'I work in the pharmacy in the High Street, and Malcolm ... worked,' (she had a little trouble using the past tense, in this reference to him) 'as a sous chef in the Italian restaurant, about three doors from the pharmacy. We worked so close together, but never came across each other until recently,' she informed the two detectives, Carmichael huddled over his notebook, his chair pulled to a slight remove from the table so as not to draw attention to his note-taking.

'Did he tell you anything about his past, or his family?'

'Not a lot. He just said he'd worked there for a few years, and that he was estranged from his family. I never met any of them.'

'Did he say why?' This had interested Falconer.

At this question, she flicked her eyes away from the table and took a deep breath. 'We never discussed it,' she answered abruptly.

'What, never?' Falconer was definitely interested.

'He said he didn't want to talk about it: that it had been some silly adolescent squabble, and that it wasn't relevant to his life anymore. I took him at his word.'

'Do you know where his family lives?'

'I'm afraid not,' Chelsea answered, shaking her head to emphasise this negative.

'Did he have brothers and sisters?'

'I've no idea,' she said, again shaking her head.

'You really knew very little about him, then,' Falconer stated.

'People's pasts don't concern me; only their presents and futures,' she stated emphatically, as if this were really important to her.

'But surely what has happened to us makes us who we are today'?' commented the inspector.

Chelsea's answer consisted of just two words, 'Not necessarily,' and then she clamped her mouth shut, and stared down at the table blankly.

'I think we'll leave it there for now, thank you, Miss Fairfield. We'll be in touch when we have any more news or information. Thank you for your time, and thank you again, Mrs Jenkins, for the refreshments.'

They rose to leave but, just as they were passing through the kitchen door, Falconer looked back and caught a sideways glance after them that expressed extreme relief, on Chelsea Fairfield's face. It could just be a normal reaction. It could be that she was concealing something. He didn't know which, but he intended to find out.

<u>Chapter Four</u>

16th February

In the office the next morning, Falconer and Carmichael fell into a casual chat as they waited for various pieces of information to filter through to them which would allow them to continue their investigation.

'Buying that cottage next door to Kerry's was the best thing I ever did,' Carmichael threw out casually.

'It was originally bought by a couple of weekenders, wasn't it, after that first case we worked together?' asked Falconer.

'That's right, sir. With two very noisy dogs. I don't think the Brigadier knew what had hit him when they bought it. He did nothing but complain to them when they were down for the weekend, and even went to the Parish Council to see if anything could be done about it, but they said he'd just have to put up with it or get the noise abatement officer in from the council if he wanted to take it any further.'

'So they didn't settle?' Falconer had never heard the full story, and was in just the right sort of mood to have his mind distracted while he waited. 'They can't have felt very welcome. I've met the Brigadier, and he can be a fearsome character.'

'They only came down for a few weekends. Kerry left it as it was, telling them that she'd been through it, and they could keep anything they thought was of any interest to them, but the state of the place just defeated them.

'Not only was there a tremendous amount of work to do, but they had constant complaints about their dogs barking, and there was nothing to do in the village, and only the village pub and the tea-shop to amuse them.

'They soon got fed up with spending every weekend they came down clearing out and cleaning, and when Kerry and I had a talk about it, and I offered to buy it from them at the price they'd paid for it, they jumped at the chance.

'Kerry and I knew we'd get married even then, so it seemed like an ideal opportunity for me to take out a mortgage and buy the place, so that we could enlarge the living quarters, without all the upheaval of having to move. And with me buying it, it left Kerry's nest-egg intact for anything big that came up in the future. It was a form of being joined together before we actually tied the knot.'

'Smart move, Carmichael. So now *you've* got to do all the clearing out and renovation.'

'No problem, sir. One of my brothers has got a flat-bed truck, so it'll be easy to get all the rubbish to the tip, and everyone in my family's a dab-hand with a paint brush. We'll get there, and it's a bit of an adventure, too, all the funny little personal bits and pieces we come across, and all the old photos.'

'So, life's being good to you at the moment, Carmichael?' asked Falconer.

'It's just got better and better, since we've worked together,' Carmichael stated, without a whit of embarrassment.

'You soppy old sentimentalist, you!' said Falconer, nevertheless feeling pleased. They did work well together, chalk and cheese that they were, and he was beginning to feel proud of the partnership they were forging.

The telephone rang on Falconer's desk, and as he answered the call, Carmichael applied himself to his computer to carry out the check he'd promised himself he'd do first thing this morning, and had then been waylaid from his intended task by his enthusiasm for his new-found happiness.

Placing the telephone to his ear, a voice spoke without preamble. 'Get your lazy-ass butts over here now! You promised me you'd both attend the post-mortem, and I'm not starting it without *both* of you being here in person.'

He realised immediately that it was Dr Christmas, and blushed at being so remiss. Not only had he forgotten all about their agreement the day before, but it seemed, so had Carmichael. 'I'm so sorry. We both seemed to have suffered a crisis in short-term memory. We'll be over as soon as we can,' he apologised, and ended the call, indicating to Carmichael that they were going out.

'Just a minute, sir. I've got something here!'

'Can't it wait?'

'No, I don't think it can. I've just run Malcolm Standing through the records, and although he has no criminal convictions, it would seem he received a police caution in 2005,' Carmichael informed him.

'What for? Anything interesting?' asked Falconer.

'Don't know if it's relevant, sir, but I don't think it shows him up in a very satisfactory light,' said Carmichael. 'He was cautioned for interfering with a little girl – not very edifying – and it would appear that it wasn't just a one-off offence.'

'We'll see what we can dig up later,' offered Falconer, continuing, 'We haven't got time to do anything about it now. That was Christmas on the phone. We've both forgotten about his blasted post mortem. We were supposed to be there first thing, remember?'

'Oh no!' groaned Carmichael, turning pale. 'I'd completely forgotten about that.'

'So had I, but good old Dr Christmas has stayed his scalpel, until we arrive. Aren't we the lucky bunnies then?'

'No, sir,' disagreed the sergeant, reluctantly following the inspector out of the office, and on their way to an event that both of them would rather have been spared.

Market Darley was too small a town to have its own mortuary, so any bodies in need of storage or a post mortem were kept at the hospital mortuary, and it was in this direction that Harry Falconer drove his beloved Boxster now. Carmichael, beside him in the passenger seat, was unusually quiet, and Falconer enquired if he was all right.

'Not really, sir. I've got a rather delicate stomach.'

'What, with a physique like yours?'

'Can't help it. I've always been like it.'

'Well, I expect Dr Christmas will have the odd bowl or bucket lying around, should you need one. He's always got things like that on hand, for the various bits and pieces he removes from the bodies.'

'Gee, thanks, sir! And I had a really good fry-up this morning, too,' replied Carmichael in a sepulchral voice.

At the hospital, Dr Christmas was already scrubbed-up, gowned, and gloved, practically trembling with his eagerness to wield his various knives, saws, and maybe even a chisel or two. He enjoyed a great deal of Schadenfreude from observing others observing him carrying out this routine task.

Their reactions were so different, and he could never predict who would be sick, who would pass out cold, and who would just observe, and take an intelligent interest, without any reaction at all, to the various bits that were usually on the inside of a body, being delivered, like bastard deformed creatures, to the outside. Sometimes he'd have a little bet with himself, but he hardly ever won. There was nowt so queer as folk, in his opinion.

Falconer heartily disliked seeing people sliced and diced, as if they were in some sort of bizarre cannibal kitchen, but he could cope with it, because of what he had experienced on active duty in the army.

Carmichael was not quite so worldly-wise, and was unusually squeamish when it came to a lot of substances – inside things being outside, blood, and bones being three of them. He also could not deal with vomit, but predicted that it would only be his own that upset his stomach today.

It was the great Y-shaped cut that set Carmichael off: that and the cutting of the ribs to reveal the contents of the chest cavity. Taking a few steps back from the proceedings, he bent nearly double and gave an enormous heave. Dr Christmas's assistant was more than prepared, however, and managed to pop a bucket under his mouth just before a great whoosh of breakfast sprayed out of the sergeant's mouth.

'Ups-a-daisy!' this anonymous individual encouraged him, and stood there stolidly until the gauge on Carmichael's stomach was registering 'empty'. This was all carried out as quietly as possible, as Dr Christmas was speaking into a small suspended microphone, as he noted his findings.

Carmichael was led solicitously away, and settled down somewhere where he could not see what was being carried out, before being offered a large mug of heavily-sugared tea to settle his stomach.

He was just finishing this, and feeling a shade more human, when Falconer and Dr Christmas entered the room, both of them looking perfectly well and not the slightest bit wobbly. 'Please don't discuss it while I'm here,' he begged them. 'If you want to talk about, I'd rather go outside and get some air, and wait for you there.'

'I'll be there in a few minutes,' Falconer assured him, and he left them to their post-post mortem discussion.

Carmichael sat himself down on the boundary wall of the little mortuary car park, and sucked in mouthful after mouthful of clean, living air, and Falconer, true to his word, joined him within ten minutes. In his hand he held an empty carrier bag, which he handed to Carmichael. 'Here you are!' he said.

'What's that for?' asked Carmichael.

'To keep under your mouth on the drive back to the station. After this start to the day, if we go out again, we'll take your car. I will not tolerate you being sick in my Boxster, and that's that! If you're sick at the wheel of your own car, I'll happily hold the bag over the steering wheel for you, but I will not allow even the chance of you 'chucking up' in my beauty.'

Back at the station, Falconer had a word with Bob Bryant about the information that Carmichael had turned up on the computer before they had been peremptorily summoned to the mortuary. 'This dead chap, Bob,' he explained. 'Name of Malcolm Standing. It seems he received a caution for child abuse in 2005, when he was in his early twenties. I wondered if there was anything you could dig out about it for me.'

'Seems to ring a bell, but I don't know if the details will be on the computer yet,' Bob answered, his expression one of careful thought. 'I'll see what I can dig up – or get dug up – for you. I'll also ask around, see if anyone remembers it, or was involved. I'll send up anything I find to you, 'ASAP.'

'Thanks, Bob. I owe you one.' If you wanted to know anything about past cases, or even police gossip, you consulted Bob Bryant, who seemed to have worked on the desk forever, and knew every little thing that happened, as if it reached out to him from the past out of the ether.

Upstairs in the office, he found Carmichael sprawled backwards in his chair, still an unnatural colour, and insisted his sergeant took an early lunch, as his tank was obviously out of fuel, and he wouldn't be able to think straight without it. Carmichael smiled at him wanly and ambled off, still looking unhappy, in search of nourishment and a happier tummy.

Chapter Five

15th February – afternoon

When Carmichael returned to the office, he looked a lot more like his normal self and, as Falconer had just stopped to eat his own healthy lunch – a box of salad and a wholemeal bap, followed by an apple and a banana – he took the opportunity to find out a little more about Carmichael's family, the members of which he had met at the sergeant's and Kerry's wedding at the very beginning of the year, but had been rather 'blurred' at the time, and he was now unable to recall them very clearly.

'Well, there's six of us,' Carmichael started. 'Four boys and two girls.'

'And where do you come in that order?' Falconer enquired.

'I'm the fourth and last boy, then come my two sisters.'

'And their names – all of them?'

'My oldest brother's called Romeo, but everybody calls him 'Rome'. He's a builder. Gave me a bit of a hand when I built my little hideaway, when I lived at home. Then there's Hamlet – I told you my ma had this Shakespearian thing about names. He's known as Ham, and he works on a farm.

'Number three is Mercutio – just called Merc, like the car. He's a sort of 'man with a van'. He does small removals, house clearance, odd jobs, and gardening. He reckons the variety of jobs is good for him and stops him getting bored. Then it's me, but you know about me, because we work together,' said Carmichael, stating the bleedin' obvious. 'I got the Ralph bit, because my ma was really taken with an actor at the time – some fellow called Richardson.'

'Tell me, Carmichael, is your 'ma'' (Falconer suppressed a wince at this mode of maternal address) 'a great Shakespeare fan, then?'

'Not really. She just liked the names he used in his plays. Said they had a sort of 'ring' to them, like, but I'd better finish my family run-down.

'Next come the two girls. Juliet's the elder, and she's a hairdresser and beautician. Then, finally, there's Imogen, who's a librarian. She's done really well, passing all her exams and everything, and we're all very proud of her.'

'I should think they're all very proud of you, too,' Falconer commented.

'Yes, well, sort of,' replied Carmichael.

'What do you mean, sort of?' asked Falconer, not quite understanding why his family should not be really happy about what he was doing.

'Not everyone likes having a member of 'the fuzz' in their immediate family,' the sergeant stated baldly, turning slightly red, and avoiding Falconer's gaze.

''Nuff said, Carmichael. No further explanation needed or sought,' Falconer added, hoping to dispel the younger man's evident embarrassment, as he remembered the uncle who used to go out 'lamping' for rabbits. That was, no doubt, one of his more innocent pastimes. What he didn't know couldn't hurt him, and he'd pry no further. 'What about your parents? How did they cope with such a large brood?' 'Dad's a lot older than Ma. He's retired now, but he used to be a bus driver, then a coach driver. He always said he liked the long continental coach trips, 'cos at least it gave him the security of knowing that he couldn't get Ma in pod again while he was away. He swears that most of us kids were conceived just from him kissing her goodbye on the cheek when he went to work in the mornings.

'Ma married him at sixteen, in a bit of a hurry, and she's never had a proper, paid job. She said she always had too much to do just keeping house and home together, and preventing us kids from overthrowing western society, but I think she was joking about that last bit,' he concluded.

'I should hope so!' exclaimed Falconer, trying to digest the plethora of facts he had just been offered. By crikey! He bet their

Christmases were good, if Carmichael's wedding had been anything to go by. He just hoped that he was never asked to join their celebrations.

'Ma says that after six kids, her pelvic floor's so riddled with woodworm, that if one more kid trod on it, they'd go right through,' Carmichael added as an afterthought, and Falconer wrinkled his nose in disgust, determined to change the subject at all costs. He had no wish whatsoever to learn anything further about Mrs Carmichael senior's insides, having just had an intimate encounter with those of Malcolm Standing that morning.

'And how are the two little dogs you got last month? I'm sorry, I can't remember their names offhand.'

'Fang and Mr Knuckles,' declaimed Carmichael with pride, suitably distracted. Fang was a Chihuahua puppy, and Mr Knuckles a miniature Yorkshire terrier. When Falconer had first seen them they were tiny balls of fluff, which looked ridiculous cradled by the enormous Carmichael.

'They're getting on great! The boys love them, and they get more walks than they can cope with, poor little things. They slot right into the family, as if a gap has been waiting for them for some time. You must come and visit them sometime, sir.'

'We'll see, Carmichael. Not when we're in the middle of an investigation.'

Later that afternoon, Bob Bryant came upstairs with a dog-eared buff folder for Falconer, this being the file on Malcolm Standing's official caution. 'There were, apparently, some newspaper cuttings supposed to be in here, too, but they seem to have gone missing. I know there was a bit of a fuss about it at the time.

'We don't know who leaked it to the press, but that's the sort of thing that happens when it's a case of interfering with little kids. People get upset and can't bear to see it brushed under the carpet, even if there's no court case or prosecution,' he explained, having handed over the slim folder.

'Thanks for that, Bob. I'll have a little read of this, see if it throws any light on anything.'

There was very little in the case notes to help, but there were references on a separate sheet of paper to local newspaper reports which sensationalised the caution, blowing it out of all proportion and demonising the young Malcolm Standing.

It had all been five years ago now, and the dust must have settled, as Malcolm had been in the last job he was ever to hold for three years. It made him think of something someone had said when he was a child, and which had impressed itself on his memory, although he didn't completely understand it at the time. 'Good times, bad times, all times pass over.'

This sensation of its time had also passed over, and allowed the younger Standing to get whatever it was that had driven him to it out of his system, and try to lead a more normal life thereafter.

Many of Falconer's dealings with the local press in the past had been with the *Carsfold Gazette*, but this had happened in Market Darley and, after checking the telephone number, he put through a call to the *Market Darley Post* – a local newspaper that was more likely to have carried the story – asking for the editor when his call was answered.

'Good morning. I am Detective Inspector Falconer from Market Darley CID, and I was wondering if I could have a rummage through your archives for some information that may be pertinent to a case I'm working on at the moment?' he asked.

'Good morning, Chief Inspector Falconer. My name's Garry Mathers – that's two 'r's in Garry – and I should be delighted to be of assistance to the constabulary, provided, of course, that I get a scoop on whatever story is about to break.'

'Typical press!' thought Falconer, before replying, 'There might not be any case to break, but whatever comes of it, I promise that you will be the first to know. Is it all right if I pop over now? Time is always rather pressing during an investigation.'

'No problemo, squire! I am here to serve my community.'

Oh boy! He had a feeling he wasn't going to like this, but it had to be done.

Half an hour later found Falconer sitting in a back room at the offices of the *Market Darley Post*, scrolling through records of back numbers of the newspaper. Garry Mathers had provided him with the relevant year, and he knew the date of the official caution, so he worked from that date onwards, scrutinising each issue with a view to identifying any and every paragraph about Malcolm Standing's misdemeanour.

It seemed that the local press had made rather a large meal of the event, and headlines proclaimed the presence in the streets of Market Darley of a young and dangerous paedophile, stalking his victims at will, and, as yet, not behind bars. There were follow-up articles about the public outcry, and a special double-page letters section, allowing the town's residents to have their say, and it didn't make pleasant reading.

There was mention of another child being questioned about whether she had been assaulted or approached by Standing, but her (it was made obvious that this was a 'she') name was never mentioned. The identity of the child, concerning whom the caution had been issued, was also not published for legal reasons, so the articles were not a great deal of help to him. All they really did was to clarify the public hostility the young man must have endured at the time, and how difficult it must have been for him to live this down and start afresh, trying to live a more normal life after all the publicity had been superseded by more current events.

He'd rather naively pinned his hopes on learning something from this outdated reportage, forgetting that the young victim of any sort of abuse was guaranteed anonymity, and he supposed he must have hoped that someone would have let a name 'slip' at the time. Even if they had, the newspaper had not had the temerity to print it, no doubt fearing prosecution should they have done so.

Before he left, he even sought out Garry (with two 'r's!) in his office, to see if he could give him a name on the Q.T. but that was no-go, either. He'd only been there a year, and had no knowledge of events in Market Darley that long ago. 'I moved down from Town,' he explained. 'Thought I'd rather be a big fish in a small pond, than a minnow in the shark-infested waters of the capital.'

So, that was that! Dead end! What now? He decided to go back to Bob Bryant, and see what he could winkle out of the darker corners of his memory.

'Anything you can drag up, Bob,' he pleaded with the desk sergeant, as he entered the station, after his abortive treasure hunt.

'Leave it with me, and I'll give you a tinkle as soon as anything comes back to me,' he promised, and Falconer had to be content with that.

When he got back to his own office, he found a message to contact Dr Christmas, an activity he carried out without delay. He might have identified the substance that caused Standing's death, and that might give them a clue as to who had administered it. Although Chelsea Fairfield was the obvious choice, she had not struck him as a murderer, and Malcolm Standing had had a lot of enemies from the past.

He was in luck, as Christmas answered on the third ring. 'Hello there, Harry. I've got some news for you, my boy.' Bingo! And the doctor sounded happy, so it looked like Falconer was finally going to learn something solid about the case.

'The lab's identified what that young chap ingested. You'll never guess what it was.'

'Don't tease me, please. I can hardly stand the suspense,' Falconer pleaded.

'It was a whacking great dose of good old-fashioned valium. If that girl had called for help when he first started feeling strange, they could have saved him, but valium is a muscle relaxant, and it works on the chest muscles as well and suppresses breathing. If she'd have summoned an ambulance, they could have got him pumped out and stabilised him. As it was, he died of suffocation.'

'I don't really know that I want to tell her that,' Falconer replied. 'She's worried enough about whether he would have been all right if she'd called a doctor the night before. This news would probably destroy her.'

'I'll leave that particular moral dilemma with you. My job is just to identify the cause of death, and pass on that information. Good luck!'

'Thanks, Philip. Goodbye.' Falconer put down the telephone, now faced with a new problem: to tell, or not to tell, that was the question.

While he was mulling this over, the internal phone system trilled, and he found Bob Bryant on the other end of the line. 'So soon?' he queried, knowing that Bob would know what he was talking about.

'I just remembered who administered the official caution, and you're not going to believe this, but it was our very own darling Superintendent 'Jelly' Chivers. It was just before he was promoted from detective chief inspector, and he must have frightened seven shades of shite out of that young lad, for he never reoffended, as far as I know.'

'Language, Bob!'

'I know, but put yourself in the lad's position. Yes, you've done something terrible, and now here you are in front of this terrifying monster while he roars the caution at you and delivers a hell-fire and brimstone lecture to you at the same time. I bet he wished the earth would open up and swallow him.'

'That doesn't detract from the seriousness of the matter, though, Bob,' Falconer felt compelled to point out.

'I realise that, but I bet if he was used on young offenders of any sort, he'd be a better deterrent than these soft Youth Detention Centres they put them in nowadays. I'd be willing to bet that anyone who's ever been cautioned by old Jelly has never reoffended, nor even considered it.' This was Bob Bryant's personal opinion, and nothing would sway him from his belief.

'You could be right, at that, Bob,' agreed Falconer, imagining how he'd felt in the past, when Chivers had given him a good bawling-out over something.

'So I've booked an appointment for you to see the great man himself, at 9.30 tomorrow morning.'

'Thanks a bunch, Bob. Do I get a last request before I enter his office, like a man facing a firing squad?'

'I should advise you to step warily. He's going to a golf club dinner tonight, and he's liable to have a sore head.'

'Great! So, not long after I get in tomorrow, I have to enter the den of a bear with a sore head, and try to get him to think back to something that happened five years ago?'

'That's about the size of it, Harry. Good luck! And let me see the wounds afterwards, won't you?'

Falconer finished the call with just one word, 'Rat!' but he heard Bob Bryant's chuckle. before the line went dead.

<u>Chapter Six</u>

16th February

The next morning, having dressed and carried out his daily grooming with especial care, Falconer found himself outside Superintendent Chivers' office with thirty seconds to spare. Counting them down conscientiously on his watch, he mouthed, 'Three, two, one,' and raised his hand to rap on the door when it unexpectedly opened, and he found himself apparently brandishing a fist in the superintendent's face.

'Sorry, sir,' he mumbled in apology, letting his hand drop.

'I was just coming out to see where the devil you'd got to,' snapped Chivers, striding back into his office and throwing himself, like a large sack of potatoes, into his chair. 'What do you want?'

'I need to talk to you about an official caution you delivered about five years ago,' Falconer began, only to be nearly blasted out of his socks by the voice of a volcano.

'Five years ago? How the devil am I supposed to remember something I did five years ago? Are you mad, man?'

'I think you'll remember this one, sir,' Falconer suggested humbly, glad that he hadn't been flattened in the blast. 'It concerns a young man called Malcolm Standing, and you were dealing with a case of interfering with a little girl. The parents didn't want to put their daughter through the trauma of a trial, I presume, but the press got hold of it somehow, and created a nine days' sensation out of it.'

Chivers sat in silence for a few seconds, then, it seemed, from his expression, that light had dawned. 'I do remember that one. Nasty business, very nasty indeed. I gave the little toe-rag a right dressing down, and it left me feeling physically sick to think what he'd done.'

'It's just that I need to know as much as I can about who was involved, with reference to a case I'm working on now. Standing has been murdered, and I wondered if it could have been done by someone connected with his misdemeanour back then.'

'I see,' said Chivers, thoughtfully. 'The child's family name was, I seem to remember, Ifield. She was their only child, Eileen, who was sinned against. She was thirteen when it finally came out. I don't know what the catalyst was, but she suddenly confessed to her mother, and it would seem that the abuse had been going on from when she was just seven years old until the previous year.'

'Is it possible that you still have an address for the Ifields? I'd like to speak to them, and to Eileen, about Standing. I wouldn't normally rake up something like this, but I need to catch whoever murdered him.'

'I'm afraid you're out of luck with all the members of the family. Mr and Mrs Ifield moved away from the area after their daughter committed suicide a couple of years ago.'

'She killed herself?' Falconer asked, aghast.

'That's right, and only sixteen years of age,' replied Superintendent Chivers, a shadow passing across his expression, as he remembered the sad event.

'How did she do it, sir?'

'With tablets. Something the doctor had prescribed for her. It was all that little bastard's doing, you know. She was never the same after that, her parents told me. I went to the funeral. Felt I had to; show some respect, and the support of the police.'

'I don't suppose you know what tablets she used, or who her doctor was at the time, sir?' Falconer was determined that there was a connection, and he wanted to get to the bottom of it.

'That I can't recall, but it was reported in the local paper. It might be worth your while trawling through their back issues for 2008. I seem to remember that they made a bit of a song and dance about it. Poor little abused girl, couldn't forget and get on with her life – you know the sort of melodramatic crap the media churn out. 'Probably hoped to start off the same old witch hunt again, but the general opinion seemed to be to let the past rest in peace. Raking it all up again wouldn't bring her back, or restore her innocence.

'We had a few calls from members of the public, asking us why we hadn't locked him up and thrown away the key, but I put out a press statement, informing them that the poor girl's life would have been even more blighted by having to go through the trauma of a court case. That soon shut them up. Sorry I can't be of more help, Harry.'

'You've been very helpful indeed. I'll drop in at the *Market Darley Post* offices, and have a look at 2008; see what they reported at the time of her suicide.'

'Good man. And good luck!'

Returning once more in the back room of the local newspaper offices, Falconer metaphorically shook himself free of the invisible slime that Garry Mathers had seemed to coat him in when he had first arrived, then set to work to hunt out the articles he was after.

It didn't take him long to find them, for the story had made the front page: the press, as usual, braying for someone's blood, and not caring in this case whether it came from the local constabulary or Malcolm Standing himself.

Reading the articles written at that time, and the statement issued by Chivers himself, he finally, just out of idle curiosity, began to hunt for the death notices of the young girl, or perhaps he should refer to her as a young woman, at sixteen years of age?

These he found without difficulty. Many of her friends and relatives had put separate announcements in, and he scanned the column conscientiously, his eyes widening with surprise as he read the last announcement, hardly able to believe what he was seeing.

With an expression of infinite sadness in his eyes, he packed up his notebook and left the building, towards the inevitable end of this case.

Back at the office once more, he collected Carmichael and requested that PC Linda 'Twinkle' Starr accompany him on his mission. To neither of them did he say anything, just asking them to take their lead from him, and follow standard police procedure.

He drove, and it wasn't long before they stopped outside Coronation Terrace. Number twelve was their destination, and his steps were slow and heavy as he walked up the garden path. PC Starr accompanied him: Carmichael had been instructed to go round to the back of the property, in case there was a last-minute escape attempt.

Chelsea Fairfield answered the door, her face a picture of panic and despair when she saw who was waiting for her. She'd been a great little actress up till now, but she realised the game was up.

'I think you know why we're here, don't you, Miss Fairfield?' Falconer asked, his voice thick with emotion at the waste of another young life.

'You'd better come in,' she said, as if she cared what the neighbours would think!

When Carmichael was alerted that they had gained entrance, he went next door to number ten and asked Mrs Jenkins to join them. She would be support for Chelsea in her hour of need, and she also made exceedingly good tea. If he was lucky, she might even bring some biscuits round with her. No matter how grave the circumstances, Carmichael was always hungry!

But Ida Jenkins went one better, and appeared at the front door with a cake tin. 'Just a little something I made yesterday,' she announced. 'Nothing like a bit of sugar to make you feel a bit stronger when times is trying, is there?' she asked of no one in particular.

She bustled around in the kitchen area in Chelsea's, clattering crockery and boiling the kettle, while Falconer got on with what he had come here for.

'Why did you do it?' he asked the young woman, who had not yet shed a tear at their discovery of her crime.

'She told me about what Malcolm had done when she was about eleven,' she said. 'And I told her that she had to do something about it, but she said she couldn't tell her mum. I used to go and stay there for a while, in the summer holidays, because we were both only children and they lived out of town. It didn't matter about the age difference: she was like a little sister to me.

'The next year, when I went back, I found out it was still going on and I was furious. Of course, by then, I wasn't staying there for long in the summer. I was seventeen years old, and I'd discovered boys and parties and I wanted to be with people my own age. Young people can be so selfish,' she finished, not noting the irony that she was still one of those young people. Maybe she'd had to grow up faster than most, though.

'I didn't want to get involved, but I asked her to show me where he lived, and I wrote him an anonymous letter telling him I'd castrate him if he ever laid a finger on her again, and it seemed that he did stop, but it was also me that told her parents she had something disturbing to tell them, and that they'd better get her to talk to them.

'Time went by so fast that we hardly spoke again until just before she took her own life. I think she'd discovered boys, and found that what he'd done to her had changed her. She didn't think she'd ever be able to have a boyfriend like normal girls do. It was all so sad. She'd lost so much weight. She used to be a chubby, laughing little child, but by the end, she looked like a skeleton. *He* did that to her!

'For me, it was over when I sent that letter and he left her alone, but it had haunted her ever since. As soon as I heard what she'd done, I went over there to see Auntie Maureen and Uncle Brian, and that's when I did it.'

'Did what?' Falconer asked her, his voice muted, his face careworn.

'I took the tablets she hadn't taken.'

'So it wasn't something you got from the pharmacy where you work?' Falconer asked.

'No. I took what was available at the time, and just hung on to them, because I decided there and then that I'd hunt that evil bastard down and somehow get even for her. And that's exactly what I did. Of course, I had to get on with my own life. Then I had to find him, and strike up some sort of relationship with him. Perhaps now you'll understand why I kept him waiting for you-know-what!

'I can't tell you how unbearable it felt, to have that creep slobbering all over me, and trying to get into my knickers for those three weeks.

'There was no way I was ever going to go to bed with that evil little pervert, but I was going to deliver justice to him – a life for a life!'

'Did you know what those tablets would do to him?' Falconer interjected at this juncture.

'I knew what they'd done to my cousin, and I just wanted the same thing to happen to him. I ground them up with my pestle and mortar, and dissolved them as best as I could before he arrived, then I split the suspension between two drinks, hurrying him through the first one so that I could get him to drink the second one before he lost consciousness.

'Of course, when I saw the reality of what I'd done, and phoned the station, I really was hysterical. I couldn't believe it! The seriousness of actually taking a life. But later, I remembered all that poor little Eileen had gone through, and I was glad.'

Her voice trailed off into silence, and Mrs Jenkins erupted into that silence, carrying a tray, and carolling, 'Tea and cake for everybody. Just the thing to lift the spirits, that's what I always say.'

THE END

Battered To Death

DI Falconer and DS Carmichael are both enjoying a well-earned rest day, when they are summoned to a most distressing incident that has occurred at a chip shop on the parade of shops in Upper Darley.

It was obviously murder, but was it something to do with the robust behaviour of some of the more aggressive customers from the night before or was it closer to home?

PORTION ONE

<u>Friday 16th April</u>

It was after ten o'clock on a mild evening, and the rather pathetically-named shop unit called Chish and Fips was doing its usual roaring trade for a Friday night. The shop was packed with customers being served and waiting to be served, with even one or two customers standing outside, waiting for the queue to get a little shorter, so that they could join it on the other side of the door.

The heat in the little unit was furnace-like, the faces of the customers nearest to the counter a bright red as the fryers belched out heat and clouds of steam. From outside, the little unit was a beacon of smeared colours, like a work of abstract art, behind its condensation-clouded and dripping plate-glass window. The face behind the counter, trying to cope on its own, was of a similar hue to that of its closest customers, but with the features down-turned and cross. The owner, Frank Carrington, had promised to come in at half-past nine to give her a hand, and had still not shown up.

'Who's next?' queried the cross-faced figure, Sylvia Beeton by name, trying to serve, wrap orders, rescue cooked food from the fryers, take money, give change, and put fresh food on to fry, all at the same time, and getting mighty fed-up with the gargantuan effort she was putting in for what was just a smidgen over the minimum wage.

As a voice shouted out for two cod and chips, and to make it quick, she shouted back, without diverting her gaze in the voice's direction, 'You wait your turn like everyone else, Sanjeev Khan. Just because your dad's on the council doesn't give you priority over anyone else.'

'Two cod and chips, one double battered sausage and chips, and one meat and potato pie and chips,' the next customer called out, while she was still adding up two burgers and chips, two pickled onions, a pineapple fritter, and a portion of chicken with extra chips.

'I'll be with you as soon as I can. I've only got one pair of hands, and I've not taken for this lot yet,' she called out, handing over a bulging carrier bag and taking, in exchange, a high denomination note. 'Haven't you got anything smaller, sir?' she asked. 'Oh, well, can't be helped.' She sighed, then raised her voice to the rest of the gaggle in the shop, 'Correct money if you can, or as near as possible. I'm not a bank, and I've nearly run out of change. If you can't, I may have to refuse to serve you.'

As she got on with serving the next order, throwing an extra load of chips into the fryer and pulling a dozen pieces of fish out of the batter tray and throwing them into another receptacle of boiling fat (for everything was fried in lard in this establishment, in the old-fashioned way), there was a muttering amongst the customers, and some, who knew each other, got wallets out and rummaged around in pockets to see if they had the exact money, or could help out friends, who looked woebegone, when they flashed a twenty-pound note at them, and felt devastated at possibly having to forego their supper just because of lack of change.

The queue shortened slowly, as the lull before 'chucking-out' time at the pubs arrived and from the flat upstairs there suddenly boomed an almighty racket of drum and bass music, shaking the fluorescent light fitting on the ceiling and causing some customers to cover their ears.

'It's all right,' Sylvia shouted. 'I'll just go up and give them a blasting. I can't take orders with this racket going on,' and with that, she was off, through a door at the back, and could be heard thumping up a flight of stairs to the first floor. There was then a roar that rose even above the music, the deafening racket was turned down to a reasonable volume, and Sylvia returned, a look of triumph on her face.

'That's sorted *them* out!' she said, with satisfaction, rubbing her plump hands together with satisfaction. 'Now, who's next? Curry Khan, you put that can of drink back in the fridge where it belongs. If I know you, you'll high-tail off with it before I get to your order. You can take one then, and not before.'

'But I'm thirsty, Mrs Beeton.'

'Then squeeze to the front and put the exact money on the counter, and I'll let you take it now, and then you can wait for your order like everybody else here. But no pay, no drink. Got it?'

'Got it, Ma,' agreed Curry, the son of the owner of the local Indian restaurant, and leaned through and put a pound piece on the serving bar. 'I'll get my change when I order,' he shouted to Sylvia, then removed his cold drink and began to gulp at the contents.

'Who's two haddock and chips?' Sylvia shouted above the sizzling and bubbling of yet another load of fish fresh into the fryer, and a cloud of steam enveloped her for a second or two, making her invisible.

'Over here! And I've got the right money,' called a voice from the other side of the counter, and an arm extended, hand clasping a pile of change, and the paper wrapped packet was given in exchange.

She had almost dealt with this deluge of customers, and there were only three people waiting to be served, when Frank Carrington strolled in. 'I thought I'd come in and give you a hand during the rush,' he announced, as if he were doing her a favour, rather than working in his own business to line his pocket, not hers.

'You know damned well we have a rush at ten, then another one just after eleven. Where were you at ten o'clock? I was in here getting broiled and working my guts out, just so as you can go on a nice holiday in the summer then swank about how well your business is doing.'

'Well, if you're not up to it anymore, Sylvia ...' he said, and left the sentence hanging.

'Don't you threaten me! You wouldn't get a fraction of the work out of a young 'un as you get out of me, and you know it. I'm more than value for money, and don't you forget it.'

'Only pulling your leg, Sylv. Don't get all hot and bothered about it.'

'Don't get all hot and bothered? Just look at the colour of my face, and my hair's dripping under this hat. You wouldn't know hot and bothered unless it had a sauna attached to it, you wouldn't.'

'Look, I'm here now, so let's not argue about it. The after-hours rush will be here any minute now, so make sure you've got enough chips ready, and plenty of batter. We can get on with some of the frying before they get here, so that at least we can serve the first dozen or so customers with what we pre-fry, then the next lot will be ready for the queue behind.'

'Makes sense to me. Get your coat and hat on then, and we'll get started for the first wave,' replied Sylvia, scooping the last of the chips out of the fat and adding a new batch.

The next wave arrived just a few minutes after eleven. and was the most difficult to deal with, because it consisted of those who had been in the pub just that little bit longer.

The queue was, unsurprisingly, not so well-behaved with the new batch of customers, and there was a fair amount of shoving and barging for position, and quite a few angry words exchanged as they waited.

Sylvia let fly. 'Get yourselves into a proper queue and act like civilised human beings. I don't care how much you've had to drink! If you want your chips from here, you can bloody well behave, or I'll chuck you out myself!'

She received some unexpected support from Frank Carrington, who raised his voice above the hubbub, and shouted, 'You'd better to listen to our Sylvia, because she means it, and I'm here to re-enforce her decisions.'

'Bloody little Hitler!' came from the middle of the queue, and Sylvia was on to it immediately. 'Dogger Ferguson, you get out of here this minute. I won't have talk like that in this chip shop, and you're barred.'

'You can't bar me! This is a chip shop, not a pub,' he replied, not really bothered by her threat.

'No, but *I* can!' This was Frank Carrington's voice, 'and *I'm* barring you. Get out now, and go quietly, or I'll call the police. I will not have insults like that bandied about in my chip shop. And if any of you think that's unfair, you can go too!'

'So where am I supposed to get my chips then,' the youth shouted back, now not looking so sure of himself.

'You'll just have to go into the town centre, won't you? Come back in six months, and I'll see if you've learnt any manners. Until then, don't come back!' This was from Sylvia, who was usually the one to restore order, if trouble seemed to be about to break out.

'Chalky White, you come back here this minute! Not only have you short-changed me, but one of the fifty pees is an old Irish one. You get back here, or I'll tell your mother!'

A dark-skinned youth wove his way back to the counter and corrected the transaction. 'God, I'm glad you're not my mother,' he said, as he left the counter.

'So am I!' called back Sylvia, giving as good as she got, 'Because if you were mine, I'd have drowned you at birth!'

'Old bitch!'

'I heard that!'

The rest of the evening was unusually aggressive, and by the time they had cleared up, prepped for the next day which, being Saturday, was a busy one, both she and Frank were exhausted.

'Where do they get it from? That's what I want to know,' said Sylvia, pulling on the old coat she always wore to work because she didn't want to smell like the lady from the chip shop wherever she went. This way, she didn't have to have any of her other coats sullied by the tell-tale smell of where she worked.

'The telly?' offered Frank. 'School?'

'More like the fact that their mums were only just out of school when they had 'em, and don't know a thing about bringing up a child to have good manners,' was Sylvia's considered opinion, and on this thought, Frank locked up. Sylvia got her bike out of the back hall and made her way home, another Friday evening over and done with. And good riddance to it, too, she thought, puffing and blowing her way back.

PORTION TWO

<u>Saturday 17th April – morning</u>

Detective Inspector Harry Falconer of the Market Darley CID was having a well-earned day off. Apart from other crimes, he had already dealt with three murder cases since his explosive entry to the New Year, courtesy of Carmichael's pantomime-themed wedding, and more booze than he'd ever indulged in in his life before, and that included his time in the army. He really needed a day away from the office and work, and had decided to indulge himself in one of his lazy days.

He'd not risen until half-past eight, a veritable lie-in for him, then treated himself to a fried breakfast, sharing the last rasher of bacon between his three cats, Mycroft, Tar Baby, and Ruby, who had all begged very nicely to share his unaccustomed treat.

After that, he'd spread the main body of his Saturday newspaper on the floor, laid down at the bottom of it, and begun to read. He was usually much more grown-up about this activity, but occasionally indulged in this sort of lounge on the floor because he enjoyed it, and holding up the paper (which was a broadsheet) made his arms ache, and, folding it, his temper ache.

He knew he wouldn't be able to stay in this position for long, because the cats so loved to play with the corners of the pages, stalking and pouncing on them, then chewing them a bit, and eventually, clawing them. He reckoned he had a good half an hour of shooing them off before he had to transfer the newspaper to the dining table. After that, he intended to watch an old black and white movie he had recorded weeks ago, and hadn't yet had the time to look at. And after that? Who knows? He might even go for a walk, or take a trip to the local garden centre.

In Castle Farthing, Detective Sergeant 'Davey' Carmichael was also enjoying a day off, and spending it with his wife, Kerry, and her two sons, Kyle and Dean. In his opinion, there was no better way to spend his leisure time than with these three dearest of people. They had also, recently, become the proud owners of two tiny dogs that the boys had named: a Chihuahua called Fang, and a miniature Yorkshire terrier called Mr Knuckles.

After an enormous breakfast – for, if Carmichael were a car, he'd be a gas guzzler, given his size and fuel consumption – he suggested that they all go out on to the village green and throw a stick and a ball around for the dogs. They had managed to find a very small ball in the pet shop that the young dogs could get their jaws round, and a twig sufficed, in their case, as a stick.

The boys were very enthusiastic, as were the dogs, for they loved getting out of the house and having a mad run around with the big man, and the green was so big to them. Kerry, however, pleaded household duties and, after closing the door on them gratefully, put on the washing machine, and sat down in her favourite armchair with a magazine and a cup of coffee. She already had a stew cooking away for their evening meal in the slow cooker, and felt that this was about as much as she wanted to do this morning.

Through the open window, it being such a fair day, she could hear the high-pitched yips of the dogs' excitement, and the voices of the boys calling after their pets. Occasionally her husband's voice boomed out with an instruction, but more often with laughter so, it seemed to her, that they were all having a jolly nice time, including herself in this thought.

Harry Falconer had finished with his newspaper for the time being, and was having a pre-luncheon doze on the sofa, covered in three furry bodies, joining him in this unexpected opportunity to use his body heat, when the phone rang. He started awake and sat up immediately, scattering cats as he got to his feet. This had better be a cold call. And if it was work, it'd better be good, disturbing him on the first day off he'd had for a fortnight.

'Falconer. What?' he answered, peremptorily.

'Harry, I'm so sorry to disturb you,' said the voice of Bob Bryant from the station, 'but there's been a very nasty death in Upper Darley. I think you need to get out there. And Carmichael.'

'What's happened? And why can't someone else handle it for a change?'

'I've spoken to Superintendent Chivers, and *he* wants you out there.'

'Sadistic bastard! Right! Where is it, and what happened?'

'It's at the chip shop on the Riverside Parade, in Upper Darley, and it's a nasty one. I don't even want to describe it. It turns my stomach.'

'And yet you want me to go out and *look* at it?'

'Sorry, Harry, but it is your job. Get yourself out there, and I'll send Carmichael to join you.'

'I'm on my way,' sighed Falconer. It was half-past twelve, and he now wouldn't have time for any lunch. And on his day off, too! Maybe he could snaffle a bag of chips when he got there.

The two little dogs, now exhausted, were having a nap on Kerry's lap when the phone rang in Jasmine Cottage, in Castle Farthing's High Street. Sliding them carefully off her, she rose to answer the phone. 'Hello, Bob,' she greeted the sergeant. 'Surely you're not going to disturb Davey on his day off? He hasn't had one for a couple of weeks, and he's out on the green, now, playing football with the boys.'

'Sorry, Mrs Carmichael. I wouldn't have called if the super hadn't insisted. Can you call him in, so that I can have a word?' asked Bryant, apologetically.

'Of course I can, and call me Kerry. Everyone else does. Hang on a moment,' she said, and put the receiver down on the little table where the phone base lived.

Opening the cottage door, she put her hands to her mouth, to create an improvised loud-hailer, and called, 'Davey – phone. Urgent!' and watched as he said a few words to the boys and sprinted back to the cottage, the boys trailing in his wake, evidently disappointed that their fun had been cut short on their day with Daddy Davey.

'Carmichael here,' said the sergeant, picking up the phone, wondering what could be so urgent on his day off.

'Davey, it's Bob from the station. There's been a nasty death at the chip shop, on that parade of shops at Upper Darley. Do you know the one? Good! The super wants you to meet Harry out there. You'll find out the details when you arrive.'

'But, what's hap ...' Carmichael started to ask, but Bob Bryant had cut him off, without a shred of detail. He'd just have to get himself over there as quickly as he could, and find out what had happened when he got there.

Falconer, living on the outskirts of Market Darley, was the first one to arrive on the scene, and found a crowd of would-be customers, now turned rubber-neckers, outside the plate glass window. Crime-scene tape had already been stretched across the front of the shop, and PC Merv Green was on duty at the door to keep sight-seers away, as far as was humanly possible. There was always an audience at the site of any public death. It was simple human nature, but not a nice side of it.

Pushing his way through the people gawking for a look through the window, he held out his warrant card and pushed his way through to where PC Green stood guard. 'Know what's happened in there?' he asked, before entering.

'Very nasty one, sir,' replied Green, his face in agreement with his name. 'I'm not usually squeamish, but this is a very unpleasant one. I think you'd better go inside and see for yourself. I don't want to think about it, let alone talk about it. Sorry, sir.'

This was unlike Green, and Bob Bryant had been reluctant to give any details either. Falconer's insides gave a little flip of apprehension as these two thoughts collided. These were both experienced policemen. Whatever could have given *them* such a fit of the heebie-jeebies? Wondering if Dr Christmas had already arrived, or was still on his way, he pushed open the glass door and went inside the chip shop, preparing for the worst.

'Hello, Harry,' said a familiar voice, and Falconer became aware of Dr Phillip Christmas and another man, standing at the back of the shop, well away from the fryers. 'May I introduce you to Frank Carrington, the owner of this establishment?'

Falconer approached and shook the man's hand, taking the opportunity to introduce himself at the same time. 'So, what have we got here?' he asked, and was surprised when the owner just pointed at the counter of the shop. After staring at this for a few seconds, Mr Carrington finally spoke, his voice a hoarse whisper. 'It's behind there!' he croaked. 'At the chip fryer.'

Christmas gave Falconer a look, and added, 'I hope you haven't already had your lunch, Harry. It's gruesome!'

'I haven't, as a matter of fact,' Falconer informed them, and then, finally reaching the other side of the counter, stopped dead, his mouth opening in surprise and horror, his eyes involuntarily closing to shut out what was in front of them.

Turning back to look at the other two men present, he opened his eyes again, and said, 'I think I might give lunch a miss today. Who the hell did this? It's iniquitous! What a bloody awful way to die!'

'Sorry, Harry. Wish I could have spared you this one,' sympathised Christmas. 'Maybe it'd be better if I told you what happened, rather than you poke around for yourself.'

'I think that's a very good idea. I don't fancy going any nearer to 'that' than I have to, and the thought of 'poking around', makes me positively queasy,' replied Falconer, joining them at the other end of the shop, well away from the fryers, where a couple of grotty tables and a few mismatched chairs were placed for anyone who wanted to dine-in.

'Take a seat, first, Harry. In fact, let's all sit down. It's not a nice subject for discussion, and I think we'd be better off seated once I start going into details.'

'Do I have to stay?' asked Carrington. 'After all, I found her, and I feel as sick as a dog.'

'Make a note of your name and address, and leave it on the counter, and I'll be in touch later,' Falconer told him, then waited until he'd complied before turning back to Dr Christmas. 'Come on, out with it. You know you've got to tell me sometime,' he said, looking apprehensive. 'Who? How? And when? And why, for God's sake. That's sick, and it took some doing. We'll work out who is responsible, when we've got something more to go on.'

Christmas drew a deep breath, and commenced his grisly tale. '"Who" is easy. The victim is a Mrs Sylvia Beeton, who had worked part-time here for years. I got her address from Mr Carrington, so you don't need to worry about that.

'"When" isn't too difficult, either, as she was supposed to arrive at work to get everything started at about eleven-thirty this morning, and open up at noon. Mr Carrington arrived just after opening time, and found customers waiting outside, unable to get in – she'd have locked the door while she did her preparation, and then not unlocked it again until opening time.'

'That seems straightforward enough, so far,' Falconer interrupted the doctor, in a vain effort to delay what he knew would follow next.

'Oh, it is, but it's the 'how' that's the stomach-churner.' Here it came then. Falconer steeled himself for the grisly details. 'From what I could glean from an examination of the scene, when I arrived about fifteen minutes ago, someone dumped the large container of batter over her head, then pushed her head into the chip fryer, and held her down with the large chip scoop. As she was due to start pre-frying chips, the oil was up to temperature, and I'm afraid that's not very good for the complexion.'

'Oh, my good God!' exclaimed Falconer, unable to quite comprehend what he had been told. 'I'll have to take a look, for the sake of procedure, but now I know what happened, I know I'm not going to like it one little bit.'

Slowly, like a child who is afraid that someone might jump out at him, Falconer approached the other side of the counter, and moved towards the huge bulk of what, until nearly midday today, been Mrs Sylvia Beeton.

'Can you give me a hand to turn her over?' he called to Christmas. 'How did you manage it? She's a very big woman.'

'I got Green to help me,' explained the Doc, and followed Falconer behind the counter.

'That would explain why he looked so bilious when I got here,' replied Falconer, more as something to say to keep his mind off what he was about to see.

The two of them manhandled the body, so that they could look at its face, and Falconer came out in a cold sweat. 'Whoever it was, has literally fried her face, and in batter, too,' he managed, in a rather high-pitched voice, letting go his hold on his half of the mighty Mrs Beeton.

Christmas lowered his end too, and said, with a nervous little giggle, 'She's definitely been battered to death, then! And it looks like she was held down in there at the back of the neck, as I just said, with the chip scoop. I haven't touched it, just left it for you to put into an evidence bag, in case it's got fingerprints on it.'

'Don't joke about it, Philip. It only makes it worse. And I'll just get that scoop bagged up now. Thanks for noticing that. God, what a ghastly way to end up!'

'What a dreadful thing even to contemplate doing to another human being,' commented the medical man, and they both fell silent, and stared off into nothingness, horrified by this seemingly random and unspeakable act.

So deep were they in a brown study that they didn't hear the door open, and before either of them could do anything about it, Carmichael sprung up like a jack-in-the-box beside them, full of enthusiasm, as usual, to see what was afoot; and, unfortunately, from this distance, he could do just that.

As he began to heave, Falconer yelled, 'Nooo!' and rushed, over in the vain hope that he could stem the inevitable flow. 'Footprints, man!' he shouted. 'Evidence!'

Hearing the inspector's voice, Carmichael swivelled his noxious spray a hundred and eighty degrees, and the last of his offering landed on the highly polished tops of Falconer's immaculate shoes.

'Now look what you've done, Sergeant! Muddied any forensic evidence on the floor. And just look at my shoes,' he finished, reaching for a roll of kitchen paper that sat on the shelf behind the counter. 'Why on earth didn't you wait?'

'Urgh!' groaned Carmichael, took a step forward to assist Falconer and slipped, landing on his back on his contribution to 'Dirty Floor Day.'

'And now you've fallen in it! Get yourself into the little cloakroom out the back, and see what you can do about cleaning yourself up!'

'You know I've got a dicky tummy, sir,' Carmichael pleaded, then, thinking again of what he had just seen, and went for it again with enthusiasm. But there was no ammunition left for him to shoot, and he stood there, in a pool of his own breakfast, dry-heaving like a pump fresh out of water.

'Sometimes I wonder why you joined the force!' snapped his boss, wiping lumps of the vile substance from his shoes, making a little moue of distaste, and making sure that he was breathing only through his mouth.

'Because I wanted to catch criminals, sir,' answered the sergeant, gingerly making his way towards the indicated cloakroom, and removing his jacket as he went.

'Well, that's ruined any evidence of footprints, this side of the counter!' said Falconer, a little later, looking daggers at his sergeant, who was perched on one of the old chairs at the back of the shop, his head between his knees. 'Why couldn't you have had a light breakfast for, once? Just look at the mess you've made of the crime scene!'

'Sorry, sir,' replied the ghost of Carmichael's voice. 'I couldn't help it. I'm surprised it didn't have the same effect on you, too.'

'Leave it, sergeant. I suppose *I'll* have to clear this away as best as I can before the SOCO team arrives, and I'd rather hoped to warn you to stay the other side of the counter before you came round here, but you just appeared out of nowhere, and it was too late by then.'

'What sort of evil person does that to someone?' Carmichael managed, his thought processes slowly re-gathering, his rinsed-off jacket in a chip shop plastic carrier bag at his feet. 'What sort of imagination could even think of doing something like that?'

'Don't ask me, Carmichael. Most people are all right, but a few of them, out there, are mad, bad, and dangerous to know, to coin a cliché. They're either just pure evil, or off their heads.'

'Hear, hear!' sounded, from where Philip Christmas was seated at another table, talking quietly into a recording device to aid his post mortem sometime later.

PORTION THREE

<u>Saturday 17th April – afternoon</u>

Neither Falconer nor Carmichael had been able to face any lunch, and when the SOCO team had arrived they left them to it and called into a coffee shop at the other end of the parade for a shot of caffeine.

'Oh, God, sir! I've never seen anything like that in my life before,' Carmichael almost breathed. 'All that bubbling! And her eyes! Bugger!' He suddenly went silent, and seemed to have a silent conversation with his innards, eventually adding, 'I think that's going to give me nightmares! Sorry about the language, sir.'

'Don't give it another thought, Carmichael. I think you've earned a bit of a swear after what you've witnessed this morning. Me, I think it was the batter that made it worse,' Falconer opined, in a low voice, so as not to alert too many people already in the coffee shop that they were police. 'And I agree with you. I think my sleep might be a bit disturbed for a few nights after this morning's little adventure.'

As Carmichael made a characteristic shrugging motion identical to the one he had made only a minute ago, Falconer looked at him in alarm, and hissed, 'And don't you dare be sick again. You can't have anything left after that magnificent demonstration back there!'

The sergeant sat as still as a statue for almost thirty seconds, his eyes closed, making a herculean effort to regain control of his internal muscles, then took a sip of coffee. 'So, where do we start, sir?' he asked. The spirit was willing, and the flesh recovering, at last.

'We ought to start with the owner, see if she made any enemies out of the customers. And I believe there are tenants in the upstairs flat. It might be worth having a word with them. Then we're going to have to have a look at where she lived: the usual stuff, although it was anything but a usual death, even for a murder.'

'While you were in that cloakroom, I got the address of the owner, and of Mrs Beeton, the – er – deceased. I think we should pay a little visit to Mr Carrington and ask if he remembers anything from last night that might have led to what we found this morning. There might also be regulars that she had fallen out with. He said she didn't mince her words, so that looks like our starting point, after the upstairs flat.'

'Mmph, sir.' Carmichael was still working on that internal control.

As the occupiers of the first floor flat above the chip shop were both office workers, they were at home, and not surprised to see the police after all the fuss that had been taking place downstairs since just before midday.

Before either of them could say anything, after the flat door had been opened, the young man who opened it asked, 'It's not about last night, is it? The music and everything?'

Falconer, not understanding what he was talking about merely echoed, 'Music?'

'We sometimes get a bit carried away on a Friday and Saturday night, and you can tell Mrs Beeton that we're really sorry. We'll think about other people in the future. We don't want to lose this flat, as we've only been here six months, and it's perfect for somewhere we can walk to work from.'

'Mrs Beeton asked you to turn your music down last night?' Falconer bluffed.

'Yeah! She was furious, because she had a rush on, and she couldn't hear the orders with us blaring out with the CD player. We're really sorry, and we'll apologise to her when we see her again. She was a bit of a dragon, though, which you'll know, if you've met her.'

'I'm afraid I haven't had that pleasure, sir. May I take your name, and that of your flatmate?'

'I'm Mark Manners, and my wife's name is Melanie,' he offered, and Falconer was surprised at the use of the term wife. The young man couldn't have been more than twenty-one or two.

'Well, Mr Manners, I'm afraid that Mrs Beeton was murdered a little before midday today, and I'm here to ask you whether you heard or saw anything about that time,' (and to see if her coming up here constantly to get you to turn your music down was enough to enrage you sufficiently to fry her face, he thought, but didn't vocalise).

Manners took a step backwards in surprise, and called over his shoulder, 'Mel, that chip shop woman has been murdered.'

There was a scuffling noise from the interior of the flat, and a young woman joined them, wearing only a dressing gown and slippers, yesterday's make-up a series of smears on her face, and her hair tousled and standing on end. 'What, that old moaning minnie who came up here last night? I don't believe it! Where did it happen? In the actual shop?'

'That's right, Mrs Manners. Just before midday.'

'I was asleep,' she stated baldly. 'Is that what you were trying to wake me up and tell me about, Mark?'

While they were speaking, Falconer had been thinking, and decided that, for now, they were wasting their time here. They could always call again and, if necessary, bring them down to the station for further questioning. If their noise nuisance had been persistent, and they were worried they might lose their tenancy, this might prove sufficient motive for doing away with the complainer.

After all, the owner probably wasn't on duty for the same number of hours that Sylvia Beeton was. What was the use of having a dog, and barking yourself? Maybe this very young couple had decided to take matters into their own hands before things came to a head, and Sylvia told the owner how often she had to go upstairs to tell them to turn the volume down. It was food for thought, at least.

Frank Carrington lived just a few streets away in Crescent Road, a pleasant curved development of detached 1930s houses, his being number nineteen. The garden was positively manicured, a car less than a year old stood on the drive, and pristine white net curtains showed at all the front windows.

'Very tidy!' commented Falconer, as they drew up at the kerb. 'Can't be too much of a hardship, serving fish and chips to the sort of rabble that buy them after chucking-out time, but I wouldn't fancy it on a Friday or Saturday night.'

'Me neither, but I wouldn't mind a couple of portions of his produce after work,' was Carmichael's reply, showing that he had obviously recovered from his unpleasant little outburst of Technicolor conceptual art.

'He did rather give the impression that he had employed Mrs Beeton for her strong personality, shall we say. Anyway, let's see what he can remember about who was in last night, shall we?'

Carrington answered the door almost before Falconer had taken his finger from the bell, and invited them into a house as immaculately kept as the garden. 'I'll just put the kettle on, then we can sit down with a cup of tea or coffee, and I'll tell you everything I know. I want whoever did this caught. Sylvia's been working part-time for me for as long as I can remember, and I want whoever did this locked away for a very long time.

'She started when her husband left her and she still had the kids at home, and when they left, she just carried on. Oh, but she was a good one with handling trouble. I've seen her pick some troublesome lad up by the scruff of the neck and hurl him out of the door without batting an eyelid. I won't be a minute. Go in and make yourselves comfortable,' he concluded, disappearing off into what they could see was the kitchen, another room that sparkled with loving buffing and cleaning.

The two detectives went through a door that evidently led to the sitting room, and found it furnished with plush leather furniture at one end, and an antique dining table and chairs at the other. Settling, each of them, into an armchair, and almost disappearing into its feather-filled cushions, they waited in silence until Carrington returned, a large tray in his hands.

'I didn't ask you what you wanted, but I thought tea would be all right? I can make coffee if you prefer, though,' he declared, setting down the tray on a marble coffee table.

'Tea's fine,' confirmed Carmichael.

'Just the ticket,' agreed Falconer, and Carrington began to dispense the fragrant liquid.

'Milk? Yes? Right. Help yourselves to sugar,' he suggested, as he handed them their cups, then stared on in disbelief as Carmichael added six spoonfuls of sugar to his cup, nearly emptying the little sugar bowl.

'Don't worry about me,' Falconer hastily stated. 'I don't take sugar,' as if this would be consolation enough to their host. He was used by now to Carmichael's preference for sticky tea that could almost, but not quite, be sliced.

'Me neither,' muttered Carrington. 'Now,' at a more normal volume, 'How can I be of assistance? I've made a note of anyone I saw or heard misbehaving yesterday evening, and of any Sylvia mentioned when we were chatting, clearing up. It's the usual suspects, I'm afraid, and she actually had to take the unusual step of barring one of them, 'Dogger' Ferguson, last night. I don't think I've known her ever do that before, but I don't know whether I can back that up, now she's gone.'

So, Sylvia Beeton had been employed to be the chip shop 'heavy', and Mr Carrington was one of those weak men whom he would like to advise to 'grow a backbone'. Hiding behind the stronger personality of a woman was despicable, in his opinion.

Suddenly, Carrington looked woebegone and lost, and Falconer realised how much he would miss the woman, if she had worked for him for as long as he said she had. 'Let's have those names then, sir,' he requested, and Carmichael extracted his notebook, after having made short work of the plate of biscuits that had also sat on the tray, and was now sadly decorated with only a few crumbs.

Noticing this for the first time, Falconer exclaimed, 'Carmichael! You've eaten *all* the biscuits!'

'Oh, sorry Mr Carrington, but I lost my breakfast,' he shuddered as he remembered, 'and I didn't feel like any lunch.'

'Don't worry, Sergeant. A few biscuits isn't going to bankrupt me. I've got a little list here: 'Spike' Ellis, 'Dogger' Ferguson, 'Troll' Norman, 'Darkie' Collins, 'Chalky' White, and 'Curry' Khan. They were the main offenders. I've known them all since their mums used to bring them along in their prams and pushchairs to get a bag of chips for their tea.

'And nice kids they were, too, but you know what happens to them these days, once they get to a certain age. Once the acne gets them, they discover fags, booze, joints, and girls, and suddenly they're all like Jekyll and Hyde, especially on Friday and Saturday nights. They've got really mouthy over the last year or so.'

'But Mrs Beeton kept them in line, did she?' asked Falconer.

'As best she could, but they were getting worse. She wouldn't stand for any nonsense when she was serving, and she gave as good as she got. Her father was a sailor, and, boy, could he cuss! She learnt well from him.'

'Anyone else you can think of who might bear her a grudge?' was his final question.

'No one. She was a fine specimen of her kind, and she'll be sorely missed in the shop.'

Back in the car, Falconer turned a suddenly optimistic face to Carmichael, and said, 'I recognise most of those names. They've all been in trouble at some time or other over the last eighteen months or so, so we'll have no problem with their addresses, and the ones not known to the police will be easy to find, because we'll make sure we get their addresses from the others.'

'That'll save a lot of time. We can just look them up on the computer, and we'll be able to go there knowing what they've already been up to.'

'Just so! Forewarned is forearmed!'

PORTION FOUR

<u>Saturday 17th April, – later</u>

Back at the station, they looked up the records of the names of the four youths that both of them were familiar with, and it was the usual story of the times, for between them they had been brought in for: taking a motor vehicle without the owner's consent, being drunk and disorderly, breach of the peace, brawling, possession of cannabis, and a bit of shop-lifting, just to add spice to the mix.

Dogger Ferguson had narrowly missed being prosecuted for assaulting a police officer, but as the officer was PC Merv Green, who was soft-hearted underneath his gruff exterior, he had not pressed charges, and the incident merely remained on file.

The two names currently unknown to the police were Darkie Collins and Curry Khan, but Falconer had every confidence that they would pick up their addresses from their mates. The other four all lived on an estate consisting mostly of blocks of flats; not high-rises – only four floors – but even these were a blot on the Market Darley/Upper Darley landscape, and a source of much of the trouble caused by teenagers and tearaways in the town and in the surrounding area.

Their first call was to the home of Spike Ellis, seventeen years old, and with three convictions for shoplifting to his name. The flat was in Robin House, as this was the Wild Birds Estate, and on the top floor, the lift, or course, being out of order. The entrance hall smelt of vomit and urine, and Carmichael clapped his handkerchief to his mouth and nose as soon as they entered.

'Don't touch the bannister rail,' warned Falconer, who had been caught like this before. Some clever individuals, in their cups, found it hilarious to smear bannister rails with faeces, and others, of a more pathological bent, liked to embed bits of broken glass in them, or even razor blades.

The top landing had four doors, all desperately in need of a coat of paint and, from the door with the number sixteen on it, (in drunken brass numerals, their original quota of fixing screws now reduced to one each) blared loud music, the sound of a baby yelling, and a female voice shouting abuse at one of the other occupants.

Falconer left it for Carmichael to use his mighty fist to knock, and when that produced no reaction from within, shouted himself, 'Open up. Police!'

There was a sudden silence within, with the exception of the wails of the baby, and a woman with dyed blonde hair, her roots almost half its length, and last night's heavy make-up making an artist's palette of her face, opened the door and grunted, 'Wotcher want? My Spike ain't done nuffink! Whenever it was, 'e was 'ere wiv me. Gottit?'

'Good morning Mrs Ellis,' Falconer opened for his side, and immediately had the legs cut from under him.

'That's *Miss* Ellis. Spike's old man did a runner when 'e found out I was up the duff, and I ain't seen 'im since, if yer must know.'

Falconer tried again. 'Good morning *Miss* Ellis. I wonder if we could have a word with your son – er – Spike, if it's not too much trouble. It won't take a minute, if we could just step inside.'

Miss Ellis turned, and bellowed, 'Spike, you get your arse out 'ere this minute. Wot you been up to now, yer little bastard?'

As they entered the flat, Carmichael wishing he could use his handkerchief here, too, a spindly, spotty youth with his hair dyed orange came out of one of the doors and stared at the visitors, perplexed.

Falconer took a moment to adjust to the smell and, surreptitiously looking round what he could see of the flat, took in overflowing ashtrays, empty beer and lager cans, and at least three rolled-up and very used disposable nappies just lying on the floor, un-regarded. The curtains were still drawn, there were newspapers and baby toys scattered across the floor and the furniture, and a collection of mugs and plates, unwashed and discarded after use.

''E's only seventeen. You've gotta 'ave me present, cos I'm what they call an appropriate adult,' Miss Ellis informed them, picking up the baby and lighting a cigarette at the same time.

How well their social workers taught them these days, thought Falconer, before turning his full attention to Spike, who looked very wary now, and beat him to it, by announcing, 'I ain't done nuffink! You can't pin anyfink on me, cos I ain't done nuffink.'

'I only want to know where you were first thing this morning, Spike, and to confirm where you were yesterday evening.'

'D'yer wanna sit down?' interrupted Miss Ellis, intent on being as much of a nuisance as she could. She might have been yelling her head off at Spike just a few minutes before, but he was her baby, and she would protect him fiercely to the end.

'No, thank you,' squeaked Carmichael, determined not to draw a deep breath in this flat.

'Spike?' Falconer encouraged the youth.

'I've only just woke up,' Spike mumbled. 'That's what me mum was yellin' about when you come knockin' on the door just now.'

''E's a real lazy little sod sometimes,' added his mother, as an aside, then added, ''e didn't come in till Gawd knows what time last night, then 'e can't get up in the mornin'. Just like 'is dad, 'e'll turn out. Never 'old down a job, nor nuffink like that. Waste o' space, 'e is at the moment.'

'I'd rather you didn't interrupt during questioning, if you don't mind, Miss Ellis. It's Spike I would like to give me information,' said Falconer, his temper rising.

'Sorry for breavin', Spike's mother snapped back at him, and sat down in a filthy, food-stained armchair and stubbed out her cigarette on a ketchup-stained plate.

'Where did you get up to yesterday evening, Spike?' Falconer asked, mentally keeping his fingers crossed that the youth's mother would butt out of the conversation and let him get on with his job in peace.

'Not a lot,' Spike answered. 'We got Dogger to blag some extra-strong cider from the 'offie', and some real head-bangin' lagers. We drunk a few, then went round the old car ports and smoked a joint or two' – this young man knew about the changes in the law that no longer made smoking a little cannabis a prosecutable offence – 'then o' course, we got the munchies, so we stashed the booze, and went down the chippie on the parade.

'After that, we went back to the car ports, and finished off the booze. I was wasted when I got in, and I've just woke up, like I told yer.'

'And who was with you?'

'Dogger, like I said, Troll, Chalky, Darkie, and old Curry. That's us. The cool dudes!'

'So, let me get this straight. You got one of your friends to buy alcohol from the off-licence, for under-age drinkers, then you smoked some drugs, then went to the chip shop, came back to the estate, and continued to drink until you came home.'

'That's it. Wot else d'yer wanna know?'

'Did you wake up earlier than just now, and go to the parade to visit the chip shop again, possibly because of something that happened when you were there yesterday evening?'

'Shit! I told yer. I dinn't wake up till just now. 'Ow could I 'ave gone out, when I never woke up?'

'Thank you very much. We'll be on our way, then. Goodbye.'

'So much for family life in the enlightened twenty-first century,' Falconer commented to Carmichael as they finally reached the blessed fresh air again, and headed for the car.

'How can they live like that?' asked Carmichael. 'No wonder we have so much trouble with the kids today, if they come from places like that. And she's got a baby. Imagine having to get a pram or pushchair up and down all those stairs, when the lifts are out of order!'

'Which is always,' said Falconer, concluding the conversation.

Four more of the names they had been given came from similar blocks on the same estate, and the interviews began with either a youth only just risen, or, in two cases, not even out of bed yet, and the day was getting on. Their trail led them variously to Blackbird House, Starling House, Goldfinch House, and Jackdaw House, and each block was as depressing as the first had been.

The only positive information that they received were the addresses of Darkie Collins and Curry Khan, neither of whom lived on the Wild Birds, and which they decided to visit after they had had a look at Sylvia Beeton's house and spoken to her neighbours.

They had obtained the keys of her house from her handbag at the chip shop, and set off now for Meadow Road which, now that they thought about it, wasn't too far from Crescent Road, so they should, logically, have gone there first, before taking themselves off to the Wild Birds Estate.

Meadow Road was a little less up-market than Crescent Road, but was comprised of tidy pairs of thirties semis. Sylvia's was a left-handed one, as one looked at the pair, and was in stark contrast to the condition of its mirror twin.

In fact, the gardens all along that side of the road were well-kept, with flower beds, displays of roses and shrubs, and lawns green and rich. Sylvia's was the exception. The beds that existed had only shrubs in them, although they were not overgrown and neglected, and the lawn, though neatly trimmed, was more weeds and moss than grass. It was perfectly tidy; just not planted and pandered to with the obsessiveness evident in the neighbouring gardens.

To the right of the boundary with the right-hand semi rose a veritable Everest of Leylandii hedging, beautifully trimmed right up to the edge of the path next door, but sprawling right over the path leading to the door of Sylvia's house, and even infringing on the lawn in the middle of its length.

'Definitely not an avid gardener, then, like her neighbours,' commented Falconer, picking his way to the door. 'More 'just keeping it tidy', like the average mortal.'

'Surprised she could get her bike up the path,' added Carmichael, thinking of the bicycle that still resided in the area at the back of the chip shop.

'You can see the tracks of her tyres on the lawn from where it was wet earlier in the week,' Falconer pointed out, removing her door key from his pocket and opening the door. 'I don't know what we expect to find in here, but we'd better have a look around, in case she had any threatening letters or anything like that.'

'Wouldn't she have confided in Mr Carrington?' asked Carmichael. 'They'd worked together for years.'

'You're probably right, but let's just take a quick look round, then we can pay a call on the neighbours and find out what they have to say about her.'

The inside of the property was in much better order than the garden, and it appeared that Sylvia Beeton had led a clean and tidy life behind closed doors. Even the cup and bowl that she had presumably used for her breakfast this morning were standing, rinsed, and upside down on the draining board, the dish-cloth hung over the mixer tap to dry.

After less than half an hour of poking and prying, Falconer called it a day. 'Come on, Carmichael,' he said, summoning the sergeant from working his way through the sideboard. 'We'll go next door and find out what sort of a neighbour she was.'

A cold welcome awaited them at the property to the right of Sylvia's house; the one with the regimented garden that looked like it had had its lawn trimmed with a manicure set. Its owner, David Mortimer, was a man who appeared to be in his mid-fifties, his grey hair close-trimmed, rather like his grass. He had a small toothbrush moustache and wore a cardigan and slippers, highlighting, thought Falconer, the fact that this was a Saturday and, for him, at least, a day of leisure.

'I'm calling about your neighbour, Mrs Sylvia Beeton. I don't know whether it's been on local radio yet ...?' Falconer began his questioning, after introductions had been carried out.

'It has, but I really have no opinion on the matter,' replied Mortimer, his eyes cold and disinterested.

'We just wanted to get an idea of what she was like as a neighbour – you know the sort of thing. Had she fallen out with anybody, to your knowledge? Had there been any trouble at the house, recently?'

'I keep myself to myself, Inspector. I do not waste time gossiping with the neighbours, and have no interest whatsoever in the ins and outs of their private lives. I'm afraid I can't help you at all,' he announced, and swiftly closed the door in their faces.

'What a miserable old sod,' said Falconer. 'People aren't usually that unhelpful.'

At the house to the left of Sylvia's, the occupant introduced herself as Mrs Hare (but call me Maude, everybody else does), who patted at her hair in a coquettish way as she spoke to them, even though she proved to be a widow, and was in her early eighties.

'And what can I do for you two young gentlemen?' she asked them, smoothing down the wrinkles in her skirt.

'We're here about your neighbour, Sylvia Beeton,' Falconer informed her.

'What? You'll have to speak up, young man. I don't hear as well as I used to.'

'SYLVIA BEETON,' Falconer repeated.

'Oh, you'll be asking about that hedge at her property,' said Mrs Hare, with a knowing nod of her head. 'Well, I don't get involved with anything of that sort.'

'NO!' roared Falconer, SHE'S DEAD!'

'She's done what, dearie?' asked the elderly woman, cupping a hand to an ear and leaning forward.

'SHE'S BEEN MURDERED!' shouted Falconer.

'Oh, that's nice for her. I hope she enjoys herself. Well, I mustn't stand here on the doorstep gossiping and letting the heat out. Thank you for telling me, young man,' and with that, Mrs Hare closed the door with a smile, and just the hint of a twinkle in her faded old eyes.

'Bloody marvellous!' exclaimed Falconer. 'We come out here to find out about the woman's character, and one neighbour lives like a recluse, and the other's as deaf as a post. Let's get off to those other two addresses, and call it a day for today.'

PORTION FIVE

Saturday 17th April – even later

Darkie Collins lived in Jubilee Terrace, a string of houses dating from the turn of the twentieth century, and obviously built to celebrate Queen Victoria's Diamond Jubilee. Forming the other side of the street was Victoria Terrace, dating from the same era. The front gardens were minimal, consisting of only a few feet of land between the boundary and the house, but this area of number thirteen was full of spring flowers in pots and tubs.

The woman who opened the door was very dark skinned, and had one of the widest smiles Falconer had ever seen. How could anyone get so many teeth into one mouth? he thought, as she beamed a welcome at them. 'Mrs Collins?' he enquired, hopefully, and she immediately corrected him,

'Miss Collins. I haven't yet persuaded a good man to put a ring on my finger,' she informed him, and smiled again, as if this was one of the most amusing things she had ever said.

'Miss Collins. I'm here to speak to your son, if he's at home. Is that possible?'

'Winston? What's he done?' she asked, and turned her head back inside the narrow hall and yelled, 'Winston, you get yo' ass down here. Now!' then turned her hundred watt smile back round to the two detectives and said, as sweetly as they could have wished, 'Would you like to come inside for a cup of tea?'

She showed them into a tiny sitting room, where the chairs and sofa were covered with bright throws, and vividly-coloured abstract paintings hung from the walls. As she disappeared off to the kitchen, a clattering down the stairs announced the arrival of Winston, and he came straight in to see what was happening.

Winston proved to be much lighter-skinned than his mother, but his complexion confirmed why his friends called him Darkie. When asked why he tolerated this, his reply was pragmatic. 'Well, it's better than "nigger", which was what they called me before they got to know me. And you've got to be part of the hard crew, or you get beaten up. It's self-protection, innit, mate?'

His mother reappeared carrying a tin tray with four mugs on it. 'I made one for you, too, Winston,' she informed her son, then continued, 'What you been up to, boy? You in trouble?'

'I just want to know where your son was this morning, Miss Collins,' Falconer informed her.

'He's old enough to speak for himself now,' she said, looking at her son as he lounged in a chair. 'And sit up straight when we've got visitors.'

Winston hauled himself into a vaguely upright position, and replied to Falconer's query. 'I've been upstairs all morning doing my homework.' His accent had definitely lost that twang of Jamaican that it had had when he had first spoken.

'Did you know Mrs Beeton, who served in the chip shop, on the parade?'

'Sure I know her. I've known her since I was a little tiny kid. She shouts loud, but she don't mean nothin' by it.'

'Did you see her last night?' Falconer was approaching the nub of the matter.

'Sure I saw her last night. Me and my mates went there for some chips, and to hang out and chill,' he replied, without any hint that he knew what had happened.

'Did you and your mates fall out with her?'

'Sure, we had words, but dat's de game, innit? It don't mean a ting, man. Jost de banter and stoff.'

'Winston, don't you use that silly accent under my roof. I've told you before, you've been brought up properly, so you speak properly too.'

'Sorry, Ma,' he apologised, then disarmed his mother with a huge grin. 'Gotcha!'

Interrupting this tender parent/child moment, Falconer asked, 'Did you know she was dead, Winston?'

'No way!' he shouted.

'She can't be,' exclaimed his mother. 'Was it an accident, or a heart attack, or something like that. She was one big woman.'

'I'm sorry to have to tell you that she was murdered, late this morning.'

There was a silence that threatened to cause a real hiatus in the interview, until Falconer gave it a little nudge by asking, 'Did you, by any chance, slip down to the parade this morning, Winston?'

Two voices angrily assured both policemen that the boy hadn't left his room, except for two cups of coffee and a bathroom break.

'Did any of your friends have a particular grudge against her, for something she'd said or done?' he continued.

'Nuh! But Dogger Ferguson did say more than once that she needed a good slap, like all women.'

'Winston!'

'Well, he did! He's an animal, and always saying things like that, but he doesn't mean anything by it.'

Three heavy sighs followed this casual reference to violence and women, and this time it was Miss Collins who broke it. 'It's that estate!' she said, obviously referring to the Wild Birds. 'We used to live there too, when I was left on my own with Winston, but I scrimped and saved to do an Open University degree, and then trained as a social worker so that we could have a better life.

'I bought this house for a song, seeing as it was number thirteen, and so many people have silly superstitious natures. We moved here three years ago, but Winston still hangs around with the old crowd from the blocks.

'I can't believe old Sylvie's dead, though. She's been serving me since Winston was in his pushchair.'

'Mum!'

'And you're absolutely certain that Winston never set foot outside this house this morning, Mrs Collins?'

'I would swear it on the Bible, Inspector.'

'And you can't think of anything that happened, that might have triggered off a fit of rage in one of your friends, Winston?'

'No, man! Not even Dogger would waste anyone!'

Curry Khan lived in a large modern detached house in the fairly new development: King's Acre. There was a Mercedes parked on one side of the double drive, a BMW on the other, and an elderly man working away in the garden, clearing away dead growth so that the spring flowers could grow uninhibited.

'Very nice,' was Falconer's comment, as they parked.

'Too flash!' was Carmichael's simultaneous opinion.

The door was opened by a tiny woman in a sari, who immediately went to fetch a man they presumed was their husband. 'Mr Khan?' enquired Falconer, holding out his hand in greeting.

His assumption was correct, and soon they were all four seated in the large sitting room at the back of the house, from which a fair-sized conservatory opened out.

'I wonder if I could speak to your son, Mr Khan. I'm afraid I don't know his real Chr ... hrmph! His forename, as we've only ever heard him referred to by his, um, nickname.' Falconer had nearly put his foot right in it, by referring to the man's son's Christian name. Life was so much more complicated these days!

'What? Curry?' asked Mr Khan, his face beaming at them, as he said this. 'They might call him that because of his ethnic origins, but if they knew how much I make from my Indian restaurants – I've got three, you know – they might use it as a term of respect, for he will have a very good inheritance.'

'How lovely!' Falconer congratulated him, not quite knowing how to respond to a reference to circumstances under which his current host would be dead. 'Is it possible for us to have a word with him?'

'Of course, Inspector. He is in his study, doing his schoolwork. Indira will fetch him for you.' The tiny woman left the room on this errand, returning shortly with a slim and elegant young man who introduced himself as Sanjeev, and took a seat looking expectantly at the two visitors.

'Good afternoon,' Falconer greeted him formally. It seemed like that sort of household, to him. 'I wonder if you could tell me where you have been this morning – all of it,' he added, in case the lad had slipped out before attending to his homework.

'I had a shower and ate my breakfast,' Sanjeev began, talking the question literally, 'Then, I went to my study to attend to my homework. When I had finished that, my mother brought me a cup of tea, and I did some research on the internet. I was still engaged in that activity when you rang the doorbell,' he explained, precisely and succinctly.

'You didn't leave the house at all?'

'Not even for one minute, I assure you.'

'What does this questioning concern, Inspector? I would like to know why you are visiting my house today,' asked Sanjeev's father.

'A woman who worked at the chip shop on the parade has, most unfortunately, been found dead this morning, and we are of the opinion that she was murdered, and that your son was in the chip shop last night.'

'No! Sanjeev?' shouted Mr Khan, rising from his seat.

'I'm so sorry, Papa! I'm so sorry!'

The boy's face was crumpled in anguish, and anger suffused his father's expression, his face red and his fists clenched.

Falconer's eyes widened at what was unfolding in front of him, and Carmichael was so startled in the change of atmosphere that he dropped his pencil, and had to grovel around under the wooden dining chair on which he was sitting to find it again.

The inspector began to rise from his seat, steeling himself to administer a caution before arrest, when Mr Khan spoke again. 'So, you have been buying chips again; when I have three restaurants from which you could get free food whenever you wanted it. My *son*! *My* son, buying chips! Oh, the shame of it!'

'I am so sorry, Papa. It was only because I was with my friends. I won't go in there again. I promise. I promise you, on my word of honour, Papa!'

Falconer sank back into his chair again, and gave a small cough of embarrassment. 'I think I have all the information I need from your son, and we'll take our leave of you now. Don't worry: we can see ourselves out,' he squeaked, and he and Carmichael fairly scarpered back to the car.

Once back behind the wheel, Carmichael gave Falconer a long stare of bewilderment, and the inspector turned to him and said, 'There are some cultural gaps too wide to cross, Carmichael.'

Back at the station, Falconer asked his sergeant to go through his notes to see if there was anything in there to give them a pointer. The four interviews he had conducted on the Wild Birds Estate had left his head in a whirl, with all the shouting, the bad language, and the squalor and he could remember little of what was actually said.

'Well, nobody actually owned up to anything, and I don't have a lot of notes, because I left out all the swear words.'

'There are decent people living in those blocks, Carmichael. It just happens that the ones we spoke to today are particularly, um, deprived,' Falconer stated, being absolutely fair. This morning visits only represented a minority of the flats' tenants.

'None of them liked her that much. They all thought she was loud and mouthy. And bossy, too. And that couple who lived over the shop weren't too keen, either.'

'She had to be, working in a place like that. I expect that was why Mr Carrington has kept her on for so long. He needs, or needed, someone who could not only serve and give change, but could act as a bouncer as well. It would seem that Sylvia Beeton fulfilled all these criteria.'

At that moment, the telephone rang, and Falconer grabbed at the receiver. 'Inspector Falconer: Market Darley CID. How may I help you? Oh, Philip it's you. If I'd known it was you, I'd have blown my whistle down the phone and hung up.'

'Ha ha! Very funny! You're only sulking because of what happened to your shoes at the locus. You can't fool me, Harry, old boy,' replied the doctor.

'What can I do for you?'

'I just felt I had to phone you, to say that I've never had a body before that I didn't know whether to douse in salt and vinegar or examine. I shall dine out on this story for months, thanks to you.'

'Philip?'

'Yes, Harry?'

'Go away, before I commit another murder in the area; one that you won't be able to be around to deal with,' he threatened, and hung up.

'What did the doc want?' asked Carmichael.

'Nothing. It wasn't important.' If he'd told Carmichael what Philip Christmas had just said, there was no telling how the sergeant would react, and he'd only just got his shoes clean again. 'Have we got anything at all?'

I don't think so, sir. It must have been some passing nutter, I suppose.'

'I don't buy that, Carmichael. There's more to this than meets the eye, and I'm going to get to the bottom of it, if it's the last thing I do.'

PORTION SIX

<u>Monday 18th April</u>

Over the weekend, Falconer had had a recurring dream: one that forced him to revisit Sylvia Beeton's house and stare at it long and hard. There was something tickling at the back of his mind, and he needed it to jump forward and declare itself. The answer was within his grasp: he just hadn't recognised it yet.

Monday morning found him in the office very early, making a list of telephone numbers, which he worked his way through shortly after arriving at the station, hoping to catch people before they left for work.

He hit pay dirt on his fourth call, then made another call, to round off his activities for the morning, being passed from department to department until he found what he was after. After a few minutes' reflection, he dialled again, to ascertain that he would be able to carry out what he wanted to do, then sat twiddling his thumbs until Carmichael arrived, too excited to settle to do anything, yet exasperated at how slowly time was crawling by. The sergeant wasn't due on duty until nine thirty this morning, and Falconer snorted his disgust and chagrin that the man had not been rostered for an earlier shift.

The hands of the clock slowly ground their way round to five, four, three, two minutes to the half hour, then the door of the office burst open, and a bright and sunny figure lolloped into the room, shedding its jacket as it went. 'Morning, sir. Anything happening?' it asked.

The tension suddenly left Falconer's body now that his partner was there, and he slumped in his chair. 'Yes, Carmichael. I've solved the case!'

'You've done what?'

'I know who killed Mrs Beeton from the chip shop!'

'You what?'

'I know who did it, Carmichael. Am I speaking Swahili or something today, or are you just incapable of understanding me anymore?'

'Sorry, sir,' said Carmichael, sitting down.

'Now, you listen up, my lad, and listen good. I'm going to tell you a little story – but not all of it, yet – then we're going out to make an arrest,' Falconer declared, and proceeded so to do.

David Mortimer submitted, without fuss, to being arrested, merely taking one more look at his immaculate garden as he was led away, and pausing to spit over the garden gate at his next door neighbour Sylvia Beeton's house. There had been no resistance at all, and he had readily admitted what he had done in a fit of rage and depression.

'So it was as simple as that, was it?' asked Carmichael, after Mortimer had been taken away in a squad car, and they were driving back to the station.

'We got nothing from those boys, no matter how intimidating their behaviour might have been, when they're out in public, and I couldn't see any signs of guilt from any one of them. The only thing that stuck in my mind was what that deaf old lady – what was her name? Maude Hare, I think – said when we arrived.

'She thought we'd come about a hedge. I thought she was just rambling, because of her age and lack of hearing, but I did notice that she had a neat little privet hedge, and Mrs Beeton had a fence, so I just dismissed what she'd said. And then, both nights at the weekend, I dreamt I was being consumed by a giant hedge, and I couldn't find any way out of it. It wasn't like a maze, you understand: just a huge hedge.

'Well, then I remembered that, at Mrs Beeton's house, the hedge between her property and the one on the right was a huge monstrosity of Leylandii, and that her side of it grew right across the pathway, but on the other side, it was carefully trimmed and kept in shape.

'Did Mrs Hare think we were from the Council, I wondered, and today, after I'd made a few other calls, I phoned up the local authority, and got myself on a real merry-go-round of extensions, until I found out that a complaint had been lodged some time ago.

'I'd already phoned the tree surgeons I was able to find in the Yellow Pages, and, on the fourth call, I found one who had an appointment to go to Mrs Beeton's house this week and cut down a hedge of Leylandii. The council had told me there was nothing they could do for the woman, and advised her to go to the Citizens Advice Bureau. It wasn't her hedge you see.

'They'd told her she could trim the offending branches, and even put the cuttings on to her neighbour's land, to prove that she hadn't stolen his property, but she wanted to find a way to get rid of the hedge altogether, because it blocked so much light from the front of her house, and it looks like she was willing to pay to get the job done without permission.

'A further search of her house produced a file of letters between their solicitors about removing the light-blocking eyesore. They were in that sideboard I called you away from, when I mistakenly thought there was nothing there for us. The situation had come to an impasse, however, and another visit to Mrs Hare, with the word 'hedge' shouted very loudly, produced the information that they – Mrs Beeton and Mr Mortimer – were frequently going hammer-and-tongs at it about the hedge, out on the street.

'Mortimer said – you heard him yourself – that she told him this morning that she was 'going to have the bloody things cut down and burnt', and she'd like to see him stop her. He spent a couple of hours working himself into a real rage and downing shots of scotch, then went round to the chip shop and confronted her, and that was that.

What a waste of both lives! And the fool had left his fingerprints all over the chip scoop, so there was no chance of him bluffing his way out of it.'

They were just passing the end of the pedestrian High Street, when Carmichael suddenly yelled, 'Stop!'

Falconer did a fairly good impression of an emergency stop, and looked at his partner quizzically. Whatever is it, Sergeant? What's the matter?'

'I just fancied a bag of chips, and there's a chip shop on that corner back there. I might even have a battered burger with it.'

'Well, it has been at least two hours since your breakfast,' replied Falconer, then leaned out of the car window and shouted, 'Could you get the same for me as well; and lots of vinegar, Carmichael.'

THE END

Toxic Gossip

DI Falconer becomes involved in a gossip-fuelled hate crime, only to find himself questioning his own judgement when it comes to protecting Miriam Darling from her anonymous persecutors...

Chapter One

Friday 6th August

Miriam Darling stood in her new sitting room, missing suddenly the hurly-burly of the removal men and their cheery banter as they had transferred all her worldly goods into her new home.

Since yesterday afternoon, her world had been filled with these energetic and talkative men. First, as they packed her precious breakables, and loaded most of her furniture into their large van, leaving her only a bed and the means of making them all a cup of tea in the morning, and again today, as they moved her two hundred miles to her new address.

At first, she had found their inconsequential chatter a nuisance, and had taken herself off to the garden to sit on an old stool on the patio, but, as the afternoon wore on, she had found herself going indoors more frequently, coming, little by little, to enjoy the sound of life in the home that she would be leaving the next day, forever.

By mid-afternoon, she found herself in the kitchen, brewing a pot of tea, and scrabbling round in her almost bare cupboards for a packet of biscuits. Sugar for energy, she thought, as her searching hand fell upon a packet of chocolate digestives she didn't realise she still had.

A tea-break meant a sit-down, and they settled themselves happily on the sitting room floor, now bare of its furniture and all its decorative trappings and pictures. She was just about to leave them to enjoy their tea and biscuits in peace when one of them called to her to join them if she wanted to, and, quite unexpectedly, she found that she did want to sit down with them, and engage in a normal conversation, for the first time in months.

They really were a jolly crew, who clearly enjoyed their work and their travels, and got on well with each other. As she sipped at her hot drink and nibbled on a biscuit, they regaled her with tales from their various trips together, exaggerating the mishaps and disasters to such an extent that she found herself laughing, and was grateful for their happy banter.

When they finished for the evening and took a taxi to a local public house to eat their evening meal, she threw the last of her left-over food together for a make-shift meal and contemplated the fact that, after today, this house would no longer be her home. That a new start was a good idea, she had no doubt, but she had lived at the same address for so long that not having the address any more would feel like an amputation – a new telephone number in her head, like a betrayal of who she was and how she had got to be this woman called Miriam Darling.

A new area would allow her to become someone new – someone whom nobody pitied and no one sought to comfort, or pointed out in the street, whispering to their companion about her history. Somewhere else, she would just be 'that woman who'd just moved into the house on the corner'. She could be anonymous, and start life afresh, with a clean sheet, provided she could banish the memories and, somehow, suppress the nightmares.

Today had started in a whirl of activity, making sure that the old house was in a fit and presentable state to greet its new owners, and that nothing had been forgotten. At the last minute, she had grabbed the old kitchen clock from the wall, where it had been abandoned for no good reason, and carried it out to her car, to put it safely on the back seat where it would not be jostled around too much.

And then they were off, at six o'clock on a Friday morning, heading for pastures new; leaving everything familiar and previously comforting behind. Following the removal van, she let her mind wander as she kept the vehicle in easy sight, due to its sheer bulk. She tried to remember all she could of the town and street she had chosen for the next phase of her life, and the few people she had met so far in her visits to the new address.

These, given the distance between the two places and the infrequency of her visits, consisted only of the estate agent and his assistant, and the two next-door neighbours, one beside her new home, the other round the corner, on the rear perimeter of the garden. They had seemed nice enough, and she supposed that people were the same just about everywhere. It was one's attitude to them, and theirs to you that really decided whether you sank or swam in a community. Then she nearly bit off her tongue at the inappropriateness of the wording of her last thought.

Silently chiding herself for being over-sensitive, she focused on the rear doors of the van, once more, and made her mind a blank for the next fifty miles. It was suddenly catapulted back to the present as she saw the van indicate to turn left. It pulled off up a slip-road towards a gathering of establishments that comprised a service stop with wide swathes of parking spaces, and a variety of eating places.

The removal men had had only a cup of tea from her this morning, and she presumed they were hungry and in need of a proper breakfast. She didn't feel in the least like eating, herself, but knew it would make good sense to put something in her belly, to give her some energy for dealing with the unloading and directing at the other end. Thus decided, she joined them in the queue for the till with a tray loaded with a full English breakfast, a pot of yoghurt, and a mug for tea.

She initially seated herself at a separate table, but was urged, before she had even sat down properly, to come and join the merry gang at a larger table at the rear of the dining area. Since their arrival the previous day, this small group of strangers had offered her a re-entry into human affairs, and she realised how much she appreciated it, when, on joining them, the 'head honcho' and owner of the van said that he had a bottle of champagne in his cab, to be cracked when all her possessions were in the new house.

He was of the opinion that all house moves should be celebrated as a moving on in life, and did this on a regular basis, unless he suspected that the couple were breaking up, or moving down-market due to financial problems. This gave her another reason to be glad that she had chosen this one-man-band to move her, and not one of the faceless large companies.

The last half of the journey passed without mishap, and it was only eleven o'clock when they pulled up outside number 45 Essex Road, in Market Darley. She had realised, about forty or fifty miles ago, how beautiful the countryside was becoming, and reached the town, from which she would commute to her job the three days of the week that she worked, with thoughts of appreciation of its architecture and surroundings.

It was an old market town, with a market cross and square, and many of its shops, if one raised one's eyes above display window level, clearly advertised their age. It looked like a place she could learn to forget and start life anew, and this made her smile, as the two vehicles in the tiny convoy pulled up outside her new home.

The rest of the day had been a whirlwind of activity for, although she was not involved in the unloading or transfer of her furniture and the boxes containing her smaller possessions, she was the one 'directing traffic', as it were. Yesterday afternoon, she had tried to keep abreast of the efficient and swift packing, to mark each box before it was loaded on to the van, but she had not managed to label them all, and she also wanted the furniture to go into the correct rooms while she had sufficient muscle to put it in place. Once they had gone, and she was on her own again, anything heavy in a wrong room would have to stay there until she had got to know someone with enough muscle-power to help her shift it to its correct position.

At lunchtime – about one-thirty, by choice of the removal men – she drove off to the local parade of shops which she had discovered on a previous visit, and bought enough fish and chips to feed them all, no matter how big their appetites proved to be. It was the least she could do, after all their friendly overtures to her, and she was saddened to think that she would never see those same faces again. They would just retreat into her past, after today, for they were not local, and would become just another memory, but a happy one this time.

Even her reception in the chip shop had been positive, with the man behind the counter, who turned out to be the owner, spotting a new face and asking her if she was just visiting – then wishing her the best of luck when she explained that she was only that day moving to the town.

When she arrived back with the food, the removal men had set up the dining table, attaching the top to the legs after its journey, had rooted out the dining chairs, and escorted her to what they had assumed (correctly) would be the dining room. They received their parcels of greasily steaming sustenance with suitable gestures of appreciation and gratitude, and set to, to make short work of her offerings.

As she scrunched up the empty papers to put in a black plastic bag from a roll she had, with forethought, brought with her in the car, she called out to see who wanted tea, and, after receiving a volley of affirmatives, entered the kitchen to find the kettle in pride of place, together with the box packed last, with mugs, tea, coffee, and sugar in it, waiting for her on the work surface. The milk, they had thoughtfully removed from the box in which it had been packed, and put into the newly brought-in and connected fridge.

After a flurry of, 'Left hand down a bit,' 'No, lift, not push,' 'Twist it so that we can get it through,' and 'Mind the doorframe, you donkey,' while the tea brewed, they came to collect their steaming mugs with gratitude, and not a little horse-play, more for her entertainment, she thought, than their own.

She had wondered if cold drinks would be more appropriate on an afternoon in August, but the British weather was behaving true to form, and a thick blanket of clouds hid the sky and smothered the heat of the sun, so it was quite a cool day, a good prod to her to check out the central heating system before autumn arrived, as it was likely to do, well before its traditional date, in this country.

The men had finally left at seven-thirty, wishing her good luck to a man, and waving frantically out of the cab window as the van drove away, an almost intimate part of her life for a day and a half, and she hadn't even known their names. And suddenly she was alone again, in a strange town where she had no friends or relatives, and just herself to bother about.

Chapter Two

Friday 6th August, 2010 – evening and onwards

Shaking herself back to the present, she began, slowly, to move from room to room, inspecting her new home with a critical eye. All in all, it was a good house, although just a bit too big for her on her own, but it was in good decorative order, if not to her taste, and it had been well maintained by its previous owners.

It had also been left immaculately clean and for this she was grateful. Her energy levels had been sapped and she no longer had the enthusiasm for the mundane jobs previously undertaken without thought. She considered that it was possible that she would be happy here, and looked forward to the time when this would be so, and she could feel like an ordinary person again.

Maybe she should get a dog or a cat, she wondered, just so that there was an extra heartbeat in the house, and something to talk to, so that she didn't feel as if she were going mad any more, when she talked to herself. A cat would be best, she decided, with her having to go to work three days a week. Dogs needed to be exercised, but a cat, although it walked to the beat of its own drum, could come and go as it pleased, with the addition of a cat flap, and would be an additional comfort to her on cold evenings, sitting on her lap and purring.

Oh! There was already a cat flap in the kitchen door, something she had not noted on any of her trips to view and measure up. Well, that was that decision made, then, and she determined to look in the Yellow Pages to try to locate a rescue centre from where she could choose a homeless animal to take in, and give the love and care it needed. Two waifs and strays together. What a team they would make!

Having ended her tour in the kitchen, having ascertained that all the bulky items of furniture were where they should be, she remembered that there had been a portion of chips, a saveloy, and a battered burger left at lunchtime, and she was glad she had not thrown them away. It was too late to look for shops open, and she was physically and emotionally exhausted from the rigours of the day. A few minutes on a plate in the microwave, and she could eat good old English comfort food, and go up to make up her bed for the night.

As she finished eating, however, there was a sharp rap at the front door, and she opened it to find the woman she had met previously, from the house next door, on her step. Introducing herself as Carole Winter, she extended an invitation to come round to her house for a glass of sherry.

Miriam was taking her first step into what was to be a period of whirling activity, as she was rapidly introduced by Mrs Winter, to the Women's Institute, where a young-for-her-years lady called Mabel Monaghan showed her their programme of events for the following autumn, and urged her to attend the special summer-break meetings. These were all talks by local people, about their particular interests, including local history, and the decline, rise and decline again, of agriculture in the surrounding area.

This sounded a good way to learn about where she was to make her new life, and she agreed, with alacrity, to attend the meetings, and join as soon as she was given the opportunity.

A meeting of the local book club, which this month was held at the home of a woman in her mid-thirties called Justine Cooper, introduced her to women a little closer to her own age, and she was fascinated that their list of books for the coming months included some quite racy titles.

She sat with them for two hours while they discussed the current volume under scrutiny, and found their impressions and insights intelligent and informative. Invited to the next meeting, she accepted immediately, and made a note of the book they were discussing earlier, so that she could get a copy, and add her own impressions to the general pot of opinions.

The ladies of the library, Liz and Becky, bade her a similar welcome to their world of literature, and provided her with a temporary ticket on the spot, informing her that she would receive her permanent ticket through the post, and telling her that they looked forward to seeing her again in the near future

In that first week, Carole was very dedicated, taking her to many other organisations, introducing her each time to the individual who ran it, and making her head spin with the plethora of new names she felt she needed to commit to memory. Mrs Winter seemed to know everyone in Market Darley, and so she should have done, having moved there from the north thirty-five years ago, on her marriage. She had lost almost all the accent that had identified her origins up until her move south.

Carole had also insisted on taking her to the local church on Sunday to meet the congregation, even introducing her to the members of the choir. The vicar welcomed her warmly to his parish, expressed the hope that she would become one of his flock, and join in with all the parish activities, which didn't seem impossible to Miriam, once she had met everyone that morning. His congregation was young, and the notice board in the entrance filled with notices of meetings, groups and social events. Maybe life would be kind to here, in this, her new start.

So busy and pleasant had her first days become in this new setting that she found herself, one evening, arranging a couple of vases of fresh flowers, one each to brighten up the dining and sitting rooms, and humming a tune as she cocked her head to one side to consider the balance of her arrangements. Without her realising it, she had moved from feeling numb to a sense of happiness and contentment, so long missing from her existence that she hardly recognised it.

Her commute to work was about the same as it had been from her old address, the transfer to another branch going without a hitch, and it seemed that life now held some promise for her. Her telephone started to ring with invitations from new friends, and her social life became almost as busy as it had been many years ago, when she had been young and carefree, and had no idea of the blow that life would one day deal her.

Carole Winter was an avid gardener, and began to help Miriam plan her own little piece of land. At the moment it was all laid to lawn, without a bed to break the runs of grass at front and back, and they began to go out to garden centres to see what was available for autumn planting, and what bulbs would go in in the autumn for the next spring.

Books from the library accelerated Miriam's interest in this hitherto unconsidered pastime, and she began to watch gardening programmes on the television, becoming hooked on the subject within a very short time. This, she considered, was because she had lived her life in limbo for so long. She could feel herself waking up, as if from a long hibernation, and it felt good to be part of everyday life again.

She also began to make friends at work, and sometimes spurned her usual home-coming train in favour of going out for a few drinks with colleagues from the office, returning home much later than usual, and feeling quite young again. Locally, she joined the reading group and attended a couple of meetings of the WI, as time-fillers, and found to her surprise that she enjoyed them, adding them to her list of regular outings. It seemed that, at last, she would be left in peace to lead as normal a life as she could, without all the hassle she had left behind when she had moved away.

She and Carole next door, who seemed to be relieved to spend a little time away from her husband, who was now retired, and whom she said got under her feet all the time, were happy to go into Market Darley on a Saturday afternoon to window shop and have a coffee and cake in the local coffee shop.

On Sunday mornings they walked to church together, even though Miriam had never been a regular church-goer in her life before. She even said her very first sincere prayer – one of thanks and gratitude that her nightmare seemed to be over, and that she was starting life anew.

On Sunday afternoons, Miriam drove while Carole sat in the passenger seat, and they toured round the various garden centres that seemed to surround the town, all of them hard to get to without a car. Carole had almost convinced her to dig a little vegetable patch, or even grow vegetables in pots, as there was nothing like food straight from garden to plate, she said.

It was on one such afternoon, just over a month since she had moved in, when they were discussing whether to go to all the trouble of turning over a patch of ground, or whether to use troughs, pots and planters for tomatoes, courgettes, strawberries and the like, and even maybe a plastic dustbin for new potatoes, that Miriam realised that she was doing most of the talking, and that Carole was uncharacteristically quiet.

'Are you OK?' she asked, wondering if maybe Carole and her husband had had a disagreement between the church service and now, or whether she just had a headache, or something similar, that was making her feel under par.

'I'm fine,' was the curt answer, and she lapsed back into a silence that soon became awkward for both of them.

'What is it?' Miriam risked another question, wondering if something she'd done had unintentionally upset her new friend.

'Nothing. You carry on with your plans,' her passenger replied, but there was the very slightest of chills in her voice, and the rest of the journey to the garden centre passed in silence.

Carole was equally distant as they walked around the area where packets of vegetable seeds were sold. She indicated, with a pointing finger, the varieties she recommended for container growing, hardly communicating at all, and leaving Miriam upset and mystified at what could have caused this sudden change in her previously very friendly neighbour.

Asking her brought forth nothing more than denial that there was anything wrong, and, in the end, Miriam suggested that they go back home early, without going on to a second establishment, because she had a headache – which wasn't a lie. The replacement of her normally irrepressible and ebullient friend by this uncommunicative and distant stranger had affected her considerably, and her temples were beginning to throb with pain.

Back home, Carole bade her a less than enthusiastic goodbye, with no comment that she would see her soon, and disappeared through her own front door without turning to wave, or thanking Miriam for the lift. Miriam entered her own house in considerable puzzlement. Her neighbour had seemed fine that morning at church, but by the afternoon, she had appeared not to be comfortable in her company any more. What on earth had she done?

Chapter Three

<u>Monday 13th September</u>

Miriam had not spoken to her neighbour again the day before, and left for work on Monday morning as confused as she had been the previous day. Her work and colleagues proved sufficient distraction during working hours, and she gladly forgot about this little glitch in her friendship with her neighbour. She agreed to go for a drink after work, partly because she knew she'd enjoy it, and partly because she was delaying going home; shelving the coolness that had so unexpectedly arisen between her and Carole.

Six of them went to the Jack of Three Sides, an old pub just off the town centre, situated on a small triangular island of land where the roads were unusually convoluted. It was an old building that had stayed in character, and to which she had never gone before.

The inside looked less contemporary than many of the public houses in the town where she now worked, and more like the establishment as it had existed many years ago. Every piece of wall was covered with pictures, framed sepia photographs and newspaper cuttings relating to the tiny area in which the pub stood. Pewter tankards hung from the beams, just below the very darkly nicotine-stained ceiling, and even this surface was not neglected, as some inventive soul had found a way to fasten pictures and paintings to the ceiling, so that even looking up was a delight.

The chairs and tables were, similarly, a mishmash of styles, but none of them new or out of place, and she stood at the bar just looking round in admiration at the fact that there was no dust. In a bar crammed with memories, there was nowhere one could see a plain surface, and yet everything was wonderfully clean.

Living near the station in Market Darley as she did, there was nothing to stop her having three glasses of wine, as she would not have to drive when she de-trained, and she thoroughly enjoyed herself that evening, sipping her chilled drinks, and gossiping with the others with whom she now shared her working life.

When her train finally arrived at her destination, it was much later than she usually arrived home, even after staying on for a drink, but she was relaxed and happy after the little boost of alcohol, and the bonhomie she had shared. It fleetingly crossed her mind to just dump her bags and knock on Carole's door and confront her, asking her outright how she seemed to have alienated her friend, but given the lateness of the hour, and the lovely relaxed feeling she was enjoying, she slid her key into the door, and dismissed the idea from her mind. A long, relaxing bath and then to bed with a book would round off the day very nicely, and she didn't want to spoil how she felt now with any bad-feeling.

That feeling evaporated completely when, picking up her mail from the hall carpet, she noticed that the top envelope had a very badly hand-written name, and no address, implying that it had been delivered by hand: and it was to Mrs Miriam Stourton, not Ms Darling.

Her hands immediately began to shake, and she sank down on to the carpet as her legs threatened to betray how she felt. No! Not here! Not again! she thought. It can't have followed me here! Letting go of the envelopes she held in her unsteady hand, she put her hands to her face, and began to sob. Her recent euphoria had completely evaporated with this one small discovery.

Monday 20th September

A steady flow of letters began to arrive, some in the naive hand of the first one, others in letters cut from newspapers and magazines. Some came in the post, others were dropped through her letterbox at night, and Miriam's newly minted self-confidence and happiness disappeared, from the receipt of that first missive.

Her applications to join various organisations were suddenly turned down, with no explanation given, invitations were withdrawn and, eventually, stopped being issued at all. Even at church, the previous morning, Carole had pleaded an upset stomach, and Miriam had found herself blanked and shunned by members of the congregation who had previously appeared friendly towards her. Even the vicar shook her hand very limply after the service, and moved on to the next person quickly, to rid himself of her company, it seemed to Miriam.

After a month of contentment and comparative happiness, within a week she had been reduced to a social pariah, and she knew it had started all over again, but this time she'd have to do something about it. She'd lived with it in her old home, but this time she was going to involve the police. She couldn't live the rest of her life constantly running away. She had to find a platform from which to plead her case, this time with the help and support, maybe even the protection, if things escalated, of the forces of law and order.

Detective Inspector Harry Falconer of the Market Darley CID was just scanning his diary for the week and exchanging morning pleasantries with his detective sergeant, 'Davey' Carmichael, when the telephone shrilled on his desk and, with a sigh of 'here we go again', he answered the call, holding up his free hand to stem the flow of Carmichael's enthusiastic conversation.

The woman on the other end of the line was almost hysterical, and it was a few minutes before he could calm her enough to be able to comprehend anything she said. She was obviously in a highly emotional state and, given that he had little in his diary for the day – and the state she was in, he decided, in the circumstances, that the situation merited a trip to her home, to interview her in privacy without the necessity of her making a trip to the police station.

'Come on, sunshine,' he cajoled his sergeant, as he ended the call. 'We've got a damsel in distress to rescue. Get your armour on, and we'll ride over to her tower and see what we can do for her.'

'What armour, sir? What tower? Ride? I don't know what you're talking about,' was his sergeant's reply.

'I know you don't, Carmichael, but that's about par for the course.'

'Why are you talking about golf now?'

'Come on, you. We've got the beginnings of a nasty case here. Make sure you've got your notebook, and I'll explain in the car on the way over. It's not far.'

'But where are we going? I don't underst ...' Carmichael's questions echoed all the way down the stairwell, as they made their way out of the station and into the car park.

Once safely strapped into Falconer's ritzy little Boxster, he began to relate what he had learned from the hysterical woman on the phone.

'Something's evidently happened in her life, in the past, that she's moved here to forget, but it seems that her story has followed her and caught up with her, and now she's receiving hate mail. I don't know any more details than that at the moment, but it sounded like she wasn't in a fit state to drive to the station, so I said we'd come to her. Somehow, although I don't have the whole story, this one doesn't feel like a storm in a teacup to me. It feels nasty.

'She says she's had abusive phone calls – numbers withheld, of course – silent phone calls in the middle of the night, and about seventy-odd letters, threatening her with all sorts of things. I don't know what happened yet, in her past, but it seems to have caused a furious reaction amongst those she's met and become friendly with, since she moved here.'

'She must be terrified, sir,' Carmichael commented, his brow furrowed with the effort to imagine his own wife in a similar situation.

'Well, she certainly sounded it on the phone.'

Chapter Four

Monday 20th September

When Falconer knocked smartly on the door of Miriam's house, there was a delay, during which they noticed the net curtains twitch, to establish who was calling, no doubt. Then there was the sound of bolts being drawn back and keys turned, before the front door opened just a crack, to the extent of its security chain, at which point they displayed their warrant cards to identify themselves.

The face that greeted them was blotchy and swollen, the eyes, as they surveyed their identification, red, and full of fear. In silence, the woman stood back and allowed the door to open just enough to admit them, before closing it again, and locking and bolting it behind them. Miriam Darling was still in her dressing gown, her hair tousled and wild, and she looked to be in the extremes of anxiety, as she preceded them into the living room.

The first thing that confronted them was a sofa completely covered in pieces of paper, some in scrawled childlike handwriting, others with cut-out letters to spell out their messages. There were dozens of the things, completely swamping the green leather surface, and Miriam simply looked at them, and then at her two visitors.

At that moment, the telephone rang, and, as she dragged herself across the room to answer it, Falconer looked at Carmichael, whose face was scrunched up in anger at this material evidence of hatred and spite.

She listened for a moment, then cried, 'Who are you? What do you want? Why don't you say something?' Her voice was shrill and harsh in the silence of the house. She slammed down the handset, pulling the plug from the wall in her impotent anger and frustration, then just wandered back to them, before collapsing into an armchair.

'What am I going to do?' she asked, in a voice hoarse with weeping. 'I can't keep on running. I've already gone back to my maiden name, but someone's found out. Am I never to be free of it? I haven't done anything wrong. It was just a tragic accident, and as if that wasn't enough, here I am being hounded again, like some sort of criminal.'

Falconer nodded at Carmichael and the letters. The sergeant, in complete silent understanding, donned a pair of latex gloves, and began collecting together the sheets of paper and putting them in evidence bags, to be checked later for fingerprints. The inspector took a seat in the armchair on the other side of the fireplace and gathered his reserves for interviewing this deeply distressed woman.

Miriam just sat in her chair, her hands in her lap, her head drooping, like a marionette that had had all its strings cut. She was evidently steeling herself, too, for the ordeal to come.

His task swiftly completed, Carmichael sank down on the now unencumbered sofa and removed his notepad from his pocket, ready to record what the woman had to say. He waited in silence for Falconer to commence his questioning.

'I'd like you to tell me what it is in your past that has 'followed' you here, and why the reaction is so extreme. There's no need to rush. Just tell it in your own time, so that we can understand what has been happening to you recently,' he said, his voice quiet and almost tender.

'It was something that happened just over a year ago.' Miriam's voice was so low, they could hardly catch what she was saying, but after clearing her throat and shaking her head, she continued at a more easily discernible volume.

'One year, one month, and six days ago, to be precise – I can't seem to stop counting the time that has elapsed. I was married then, and we had a son. Mark, my husband's name was, and Ben was our son, only four years old, and full of life.' Here she had to break off, as her voice cracked, and tears began to track down her cheeks.

'My parents moved to Spain three years ago, when Dad took early retirement, so we went out to visit them in the summer, and at Christmas. Although it was rather expensive, it was cheaper than taking a break through a travel agent, and it meant that at least they saw their grandson twice a year. We used Skype, of course, but Mum wanted to cuddle Ben, and Dad wanted to take him to the beach and play football and all those sort of grandfatherly things.

'It was when we went out last summer that *it* happened, and my nightmare began, although I didn't realise people were so cruel, and it would go on for so long that I wouldn't have time to come to terms with it in peace, and mourn them in privacy.'

'What was *it*?' asked Falconer, feeling that they weren't really getting anywhere, and he needed to get to the nub of the matter, and discover the details of the mystery event.

'We had planned to go along the coast to a little cove that was very beautiful, but usually completely empty of holiday-makers. Ben was excited at the thought of getting a bit of beach to himself, so that he could make his sandcastles without a game of football being played through his efforts, and people's dogs arriving to dig in his turrets.

'I suggested that we walk along the cliffs to get to it, as there was a rudimentary set of steps there, although they were difficult to descend, having been cut out of the cliffs, but Mark had very different ideas. He'd been a bit scratchy that holiday, and I didn't want another argument – we'd already had quite a few blow-ups, and I knew he was fed up to the back teeth of always going to the same place, and having to stay with my parents.

'I was determined that we wouldn't fall out that day, and that maybe the deserted cove would work its magic on him, and put him in a good mood for once. How naive I was; and how little foresight I managed to display, when you consider the outcome.'

Carmichael was scribbling like fury, but found a second or two to look at the inspector, and roll his eyes at the prolonged explanation of what had happened; that event still seeming a long way away, buried in this miasma of memories, as it was. Falconer acknowledged his partner's rolling eyes by pulling a face in reply. Miriam Darling sat with her head down, twisting her fingers together in her lap, lost in the past.

'So, what actually happened when you got to the beach?'

'Oh, Mark insisted that we go to the main beach and hire a little boat. He said that would be a much more picturesque way of approaching the cove, and would mean we didn't have to risk the old steps down from the cliff top.

'I wasn't sure, not knowing what the water was like round the slight headland, and disagreed, saying that we could take the utmost care on the steps, and pointed out to him that unknown waters could be dangerous. That was when we had our little row – the one I'd been desperate to avoid – with hordes of witnesses. In the end, I said I didn't want to go, if Mark insisted on hiring a boat.

'That was like a red rag to a bull for him, and he took Ben's hand and stomped off towards the man who rented out the small craft. I just stood by, feeling helpless as usual, but supposing that everything would turn out all right in the end, and thinking Mark might even be in a good mood if he got his own way on this one. If only, just that once, I hadn't played the part of the compliant wife!

'And so we set off. It really was a small boat – a wooden one. Do they call those little things 'clinker-built'? – and Mark, of course, took charge of the oars, being the man of the family. It seemed a perfectly charming way to reach our destination at first, but, as we rounded the headland, the going got more difficult, and Mark started to struggle to keep control of the little boat.

'When I realised he was in difficulties, I offered to take a turn on one of the oars, so that we could row together, and double our power to fight the current, but he would have none of that. He was always stubborn, and hated to fail at anything. At that point, this was a test of his manhood, in his mind, and he struggled on, but the further we disappeared from sight of the busy beach, the more unruly the sea became.

'That was when I got really frightened, and told him he ought to turn back, as the sea was getting far too rough. The wind had got up, too, and we were rolling all over the place, with the waves breaking over the boat and swamping us. Ben was crying and I was holding him, trying to comfort him, and telling him that Daddy would soon get us back to the nice beach where he always played.

'That was the last coherent thought I had. There was a gust of wind, and a particularly large wave engulfed our tiny boat, and it capsized, throwing the three of us, plunging, into the roughness of the sea.

'There were incredibly strong currents there, and all I could think of was to catch hold of the underside of the boat and scream for help, although I knew my cries would be blown away by the wind. By the time I had a firm hold of it, I looked round, and both Mark and Ben were gone. That's when I really started screaming. I hadn't realised how one's life could be turned upside down in just a couple of seconds, the status quo irretrievably lost, the future completely blank and needing to be rewritten.

'I was the lucky one. Someone on the top of the headland, looking at the seabirds swirling around the inshore waters, happened to catch sight of my precarious situation, he alerted the coastguard – and I was rescued.'

Miriam paused here, to gather her strength for the end of the tragic tale. 'Mark's and Ben's bodies were washed ashore further along the coastline two days later; and my life effectively ended. I might as well have drowned with them. I feel like I'm already dead and suffering in hell, with all that's happened since, and now it's happening all over again.'

'And all the sorts of things that have occurred here, happened where you used to live?'

'Live? Huh! Existed, more like. But, yes, I was held in custody in Spain by the police. People remembered, you see, how we'd argued on the beach. My mother's neighbours remembered how we'd argued at her house – those villas are jerry-built, and the sound-proofing is non-existent. They thought I'd pushed them out of the boat, and that was the reason it capsized. I was cast in the role of a murdering wife and mother.

'I can't speak Spanish, and neither can my parents beyond a few words of greeting and 'please' and 'thank you', and I was dazed with my loss, and bewildered as to what was going on around me. It was a complete nightmare. There I was, locked away from the only comfort available to me – my parents – and I didn't understand a word of what was being said to me.

'Of course, eventually they brought in an interpreter, but it was a resort mainly for the Spanish themselves, and the interpreter, although she could speak some English, could not understand what I was saying, and seemed to make up her own mind as to what I had told her.'

'So what set off this toxic gossip, then?' asked Falconer, still pursuing his fox, but feeling that the further he moved forward the further away he was from his quarry.

'It started with the Spanish press. It was quiet in the journalistic world, it being holiday time; they seized my tragedy as a terrier seizes a rat, and I made the front page, painted as black as night. Just to add to my misfortunes, there was an English journalist on holiday about fifty kilometres away. He saw the story and descended on my parents and their neighbours like a wolf on the fold.

'He couldn't get to see me, but he did trace several people who had been on the beach that day – isn't it ironic that he spoke the lingo? Of course, he phoned it in, and started the same hare running in the English press. By the time I got back, I was branded as a murderess, and nothing I could say would change that, even though the Spanish police had traced someone on a fishing boat who had actually seen us capsize.

'I was harassed in my home by journalists. I started receiving anonymous threatening letters and silent phone calls, just like now. My car had paint-stripper thrown over it, people I'd known all my life, shunned me in the street. Some of them even spat at me, and one joker poured weedkiller over my front lawn one night, to spell out 'murderer'. That's when I knew what it was to be in hell.

'I took all the precautions I could to get away from it all. I moved to a rented property fifty miles away, adopting my maiden name, dying my hair and having it cut really short. I changed the way I dressed, and started not wearing make-up – anything so that I was not connected to what had befallen my family on that dreadful holiday.

'Eventually I moved here, and I seemed to have made a really solid start on a new and normal life. Carole Winter next door befriended me and introduced me to a host of people and organisations where I was made to feel really welcome. I'd applied to join the WI, I'd been invited to join a book club, I'd met the ladies of the church, the choir and the library, and Carole, who is a keen gardener, was helping me plan my little plot out at the back. Sundays were fun. We used to go to the service together, then go off in my car and stroll round the garden centres, looking for bulbs, seeds and plants that would be suitable for what had become my new hobby: gardening.

'Then, one day, she just 'cut' me: 'blanked' me as if she had never met me before. I found I was *persona non grata* wherever I went, and then it just started all over again. I don't know who made the connection, or why they passed it on, but I'm right back to square one, and now there's nowhere else to go,' she concluded on a mournful note.

'You *have* been through the mill, haven't you? Let me think a while and see what I can come up with. Do you work outside the home at all?'

'Yes. I work for a bank – Mondays, Wednesdays, and Fridays.'

'And has there been any trouble there?'

'Not so far, but I commute, and mix with a totally different set of people there. It's the only part of my life with some sanity left in it, the only place where I get treated like a normal human being. I'm not giving that up,' she stated in a firmer voice.

'OK. For now,' Falconer replied, 'what I can do is have a patrol car pass your house when you're at home, to make sure there's no physical attack on you, and put one of the uniformed constables to patrol this area, giving us a man on the ground.

'In the meantime you're going to have to consider changing your identity completely, perhaps disappear into the anonymity of a large city. Market Darley's fairly small, and people are nosier about their neighbours than they are in the sprawling confusion of a city.'

'I see your point,' she agreed. 'I do exactly as I planned before, but become the needle in a much bigger haystack.'

'Spot on! Now, I'll give you my card, and I'll write my home number on the back, so that you can get hold of me anytime. I hate bullying, especially the cowardly, anonymous kind, and when it's completely unfounded, it really gets my goat,' the inspector growled with great sincerity. 'There it is. Any time, day or night! And I mean that! I don't live far away – in fact I'm closer to you than I am to the police station, and I can be here in a few minutes, and alert the boys in blue on my way.

'In the meantime, may I suggest that when you are here you keep away from the windows. I know you've got net curtains and I don't want to frighten you, but I also don't want you to make yourself an unwitting target for some nutter.'

'Thank you for taking me so seriously,' she murmured, as she saw them out of the front door, opening it only wide enough to allow them to squeeze through it, and they heard her lock and bolt it again, as she had when they arrived.

Chapter Five

<u>Tuesday 21st September</u>

Falconer's home phone rang shrilly at just after half-past six that morning, rousing him from a light doze in which he dreamt of a woman he had glimpsed, briefly but devastatingly, earlier that year. She had skin the colour of ebony and was, in his opinion, the most beautiful woman he had ever set eyes on.

Things were going well in the dream, and they were sipping cocktails at some function or other, when the trilling of the telephone began to break up the conviviality of the occasion. As if a herald of the bad news that was to come in his dream, his old Nanny Vogel approached the bar, stopped by his side, and gave him her cruel and knowing smile, while the attractive woman, Dr Dubois, turned into a pillar of smoke and began to disperse.

Arriving suddenly to full wakefulness, he felt both cheated and disturbed as he reached for the handset beside his bed, answering it with an uncharacteristically blunt 'Yes?'

'Is that you, Inspector Falconer,' a distressed and tearful voice enquired. 'Only things have got worse.'

Recognising Miriam Darling's voice immediately, he pulled himself together, to treat her with a more professional attitude, even if he was in his pyjamas and lying in bed. These things mattered! 'What's happened now?' he asked her gently, hoping she hadn't been injured.

'I got a brick through my front window yesterday – well, during the night, actually – but as the curtains were drawn, it didn't really do any damage, but when I opened the door to take in the milk this morning, someone had sprayed 'killer' on my front door in black paint. I simply don't know what to do. Please help me, Inspector. I'm at my wits' end.'

'I'll get an officer over to take samples of the paint, and he'll take away the brick as evidence, although there's little likelihood it will offer anything useful as to who threw it. I'll get that organised, and I'll be with you in less than an hour to take another statement. I'll also arrange for a female PC to be billeted with you, as I seem to remember that you don't work on a Tuesday.'

'That's very kind of you, Inspector. I shall feel a lot safer for seeing you again, and a PC in the house will be a great relief. At least I'll have a witness to anything else that happens, and an ally, if I need physical help.' She sounded calmer already, and Falconer was pleased with his idea of having a PC in residence. If the officer herself made her presence known, maybe it would act as a deterrent.

'I'll be with you as soon as I can, Ms Darling, and I'll get on the phone straight after this call and set the wheels in motion for a SOCO officer and a PC to be dispatched.'

As soon as he ended the call, he rang the station with a cheery, 'Hello, Bob. How's tricks?' only to find that Bob Bryant – *Bob Bryant* – had taken a *day's leave*, and he was talking to PC Barry Sugden, more usually to be found booking in 'guests' in the custody suite.

'Sorry about that,' he apologised, 'only it always *is* Bob Bryant, so I simply wasn't prepared to find someone else answering the phone.'

'Don't apologise, sir – everyone else has said the same thing. I've just told them that, as one of the Immortals, Bob sometimes has to report to the planet Zog on what he has discovered in his current role, and then he'll get his transfer to another location round about the year 2073. Nobody's questioned my answer yet, but for your personal information, he's going to have a tooth out, and wants to slink back home and suffer in peace, but don't tell anyone else. The new boys, in particular, will be devastated, if they find out the reason for his day away from the station is such a mundane affair.'

Falconer knew only too well the web of bantering fantasy that existed between the younger members of the uniformed branch about the ever-present desk sergeant who, it was rumoured by these junior members of the force, had been there from the beginning of time, and would remain there, as an Immortal, until the end of the universe.

'Look, Barry, I need someone to come out to scout for evidence at the site of what I can only describe as a 'hate crime', and I need a PC – get me Starr if you can – to join me here.' After a little more explanation and giving the address, he hung up and got ready as speedily as he could, to visit Miriam Darling again. He could only imagine her distress and fear, and wanted to do what he could to reassure her as quickly as possible.

He arrived there less than half an hour after her distress call. When the door was opened by an even smaller crack than it had been on his last visit, he looked straight at her face, and, on gaining admittance, saw that she was already petrified with the escalation of events. He sat with her, giving what comfort he could, until PC Starr arrived and distracted her by asking to show the policewoman where everything was in the kitchen, so that she should be familiar with everything she needed to make tea, coffee and sandwiches.

Falconer left the two of them in the kitchen, opening and closing cupboard doors. Miriam seemed distracted enough to carry out this simple task; evidently feeling more confident now she had someone with her for the day.

Back at the station, he found that no activity in the immediate vicinity of the address had been reported by either foot patrol or passing patrol cars, and cudgelled his brain at how to get at the root of this spiteful behaviour. The neighbours were an obvious starting point, but he felt that they would be better left until Miriam went to work tomorrow, so that they would have had time to cool off, after being questioned, before she returned home from work.

Falconer got another early reveille the next morning – this time at 6.10, and from the familiar but unusually muffled voice of Bob Bryant; he must still have cotton wool in his mouth after his extraction the day before. Without preamble, the sergeant went straight into his story. 'One of yours, I believe, Harry. A Ms Darling. Been receiving hate mail, nasty phone calls and a brick through the window.'

When Falconer confirmed that this was his baby, the sergeant continued, 'Well, she's had another faceless visitor. Apparently she came down this morning at half-past five because she couldn't sleep, and decided a cup of tea would be a good thing. She hadn't had any more phone calls and was feeling quite cheerful, she said, when she started off down the stairs.

'That was when she smelled it. Someone had inserted a substantial amount of dog-shit through her letterbox, and then thrown the accompanying note, to land it clear of the first offering.'

'Nasty!' was the inspector's only comment.

'Quite!' countered the desk sergeant. 'But the note was much worse. It informed her that the next time it would be petrol-soaked rags, and that the author of the note always carried a box of matches or a lighter, so that he was never short of a flame. He then ended it by referring to her as a murdering bitch who wasn't going to get away with it, even if the law couldn't touch her.'

'I'm on my way, Bob, see if I can catch her before she leaves for work. Have we got anywhere we could use as a safe house for her at short notice? It would only be until she can find something to rent well away from here.'

'I'll see what I can do,' Bob assured him, and ended the call.

Miriam Darling was getting ready to leave for work when Falconer arrived, no longer shaking and crying, but showing a cold, hard side to her character that he had not seen before.

Allowing him a brief fifteen minutes, the most she could, to keep herself on schedule for catching her usual train, she sat down with him in the living room and listened to his suggestion about her moving temporarily to a safe house. Once she had chosen somewhere else to live, if she so desired, he could inform the local police station of her background, and get them to keep a discreet eye on her.

'I don't think that will be necessary, Inspector, although I'm very grateful for what you've done for me, but I think it's time for me to plough my own furrow now, don't you?'

He left her home that day more puzzled than reassured, and feeling that she was being blasé about the escalating danger to her, but there was nothing he could do about it. He could only provide the help and protection that he thought she needed if she was willing to accept it, and she'd been unbelievably distant when she'd spoken to him; almost as if she'd been a different person.

He didn't bother going home again, as it simply wasn't worth the extra to-ing and fro-ing, and seven thirty saw him behind his desk sorting through the paperwork that had accumulated since he had last sat there, and mulling over what had been happening in Ms Darling's life over the past couple of weeks.

It was the telephone that disturbed his reverie, but what an interruption it proved to be. PC Merv Green had been on duty in and around the railway station that morning, keeping an eye on vehicles in the station car park, and walking round the station periodically to make sure that there wasn't a pickpocket at work. Cities didn't have a monopoly on petty crime like this. It happened in relatively small places too.

He had been making his way along one of the platforms where the usually jostling crowd of commuters was waiting for the arrival of their morning train, all trying to be in a position to get into a compartment first and bag the best – or maybe the only – seat. As the train approached the station, there had been a yell from the furthest end of the platform, and cries went up: 'Woman under the train!' 'Someone pushed her! I saw!' 'I never saw her jump!' 'Get an ambulance!' and from one anonymous wag: 'Get a bucket and shovel!'

Green ran, pushing people out of his way in his anxiety to confirm what he had heard shouted; and they weren't wrong. The train was not so long that it still covered what was left of whoever had gone under it, and Green came perilously close to losing the contents of his stomach, just avoiding an unexpected rebate on his breakfast.

When Green called it in, although he had no name for the victim, or even confirmation of the sex, Bob Bryant had a gut feeling that this one was for Falconer, and called it through to him.

The inspector's response was unusually coarse and unexpectedly heartfelt: 'No! No! No, no, no! Damn! Damn it! No! Oh, shit! Bugger!' he yelled, to himself, rather than to Bob Bryant on the other end of the line. 'I should have waited, and escorted her to the train this morning, after what happened during the night. Bugger! Arse! What a negligent fool I am!'

'If it's her, Harry, it's hardly your fault, is it?' asked Bob Bryant, trying to dispel Falconer's feelings of guilt and anguish.

'But the threat in that last letter was chilling, and we should – *I should* – have taken it more seriously. That wasn't just a case of name-calling; that was a threat to her life, and even *I* didn't take it seriously enough. I suppose I thought that her tormentor would only act on his evil impulses when she was in her own home. Why didn't I consider her safety in going to work, or rather the danger she was in when she was in transit? I'm an absolute fool!'

'I should get yourself down to the railway station, and make sure it's her first, before you start beating your breast and tearing out your hair,' was the calm advice of the desk sergeant. Falconer took it at its worth, and calmed himself with difficulty while preparing to go to see the remains.

When he arrived at the railway station and sought out the correct platform, he realised what a good job Green had done. The man had used his loaf, and requested that the train be moved as far as it could along the track, allowing a clear view of where the victim had landed, getting those who were alighting at Market Darley to use the far exit, so as not to contaminate what must now be considered a crime scene.

The passengers waiting to board had been crowded into the station's waiting room, and were now waiting to be interviewed, bleating like sheep at how late they would be for work, meetings and the like, while yelling into their respective mobile phones trying to 'big up' what they were now declaring to be a bloody nuisance. But perhaps secretly believing that the morning's experience would be something that they could dine out on for months.

The area of platform itself had been isolated with blue-and-white crime tape, which now fluttered in the slightly chilly September breeze. Thus was the situation when Falconer arrived, in the sure and certain knowledge that Carmichael was not far behind him. That was cold comfort, however, as he felt he should have been able to save this poor, persecuted woman from having to pay the ultimate price for what was, in fact, an accident, blown out of all proportion and sensationalised by the press.

After Carmichael arrived, his face a woeful mask, it took the two of them an hour and a half to gather all the names, addresses and telephone numbers of the daily commuters, leaving them to reassemble at the far end of the platform in anticipation of the next train, all chattering like starlings about this unexpected interruption to their usual boring daily schedule.

There were already white-suited officers at work where the commuter had gone under the train: Falconer was able to give an adequate identification from scraps of torn clothing that had matched what she was wearing when he had visited her before she left for the station, but there was nothing really for them to find. What evidence does a little push leave? What trace could there be of the little shove, that just tips a person's balance, and causes them to fall?

Although all the other would-be passengers on that train would need to be interviewed, to see if anyone owned up to standing close enough to Miriam Darling to have witnessed whether she propelled herself in front of that train, or whether she was given a helping hand, it was a job they would leave to the uniformed branch. They would try to uncover the network of rumour and lies that had made Miriam's life such a misery before today, hoping against hope that they would be able to trace it to its original source in the town, but it would be a thankless task, and one unlikely to be successfully concluded.

Falconer finally left feeling very downhearted, and Carmichael had a glum expression that clearly indicated his feeling that they were facing a hopeless task. 'I don't know who is responsible for what that poor woman went through,' commented Falconer as they arrived back at their cars, 'but they might as well have handed her a chalice of poison and bade her drink it, for the outcome would have been the same.'

Chapter Six

Wednesday 22nd September

Falconer and Carmichael had spent the previous afternoon clearing their desks as best as they could to give them a free run at the new case, and had decided to start their investigations with the neighbours. Rumour and gossip usually emanated from someone close to the 'target' and, as Miriam had not lived in the area long, they had decided to start with those who had been physically close to her.

Their first visit was to Carole Winter, whom Falconer knew had befriended her new neighbour. If not involved herself, maybe she could give them some leads as to whom she had introduced Miriam to.

Carole's face 'closed' when she saw who was at her door, and they were invited inside reluctantly, her face bearing an icy smile that did not touch her eyes.

After introducing themselves, Falconer explained why they were there, although he had little doubt that she had realised that as soon as they had displayed their warrant cards.

'I was good to that girl,' she spat at them, defensively. 'I toted her around everywhere with me, introducing her to everyone I know, and then I found out what she had done – and not even a whisper to me that she had a past.' Mrs Winter sat bolt upright in an armchair, her hands clasped in her lap, a look of defiance on her face.

'She'd lied to me by her silence, and I wasn't having that – not having found out what she'd done and got away with.'

'Who told you?' asked Falconer, keeping his question as brief as possible so as not to prompt the flow of indignation and self-righteousness often found in some church-goers who would happily 'cast the first stone', and considered that they themselves were incapable of sin.

'It was Liz from the library. If she's bored, when the library's not busy, she amuses herself by 'Googling' new ticket-holders. The poor girl got much more than she bargained for when she searched for Miriam Stourton, nee Darling. And, before you ask, the application form to join the library service has a lot of seemingly irrelevant questions on it, including maiden name, and she had inadvertently put her married name in that space.

'Well, that really set the cat among the pigeons, and we had a long talk about what to do. It was Liz's suggestion – that's Elizabeth Beckett – that we spread the word that the woman was a danger to society. She should've been locked away, and the key thrown over a cliff. What a wicked deed, to kill her husband and her own child like that! She deserved to burn in hell, and I hope she is doing just that, now.'

'Crikey!' Carmichael later exclaimed. They'd certainly stirred up a hornets' nest of resentment at this house.

'Can you give me the names of the other people to whom you introduced Ms Darling?' asked Falconer, thinking to get a head start, but he'd stirred up another spurt of contumely.

'Darling, my bum! She was no more *Ms Darling* than I am the Aga Khan! Darling, my big fat hairy arse! But I'll answer your question, and then I want you out of this house. This has been a shocking time for me, ending up with a murderer living next door, and I want to forget it as quickly as possible, and get back to my normal tranquil life. What a good actress that woman was! I'd never have guessed she had such evil in her heart!'

The rest of the interviews conducted, from the names Mrs Winter provided, were either full of the same contempt, or with a holier-than-thou attitude that made Falconer's stomach turn.

Elizabeth Beckett at the library merely displayed astonishment that she could have uncovered such duplicity, but her colleague, Becky Troughton, claimed that she had taken an instant dislike to the woman, and that she had felt from the first that there was something wrong with her. How some people strive to find something a little bit 'special' about themselves, some supernatural ability that sets them apart from others! Falconer felt that this was the case here. Had the information never become public knowledge, Ms Troughton would probably be saying that she had sensed a good soul in Miriam Darling, and had taken to her at their very first meeting. Feelings, schmeelings! he thought in disgust.

At the church, although he spoke to the incumbent, a selection of the ladies of the congregation and choir, it was the holier-than-thou, pious attitude he encountered, many offering to pray for her forgiveness, yet none who believed in her innocence, and absolutely no one who would admit to making silent phone calls or sending anonymous letters. What an upright slice of society all these people seemed to form, and yet he had counted at least seventy letters on Miriam Darling's sofa the first time he had gone to her house.

Mabel Monaghan, the head honcho at the WI, was highly indignant that such a woman should even have considered joining the organisation, and admitted that she had torn up Miriam's application as soon as she had heard about her murky past.

'And you believed it without question?' Falconer had asked her.

'There is no fire without some smoke,' she had replied, getting the quotation right where so many others mangled it.

The only positive response he got was from Justine Cooper, the nominal leader of the book club that met once a month. 'I'd thought of asking her to give us a talk about her ordeal, so that we could, maybe, find a few literary similarities with this sort of persecution, and choose our next book along those lines,' she had admitted, when questioned.

'I suppose it was a rather morbid thought, though, given what she was going through, and for the second time. And now she's dead! Still, every cloud has a silver lining. We could still discuss her situation at our next meeting, and go ahead with that as a theme without her actually being there.' Now there was a hard-faced young woman, Falconer thought, as they left her house. She should have been a journalist, the way she seized things and twisted them to her ultimate advantage.

'I don't like these people.' Carmichael, as usual, summed up his feeling succinctly. 'I don't think I've ever met such a bunch of two-faced, trouble-making people who aren't actually criminals.'

'I'm with you on that one, Carmichael,' agreed Falconer, and then noticed that his sergeant had his pen in his mouth again – a habit of which he thought he had broken him.

'Put out your tongue, Sergeant,' he ordered, at the kerb-side, in public.

Looking a mite embarrassed, Carmichael removed the ballpoint pen from his mouth and complied.

'As I thought! The colour of an aubergine! When we get back to the station, go straight to the canteen and see if you can get them to serve you up a cup of coffee from the very dregs of the urn. That's the only thing we've found that seems to strip the ink.'

'Yes, sir,' agreed Carmichael, glumly.

Nothing was gleaned from the uniformed staff who had spent the hours after the return of the commuters trailing around the addresses given at the station that morning. Oh, yes, they'd come across a few who admitted to standing near, but not directly behind, Miriam Darling, but none that would admit to having pushed, or even accidentally nudged her, and no one had seen anything to which they were willing to admit.

With a heavy heart, Falconer knew that all the officers involved would just have to start all over again, and see if they couldn't coax a reluctant memory from someone, even if not an admission of guilt, but it was going to be a long and tedious job, and he still felt himself responsible for what had happened. What had possessed him, leaving her to make her own way to the railway station? He should have accompanied her. He had been negligent, and a sorely put-upon, innocent woman had paid for his lack of forethought with her life.

If only he had advised her not to go to work until she had been installed in a safe house. If! If! If only he had driven her to the station and waited with her. He would have kept her well away from the edge of the platform and, maybe, by the time she had returned to Market Darley that evening, he could have met her from the train with the address of a safe house into which she could move with immediate effect.

The week after Miriam Darling had been mangled by an incoming train was a week of reflection, regret and soul-searching for the inspector, and he was in an unusually glum mood when he picked up a white envelope from his post, one morning and slit it open, to find it was from Miriam Darling's bank manager, and had a smaller envelope enclosed with it, marked with his name.

'Well, I'll be blowed!' he exclaimed. 'What on earth can this be?'

'This' was a letter from her bank, explaining that the enclosed envelope had been handed to the manager by Miriam Darling herself, with the instructions that it was to be kept there in safe keeping, and only sent, in the event of her death, and even then not until a week had elapsed.

'Curiouser and curiouser,' quoted Falconer, as he slit open the second and smaller envelope. Inside, he found a letter, handwritten, explaining everything, and which saddened him even more than he would have thought it could. He read:

Dear Inspector Falconer,

I apologise for all the work I must have caused you and your colleagues over the last seven days, and now is the time for explanations. If, as I have planned, I have gone under a train at the local station, then my intentions will have gone as I hoped, and I shall be dead.

I knew I couldn't face starting yet another life, because I think my past will follow me to the ends of the earth, given the information technology available today, so I have decided to join my husband and son 'on the other side'.

I didn't want to leave this life without a little bit of revenge on those who had tormented me, so I will have made my death look as much like murder as I can, and have left it for you to suspect and question those who tormented me, and I hope they are made to feel hellishly uncomfortable.

My last hope is that, with the delivery of my letter to you, the truth will be made public, so that they can feel the guilt they share in my carrying out of this act of self-destruction. I don't wish to carry on as things are, and I hope that what I did will give them cause to think, next time they are in receipt of a juicy piece of gossip, and maybe hold back, when they are tempted to pass it on.

Many thanks for your help and support, and to your colleagues who did their best to keep me safe,

Miriam Stourton, nee Darling

Falconer's throat was almost closed with emotion as he finished reading and, putting the letter on Carmichael's desk, in full view, where he would find it as soon as he sat down, he left the office and went for a walk in the clean, clear air of a beautiful September morning.

THE END

Driven To It

Abigail Wentworth is looking forward to her reunion lunch with Alison Fairweather. They are old schoolfriends who met twice a year, usually for Alison to dish the dirt on the others they had known when they were younger - and for Abigail to gloat over their 'inferior' circumstances, in comparison to her own respectable existence.

During one such lunch, though, Abigail recognizes a face from the past - and from that moment onward, her life skids completely out of control...

Chapter One

Friday 26th November 2010 – lunchtime

Mrs Abigail Wentworth capped her lipstick, fluffed up her tinted beige curls, and looked at herself in the mirror. Sadly, it was still her mother's face that looked back at her, but as there is no escape from that cruel beast, Anno Domini, she merely picked up her perfume atomiser and sprayed herself generously with a fine flower-scented mist. She was as ready as she could be for lunch with her old schoolfriend, Alison Fairweather, who would be visiting Market Darley that day for their annual luncheon in the town.

Although they didn't live very far apart geographically, their lives were so different that this meeting was one of only two that took place each year, the other being in a hotel or restaurant in the vicinity of Alison's home. Thus they hadn't seen each other for six months, and Abigail wanted to look her absolute best, to show that she wasn't ageing as fast as her friend. It was a matter of pride to her that she appeared just that little bit more youthful than Alison.

Scrutinising herself in the full-length mirror on the wardrobe door, she thought how well she had retained her figure over the years, whereas Alison had allowed her body first to swell, then to sag, as the years took their toll. Well, there was nothing about Abigail's body that a well-made corset couldn't set to rights, and she had one of these on for today's luncheon. Although it wouldn't allow her to eat much, it did ensure that she could get into a dress a size smaller than she wore on a day-to-day basis, and this pleased her enormously.

Having not grown much heavier with the years, it meant she was also still able to walk in relatively high heels, and this, of course, would emphasize the difference in their builds. Alison always wore trainers these days, something that Abigail wouldn't be seen dead in. At least *she* hadn't let herself go over the years and still tried to retain

a little grace and elegance, particularly when she was to see her old
friend.

She particularly looked forward to these six-monthly lunch
meetings with Alison, as it always brought news of other old school
chums. They had all started on a level playing field at St Hilda's,
but the winds of life had scattered them in completely different
directions, and Abigail revelled in the fact that so many of them had
failed to reach their true potential.

Sally Carter had screwed up big-time, producing five illegitimate
children one after the other, and all with different fathers. At school,
she had been the romantic, and fell in love at the drop of a hat.
As far as Abigail had been informed, she now lived in some sort
of hippie commune, amongst all the other dross of the late sixties
that had never adapted to the conventions and responsibilities of
adult life. Alison said that, even at her advancing years, she still
wore flowing kaftans and numerous strings of beads, and plaited her
hair in the hope that what sparse growth there was left would turn
into dreadlocks if she waited long enough. Alison reckoned that the
whole lot would fall out before that happened.

Suzie Beeton had gone to the other extreme, marrying a man
of the cloth, and lived an impoverished life in a house rented from
the Church of England, now that her husband had retired, forever
waiting for the odd occasion when he was asked to undertake locum
work, to bring in a small addition to their meagre income.

Mary Dibley had had ambitions to be a career woman, but
without a chance of even sighting the glass ceiling above her. Always
a slow, almost bovine, character, she had worked her way to level
two in administration at a large company, and there she had stayed,
doggedly working away, year after year, always hoping for but not
quite achieving promotion.

And finally there was Lesley Lovelace, an impatient girl who had
never wanted to wait for anything, and who couldn't stick to one

subject for more than twenty minutes before she started to fidget and generally cause havoc in whichever classroom her lesson was taking place.

Over the years Abigail had listened avidly as Alison had told her of Lesley's five marriages and four divorces, and she was eager to hear whether Lesley was still with the last partner she had heard about, or had moved on to number six yet. She had also had, to Abigail's knowledge, two face-lifts, and this was another subject on which she yearned for information. Had number two sagged yet, or had she gone for number three, and ended up looking like some sort of over-stretched monster?

In Abigail's opinion, she herself was the only one of the old crowd who had prospered and lived a respectable life, taking care of her social position, and dealing with the ravages of time with dignity. Who would have thought that it would have been her, Abigail Thorogood, as she was known back then, who would have the delightful detached house, the sleek Mercedes, and the membership of the country club – with a holiday home in Brittany too?

Oh, how she loved these reunion lunches with Alison!

Alison, as usual, was waiting in the bar for her, as parking in Market Darley was getting to be a nightmare these days, and the hotel car park had been full, forcing Abigail to seek on-street parking, making her arrival a little tardy. But nothing could dampen her good mood today, and she made her entrance to the bar, trailing clouds of Chanel 19 in her wake, a smile of welcome on her face, and a great ball of *Schadenfreude* in her heart, waiting to be satisfied.

Lunch was its usual avalanche of news, Alison doing most of the talking, Abigail making suitably smug comments.

'She hasn't! Not a third one! She must look almost oriental with everything stretched so much.' 'Like a wild cat? How appropriate! Lesley always was the catty one at school.'

'Twenty grandchildren? Where on earth does she put them
when they visit? It's just as well she lives in a commune, otherwise
she'd need a mansion.'

'Oh, they all get slotted in somewhere. They don't think
anything of it, being brought up as they were,' explained Alison.

'What a complete whirlwind it must be with their parents
visiting a well. Poor old Sally!'

'Suzie, shopping at jumble sales? I thought they'd be better off
when her husband retired, but you say the pension is small, and
they haven't got any savings? What a shame. She always dressed so
fashionably at school. It must be such a disappointment for her to
have to acquire her clothes that way.'

'Still hoping for promotion? At her age? Mary must live in a
different world to everyone else – one filled with false hopes and
impossible ambitions. She'll be retiring soon. How can she go on
chasing promotion when she's headed for her pension?'

On and on it went, Abigail's self-satisfied comments coming
faster and faster. Alison thanked her lucky stars that it had been an all
girls' school. Having to provide progress reports on a crowd of boys
too, would have been too much. Sometimes she thought that Abigail
enjoyed the misfortunes of her old friends just a little too much for
comfort, and knew that she thoroughly disapproved of the way she
herself dressed.

Being who she was, though, Alison didn't care a fig. She dressed
comfortably, and was at peace with her life. If she hadn't been, she
would never have continued these lunches for so long, knowing that
Abigail merely used them to make herself feel superior.

There was only one interruption to the flow of their
conversation, and that was when Abigail stared beady-eyed across
the room, over Alison's shoulder, and said, very quietly, 'I'm sure I
know that face.'

'Who's that?' asked Alison, who had been interrupted mid-news bulletin.

'Nobody,' replied Abigail. 'I just thought I saw someone I recognised, but it doesn't matter. Carry on with what you were saying. What did she do next?'

At Market Darley Police Station, Detective Inspector Harry Falconer and Detective Sergeant 'Davey' Carmichael were deep in conversation on a very important subject, considering what next month would bring.

'For a start, your height and build would give you away instantly,' Falconer said. 'Who else could you be, but yourself? Neither of them would fall for that one. Just take them into the bedroom, like Kerry's always done before, and hope they don't wake up. If they do, at least you have the excuse that they were left downstairs, and you were just being helpful in bringing them up to their room.'

'But I so want to wear one, and it's the only opportunity I'll get in a whole year. I think I'd look great!' Carmichael almost whined, in his desire to fulfil his dream scenario.

'I think you'd look terrifying. Like the Incredible Hulk does paedophilia.'

'Sir!' The sergeant was most indignant.

'Well, how would you feel if you woke up and found a great red giant in your bedroom? And you're sure to trip over something or knock something over. You're not exactly graceful, you know.' retorted Falconer. 'It would be bad enough to find the Jolly Green Giant, without introducing a scarlet one into the mix. Anyway, do they even make them in your size? You are a bit on the huge side.'

DS Carmichael was nearly six and a half feet tall, and built like a battleship. Considering this last question, he sighed, and admitted that he would probably not be able to buy a Father Christmas outfit to fit him, and that he'd better leave it to his wife Kerry to drop the filled pillowcases into the boys' room on Christmas Eve.

'It's just not fair. Maybe I can get Kerry to run me up one. You know how good she is at making costumes,' he suggested, wistfully.

'Your wife is due to give birth to your first child in less than two months. Not only has she two boys to look after while you're at work, but she's got those two dogs of yours, one of them pregnant, and that stray cat you adopted. Don't you think she has enough to cope with for the moment? And when would she get the time to just "run something up"? The boys would be sure to catch her at it, and ask her what she was making, and then your cover would be blown before you'd even had the chance to try it out.'

'OK, OK! I get the point! But it's still not fair,' replied Carmichael, his face set glumly.

'Whoever said life was fair, Carmichael, was lying. Some things we just have to live with. Anyway, didn't you have enough of dressing-up when you had that pantomime-themed wedding last New Year?'

'That just gave me a taste for it, sir.'

'Well, it looks like it's Tough Shit City for you then, Sergeant. Come on, let's get on, or we'll never finish this paperwork today.'

Chapter Two

Friday 26th November – afternoon

Abigail left the hotel with the usual smug smile she wore after what she called one of her 'catch-ups', but the smugness was tempered with a slight feeling of unease, and she decided to take the long way home through the back streets to allow her thoughts to settle. She had a lot to think about.

Pulling out of her parking space, she turned into Abattoir Road, one of the old and narrow streets that comprised the old market heart of the town and suddenly jammed her foot on the accelerator. There was a thud as she hit a pedestrian who had appeared in front of her, and then a sickening thud, as the unfortunate man hit the road surface several feet in front of her vehicle which, as she had been so late to apply the brake, was still in motion. When the car reached the body, it did a double bump, as both front and back wheels rolled over it, and by the time Abigail managed to halt the vehicle, she was several yards in front of where her victim lay, mangled and obviously dead.

She sat for what seemed like for ever, drenched in a cold sweat at what had just happened, her heart pounding, her breath coming in short little gasps. She could hear other pedestrians calling out for an ambulance to be summoned, and for the police to be called, and finally made a shaky exit from the driving seat. What had she done?

It was a quiet time of day, just after lunchtime, and there were only three people present, at the moment, clustered around the body to see if there was any help to be given to the poor victim. 'I can't find a pulse,' said an elderly woman, who had been a first-aider in her working days.

'He's definitely not breathing,' commented a younger woman, who had a pushchair with a child in it, which she had left on the pavement in her haste to come to the victim's aid.

'No chance. He's a goner. Look at his injuries,' added a middle-aged man who had been on his way back to his office, a little late back from lunch today.

Abigail leaned against her car and tried to take deep breaths, hoping that she wasn't going to pass out. What on earth had happened back there? What had really happened? It had been all so quick, though, when she thought about it now, it happened in slow motion in her mind, making it all the more horrific. She'd killed a man. What to do? What to do, now?

Within a couple of minutes a police patrol car drew up and a man and a woman got out of it. PC Merv Green and PC 'Twinkle' Starr had been on patrol in the vicinity, and had answered the call for assistance at an RTA immediately.

They instantly took over the scene, PC Green instructed the middle-aged man to stop traffic at the end of the road – luckily it was a one-way-street, and spoke into his personal radio to ask how long they would have to wait for an ambulance. PC Starr headed straight for Abigail Wentworth, to see if she was in need of any treatment for shock, or would be capable of making a statement in the not too distant future.

The ambulance arrived in less than five minutes, loading into the vehicle what they knew would be categorised as a DOA, the state of extinction of life and the time of death determined by the doctor who received the body at the hospital.

As the ambulance team left with their grizzly cargo, PC Green gathered together the three witnesses and took down their names and addresses, asking them if they could make their way to Market Darley Police Station to make formal statements, and offering a lift to as many as they could get in the patrol car. Only the man who had been stopping traffic entering the road claimed that he really ought to pop into his office first, but promised to present himself for interview within half an hour.

PC Green had transferred his attention to Abigail, whose skin looked grey under her make-up, and every day of its fifty-eight years, immediately after the ambulance had arrived. Within the space of a few seconds, she had gone from a well-preserved, attractive and elegant woman-of-a-certain-age, to a shocked and frightened elderly lady. She was still leaning against her car, and he bent down to speak to her quietly.

'I think I ought to get you back to the station and have a doctor look at you, before we go any further with this matter, but before that, you need a nice cup of hot sweet tea. I can call another car, so that you don't have to travel to the station in the same vehicle as the witnesses to the accident. That'll be the best thing all round, don't you agree?' he asked, a frown of puzzlement making small creases on his brow. Something here didn't add up, but he had no idea what.

At the station, PC Starr had placed her witnesses in separate interview rooms and arranged for tea to be brought to all of them. The elderly woman had given her name as Madge Moth, and an address only a few streets away. The younger woman, pushchair and child still in tow, had said she lived on the other side of town, but had been visiting her mother, and was going to do some shopping before she got the bus home, when the accident had happened. The middle-aged man arrived only a quarter of an hour after the patrol car, and gave his name as Arthur Black, a deputy manager at one of Market Darley's banks.

PC Green would not be back until he had a second car in which to transport Abigail, and had summoned a SOCO team to record any evidence of the accident left on the road surface. Someone would also have to erect a 'road closed' barrier at the end of the road, and arrange to have the vehicle towed away.

PC Starr started with Mrs Moth, who was fairly calm, having seen her fair share of mishaps in her role as first aider over the years, and who had a fairly high tolerance to shocks. She was in good shape, and just wished she had more to tell than she did. She had been the only one headed in the same direction as the car and, therefore, hadn't seen its approach.

The first thing she had been aware of was the thud, as the car hit the pedestrian, then a squeal of brakes, as the car had tried to stop. She had not witnessed the actual accident, merely been present, but was facing in the wrong direction, when it happened.

The policewoman waited patiently as the woman signed her statement, and then asked her if she would like a lift home, to which she received the reply that Mrs Moth was perfectly all right, thank you very much, and knew her way home, without the necessity of suffering a police car depositing her on her own doorstep.

Next, she spoke to Arthur Black, the man who worked at the bank, to find that he had been walking towards the town on his way back to work. He had not particularly noticed the car when it turned in to the street, but had noticed that it had suddenly accelerated after it turned.

He'd thought, at the time, that maybe the driver was late for an appointment, but then the car had immediately hit a pedestrian, and he was aware, at the time, that it seemed to take longer than he thought would have been necessary, for the brakes to be applied. Events had rather overtaken thought at that point, and he had ceased to think again until after the poor man's body had been taken away from the scene of the accident.

He did admit to being rather shaken by the way that the car had not only hit the pedestrian, but had then continued on, running over the body with both sets of wheels, before coming to a halt. 'Women drivers!' he commented, with a sour look. 'And elderly drivers!' he added. 'God preserve me from both of them. They're a positive menace on the roads! It shouldn't be allowed!'

Katy Cribb, the young mother with her child, had professed to have missed the actual accident, because she was picking up a soft toy which her daughter had thrown out of the pushchair, but she had heard the screech of brakes, and had then heard noises that she didn't want to think about, but which she feared would haunt her dreams for a good while to come. Yes, she might have heard the car accelerate, but on the other hand, she might not have. She really couldn't be sure, because everything had happened so fast.

PC Starr sighed, and wondered at the all-enveloping state of motherhood. The young mother seemed more concerned lest her daughter Cassandra had seen what had happened, and whether this would scar her tiny mind for the rest of her life. Starr sighed again, and hoped that when ... if ... she and Merv made a go of things, and eventually had children, she wouldn't descend into this morass of maternal fog that blinkered her to the rest of the world and its doings.

PC Merv Green, meanwhile, had also returned to the station, with Abigail Wentworth in his custody. After the administration of tea and sympathy, he attempted to extract a simple statement from her, but found that she was more concerned with what this tragic accident would do to her social standing, than with the fact that she had killed a man.

'Whatever are people going to think of me? I've always had a spotless reputation, and now they're going to think that I'm a cold-blooded killer,' she moaned. 'I promise you that I can't remember a thing from when I left the hotel, to the moment that my car drew to a halt after ... what happened.

'It's all just a blank, and as for the man, I've never set eyes on him in my life before,' she stated, her voice a little firmer.

'How do you know, if you don't remember anything?' asked Green, logically.

'I must have glimpsed his face, and it was only that that lodged itself in my memory,' she retorted, a little acidity leaking into her voice as she made this statement. 'Who knows the mystery of how the brain works?' she asked, a challenging expression on her face.

Green took down her statement as best he could, considering the number of times she fled off on a tangent about what this would do to her social standing, took the name and address and contact numbers of the friend with whom she'd eaten lunch – 'Just so that I can confirm your mood in the hotel restaurant,' he reassured her – then got a patrol car to take her home. He had something on his mind, and he wouldn't feel at peace until he'd unburdened himself. He just needed a few other bits and pieces of information before he could do so.

Falconer and Carmichael, having not long finished a rather tricky case, were in an unusually informal mood, and Green found them throwing paper balls at each other, both convulsed with laughter. Carmichael had done wonders in relaxing Falconer's previously stern manner in the time they'd spent as partners.

After peeking round the door, Green cautiously closed it again, then knocked and waited to be invited to enter. By the time this happened, all was sober and industrious in the office, and he was glad he'd withdrawn his head before either of them had seen him. It had obviously been a private moment of celebration and triumph that he had almost walked in on a few seconds before.

It had, in fact, been nothing of the sort; merely a silly piece of horseplay when Falconer had thrown a paper ball at Carmichael, who had said something unusually crass, even for him, and Carmichael had responded with a volley of hastily rolled balls of his own making. The sergeant had, for over a year now, been trying to release the inner child in the inspector, whereas Falconer had decided that he didn't have one. In fact, as a child, he was convinced that he had an inner adult, but Carmichael had just proved him wrong.

The only sign of their recent childish behaviour was a slight grin that still hovered around both their mouths, as Falconer asked Green what he could do for him.

'RTA. It's a case of a woman running down a pedestrian earlier today, sir,' he began, not sure exactly how he could express his misgivings.

'Dead?' asked Falconer.

'As a doornail, sir.'

'And have you got the driver?'

'Yes, sir.'

'And she admits guilt?'

'Yes, sir.'

'So what is it that's bugging you?' asked the inspector, in the dark for the moment.

'One of the witnesses – we've got three – says she definitely accelerated just before she hit him, another thinks she might have heard it. The driver not only hit the victim once, but the car carried on down the road and ran both sets of wheels over him before it came to a halt.

'Nasty! Do you have confirmation from either of the other two witnesses?'

'From all three of them, sir.'

'There must be something else, Green: something you haven't told me yet.'

'There is, sir. The driver denied point-blank that she had ever set eyes on the victim before, but I'm pretty sure she'd never taken a proper look at him. She claims not to remember the accident itself, and she didn't come back down the road to see him lying in the road, but stayed leaning against her car until our patrol car arrived, so how on earth did she know she'd never seen him before?'

'Come on, man. Spit it out. There's more, isn't there?'

'Yes. I stayed with her while the paramedics examined the body, and I could see her face reflected in one of the windows of her car. When one of the ambulance men said, 'He's a goner,' she smiled, sir. She looked as pleased as the cat that's got the cream, and I think we ought to know why that was, if he was a complete stranger.'

'Well spotted, Green. I think we'd better take a look into this one, Carmichael. There's obviously more to it than meets the eye. Have you got all the relevant information – victim's details, witnesses' contact numbers and anything else we might need to know?'

'Right here, sir. I typed up a report before I came to see you, so that there wouldn't be any delay.'

'Come on, Sergeant. We're on!' called the inspector, grabbing the printed sheet from Green's hand, and heading out of the office. 'You can read that to me *en route.*'

Chapter Three

Friday 26th November – late afternoon to early evening

Green's report identified the victim as a Mr James Carling, and a wage slip had been found in one of his pockets indicating that he worked at the Swan Hotel and Restaurant. That was to become Falconer and Carmichael's first port of call, to see what sort of man James Carling had been, and whether Mrs Wentworth ate there frequently.

The receptionist, a Miss Susan Chester, had worked at the hotel for five years, and knew Abigail by sight, explaining that she ate there quite often with her various groups of women friends, but also had this one particular meal, once a year, that she ate with an old friend from her schooldays, and that she looked forward to this meal avidly.

She also told them that James Carling had only worked there for a matter of weeks, and that she knew little about him, except that he was a harmless old thing who never put a foot wrong, and went out of his way to be polite and helpful. He had seemed to settle in well, and was on good terms with the other members of staff with whom he came into contact, and there had definitely been no complaints about his service.

The manager, Ronald Wild, could not really give them any further information, except for the fact that James Carling, known by everyone as 'Jimmy', had moved up from Brighton about three months ago and had secured his position at the hotel a few weeks after that. Mr Wild knew none of the details of Jimmy's private life, and he didn't think any of the other staff would be able to help with that either.

Jimmy Carling, although always cheerful and happy, had played his cards rather close to his chest regarding his personal life, both current and before he had moved to Market Darley. Wild surmised that there might be an ex-wife or two in the past, as the man was obviously gregarious, despite his age, which was near that of retirement.

After checking the victim's address, Falconer decided that they should go and pay Mrs Abigail Wentworth a call, just to confirm what Green had written in his report, and to, sort of, scout her out on her home turf.

The house they pulled up in front of was large and detached, the garden meticulously cared for, the paintwork in pristine condition. It was an expensive property, and its owner was probably justly proud of it. The garden path too, although created from crazy-paving, sprouted no weeds between its pieces of varied-colour slabs, and the brass door furniture which greeted them in the porch shone like gold.

Abigail answered the door to them wearing a frilly, but suitably modest, housecoat, and apologised about her apparel. She had had a long hot bath when she got back from the police station, to try to soak her tensions and shock away, and had then consumed a large gin and tonic, deciding that she wouldn't be getting dressed again until the next day. She could stay as she was for the rest of today, as she wasn't expecting any visitors.

Falconer apologised, in his turn, for appearing on her doorstep on such a distressing day, but explained to her that the sooner the whole matter was sorted out, the sooner she would be able to put it all behind her and get on with her life.

She accepted this as a perfectly reasonable explanation for their presence, and ushered them into an expensively furnished, but nevertheless welcoming, sitting room, which Falconer was convinced she always referred to as her 'drawing room'. As soon as they were seated, she offered them coffee, and disappeared off to the kitchen to make it, while they sat looking around to see if the room might give them any clues to the lady's personality.

There were silver-framed photographs everywhere. Some must have been of her children and, as she had explained to Green, her late husband, as she was a widow of twenty years' standing. The loss of her husband must have caused her a great jolt, but she must have had great fortitude and courage to have survived this, and carried on to build a busy life of her own.

In solitary state, on a side-table, stood a wedding photograph, in black and white, of the couple on their wedding day, both smiling happily into the camera lens. Falconer always found such photographs sad, when encountered during the course of his investigations. His presence alone indicated that something cataclysmic had happened, either to one of the couple, or someone close to them, and he wondered at the effortless optimism on their faces, when life had as much tragedy to offer as it had joy. There was no sign that one of them would eventually be left to cope on their own, only the ecstasy that they were at last married, and their lives could now be lived together as one.

There were as many photographs of her late husband as there were of her children, and she must have worked hard to keep his memory fresh, as if he were only somewhere else in the house, perhaps in another room. Some people removed all photographs after losing a partner, as they found it too upsetting to be reminded of what had been expunged from their life for ever, but not so Mrs Wentworth.

Carmichael had settled himself down on a chair just out of view of anyone sitting on the sofa, where he had assumed that Mrs Wentworth would sit to hand out the coffee, and just awaited her return, his notebook out and open on one knee.

She re-entered the room just as Falconer had finished his consideration of her family pictures. She put a tray down on the coffee table and poured a stream of steaming liquid into three tiny porcelain coffee cups. 'Milk and sugar?' she asked, looking directly at Falconer.

'Just as it comes, please,' he replied, taking the tiny saucer from her hand, which betrayed only the tiniest indication of a tremble as she handed it to him.

'Milk and sugar?' she enquired again, this time spearing Carmichael with her eye.

'Yes, please,' he replied. 'And, oh, it's quite a small cup, so about four sugars should do it.'

'And how many do you normally take?' she asked, genuinely interested.

'Six,' he informed her, and waited for his thimbleful of coffee to be handed over.

Niceties over with, Falconer began his questioning, but could not shake her from anything she had said to Green when she had made her statement earlier. 'And you're absolutely certain that you didn't know this man before the accident?' he asked, finally.

'I have never laid eyes on that man in my life, before today,' she stated categorically.

They thanked her for the coffee, and allowed her to show them out. They might not have learned anything new from her, but Falconer felt he had her measure. She was a strong, controlled woman who wouldn't let anything slip, unless she wanted you to know it.

Back at the office, Falconer consulted Green's notes again, and dialled the number of the friend with whom Abigail Wentworth had eaten lunch earlier that day. She should have had enough time to get home by now, and, if not, he had her mobile number too. No doubt Mrs Wentworth had already been on the phone, telling her the tragic events that had occurred in the aftermath of their meal together.

He finally got her on her mobile, as she had gone on from Market Darley to visit one of her children, where she planned to stay overnight. When pressed, she admitted that she hadn't heard from Abigail, as she had only just turned on her phone, but had noticed that there were six messages which had come in during the afternoon. Falconer thanked God that his timing had been so lucky. If this woman did have anything to tell, it might have been suppressed if Abigail could have got to her first.

'I feel I need to ask you if Mrs Wentworth had a happy marriage,' he said, having had a brainwave just before he made the call. What if Jimmy Carling had been an old flame of Abigail's – or, even more damning, an old lover. Maybe all those photographs had just been a smokescreen. The fact that he had turned up in Market Darley would have given her a hell of a jolt, considering how she valued the way her peers perceived her.

'I need you to tell me if there were any affairs, or any point in the marriage where it seemed they might break up,' he said, keeping his fingers crossed under the desk.

'Not that I really know of,' replied Alison Fairweather, then added, 'There was a bit of a kerfuffle round about the same time that they found out Robert – that was her husband's name – had cancer, but I never did get to the bottom of it.

'You have to understand that Abigail and I only met twice a year – our school reunion lunches, we dubbed them – and that a lot went on in her life that I never got to hear about.'

'Was there anything during lunch today that was different about her? Anything she did, anything she said?' he tried, once more crossing his fingers.

'She seemed just as usual. We talked about our old school chums – well, I did. She just listened and passed judgement on them all, which was the way it always is when we get together. I'm a bit like 'The Old School Times', for her, as I keep in much closer touch with old friends. I'm the one with the 'gen'; she's the one with the black cap, to condemn the guilty.'

'Are you sure there was absolutely nothing. Not even a word, a phrase, or a glance?' he continued, not wanting to give up on this thread of his investigation.

'Well, there was one thing, but I don't see how it can have anything to do with anything.'

'What?' Falconer almost spat into the phone in his eagerness to be in possession of whatever information she was about to give him.

'We were just about to start dessert, when she suddenly looked up, stared across the restaurant and said, 'I'm sure I know that face,' but she never followed it up, and I had no idea who she was looking at, so I didn't pursue it. If I had, she could have had me skewered there for hours, telling me some story in which I had no interest whatsoever.'

'You don't really like Mrs Wentworth, do you?' asked Falconer, chancing his arm just a bit, but he'd got the feeling that there was a certain amount of suppressed impatience in the woman on the other end of the phone, as she talked about someone she had known for most of her life.

'Not really,' admitted Alison Fairweather. 'She does so love to hear the negative things about people, or what she considers to be negative. It makes her feel superior, and I'm afraid she's been like that ever since we were at school. If any of our crowd decided to live a life different from the pattern that Abigail had chosen for hers, she thought it was disgraceful behaviour, and pitied them.

'The people I tell her about are all very happy with the way their lives have turned out, but Abigail can't see that, so she hugs information to herself, and feels sorry for the others. I only keep up the luncheons because I actually feel sorry for *her*.'

'Thank you very much for your time, Mrs Fairweather. You've been very helpful,' he concluded, and ended the call.

'Come on, Carmichael,' he said, 'Time we went home. We've stayed late enough for one day. I want us to set out bright and early tomorrow, though. I've got the keys to Jimmy Carling's flat, and I want to take a little look round there. I've a feeling that our Mrs Wentworth had a bit of a fling with that particular gentleman.

'It would have been just about the time her husband was diagnosed with cancer, and I think, instead of leaving him, she stayed to nurse him through his last illness. I just have a bit of a hunch that our Mr Carling may have been her secret lover about twenty years ago, and she recognised him today, and thought that if he saw her he might tarnish the bright and shiny reputation of which she is so proud.'

'I'm still going to have a look to see if they do one in extra-extra-extra large,' mumbled Carmichael, still continuing a discussion they had had that morning, worrying at it, like a terrier with a bone.

After Carmichael had left, Falconer picked up all the paper balls they left scattered across the office floor after their horse-play earlier, and put them in his briefcase for the amusement of his cats when he got home. They loved nothing better than a plethora of paper balls to stalk and catch and throw in the air, and it did save him having to clear up blood from the carpet in the morning, if he wore them out thusly, and discouraged them from massacring the local wildlife.

Chapter Four

<u>Saturday 27th November – morning</u>

It was only a few minutes past eight-thirty when Falconer turned the key and they entered Jimmy Carling's flat, which was in one of the old houses that had been split into two separate dwellings in Abattoir Road.

'Cor! He'd have been a real bit of rough for Mrs Wentworth, wouldn't he, sir?' exclaimed Carmichael as he looked around the sad little flat. The furniture was a mixture of old and battered, and newer and tawdry. The bed in the bedroom was unmade, and was badly in need of its sheets changing. In the kitchenette area, the sink was stacked with unwashed pots, and the breakfast dishes from the previous day were still on the tiny breakfast bar.

'Not exactly up to Lady Muck's standards, is it, Sergeant?' Falconer replied, swivelling his eyes round to see where they might search for evidence of an old, but not forgotten, relationship. 'I'll go through the bedside cabinet, and you have a look through that old sideboard over there, and we'll see if we strike it lucky.'

Both pieces of furniture seemed to be stuffed with old envelopes and papers, and Falconer could only consider that Jimmy Carling had wasted no time on having a clear-out before he had moved here, but just stuffed everything he could into the furniture to be moved, with probably a pie-crust promise to himself that he'd go through everything when he was settled. And then hadn't!

There were plenty of papers to sort, but most of them were of the junk mail type, virtually nothing being personal. Falconer did think he'd struck gold when he found a couple of small envelopes addressed in an old-fashioned female hand, but these had turned out to be letters from the old man's mother, and he must have kept them in memory of her.

At one point, Carmichael gave a yell but this, too, was a false alarm, and produced only a couple of epistles from the man's sister, keeping him up to date on family news. After an hour they had to call it a day, and left the flat as they had found it, returning to the office glum and defeated.

Back at their desks, Falconer voiced his resolution to have another go at Abigail Wentworth, and face her with the suggestion that she and Carling had been old lovers. After all, they had nothing to lose, and, maybe, everything to gain.

Although still a little pale when they arrived, Abigail was in full make-up, and fashionably dressed, when she opened the door to them, at about ten-thirty. She looked surprised to see them again so soon after their call of the day before, but her manners were set in stone, and she asked them in with no demur, showing them once more into the room with the comfy seats, and retreating again to the kitchen, to make tea this time. Carmichael couldn't face another run-in with such a tiny cup, and had high hopes of a mug this morning, and Falconer couldn't grudge him his attempt to get his hands on a larger drinking vessel.

Sadly, the sergeant had misjudged Abigail's refinement, and the tray she bore in for them today had beautifully painted, but small, teacups on it, however, at least they were bigger than the ones in which she had served coffee yesterday.

Falconer asked for his with just a tiny splash of milk, but she looked hard at Carmichael when she enquired whether he wanted milk and sugar. 'Yes, please,' he gulped, evidently intimidated by this strong woman.

'And how much sugar would you like today, Sergeant?' she asked, her eyes daring him to give her an outrageous answer.

'Six,' replied the sergeant, who had been avoiding eye contact, and had not noticed her steely look, but he wasn't deaf, and he heard her whispered opinion. 'Ridiculous!'

When she was settled, Falconer declared that he was going to ask her a very personal question, and promptly did so. 'Did you, in your youth, or at any time during your marriage, have an affair with a Mr James Carling?'

Abigail was so startled that she sprayed tea down the front of her pretty mint green frock, and sat with her mouth open in apparent amazement. 'If you're referring to that unfortunate man that I ran over yesterday, I have already told you that I had never set eyes on him before yesterday, and I am not one to tell lies. I'd never met him before, and I told you that yesterday. Now, I'd be grateful if you'd finish your tea, then leave my house immediately. I can't think what put that idea into your head, but I am scandalised that you actually asked me that question.'

Back in the car once more, Falconer and Carmichael looked at each other, shrugged simultaneously, then burst out laughing. 'Lord, I put my foot in it that time, didn't I?'

'Big time, sir, and in size twelve uniform boots!' confirmed Carmichael.

They returned to the office, Falconer knowing he was on the right track, but somehow, he had things slightly out of kilter. Somehow, he'd muffed it. 'We'll collect those witness statements and call on the three other people who were actually at the scene of the accident. Maybe they'll have remembered something else,' decided the inspector, determined that Merv Green's hunch, and the reflection he had seen of Abigail's face in the car window, meant something important. That had been no accident, and he knew it.

As Carmichael gathered the necessary paperwork together, a thought struck him and he asked, 'Is that chap still upsetting Kerry – the one in Castle Farthing that you said is getting up everyone's nose?'

Carmichael stopped scrabbling at his desk and slumped down in his chair. 'Technically, no, sir. Kerry's Auntie Marian – you know,

Marian Warren-Browne, who used to run the post office? Her godmother. Well, she, apparently 'had a word' with him, about upsetting Kerry in her advanced state of pregnancy, but it only seems to have made things worse.'

'How could it?'

'Well, now, when he sees Kerry, he does a fake start of surprise, puts a finger to his lips, then turns around and tiptoes away in the most hammy manner imaginable, which just upsets her even more.'

'The man obviously has no idea what effect he has on her. Why don't you have a word with him?'

'I thought of that,' said Carmichael, 'but I can't imagine what I'd say. "Stop tiptoeing off when you see my wife?" It sounds so daft. And the most distressing thing is, he seems to think it's all a huge joke. I'll be glad when this baby's born, and Kerry's hormones return to normal. Maybe she won't be quite so sensitive, then. I've had just about enough of him, I can tell you, sir.'

'It won't be long now, Carmichael. Just hang on in there. Maybe he'll get bored.'

'I certainly hope so. I don't want to have to take him round the back of the pub and give him a punch up the bracket.'

'What quaint phraseology you use. But that course of action is not recommended for your career prospects, Sergeant. Now, let's get off and speak to these witnesses.'

Madge Moth lived just around the corner from Jimmy Carling's flat, in a terraced house that was slightly larger than the ones in Abattoir Street, and she lived in the whole building, not just part of it.

She was an elderly woman whose hands were gnarled with arthritis. She had a deceptively sweet, high-pitched voice; but she pulled no punches, and the sweetness of her tone belied her nature.

'You can come in if you like, but I've got nothing else to add to what I said yesterday. I think there's tea in the pot, and I've got a few biscuits left. Go through that door to your right and sit down, and I'll be through in a minute. But don't expect any revelations.'

Through that door to the right was a parlour almost as grim, but not as grubby, as Jimmy Carling's living quarters. The furniture was heavy Victorian, the carpet hectically coloured in dull orange and brown swirls. The curtains were only partly pulled open, and little natural light penetrated through the window, which faced north.

Mrs Moth joined them almost immediately, her grip on the tray unsteady, as she wrestled with her damaged hands, and Falconer got up to take the tray from her. 'I can manage perfectly well, young man,' she trilled at him. 'What do you think I do when you're not in the house to help me?'

Embarrassed, Falconer retook his seat, and accepted a cup of tea and a biscuit. Carmichael, too, was intimidated by this fierce, fragile woman, and even refused sugar in his tea – a first since Falconer had known him. It was probably a good move on his part though, as the tea was only lukewarm, and would never have dissolved the six spoonfuls of sugar that Carmichael regularly enjoyed (how?) in his beverages.

The biscuits proved to be stale, and, after an initial nibble, they both placed the soggy discs in their saucers and decided to get this over with. 'I wonder if you would be so kind as to read through the statement that you made yesterday and tell us, having had time to sleep on it, if you have remembered anything else that may prove relevant, Mrs Moth,' Falconer began.

'I shan't, you know,' she replied with such haste that he only just managed to finish his sentence.

'Nevertheless, I should be grateful if you would humour me. A man is dead, and I want to know why.'

'Because he was run over by a car. Surely that's self-evident. No one would be feeling very chipper after what happened to him.'

'Please,' Falconer almost pleaded, still holding out the statement, waiting for her to take it.

'Oh, all right. If it'll get you two out of my hair and out of my house, give it here.'

She read her statement through thoroughly, then handed it back, commenting, 'Nothing new,' almost with relish.

'Another witness mentioned that she might have heard the car accelerating. Have you any memory of that?' asked the inspector, desperate for any crumb that might come his way.

'My statement stands as it is. I have nothing to add to it,' she declared, and stood, as a signal that they should leave.

Katy Cribb's house, on the other side of Market

Darley, proved to be on a new development of houses, so recently built that the roads hadn't even been made up. Hers was a smart but small semi-detached house right near the beginning of the estate. She was in, a fact that became obvious as they reached the front door and heard the cries of her child issuing from inside, and she opened the door to them with an armful of squealing baby.

'Sorry about this,' she said, her head inclining towards her daughter. 'She had a bad night, and I'm just going to put her down for a nap. She's worn out, poor little darling. Come on in, and I'll be with you in just a minute. It's about that accident yesterday, isn't it?'

With that, she rushed up the stairs to deposit little Cassandra in her cot, where her wails would not be so intrusive. When she re-joined them, she read through her statement of the day before, and said that she'd been thinking about it and, although she'd been absorbed in retrieving Cassandra's cuddly bunny-wunny, she thought she really had heard the whine of an engine, as in increasing its revs.

Excellent! That was a tiny step closer to proving that Jimmy Carling was not the victim of an accident, but had been targeted on purpose. Of this, Falconer was absolutely convinced, and nothing would sway him from his belief.

They went straight to the bank because, even though it was a Saturday morning, they suspected that they would find Arthur Black in his office, and they were right. Banks had had to expand their hours over the years, and now offered a limited service at the weekend.

Black was absolutely sure that Abigail Wentworth's car had speeded up just before it hit Mr Carling. He had not only seen it increase its speed, but had heard the revving of the engine, and wondered why the driver had done this, and then had been so tardy in applying the brakes.

'Every little helps,' Falconer commented, as he announced that they were going to return to Abattoir road and have a final search of the victim's flat. This time they'd search the other way round. Carmichael could do the bedroom, while Falconer rummaged through the living room. Fresh eyes might see something that hadn't been spotted before, but, before that, he suggested that they take a short break for lunch, as working on an empty stomach with low blood sugar wouldn't see them performing at their best.

Chapter Five

Saturday 27th November – afternoon

After lunch in the staff canteen – a chicken salad for Falconer and double fish and chips for Carmichael, with six slices of bread and butter and lashings of ketchup – they set off for the sad little flat in a much more up-beat mood. It was amazing what food could do to the way one felt.

Once inside, Carmichael headed for the small squalid bedroom and Falconer started on the sideboard, filled with fresh hope. If there was anything to be found, it would be in this seedy little flat, and, what's more, they were going to find it today. Mrs Wentworth wasn't going to get away with what he was now convinced was cold-blooded murder.

He looked at every scrap of paper he could find, and even came across a few dog-eared black-and-white photos, that he presumed were of Carling and his family, but nothing connected to the case came to light, and he was wondering how Carmichael was getting on in the bedroom, when he heard his voice exclaim, 'Coo! There's an awful lot of colourful clothes in here!'

'What's that?' he called back.

'In this wardrobe,' replied Carmichael, with respect in his voice, for he loved to dress flamboyantly, although he'd never admit it. 'Come and have a look, sir!'

How could he resist such a tempting invitation? The inspector dropped the handful of papers that he was meticulously sorting through and joined Carmichael in the bedroom. The doors of the old walnut wardrobe, which had been held closed with an old sock the day before, now stood wide open, a positive rainbow of shirts and jumpers glowing from its inside. How had he managed to ignore the wardrobe?

Ignoring Carmichael's fascinated inspection of the clothes within, one word chimed, over and over again, in Falconer's mind: pockets! He had to look in the pockets! Here was a whole new world of possibilities.

Pushing Carmichael aside in his new-found enthusiasm, he started first with the trousers, slipping a hand into each opening, in search of the treasure that would make an arrest for murder a certainty. He didn't believe that there could possibly have been nothing between victim and murderess.

Finally, he was rewarded, and pulled out an old, battered wallet which, on being opened, proved to contain a photograph of Carling, with what looked like a very close friend. He whistled with amazement, and called Carmichael over to see what he had discovered. The sergeant's reaction was equally nonplussed. 'Wow! What a turn-up for the books.'

The jacket pockets yielded nothing more. Falconer stared round the little room, hoping for just one more piece of the jigsaw to fit into the picture. His eyes were drawn to the bedside table which he had searched so diligently the day before. On top of it lay an old book, well-thumbed, and evidently much loved, and his heart rate rose. Maybe, just maybe, the last little piece of damning evidence was within its covers.

Taking it in his hands almost reverentially, he held it by its spine and shook it. A very thin, yellowing piece of paper fluttered to the ground. Slowly, oh so slowly, he bent down to pick it up, and unfolded and held it where both of them could read it. After exclaiming, 'Well, I'll be jiggered!' he placed both items into evidence bags and gave Carmichael a smug smile.

'Got her!' declared Falconer triumphantly. 'Come on! Let's go and arrest her.'

Abigail was flabbergasted when she opened her front door to find the two policemen from the day before on her doorstep yet again. 'What do you want now?' she snapped at them, a look of distaste on her face.

'We need another word with you, Mrs Wentworth,' explained Falconer politely. No need to feed her hostility at this early stage.

'I suppose you'd better come in then, but I've offered you all the refreshments you're going to get from me.'

Back in her expensively furnished sitting room once more, Falconer asked her if she had anything more to add to her statement about the 'incident' that had occurred the day before. He purposely didn't use the word 'accident', because he knew that this was not appropriate now.

'Absolutely nothing. I told you I couldn't remember the actual event, and nothing's come back to me since. Maybe I just shoved my foot down on the wrong pedal.'

In silence, the inspector removed the evidence bag containing the photograph of Jimmy Carling and her husband, arms round each other, and just watched her face as she looked at it. 'That is your husband with the victim, isn't it? I saw several photographs of him on display in this very room just yesterday.'

Abigail's face drained of colour, and a look of horror slowly developed across her features. Improvising as if her very life depended on it, she replied, 'Robert made a good many friends through his work whom I never met. This is obviously one of them.'

'They seem rather intimate to be just friends, don't you think?' he asked, referring to the arms-entwined pose.

'He probably did it for a joke. He did have a sense of humour, you know.' She was on more of an even keel now, her mind working nineteen-to-the-dozen so that she shouldn't be caught out like that again, but she didn't know what else Falconer had found.

Removing another evidence bag from his pocket, he handed the letter across to her, and just waited for her comments. The letter that had been so carefully preserved between the pages of the book for all these years was a 'dear John', ending the affair between Abigail's late husband Robert and James Carling, citing the diagnosis of his cancer, and his very limited time left, as the reason they could not set up home together as they'd planned.

Alison Fairweather, in her phone conversation, had certainly mentioned a bit of a kerfuffle at about the time that Robert's illness had been diagnosed, and it looked like this was what they had inadvertently stumbled upon. It also gave them a twenty-four-carat motive for murder.

Abigail had managed to suppress this scandalous affair all these years, in a bid to preserve her respectability. Now it would become public property when she was prosecuted for the murder of Jimmy Carling.

There was a sudden change of mood in Abigail as her face turned purple with rage, and she leaned forward and began to thump the coffee table with her fists to punctuate what she was saying. 'After' (thump) 'all' (thump) 'these' (thump) 'years' (thump) 'of keeping' (thump) 'this' (thump) 'quiet' (thump) 'and you' (thump) 'have to' (thump) 'come' (thump) 'along' (thump) 'and ruin' (thump) 'everything' (thump).

Falconer felt his sphincter contract with trepidation, and wracked his brains to try to remember whether there was such an offence as 'scaring the pants off a police officer'. Out of the corner of his eye, he noticed that Carmichael was so rattled that he had reverted to sucking his thumb.

'Didn't you know your husband was bisexual?' he asked, knowing that he risked having his face ripped off by this furious, screeching banshee. Carmichael was silent. His mouth was full of thumb, and he'd been brought up never to talk with his mouth full.

'He wasn't bisexual!' she yelled. 'He was homosexual, and he only married me for the sake of respectability. When he told me he was going to leave me I was devastated, but that was nothing to what

I felt when he said he was leaving me for another *man*. How could he do that to me and the children?

'Then he was diagnosed, the very same day, with cancer, and I said I'd nurse him at home, if only he wouldn't leave me. He didn't have much time. It was cancer of the liver, and had spread throughout his body. So he stayed, and I've kept it quiet all these years, and then I saw that miserable little queen actually working in Market Darley – I'd found other photographs, when Robert was ill – which I of course destroyed – so I knew what he looked like.

'I had no idea what I was going to do about it, but I wasn't going to have the lid blown off this whole sordid thing, after so much time had gone by. I recognised him in the road, and my temper just snapped. How dare he turn up where I lived and just get on with his life as if nothing had happened? I made a split-second decision to get rid of him once and for all. Why should I have my reputation ruined after all this time?

'I'd already lost my husband twice. Once, when he told me he was leaving me, and the second time when he died. Why should this predatory old 'scrote' be allowed to live his life as if nothing had ever happened?'

Carmichael winced at her terminology, while Falconer realised that it was time he took charge of the situation, and got the woman cautioned, arrested, and delivered to the station where he could question her at greater length, and on tape. There was no way out of it now. He had incontrovertible proof that she had run down Jimmy Carling with malice aforethought, and she had finally admitted it.

When they had done all that they could for that day, the two detectives returned to the office to collect their coats, for it was bitingly cold out. 'Crikey!' exclaimed Carmichael. 'She was one scary lady. I nearly shat myself at her house, if you'll pardon my French, sir.'

'You're not the only one,' agreed Falconer. 'It's the first time since we started working together that I've been really worried about wearing beige trousers,' he added, diplomatically not mentioning that he had seen Carmichael sucking his thumb. 'You should've got her to have a word with that chap that's always worrying Kerry.'

'You should've suggested that before we locked her up, sir. But what bad luck, Carling turning up like that, after all those years.'

'Fatally bad luck for him, and catastrophic for her, too. I suppose if he had recognised her, it would probably have been all round the hotel like wildfire soon enough, and then done the rounds of the whole town.'

'She must have nearly choked on her pudding when she recognised him in the restaurant. And then the opportunity to get rid of him just presented itself to her when she was on her way home.'

'Yes,' agreed Falconer. 'You could almost say she was *driven to it*,' and he chuckled quietly to himself at his own wit, as Carmichael stared at him in bemusement.

THE END

All Hallows

DS Carmichael is accompanying his step-sons on their 'trick or treat' rounds in Castle Farthing, while DI Falconer holds the fort at Market Darley police station this Hallowe'en. In fact, it is DC Roberts who has drawn the evening's short straw and has been dispatched to the small town of Carsfold, to the south of the market town, for a second interview with a householder, without a clue that an unexplained explosion will not only land him in hospital yet again, but kick off another case of murder for his two colleagues.

Harry Falconer is summoned to an address in Carsfold on the evening of 31st October when a man is found dead in his garden, a hollowed-out pumpkin jammed over his head, and his garden shed blown-up and fire-damaged. Carmichael is immediately summoned to join him and, together, they interrogate the victim's neighbours, uncovering a plethora of damaged and broken relationships, in their search for his killer.

31st October – All Hallows Eve

Definitely a blanket stitch in stout black wool, she thought, surveying the vulnerability of the material as it fell to the hem of the vast floor-length garment. It was only a loose weave, and wouldn't stand up to the abuse of being dragged roughly over the unforgiving ground for hours on end without fraying away to nothing. The garment coming apart from the bottom upwards would not sustain the illusion necessary for the occasion.

Kerry Carmichael selected a ball of black nylon, unbreakable by mere human hands, cut a length from it, and threading a large-eyed needle that would work well with the open weave of the costume, she began to stitch round the bottom. Her husband, DS Davey Carmichael of the Market Darley CID, would be the best dressed Frankenstein's monster on trick or treat duty this Hallowe'en, or she was a Romanian paisley-weaver with purple dandruff.

He had not used all his considerable powers of persuasion (not to mention begging and whining) to secure this special evening for the children, off duty, to have his appearance spoilt by shoddy needlewoman-ship. She had been certain in her own mind, however, that he would not be needed to uphold the law tonight, as his immediate superior, DI Harry Falconer, although appearing stern and unyielding, was a closet pussycat. He knew full well what the children meant to his sergeant, and how much he had been looking forward to escorting them around their home village of Castle Farthing in fancy dress, hoping for the neighbours' largesse of sweets, chocolate, and even pieces of fruit from the more health-conscious amongst the inhabitants.

A roar of despair from the sitting room claimed her attention, and she called out, to find out what was amiss. 'I can't find my fake head top,' floated back a baleful bass voice, in despair. 'I was sure I'd left it on the dresser, and now I can't find it anywhere. I can't be seen out tonight without a tall flat head. I'll be laughed out of the village and the kids'll never forgive me.'

'It's in the right-hand cupboard. I slipped it in there so that one of the dogs wouldn't mistake it for a plaything and chew it. You know how long it took me to glue all the wool on to it in parallel lines so that it looked like hair.'

'Good work, Mrs Carmichael. That's the sort of intelligent thinking I'd expect from the wife of an up-and-coming detective sergeant. You *will* help me stick it on straight, won't you? I can't go out with a wonky head,' he stated with all seriousness, returning to his original task of hanging the evening's decorations from the ceiling, for the party they had planned for later, an easy job for him, as he was just about six and-a-half feet in height. He was constantly grateful that the ceilings of the two cottages knocked together, in which he and his family lived, had higher-than-average ceilings for the style and age of dwelling it was.

'I will, when it's time. Honestly, you've got hours before you go out, yet. You're worse than the boys. I'm still working on the costumes.'

'I think I'll just phone the inspector one more time. He may be working, but he might fancy driving over here on a patrol round, to see the Carmichael gang out doing their stuff. We could always find a black sheet, make a vampire cloak for him, if he's in the mood when he arrives.'

'I shouldn't waste your breath, Davey. I really can't see Inspector Falconer being in the least interested in going tricking or treating with our crew. You forget, Peter Pan, that *he* actually grew up, and lives in the adult world, as do quite a lot of other people of our acquaintance.'

'Daft rumour, woman: that's just a daft rumour,' her husband muttered darkly, as he went off in search of the bolt for his neck.

In his office in Market Darley Police Station, Inspector Harry Falconer leaned back in his leather chair with his feet up on his desk, and tranquilly sipped a cup of coffee, hot and fragrant and comforting. He'd almost forgotten how peaceful the office could be without the madcap company of that giant jumping spider of a DS, to whom he had granted a night's leave, to lead his children on a merry dance round the green in Castle Farthing, begging sweetmeats from the neighbours under the dire threat of 'trick'.

It seemed the kindlier of two acts. Carmichael would get a great deal of enjoyment from playacting with his two stepsons. Had he given a free evening to DC Roberts, that officer would only have gone to the party at the town hall, to spend the evening tomcatting around and getting blind drunk. He would then have been late into the office tomorrow, and have proven to be totally unfit for work anyway. No, Falconer thought, he had granted the free evening to the most deserving officer, who would cause the least future disruption because of his present free time.

He'd sent his DC – on duty with a very ill grace – out to interview a homeowner who had suffered an attempted burglary which had originally been investigated by PC Green, but was deemed worthy of a follow-up interview, as it was thought now to be part of a series of break-ins and attempted breakings-and-enterings. And this evening had seemed like a wonderful opportunity, not just to get that re-interview out of the diary, but to claim a little oh-so-rare peace and quiet for himself during working hours. He reckoned that, with the world of parents fully involved with organising their little darlings into bullying their respective neighbourhoods, and everyone else cowering behind their front doors with bowls full of goodies to hand out to whoever rang the bell or knocked the knocker, to avoid anything happening to the exterior of their property, car, or garden, he was guaranteed to be left alone.

Languidly, and with the keenest anticipation, he reached out a hand towards a paper bag which sat enticingly in the very centre of his desk. Inside its sticky folds nestled the gooiest lardy cake he could find in the baker's on his way into the office, and he knew, from past experience, that sitting out on his desk for a few hours would not diminish its tacky deliciousness. It would be the perfect accompaniment to his mug of coffee and heap of peace and quiet, and he wriggled into a slightly more comfortable position in his chair, in preparation for this treat.

He had felt quite resentful, leaving behind a large heap of blissfully dozing cats before the fire when he left the house to report for duty. His home was a 1930s house with three bedrooms and two reception rooms, where he lived alone but for his five cats.

Until he had been paired with Carmichael at work (although this had nothing to do with the change in his circumstances), he had had only the one cat, a Siamese called Mycroft, but his various cases, and circumstances in general, had conspired to land four more felines on him, and now they all lived together in perfect harmony, for most of the time at least.

He smiled at the memory of Carmichael's desperate pleading to have this evening free from work, and, as his route took him past the best bakery in Market Darley, smiled again, as it revealed a golden pile of sticky lardy cakes winking seductively at him through the glass, and the purchase of one of these soon allowed him to look forward to the rest of the evening with greedy anticipation, and generally count his blessings.

DC Roberts had no sooner said 'good evening' to the inspector, than he found himself back outside in the cold and dark, on his way to conduct a second interview with a householder who had surprised a miscreant trying to break into his house, no doubt for nefarious purposes.

He resented working this evening, as there was a damned good Hallowe'en party going on at the town hall for which he had intended to purchase a ticket, and had even put together the vestiges of a zombie costume. Why should that shambling lump Carmichael get the evening free? He'd've thought the man's wife would have been perfectly capable of dragging a couple of kids round a few houses begging for 'candy' – in his mind he used the American word to indicate irony.

Why did their father need to be present, thus preventing him, DC Chris Roberts – super-sleuth and secret love-machine – from granting the boon of his presence; superb body and amazing mind, to the chicks at the town hall for the evening's thrash?

Well, he hoped one of the beleaguered Castle Farthing pensioners took offence at having that great lump on his doorstep, and threw some eggs at him – they say free-range are better for you! It wasn't that Roberts didn't get on with Carmichael; he was just so disappointed at not being able to go out on the pull in legitimate disguise, later that evening. It was the one night of the year when a red-blooded male, who was normally recognizable as a representative of the forces of law and order, could carry out lightning snogging attacks and remain unidentified because of make-up and fancy dress.

Bum! In fact, double bum!

In his garden shed, Larry Jordan lay back on a pile of dusty sacks which had once held potatoes and bulbs, lifted the scotch bottle to his lips, and poured a generous stream of the fiery amber liquid between them, swallowing, then blinking, at the strength of the spirit.

He was going to tie-on a good one tonight. There was no way he was staying in the house to be pestered by those bleedin' irritating estate brats in their pathetic attempts at dressing up, knocking at the door every five minutes and whining after sweets and chocolates. If his so-called loving wife was going to go out with her bit on the side every other night, with the excuse that she was going to her workmate's for a girls' night in, then he was getting the hell out of the way and drinking himself into the middle of next week. At least he wouldn't have anyone sniping and moaning about how much of the Scottish brew he was pouring down his throat, and asking if he'd ever worked out how much he spent on booze in a week. He might even be lucky enough to receive a visit from his own current piece of fluff to liven up the evening's activities.

He'd done his bit for the beautification of the neighbourhood on his way down to the shed. His garden was a jungle of weeds that reached to waist-height, and he'd run his hands through all the ripe seed-heads that hadn't already unburdened their load on to the winds, on his short walk to his hideaway. That should keep all the enthusiastic gardeners busy. It had been quite mild so far this autumn. A few of those seeds should root and prosper, courtesy of his own fair hand. He'd do his bit for the aural in a couple of hours' time, and give them a damned good drunken singsong with Status Quo on the old CD player. Oh, how he did love his neighbourhood. Carsfold was Paradise indeed!

DC Roberts slowed down and actually parked within sight of the town hall. The steps were lined with hollowed-out pumpkins' heads containing lit candles which glowed welcomingly across the road to him. Currently mounting the steps were a coven of honeys variously dressed as witches and the un-dead, and his soul longed to join them and make their evening perfect – not that he was at all vain, of course. The posters on each side of the giant Corinthian columns on each side of the town hall steps proclaimed '*Giant Halloween Party. Fancy Dress, Prizes,*' and here was he, the Market Darley Casanova, the number one local babe magnet, on his way to Carsfold, to talk to some boring old geezer about something that wasn't even a real break-in. Truly, there was no justice in life!

In the houses of the circle that made up the end of Chestnut Close, where Larry Jordan lived at number two, the other residents were settling down to a cosy evening with plenty of young ghoulish visitors, hoping that there would not be any interruption from their most unpopular neighbour, the lazy, unemployed, and drunken Jordan, who neglected his property so disgracefully, and whose wife acted like a right slapper given any opportunity. This was part of a housing association development, and a petition had already been started to have the Jordans moved away from such a respectable close.

In number one, the house with the attractively immaculate front and back gardens, Dave Weston sat before the television set watching a documentary about the origins of modern Hallowe'en traditions, with the sound turned quite low so that he could hear any rings on the doorbell. His sixteen-year-old daughter Rebecca had gone to the party at the town hall with a couple of her friends, hoping to pass for eighteen and gain entrance, having promised not to (illegally for her age) imbibe a surfeit of alcohol, and return home in the early hours in a state similar to the usual one in which they could find their next door neighbour at roughly the same time – one his mother would have described as 'stocious'.

As an echo of past thoughts, it went through his mind how much he disliked his little angel sunbathing in the back garden in the summer months, with that drunken pervert next door watching. The man would actually make a point of planting a deckchair in the wilderness that was his lawn and ogle her, while he poured a can of beer down his throat. It was disgusting for a man of his age to be looking at such a young innocent in such a lascivious way.

As the doorbell disturbed his thoughts, he rose and went into the hall where, on a side table, he had a large bowl filled with assorted goodies – including tiny bunches of healthy grapes – for the children who came to exhort him to choose 'trick or treat'.

Patrick Flanagan, sprawled on the brown corded velvet sofa in the sitting room of number three, was watching the same programme on the television, while idly picking at the bowl of sweets he had on the floor beside him, waiting for young visitors to call for contributions to their goodie bags.

He had recently retired from the bakery in Market Darley where Inspector Falconer had bought his evening lardy cake, and was enjoying the first few weeks of not having to get up for work before some young people retired to bed. Since Jordan had lived next door, his life had been a misery of broken and non-existent sleep, as his neighbour was wont to play loud rock music into the small hours of the morning, as an accompaniment to his over-enthusiastic drinking. Not only was the man in no mood to discuss his anti-social and inconsiderate behaviour at the time, but was usually unable to remember it or understand the seriousness of the transgression the following morning.

The eejit had no idea of the misery of sleep deprivation, and repeated written and telephonic exhortations to the housing association to curb his enthusiasm for Status Quo et al, had not been taken seriously. Even the one visit to the cul-de-sac by the local authority's noise abatement officer had yielded no proof of anti-social behaviour, as it had happened to coincide with a fault of twenty-four hours' duration in Jordan's audio equipment.

Although Patrick no longer had to get up at a ridiculously early hour to go to work, he still needed to sleep, and still sometimes found himself driving to his sister-in-law's house after midnight, to beg the use of her spare room. If only the man would disappear, his life would be one of happiness and contentment. With a tut of irritation at this thought, he rose from his sprawled position and headed out of the room, a man on a mission.

The small band of disguised children currently on their way round the semi-circle of houses that comprised the end of Chestnut

Close (supervised from the pavement by a responsible adult, of course) complemented their background perfectly on this particular night of the year. Each household (with the exception of the Jordans' which was number two) had good-naturedly hollowed out a pumpkin and carved a face in its flesh. In the hollow depths of each of these glowed the yellowish light of a lit candle, lending atmosphere to the normally totally nondescript development.

From behind a net curtain at the front window of number five, the baleful expression of 'petrol head' Leslie Ingram glared with disgust at the dirty, rusting heap that the residents confidently identified as Larry Jordan's disgraceful excuse for a car.

This elderly vehicle was not only rotting, and in a shocking stage of repair, but was also disgustingly dirty, and suffered from a small but constant oil-leak, which left little clusters of black kisses wherever its owner decided to park it. This, due to availability of parking space at the time, meant that quite an area of kerbside road was splattered with small black marks.

Leslie Ingram unconsciously ground his teeth together. The man could at least wash the poor old heap, and mend the oil leak. No one would think of forcing him to buy a newer car, as he was unemployed, and assumed to be short of money – although he seemed to be able to put a plentiful supply of cash across the counter at the local off licence. It was the attitude of complete 'don't care' that really gripped Leslie's shit. How much bother was it to get a bucket of water and wield a sponge? If the man could be bothered to do that, he'd mend the oil leak himself for him: after all, he had offered, even if his offer had been rebuffed. He was fed up to the back teeth with going out into the road to pour cat litter onto the spillage to soak it up, knowing that the person responsible wouldn't even notice what he'd done.

Leslie moved his hand away from the filmy material of the curtain and began to pace up and down his living room like a caged animal, remembering the one time he had complained about the state of the car and the damage it was doing to the road surface, and the trio of raw eggs that were smashed on the bonnet of his own immaculate vehicle during that night. He wasn't sure why he felt so tense tonight. Maybe it was the memories, or just the atmosphere of the date getting to him.

Lying back apparently relaxed in a reclining armchair in the lounge of number four Chestnut Close, Peter Sage watched his wife Deborah carefully, as she got her regular fix of a long-running soap opera. The episode was almost over and she had already begun to fidget. Well, she could forget sneaking off out to meet that bastard Jordan for one of their filthy little assignations. He was on to them now, and while he was home, at least, there would be no more behaviour of that sort.

Unfortunately he was only home at weekends, finances forcing him to work away from home during the week, to do a job that paid enough to cover the household bills and his wife's somewhat reckless spending on clothes and make-up. Add that to a new three-piece suite every twelve to eighteen months, and complete redecoration of the lounge on an annual basis, and it began to become obvious why he couldn't just take a less well-paid job locally, and sleep in his own bed every night, like other, *normal*, men.

Life, in its many everyday variations, went on in Chestnut Close behind closed doors, and events, having a schedule to keep to, wended on their inevitable way towards what would be the climax of this Hallowe'en evening in the vicinity.

Life also went on in Castle Farthing, which was a very attractive village with most of its housing clustered around a central green which had, at its centre, a pond and benches on which to rest weary limbs on warm days. It had its own church, and was the possessor of a pretty, thatched public house, 'The Fisherman's Flies'. It also had a village store and, just outside its centre, the ruins of the Castle from which its name derived. The Carmichael family lived in the amalgamation of the two dwellings that had been named individually, Jasmine Cottage and Crab Apple Cottage.

At this very moment, DS Davey Carmichael was mustering his stepsons for their series of house-calls round the green of that village centre. Kerry was just finishing helping them into their costumes as ghosts – not too challenging on the sewing front for a busy mother who had a dearth of spare time but a surfeit of white sheets.

'Can you give me a hand with the bolt in my neck, and make sure the top of my head's fixed on properly?' her husband asked her, as she stepped away to look at her sons in their simple disguises.

'Bend down a bit, then, so's I can reach your top bits,' she urged him, being only of average height herself, and not blessed with a multitude of inches (or centimetres, she supposed, nowadays) like her husband. She thought how odd it was, in a metric society, that men's heights were never expressed in anything but feet and inches, and supposed that some things would never change. Mothercare had taken care of everyone thinking of babies' lengths and children's heights in centimetres, but no one could alter how society expressed the height of its male warriors.

As she gratefully closed the front door on the trio of giggling conspirators a few minutes later, her husband's face glowed with anticipation and excitement behind his disguise. She had been right to call him Peter Pan, for he still derived a huge amount of pleasure from childish pastimes, and revelled in the company of Dean and Kyle, her sons from her first, ill-fated marriage.

The appearance, not so much of two white-sheeted faux ghosts, but of a fairly convincing and huge representation of Frankenstein's monster on the doorstep drew little squeaks of astonishment and surprise from most of their neighbours, and the boys' goodie bags soon began to look less empty. Unbelievably, so did Carmichael's!

The only neighbour who was not taken in was a similarly-outsized Great Dane rejoicing in the name of Mulligan, who had been an occasional houseguest at the Carmichael's house. He recognised the spooky visitors immediately and began to caper around them, making happy snuffling noises and surprisingly high-pitched squeaks of pleasure for such a large dog.

His owners, using only their eyes, were not so astute, and Mulligan's mistress uttered a perfect horror film squeal of alarm, and his master threw his forearms across his face, at the surprise at finding such a monster at large in the village in which he lived. He had been perfectly prepared to open the door to little witches and vampires tonight, but the sight of a huge creature with a bolt through its neck had been unexpectedly unnerving.

'Ee, Davey,' he muttered, recovering, 'You've taken six months off my life with that get-up. You should carry a written warning.'

'Sorry about that. It must look so much more realistic in low lighting. Anyway, happy Hallowe'en! The boys wanted to see Mulligan.'

'And Mulligan looks very pleased to see all three of you,' replied the Great Dane's owner, a nebulous plot beginning to hatch in the man's mind. He and his wife were getting on a bit, and they'd never expected their pet to grow quite so large. He could be a real handful at times, and needed so much exercise, as *he* was in the prime of his life. He could really do with a younger owner. He tucked the thought away for future discussion with his wife, a wistful smile now on his face, as he handed out confectionary with the good grace of the occasion.

After loading various sweet treats into their gradually filling bags, the boys immediately wanted to know when Mulligan could come to stay again, and were mentally guided, by logic and memory, to their next question: was Uncle Harry – their step-father's boss – coming to their Hallowe'en party? For Falconer had been in *such* awe of Mulligan when they had met previously ... The inspector had, surprisingly, not proved very confident in the company of canines – not even that of such tiny specimens as Mistress Fang and Mr Knuckles, the Chihuahua and Yorkshire terrier that Carmichael had chosen to augment their household.

'Sorry, boys, he's working,' replied Frankenstein's monster, using their step-father's voice and, at their groans of disappointment, explained that if Uncle Harry hadn't worked tonight, *he* would have had to go on duty. And Mummy would have been useless going trick-or-treating with them, wouldn't she? At their wholehearted agreement at this distracting thought, he managed to get them away from the Great Dane, and back on track to finish their round of visits within the hour.

DC Roberts parked outside 86 Oak Drive, and rang the doorbell of the house of John Masters, the householder whom he was to re-interview, and whose rear garden backed on to the rear access alleyway shared by the back gardens of the houses in the end semi-circle in Chestnut Close.

The door was opened promptly by Mr Masters, clutching a large plastic bowl of assorted confectionary, and who looked thoroughly flustered to find himself staring up into the face of an adult, and not the eager expressions of a group of children.

'DC Roberts, Mr Masters,' his visitor offered. 'I'm here about the attempted break-in, as arranged, if you could spare me a few minutes.'

'Of course,' John Masters replied, catching up mentally with events. 'Do come in. Would you like a candy bar?' He might as well offer, as he was holding so many of them and he didn't want to appear mean.

DC Roberts, being the possessor of a notorious sweet tooth, helped himself to a white chocolate bar with a smile, and stepped over the threshold to commence his questioning.

No sooner had they got settled in the comfort of the living room, however, than the detective pointed out towards the back garden, through the window across which the curtain was not yet drawn, and asked, 'Is that your dog out there?' Masters rose to his feet with the denial,

'I don't have a dog.'

Roberts followed him through the French windows into the night, where they both became aware of the most peculiar sound on the air. They could hear a moaning sound that seemed to be muffled or smothered in some way, and it appeared to be coming from the direction of a garden shed which lay just the other side of the rear access alleyway, in the garden of one of the houses in Chestnut Close.

'That's Larry Jordan's shed,' declared John Masters. 'It's usually drunken yells and singing you get from there, or heavy rock music.'

Roberts had already started to move in the appropriate direction to investigate, and had just exited the garden via the little gate that gave on to the alleyway, and allowed access to the properties for the weekly visit of the refuse collectors, when there was a sound that could only be described as 'whump'. The shed divided itself into several pieces, one of which felled DC Roberts, and flames licked the air.

DI Falconer had just licked the last of the lardy cake's delicious stickiness from his fingers, when the switchboard connected him with the incoherent ravings of John Masters, and he settled himself in his chair more comfortably, to learn what was afoot, this dark and spooky night.

'It just went up,' a slightly breathless voice informed him. 'We went out there, and it just went up, and he went down like a sack of spuds,' rambled John Masters, in confusion.

'I am Detective Inspector Falconer of the Market Darley CID, sir. How may I help you?' the DI intoned in a reassuring tone of voice, hoping to introduce a little sanity to the conversation, for nothing had made sense so far.

'Oh, sorry. I'm making a right dog's breakfast of this,' replied Masters, already feeling a little steadier, at the confidence at the voice that had replied to him. 'My name is John Masters, and one of your men came out to interview me again about an attempted break-in at my house, earlier this evening.'

This was more like it. Falconer could cope with narrative like this. 'And has he done this to your satisfaction, sir?' he asked.

'It's not that. It's the shed blowing up like that. He's out cold on the pathway, and the ambulance hasn't got here yet.'

'What shed, sir? And why is my officer apparently unconscious?' This was sounding rather worrying, although he had to say, it was rather typical of Roberts to end up *hors de combat* when sent out on some mission of his own. It was certainly not the first time that this had happened, and it was something he was proving to be rather good at.

'He saw this stray dog in my back garden, and when we went out to shoo it away, we heard this weird noise, like a sort of moaning. And it was coming from the direction of next door's shed.'

'I'm with you so far, Mr Masters. So what happened next?'

'Your man went across to the gate in the fence opposite the shed and, before I could make a move to join him, there was this sort of other weird noise, a bit like a cross between a bang and a whoosh, and the shed blew up. Bits went everywhere. One of them hit your man on the head, and he went down, and the flames went up, as all the neighbours came outside to see what was going on.

'That's when I left them to see to him and drag the other fella out of what remained of the shed – I rather think he was a goner – and got on the blower to do the 'three nines' bit. As I said, the ambulance is on its way and the fire engine was just drawing up in Chestnut

Close when I was put through to you. Oh, did I mention that I'm phoning from Carsfold?'

'I'll be with you, sir, as soon as I can. Don't be surprised if uniformed officers turn up before me. I'm on my way, right away.'

Staying only to dispatch PC Merv Green to secure the scene ahead of the arrival of the SOCO boys, and ring Castle Farthing to alert Kerry Carmichael that he had urgent need of her husband in Carsfold, he left the station.

In Castle Farthing, Kerry Carmichael made a note of the Carsfold address, grabbed her coat, shoved her baby daughter Harriet into the blankets of her pushchair, and went out into the night to dispatch her husband and bring back her boys. They could hardly moan at having their playtime cut short; they'd had enough time on their rounds to have visited just about every dwelling in the village centre. At least the timing was such that they hadn't missed out on the activity altogether, for which she was grateful, after all the effort she had put in to kit out the three of them for the occasion.

She found the little group at the front door of Brigadier Malpas-Graves' substantial property, gathered round the lady of the household, who was sitting on a stool, while her husband, in monstrous guise, flapped a towel before her face, and advised everyone to 'stand back and give the lady sufficient air'.

'Whatever's happened, Davey?' she asked in some concern, as she reached her gathered family.

'I'm afraid I was a little too realistic for her,' he explained, shamefacedly. 'I should have spoken sooner, so that she could have recognised my voice.'

'No matter, lad. No matter,' soothed the brigadier. 'All part of the fun. Joyce is no spoilsport, are you, dear?'

'Not at all. Very realistic costume, my dear. Ten out of ten for effort.' These remarks she addressed to Kerry, realising who was responsible for the success of the masquerade.

'You've got to go, Davey,' announced the DC's wife abruptly, 'Inspector Harry needs you down in Carsfold right away. There's a case for you,' she informed her husband, without giving away any sensitive information. 'You need to get down there immediately. Come along, boys. Let's get home and get ready for all your friends to arrive for the party.'

This last, took any sting of disappointment out of her arriving to end their evening's activity, out and about in their home village, and the two small figures began to walk behind her, happy still to have their party ahead of them.

Their father passed the hand towel to the brigadier, gave an apologetic smile at this unexpected call of duty, and set off down the road towards the green and his car, at a considerably faster pace than he would normally walk.

PC Merv Green stood in the Jordans' back garden and looked around him at the mess. The area, which was normally an untidy sea of weeds, now had considerably more to make it look disreputable. He had arrived to secure the area before any SOCO officers arrived, but it looked like any efforts on his part to do this would be a waste of time.

The rear garden was full of neighbours, taking full advantage of the opportunity to have a good nosy around at what had happened there. PC Linda Starr, (Green's fiancée, incidentally), who was on duty with him that evening, immediately began to make a note of the names of those present, and request that they return forthwith to their own homes, so that the police could get on with their job.

Merv took off his helmet and scratched his shaved-bald head. The fire brigade seemed to have had a merry old time extinguishing the blaze that had been trying to consume the boards of what had once been a garden shed, and sodden, blackened pieces of wood adorned the furthermost area of the garden. The contents of the erstwhile structure were also strewn around the desolate patch of ground, making it look even more unloved and uncared for than usual.

Towards the other side of the narrow strip of land lay what remained of its tenant: a burnt and singed figure, but still recognisably human, as the fire had not had much of a chance to take a hold, due to the ineptitude of whoever had applied the incendiary device to the wooden building. His body was not too badly disfigured, and it was obvious that fire had not been the medium which had done for him.

The PC's eyes were drawn, as if magnetically, to the figure's head, over which had been forced a large pumpkin, evidently hollowed out to get it over the bulk, and it was now blackened and charred on its skin, where it had started to cook in the heat. 'What the...?' he exclaimed in incomprehension, as he approached the unlikely apparition.

'We think someone shoved it over his head and suffocated him, then shoved in something explosive to make sure he was finished off,' sounded the voice of John Masters, the householder whom DC Roberts had been visiting when his accident had befallen him.

'And your bloke went over to investigate, and got a lump of wood blown into his head for his trouble.'

'Yes, where is he?' asked Merv, suddenly remembering that DC Roberts had been rumoured to have been on the scene before the incident occurred.

'Taken off in an ambulance about ten minutes before you got here. There's a small ambulance station in Carsfold, so they didn't have so far to come as you have now, since they bundled all the little stations together, up in Market Darley. Should never have done it, in my opinion, but then, whenever did they listen to a member of the public?'

Ignoring this rhetorical question, Merv and his partner set about having a word with the dead man's neighbours in advance of the arrival of the CID officers, still brooding on the bizarre act a man being suffocated inside a hollowed-out pumpkin. Even if it was Hallowe'en.

Falconer, on his arrival, announced, as always, that he would tackle things in a logical manner. After an initial inspection of the crime scene, he decided to start his questioning at number one Chestnut Close, advising Merv and Linda to tape off the relevant area now that it was free of rubberneckers. The commencement of his interviews was delayed, however, by the timely arrival of Dr Philip Christmas, the forensic medical examiner for the force.

'What-ho, Harry!' the medical man greeted him, approaching from the end of the alleyway. 'What have you got for me now? I say! Is that what I think it is, or are my eyes deceiving me? Can it really be a citizen of Carsfold with a pumpkin over his head, and slightly charred around the edges at that?'

'Your vision is 20/20, Philip. I reckon it'll be some time before I can figure out exactly what's happened here. SOCOs should be arriving any minute now. Get the body away as quickly as you can, will you, and let me know exactly how the poor chap died. This little caper has also put Roberts in hospital with what sounds like concussion, and is dragging Carmichael away from his Hallowe'en celebrations with his family, so there's plenty to answer for.'

'Roberts in hospital again?'

''Fraid so.'

'Par for the course, then,' answered the doctor, basing his response on past events. 'Shame about Carmichael, though. I hope he doesn't take it too hard.'

'Me too,' agreed Falconer. 'The kids'll cope. Just not sure about their stepfather.'

Number one was the home, he discovered from the notes his constables had made, of one David Weston and family, and was situated directly to the left of the property that contained the scene of the crime, as one looked at the front of the houses from the front of Chestnut Close.

At the front door, David Weston bade him enter, and invited the inspector to call him 'Dave', although no similar invitation of familiarity of address was forthcoming from the detective. He was perfectly happy to be called Inspector Falconer, and wished to invite no closer means of address.

In the light of the street lamps, Falconer had already noticed how beautifully tended and tidy the front garden of number one was. The inside of the house proved to be tended to a similar level, the house looking as if no one had ever lived in it, not a speck of dust sullying any visible surface, and not one item being out of place. Even the *Radio Times* was sitting tidily in a magazine rack, and not spread open, on a chair seat or table top.

A woman, equally spick and span, occupied a recliner chair, her legs tidily crossed at the ankles, and her hair and make-up immaculate, even though they were neither going out nor entertaining at home and, for a split-second, Falconer questioned whether he was in Carsfold, or had accidentally strayed into the unnaturally perfect community of Stepford.

'Do take a seat,' his host exhorted him, and the detective slid slowly down into a chair, wincing as he crushed the cushion it contained on his descent.

Before the man could utter another word, his smug-looking wife piped up with, 'My Dave was the first one on the scene. He was already out in the garden, and helped pull that awful man out of his burning shed.' Her mouth twitched up in a self-important smile, as she uttered this interesting snippet of information.

'Don't be ridiculous, Brenda,' barked her husband with unexpected fervour. 'Granted, I was one of the first there, but I wasn't outside when it went up. I'd gone into the garage to check

I had enough compost to put in the wallflowers for their spring showing.

'Sorry about that, Inspector. She thinks that, just because I wasn't in the room with her, I must be outside working in the garden, even at this time of night.' Dave Weston appeared flustered at his wife's remark, and was eager to move on, although he mustered up the effort to make a face that expressed the sentiment 'silly little woman,' in Falconer's direction.

'It was amazing how quickly the sound of that petrol, or whatever it was, going up, gathered a crowd in that disgusting jungle of Jordan's.'

'Don't speak ill of the dead, Dave,' Brenda simpered, looking through her heavily-mascaraed eyelashes at Falconer, to see if he noticed her fineness of feeling.

'It's hardly a state secret that he let his garden go to wrack and ruin and never lifted a finger to keep it under control,' snapped back her husband. 'Why, I should think the origin of every weed within a quarter of a mile of here is his garden. There were enough seeds blowing around from that patch to destroy a country house garden, let alone a collection of small, private gardens.'

'I gather you didn't approve of his neglect of his property,' commented Falconer quietly.

'I certainly did not!' Weston replied with fervour. 'I work hard, now I've retired, to keep our little patch looking as perfect as possible – I even have a vegetable plot at the end, and I keep all my beds as weed-free as possible, which is not an easy task, with that lazy, neglectful beggar living next door.'

'Maybe you'll be able to persuade Michelle – that's his wife, no, widow now, Inspector – to employ someone to keep it down.'

'Fat chance! She'll be even shorter of cash now, without her husband's benefits. Anyway, I've even offered to run the mower over it myself, and pour over some weed-killer in the worst areas, but he very rudely told me, in somewhat choicer words, to 'get lost.'

Feeling he was losing control of the situation, as it sank into neighbourhood ire, Falconer cleared his throat loudly and began to question the couple in a more professional manner, about their movements that evening, and anything that Dave had heard while outside, as Brenda had deemed it beneath her dignity to join her husband out at the scene of the tragedy.

It seemed simple enough. Brenda had remained in her chair watching her favourite soap opera. Dave had been, as he had claimed, checking his supply of compost in the garage, when he heard the noise of the shed blowing up, had raced down the garden to see what he could do to help, and stayed there, milling around with the other neighbours, until PC Green had arrived and dispersed them back to their own homes.

Glad to leave the clinical cleanliness of number one, Falconer called next at the house of the widow, prepared for tears and woe, and finding, instead, a thoroughly together, over-dressed, and heavily made-up woman, with a tall glass tinkling with ice-cubes in her hand. She appeared totally unfazed at her sudden plunge into widowhood.

'Come on in, Inspector,' she invited him. 'Sorry about the lack of tears and grief, but Larry and I didn't really get on that well, and I've just realised that I can move my boyfriend in now, if I can get his name put on the lease.' So much for sorrow at the loss of a life. Was no one to mourn this man, who had died in such a bizarre way?

Falconer entered the living room, noting the contrast in housekeeping standards and styles of furnishing. Things were very much more relaxed – if not actually lax – in this household, and nowhere near so spotless.

After he refused a drink, it not seeming respectful, given the circumstances, Michelle Jordan sat down herself, informing him that she and her husband had not been a proper couple for years now, and that she considered him to have been a perverted, dirty, drunken, old bastard, without a decent bone in his body, and that if this hadn't happened tonight, she'd have left him by Christmas.

What an epitaph for the man! And from his own wife!

Over the next quarter of an hour the inspector was to learn that Larry Jordan had started having casual affairs from the end of their first year of marriage, and had also begun to drink heavily about the same time. He had given up work within months of their wedding, and had existed exclusively on benefits and the odd crooked deal ever since.

If he wasn't off with one of his floozies, he was holed-up in that filthy old shed of his, to avoid her company and guzzle whisky without criticism or interruption, she explained, at length. She'd just left him to his own devices for years now. Life was easier if she just ignored him and got on with her own life.

What a joy he must have been to the neighbours, thought Falconer, having already heard the Westons' opinion of the man. Would no one have a good word to say about the man? Would no one mourn his death?

He left number two rather more abruptly than he had expected, as a piercing scream rent the air, penetrating indoors in the absence of double glazing in these properties, and he rose abruptly from his seat and rushed outside to see what was amiss, hoping that more criminal activity was not in the offing. Subliminally aware of the screech of brakes, he had already been halfway to his feet when the scream rent the air,

Outside number four (which was where Falconer had found space to park his car when he had arrived) were three figures, vaguely visible in the dim illumination from the street's lampposts. One was smaller and obviously a woman, garbed in a dressing-gown and slippers, and with a towel round her head; it was from this figure that the sounds of distress were emanating. The other two gave the impression of being male; one was much larger than the other, but was nevertheless being beaten round his oddly-shaped head with some sort of long weapon.

As he approached, the man suffering the assault seemed to catch sight of the inspector and called out, 'Can you make him stop, sir?' unbelievably in Carmichael's voice. Unbelievably, because the figure, which Falconer could now see was being soundly thrashed with a French stick, no doubt not as fresh as it could have been, appeared to be a refugee from the set of a horror film. Falconer knew it was Hallowe'en, but thought that the dressing up would have all been confined to children, and he wondered, a) how this lone adult specimen came to be on Chestnut Close? and, b) how on earth it had managed to sound exactly like his DS?

'It's me, sir,' pled the familiar voice from the very unfamiliar face, visible now that the tenant of number four had stopped hitting him round the head momentarily. 'I came straight here when Kerry passed on the message that you needed me. I didn't bother calling into the house to change: it sounded urgent.'

'Carmichael! I might have known you'd be at the centre of any disruption ...'

'You know this man?' asked the woman who had screamed.

'For my sins, I do indeed,' admitted the newcomer to the scene. 'I am Detective Inspector Falconer of the Market Darley CID, and this, in the spirit of the season, is my assistant, Detective Sergeant Carmichael, who had been celebrating the occasion of All Hallows' Eve with his children, when urgently summoned for duty, I can only assume. Please excuse his appearance. Am I correct, Carmichael?'

'Absolutely spot-on, sir.'

Falconer suppressed a private smile, remembering how much more terrifying Carmichael had looked, on occasion in the past, when he had been transferred to plain clothes. That particular young man had had no idea of the literal meaning of the word 'plain', and had turned up for duty in some hair-raising outfits. Even now he was not totally free of the affliction and had, in the not-too-distant past (shortly after he had returned to work after being off injured for some time) been seen dressed in glaring checked trousers, a pink and purple striped waistcoat under a custard-yellow jacket, and a hat that a donkey in a field somewhere was clearly missing. (During his recuperation, Carmichael had become addicted to an antiques challenge programme on daytime television, and had developed an unfortunate infatuation with the style of dress of its presenter.) The desk sergeant had had to have a short sit down after catching sight of this apparition entering the building, Falconer recalled.

Shaking his head and returning to the present moment, the inspector asked, 'And you are?'

'Deborah and Peter Sage,' declared the woman, holding out her hand in introduction. Her husband appeared to be more concerned with picking up every crumb of French stick that had broken off during his assault of DS Carmichael, than on making physical contact. As he manhandled a handful of small pieces of bread that had become detached from the mother-loaf, into the pocket of his baggy jeans, he was heard to mumble, 'Absolute lunacy, a member of the forces of law and order turning up on the doorstep of a law-abiding citizen dressed as a monster. Never heard the like in all my life. I shall be lodging a complaint.'

This last, he addressed to Falconer, his head swivelled at a severe angle to his body, so that he could look up at the more senior policeman. 'This sort of behaviour is simply not acceptable. Had my wife been elderly, she could have suffered a heart attack from the shock of seeing such an apparition on her own doorstep.'

'I can't apologise enough, sir. I'm sure DS Carmichael was only anxious to report for duty with the least possible delay, and hadn't given a thought to how he actually looked.'

Carmichael merely nodded, having been effectively silenced by a fierce glare from his superior who wanted, at all costs, to prevent his sergeant from getting involved in a convoluted and complicated explanation of how he had ended up outside their front door looking as he did.

'My car is parked outside your house. I expect he thought I could be found inside. Now, I should be grateful if we could go into your house. A rather serious incident has occurred, and we are here to investigate it, me already being a man down, as my detective constable was injured here earlier this evening.' He was glad they simply accepted this statement about Roberts, as it was much too complicated and time-consuming to explain how the DC came to be on the spot in the first place.

As they walked through the hall, Sage suddenly requested, 'Would you mind speaking to us separately, please?'

Falconer gave him an old-fashioned look, but wasn't given the opportunity to ask why. Sage offered an explanation with no coaxing. 'I'll be honest with you and tell you that we're not on speaking terms at the moment, and that's all I'm prepared to say, until I'm on my own with you.' For the first time, Falconer noticed that Mrs Sage had eyes red from weeping, and seemed to be in an emotionally fragile state.

'I'll speak to Mrs Sage first, in the sitting room, if I may?' Falconer requested, only for Mr Sage to disappear through a door that the inspector assumed was that of the kitchen, muttering under his breath.

'That's me, Mr Second-Class-Citizen. I work away all week to earn enough to keep this place going, while she's being knocked off by that drunken lunatic next door, and it's me that gets relegated to the kitchen when it comes to investigating that bloody reprobate's murder. And I'll probably be the one blamed for it.'

In the sitting room, Deborah Sage was pouring out information like a leaky tap, without a thought for getting properly dressed. She could not keep the situation to herself, and immediately admitted that she had been having an affair with Larry Jordan while her husband Peter was working away during the week. He may not have been the most savoury of characters, but she herself liked a drink or six, and he made her laugh, which was more than 'Neat Pete' did, with his fixation for everything to be just so.

Larry Jordan made her happy and he made her feel like a woman – desirable and sexy, not middle-aged and frumpy. She would have gone out to see him later tonight, if the tragedy had not occurred, and now she felt bereft. Whatever would she do for company now? To whom could she turn, now that Larry was dead – and murdered, too? When Peter was home at the weekends, he spent all his time upstairs in the spare bedroom playing with his model train set. She'd go mad with boredom and loneliness, and at this point her dressing gown began to droop open at the front, as if it felt as hopeless as its wearer.

At the party at the town hall, the Westons' daughter, Rebecca, was showing off to her friends about her own desirability. She was a fairly innocent teenager who had not yet had a boyfriend, but wanted to appear worldly-wise to her peers.

'I'm not kidding. He stood at the end of the path and put both his hands on my bum, and he squeezed hard, looked me in the eyes, and licked his lips. He's absolutely gagging for it with me, and if it weren't for my stuffy old dad always being around, I'd give it to him, too.'

'You wouldn't, Becky, would you? Really?' asked her best friend, wide-eyed.

'Without a second thought. You've got to get your experience somewhere, haven't you? And where better than from an older man?'

'Older man, yes, but that fellah next door to you must be at least a pensioner. Yuck!'

'Look, he's forty-two, okay? He's nowhere near a pensioner,' protested Rebecca Weston indignantly. 'And he's always got booze down in his shed.'

'So at least you can get pissed before you have to face doing it with him,' nodded her best friend, all understanding.

'That's not what I meant at all, and you know it!'

In number one Chestnut Close, Dave Weston was pacing the living room floor restlessly. 'What on earth made you tell that copper I was actually out in the garden when that shed went up?' he asked of his wife, who was not looking quite so smug now.

'Because you were,' she replied, aware that she had done wrong, but not quite sure how. 'You were never in the garage checking on the compost, because you've not got any out there.'

'I know that, and you know that, but that copper didn't. You should never have said I was in the garden. He might just get the idea that I was responsible for making off with that whisky-sodden waste-of-space next door, Jordan.'

'Don't be silly, Dave. He wouldn't think that of a nice respectable man like you.'

'Don't you be so sure, woman,' her husband replied. 'He's got eyes in his head. He can see perfectly well that I've got a vegetable patch at the bottom of the garden, and that there are ripe pumpkins in it. What's that going to make him think, with you blurting out that I was actually out there when the shed went up?' And if he gets to hear what I saw that filthy pervert do to our Rebecca on her way out this evening, he'll have the cuffs on me so quick, I won't know what's happening, he thought, doing another restless round of the carpet, and ignoring his wife's reassuring twittering.

Back in number four Chestnut Close, Deborah Sage went across to the coffee table to get a handkerchief out of her handbag, its gaping mouth exposing that she kept a silver – or at least silver-plated – hip flask within its cavernous depths. Seeing the direction of his gaze, she snapped it shut, no doubt jealous of the treasures and secrets she kept within.

As it seemed she had divulged all that she knew about her neighbour, including the information that she had been having an affair with him, Falconer asked her if she would be good enough to ask her husband if he would come in to speak to them. Obligingly she left the room and did as she was bidden, moving up the stairs out of the way as her husband entered the living room looking apprehensive at what the two policemen would think of him as a cuckolded husband. It was the only thought that had brought a smile to her face that evening.

As Falconer had expected, Peter Sage denied having been outside the house before the tragedy in the next-door garden, claiming, as his wife had said he would, to have been in the spare bedroom, interacting (for 'playing' would never have done as a description) with his model trains and landscape models and buildings. He had, according to his own story, been painting some new trees and shrubs, and could produce these, along with the little pots of green paint and the tiny brushes, should the inspector so wish.

As this was an easy enough alibi to set up in advance, Falconer did not take him up on his offer. It wasn't long before the two detectives found themselves outside on the pavement again, coming to a decision as to whether to back-track to number three, which had been missed out due to the upheaval caused by Carmichael's dramatic arrival, or to go on to number five, then go back afterwards.

The decision was made for them, as the tenant of number three, Patrick Flanagan, put his head out of the front door to ask if they were intending to call on him next. He had been keeping watch out of the front window since the incident with the disguised Carmichael, and had been fretting that he had been missed out.

'We'll be with you directly, sir. The route was rather disturbed by the arrival of my sergeant. I am Detective Inspector Falconer, and this is Detective Sergeant Carmichael. Please excuse his appearance, as he was celebrating Hallowe'en with his children when he was called in for duty.'

'Patrick Flanagan,' said the man, holding out his hand to shake both of theirs. 'And he's not the only one who's been doing that this evening,' he added, nodding his head in the direction of a small group of witches and wizards who were making their way into the close, accompanied by what appeared to be somebody's father. This adult, however, had not got into the spirit of the occasion by dressing up, as had Carmichael, and merely wore, boringly, jeans and a parka jacket.

'He's not playing the game,' sounded Carmichael's voice, lugubriously. 'He can't get any sweeties if he's not in costume.'

'Do come in,' invited Flanagan, not wishing to get involved in a discussion about whether adults accompanying minors on such excursions should also wear fancy dress. He had no children of his own and, while quite happy to provide those of others with sweets, did not wish to get any more deeply involved with what he considered to be a sub-species of the human race.

Although his place of birth was betrayed in his voice, the interior of his house was no different in decoration than any other average English house, and did not display large numbers of shillelaghs or shamrock-patterned carpet. It also betrayed the absence of any other occupant.

Seeing them staring round, Flanagan explained without enquiry, 'My wife's away in Ireland for a month or two. I may look as old as the hills, but I still have a mother-in-law, and she's not very well. That just leaves me here to my own devices, as I retired a couple of months ago, and I'm still trying to work out how best to occupy my time. Still, I expect it'll all work itself out when the wife gets back. At least I'll get a decent night's sleep now, with him next door gone; not wishing to speak ill of the dead, but nevertheless stating the truth.'

'What did your work used to be?' asked Falconer, in genuine interest.

'I was a baker for thirty years.'

'No doubt you had to get up at what, to the rest of us, is the middle of the night.'

'I used to have to get up before mi-laddo next door had finished playing his loud rock music,' admitted Flanagan, with feeling.

'Good God!' exclaimed Falconer. 'How on earth did you cope? Sleep deprivation is used as a method of torture!'

'Any way I could: herbal remedies, ear-plugs, sleeping tablets from the doctor. I couldn't resort to a drop of whisky because of having to get up so early, and then operate machinery,' he explained. 'As a last resort, every now and again, I used to stay at my sister-in-law's for a few nights, just to feel human again.'

'I don't think I could stand a neighbour like that,' interjected Carmichael.

'Someone else obviously agreed with you,' stated Falconer pointedly, his mind straying back to what had happened earlier that evening in the adjoining garden.

Their final port of call in Chestnut Close was at number five, the home of Leslie Ingram. From what they could see in the dim illumination of the street lamps, it was a tidily-kept property. Outside by the kerb was an immaculate and rather expensive motor car, only a couple of years old, and in complete contrast to the filthy, rusting heap that had been identified to them as that belonging to Larry Jordan.

Ingram was quick to answer their summons at the door and had obviously been awaiting their arrival. After introducing himself, he bade them enter and take a seat in the sitting room. Without preamble, he stated, 'Terrible business, this; terrible – but it couldn't have happened to a more deserving victim, although I wouldn't normally wish ill to anyone.'

'So, you're another neighbour who wasn't a fan of Mr Jordan,' stated Falconer drily.

'The man was a boor,' retorted Ingram. 'Have you seen that disgusting heap out on the road? That's the man's car, and he actually drives – used to drive,' he corrected the tense to take account of the man's untimely but hardly regretted demise, 'it on occasion. He had such a contrary character that he took great delight in parking it in a slightly different position every time he returned to the close.

'The old crate has an oil leak, so you can imagine what that did to the appearance of the road surface, this close being laid in concrete in the sixties. He's defaced the end of the road all the way round. Not only that, but the thing itself is an utter eyesore.

'I, personally, have offered, not only to mend the oil leak, but to give it a thorough clean, both inside and out, just to improve the view from my front window. And what do I get for my public-spirited attitude? He threatened to punch out my lights and, the next morning, there were eggs smashed all over the bonnet of my car. It took me ages to wash off the mess and restore the shine.'

'Mr Jordan really didn't seem to go out of his way to make friends and influence people, did he?' asked the inspector, with no expectation of an answer. 'Was there anyone in this neighbourhood who had a good word to say about Mr Jordan?' he enquired wryly.

'Deborah Sage, two doors from his place, seems to have had a soft spot for him, much to her husband Pete's disgust,' the car fanatic commented, smiling slyly behind his hand.

Feeling that this was punching rather below the belt, Falconer replied, 'Whereas you merely fell out with him to the extent of him defacing your car and offering to punch you.'

'That sounds much worse than it actually was,' squawked Ingram in protest.

'But his defacing of the road surface with motor oil infuriated you?' This did hit home.

'Do you realise that since that old heap's leaked, I've had to buy kitty litter to soak up the spillage, when I don't actually possess a cat?'

'Do you live alone, Mr Ingram?'

'I do. Not that it's any of your business, but my wife left me eighteen months ago: said she couldn't stand life with what she described as a 'petrol-head' who cared more for his car than he did for his wife. And good riddance, too. Do you know, she used actually to smoke in the car? Moaned like hell when I asked her to open a window and hold the filthy cigarette outside, for put it out she would not. It was when she changed to smoking cheroots that I really put my foot down; and that's when she packed her bags and buggered off.'

'What the hell are you doing, Carmichael?' asked Falconer, as they sat in the front of his car, and his sergeant squirmed beside him. They had sought the privacy of the vehicle to mull over what they had learnt so far about the suspects in the case, such as they were.

'Sherbet dab, sir,' replied the sergeant, flourishing his little lollipop and holding up the little bag of white powder. 'From trick-or-treating.'

'Don't tell me you actually helped yourself to sweeties too, when you went knocking on doors!'

'Of course! I was dressed up, too. I'd also gone to the trouble of escorting the boys round the village. What's wrong with me getting a few sweets as well?'

Falconer merely shrugged, feeling speechless in the face of such deathless logic, and addressed himself to their murderous problem.

'Let's discuss who could have been responsible,' he began, while Carmichael slurped away at his sherbet-coated lollipop. 'If we look at the Westons at number one, Mrs W let the cat out of the bag about her husband being in the garden at the time of the murder. He didn't like that, did he, and came up with a different story immediately, to throw us off the scent. And he's got a vegetable patch at the end of his garden which I saw when I was examining the scene of crime, and it's got pumpkins in it.'

'I bet a lot of them grow veg, sir. It's not a high income area,' contributed Carmichael, beginning to sound like a nuisance. 'And it is definitely a murder, is it, sir, and not just a suspicious death?' asked the sergeant, playing Devil's advocate, although he didn't realise it.

'I can't see anyone committing suicide by pumpkin, can you, Carmichael? And I can imagine no circumstances in which what happened to Jordan could have occurred by accident,' snapped the inspector, in indignation that such a thing should be suggested.

'Just checking, sir.'

'Well, don't! To sum up, we've got a victim who was a drunken noise nuisance – a potential victim waiting to be murdered – who didn't get on with his wife or his neighbours, and seemed to go out of his way to antagonise anyone with whom he came into contact. We've got one woman who found him a laugh and was having an affair with him, but that's the limit of his fan club.

'Her husband – Sage, that is – resented the fact that Jordan was sleeping with his wife, the guy at number one – that Weston chap – hated the fact that the man's garden was a weed-infested disgrace that seeded his own immaculate patch throughout the year, the Irish bloke, Flanagan, went through hell with sleep loss for goodness knows how long because of the loud rock music. And finally we have the car nut, Ingram, who was actually threatened by the victim. According to their states of mind, they've all got a reason to want rid of him, even his own wife, whether or not we understand it as a suitable motive for murder.'

'Would you like a liquorice wheel, sir?' Carmichael had his own inimitable way of breaking a mood.

In a metal-framed bed, in a side room in the Market Darley Hospital, a figure stirred, groaned and opened its eyes. A tongue emerged between its dry lips and attempted to moisten them, before it spoke in a croaky voice. 'Can someone get Inspector Falconer urgently?'

A nurse, just popping her head round the door to check on the patient, entered, and attempted to find out what was so pressing that only the said inspector could deal with it.

Falconer had a little difficulty removing his mobile phone from his trouser pocket while sat in the driver's seat, but the effort was worth it when Roberts had passed on the vital information with which he had regained consciousness.

'I think we'll just have a final word with Mr Masters, who was with Roberts when he was struck down, to find out if he can confirm what the DC has just told me, then we'll make a little call,' he pronounced, after relaying the contents of the short call to Carmichael. 'Oh, and wipe your top lip. There's sherbet on it, and it looks like you've been helping yourself to the Class As.'

As they exited the vehicle and headed for the alleyway leading to the rear of the properties, and also to 86 Oak Drive, where Mr Masters could be found, the DS removed a large rumpled handkerchief from the trouser pocket below his all-enveloping fancy dress costume, and scrubbed at his top lip in an embarrassed manner.

On their way to Oak Drive they were waylaid by a flustered Patrick Flanagan, desperate to unburden himself of some information that it had slipped his mind to pass on earlier, in his anxiety about being missed out of the run of questioning.

'I witnessed something earlier on this evening that I think might have some bearing on the outcome of your investigations,' he panted, losing his breath from the speed with which he had hurried after the two figures.

'It's about yon fella that got killed, and that gardening fanatic at number one,' he continued, his face red, not only from exertion, but with excitement, too. Well, he's got a daughter – young thing and quite pretty.'

'Go on,' urged Falconer, fully expecting this incident to come to nothing.

'Well, she went out this evening, all dolled up and probably heading for some party or other, and yer man Jordan waylaid her at the end of the garden path and acted like a full-blown pervert.'

'What did he do, Mr Flanagan?' Falconer's interest had been piqued.

'He only put his hands on her buttocks and gave them a good squeeze. And he put his tongue out and ran it round his lips in the most lascivious manner. The girl's an innocent abroad, and I know that during the summer he used to go out in his jungle and ogle her, when she went out in her bikini to sunbathe.'

'How very interesting, Mr Flanagan. We shall certainly bear this new information in mind as we continue with our investigations.'

Unfortunately for them, John Masters had not noticed anyone near the shed when the explosion occurred, as he had been standing further away than DC Roberts, who had been walking in the direction of the wooden structure in order to investigate the choking noises that had been emanating from it. With this unhelpful information, Falconer's mobile phone rang again, and he answered it to find Dr Christmas on the other end of the line.

'Hello, Philip,' he greeted the FME. 'You're surely not working at this time of night? ... You're that bored? ... Well, whatever floats your boat ... You've found what? ... Oh, you wonderful man!' Something else went 'click' in Falconer's head, and he saw again, in his mind's eye, something he had actually looked upon, earlier in the evening. 'I think you just may have solved this case for me. I'll be in touch.'

Ending the call and replacing the phone back in his pocket, he turned to Carmichael. 'Come along, Sergeant. We've got an arrest to make,' he announced dramatically and enigmatically, and set off once again for Chestnut Close – rear entrances, this time – leaving John Masters standing, abandoned once more by the forces of law and order.

Having knocked on the obscure glass of the back door of number four, it was Deborah Sage who opened it to them, and bade them enter. She was still attired in dressing gown and slippers, a towel still wrapped round her head. Her large handbag was open on the work surface, and she made haste to close its gaping jaws as the two detectives entered the house for the second time.

'Mrs Sage,' began Falconer. 'The night has become unseasonably cold, and I believe I just noticed a silver flask in your handbag. I don't suppose you'd care to offer me a little nip to warm my poor, cold bones?'

Deborah Sage's face drained of colour, and she clutched the large handbag to her chest possessively, her lips moving, but no sound emerging from her mouth.

'Come on, don't be mean,' he exhorted her, holding out a hand and moving closer to her. 'You saw what he did, didn't you?' he asked, apparently apropos of nothing, causing Carmichael to stare at him in incomprehension. Like a mesmerised rabbit, she slowly extended a hand clutching the bag, in offering, her eyes now closed, and her head now nodding up and down in agreement.

Falconer took the bag when it came within reach and extracted the flask from its depths. He opened it, gave an almighty sniff, which produced a smile of satisfaction as the brandy fumes hit his nostrils, closed the receptacle again, and placed the flask carefully in an evidence bag, which he handed to Carmichael for safe-keeping.

'Deborah Sage, I am arresting you for the murder of Lawrence Jordan ...'

Back at the station, Carmichael could not contain his unquenched curiosity. 'How did you know it was her, sir?' he asked, eager for enlightenment. 'She was the only one who didn't hate him.'

'Correct, Carmichael, so she was very hurt when she saw her lover feeling up someone who was little more than a child, but who, nevertheless, represented a threat to her relationship with the deceased. Someone very young, very pretty, very innocent, and very available, given her lack of disapproval of what Jordan had just done to her.'

'But, how did you work it out?'

'I had a little help. I received two phone calls. One was from Roberts, who had regained consciousness and remembered that just before he was struck on the head by a flying piece of wood, he had seen the figure of a woman near the shed – I told you about that one – and a second call from Doc Christmas, who, being easily bored, had started the post-mortem early, and discovered the presence, not just of the whisky the victim was drinking in his shed, but also of brandy and of the drug that makes up a commonly prescribed brand of sleeping tablets.

'That told me that he was drugged before he was encased in that pumpkin, which had been purloined from Dave Weston's garden earlier that evening. Mrs Sage would have fed him some of the brandy and just hung round until the drug took effect, and he fell asleep. We can prove where the pumpkin came from tomorrow by identifying the stalk from which it was cut, in Weston's vegetable patch.

'And she could easily have made up some sort of basic incendiary device, which was supposed to cover her tracks, using the fuel from her husband's lawn mower, a scrap of rag or cleaning cloth, and an empty glass bottle.

'The one clue that it had been she who had done that, would be the presence of accelerant on her skin. The only one of our possibles who had managed to fit in a bath or a shower after the tragedy was Mrs Sage, who came to the door garbed in a dressing gown when you arrived originally.'

'That's brilliant, sir.'

Falconer almost blushed. 'Not really, Carmichael. In fact, if I may borrow a phrase, 'Elementary, my dear Watson.''

'Who?' Carmichael's expression, despite his Frankenstein get-up, was blank.

Rebecca Weston closed the door of number one Chestnut Close behind her, conscious that it was almost midnight, and giggled quietly. She was just a little bit tiddly.

'Becky!' called her mother from the living room, having stayed up to see her safely back home. 'Have you missed some fun and games tonight!'

'Why? What's that?' asked Rebecca, tottering into the living room, a victim of her own slight inebriation and a pair of new, too-high heels. 'Nothing ever happens round here.'

'That waste-of-space next door has only gone and got himself murdered,' chirruped her mother, in the glee of an attack of *Schadenfreude*.

'What, Larry? Murdered?' Rebecca was absolutely astonished.

'Yes. And by that woman from number four.' Brenda was full of herself, being the bearer of such extraordinary tidings, but her bubble of self-importance was about to be burst.

'Well, poor old Larry. He was a bit of a laugh, wasn't he' was Rebecca's only comment, delivered in a very off-hand manner, before she tottered off upstairs to bed, so hard-hearted can be the young in the face of tragedy.

DS Davey Carmichael arrived home to find there were still stragglers at the Hallowe'en party at his house, the progeny of parents who did not mind their children staying up to the witching hour on such a date, the adults having settled themselves down in the Carmichael household with eagerly-accepted glasses of wine.

The man of the house's arrival had caused a small flurry of disquiet, but the visitors soon realised who he was beneath his disguise, and held out their glasses eagerly for a refill from their generous hostess.

'Hey, there're still apples!' declared the new arrival, heading towards an old tin bath, two-thirds filled with water, with apples floating in it. 'I'm going to have a 'bob'.'

As he got down on his hands and knees to indulge in the time-honoured Hallowe'en pastime of bobbing for apples, his wife shook her head in disbelief, and a large grin split her face, as she hoped that her husband would never grow up.

When Falconer next entered his sitting room, a room lit only by the dying light of the fire, he switched on a lamp and observed the tangled heap of multi-coloured fur in front of the fireplace. A head or two rose languidly to see why there was extra light, and he smiled at his heap of sleeping pets. How good it was to come home to their relaxing presence.

Crossing the room to the sideboard, he poured himself a small brandy, then moved to his favourite armchair, to sit down for a while before he retired to bed.

The pile of cats squirmed slightly to achieve total comfort, then settled back down to sleep.

THE END

Written Out

A regional television programme, Get One Over, where amateurs search for and discover antiques and valuable objects in junk shops, has captured the nation's zeitgeist and gone nationwide.

The Christmas episode is to be filmed in Market Darley, and being antiques fans, Miss Emily Jarvis, and DI Falconer and DS Carmichael plan to be in town to bump into the stars of the programme. Carmichael loves the programme for its jokey narrator, but Falconer, along with a host of other viewers, hates the man's rude and condescending commentary.

But on a crispy cold December morning, as the chase around the town to find the TV stars continues, it proves to be a terminal performance for one of their number.

ONE

Emily Jarvis sat in her favourite battered armchair in front of the fire grinding her dentures together. She was watching her favourite afternoon programme, *Get One Over.* It was a simple formula. Four antiques buffs were filmed visiting three locations to locate bargains. The venues could be jumble sales, car boot sales, even junk shops, and the point of the whole show was to decide who had got the best bargain, having thus 'got one over' on the other three.

The real twist came at the end of the show. The amateur experts were only allowed to spend a certain sum of money and, when all their purchases had been made, a professional antiques dealer was called in to value the items and work out what the amount of profit per expert should be. The items were then auctioned, and only after the profits from that had been calculated was the winner declared. When one of the amateurs had won five shows, the profits accrued from those editions were donated to a charity of their choice.

The show was very popular because it was so easy to identify with and emulate. Anyone watching could easily go treasure hunting themselves and make a profit if they so desired, but the point of the show itself was not profiteering but friendly competition, with regular sums paid to charity. Also, the 'experts' were changed twice a year, so there was plenty of opportunity to pick a new 'favourite'. Being such a popular yet low-budget production and in such a popular genre, it wasn't long before it was broadcast nationally instead of regionally, and the experts travelled to different parts of the country every week, so everybody – the antiques trade, the experts, and the happy viewers – was a winner.

Get One Over had been high on Emily Jarvis' list of favourite television shows since it had begun a few years ago, but there was one fly in her ointment. It was made by her regional TV company and so she had recognised many of the locations. She had also liked the amateur dealers that had been contracted to hunt for the best buys. What she *didn't* love was the narrator, a terribly irritating and over-the-top chap caller Peter Potter-Porter. His wordy and pun-laden scripts made her cringe and, lately, had been slowly but surely leeching out her pleasure in the little bits of one-upmanship that the show filmed by the inanity of his jolly, joking voice, and she had begun to hate him. Her dearest wish for Christmas was a button where she could mute the narrator and just watch the show for what it was.

Since she had put up the Christmas decorations and little tree that she always decorated in December, she had taken to sipping a small sherry with the programme, but this man was becoming the bane of her life. He was ruining one of the little pleasures left to her in her old age, and she found that difficult to forgive. She knew that the Christmas special was to be filmed soon in Market Darley, and had decided to go into the market town that day to see if she could see any of her favourite amateur experts – but the thought of what that idiotic narrator would make of it didn't bear thinking about.

As the show finished on a flurry of dreadful puns, some so bad they made her wince, she did something she had never done before and went over to the sideboard to refill her sherry glass. Really, this irritating young man was going to turn her into an alcoholic if he carried on behaving like this, and she didn't think she could stand it much longer.

The narrator's voice was one that seemed to talk down to the viewers, as if he considered them of very little intelligence, while simultaneously sneering at the 'experts' and putting them down too. She was so cross that she swallowed her second sherry in one gulp, and spent the rest of the afternoon muttering under her breath, 'Peter Potter-Porter picked a peck of pickled pepper ...' over and over again, and fighting her rage at how this superior young man was ruining her enjoyment of such a simple pastime.

That evening, she had three friends over for a few rubbers of bridge, and got them all talking about how this programme was being spoilt by being so patronising to both those who liked to watch it and those who took part in it.

'Fellow needs horsewhipping,' commented Theodore Matthews from a few doors down. 'Simply not cricket. Should be drummed out of the regiment.'

Emily Jarvis smiled in agreement, but reminded him that the war had been over for some time, and he had been out of the army for a couple of decades, a fact that he often forgot in his daily life. He may be a bit hazy about everyday details, but he was a devil with the cards, and could seem to memorise every one played in a hand, damn him.

'I used to like *Going for a Song*,' added Camilla Smethurst. 'Such a nice programme, except for that man with the terribly common voice.'

'Come along, chaps,' interjected Emily. 'Let's have another drink and a last rubber before we pack up. Theo, will you shuffle the cards please, and then pass them to Veronica, because I just don't trust you enough not to be able to "fix" them whilst you're shuffling them.'

As she went upstairs to bed that night she remembered with pleasure that tomorrow the crew of *Get One Over* was filming in Market Darley for the Christmas Special. She had promised herself that she would go into town and wander round likely locations, popping into the old people's day centre at midday to have a decent and inexpensive lunch. She could then recharge her batteries before having another prowl around in the afternoon, hoping to catch a glimpse of them at work. Wiping the sound of the young man's patronising voice from her mind, she went to sleep with a smile on her face, hoping that she might bump into her favourite experts and have a little chat with them.

TWO

In the police station in Market Darley, Detective Inspector Harry Falconer was having a bit of a rant. 'The beginning of December, trees and blasted coloured lights already all over the place, shoppers out in force, and tomorrow we've got a damned camera crew filming in the town. That's going to bring in extra crowds since they mentioned on the local news that the programme was being filmed here. That's all we need to give a little encouragement to pick-pockets, muggers, and shop-lifters. How could they have been so irresponsible as to have given permission for this to happen in the midst of Christmas shopping?'

Detective Sergeant 'Davey' Carmichael was chewing the cud in the form of a piece of bubble gum, which he lazily made protrude from between his lips, and blew. As the large pink bubble burst all over his face, he managed to mumble a reply. 'Is that for that *Get One Over* programme? I like that. The bloke who does the voice-over makes me laugh.'

'Well, he doesn't do that to me. He's an arrogant little swine, and I personally would like to punch him in the mouth.' This may have seemed strange, for two men who worked such long hours to be discussing a daytime programme on the television, but, so popular had it become that it was now shown in the evening the day after it aired in the afternoon, and Falconer was interested in antiques and collectables. The unlikely programme was making inroads into public popularity as far as rummaging in junk shops went, and would soon air for the first time during peak viewing time when a new series started in the New Year.

'Kerry can't stand him,' replied Carmichael, trying to remove some strings of sticky pink from his eyebrows. 'She says he's too big for his own boots.'

'Carmichael, will you please peel that horrible stuff off your face and deposit it in the bin. I'm damned if I'm going out on a call with a DS with pink eyebrows.'

'Yes, sir,' said Carmichael, sheepishly, putting the wad of brightly coloured stretchy stuff in a piece of paper, preparatory to throwing it into the waste paper bin. He had some more in his pocket, and would be able to indulge again at lunchtime, in private. Carrying on where he had left off, he said, 'Kerry says that sometimes she could strangle the bloke for the contemptible way he talks about the people in the show who do all the work finding little treasures, whilst he tells a lot of terrible jokes.'

'And they're always at someone else's expense,' added Falconer. 'I find him very irritating. It's just the way these people find things that you wouldn't look at twice and then show us how they come up with a bit of TLC that fascinates me.'

'Kerry will watch anything these days that means she doesn't have to drag her bump around with her. She's getting really tired, even though the twins aren't due for a few months yet.'

'Well, Carmichael, it was your choice to have even more children. Do you fancy having a bit of a walk round the streets, just to see if we can spot any of the filming?' asked Falconer, who was secretly excited about seeing some of the corners of his adopted home town shown on the television.

'Yes, please. I wonder if we can get any autographs. I'd love one of that narrator.'

'Carmichael, you are an enigma.'

THREE

Emily Jarvis had woken up in a good mood, definitely looking forward to her little jaunt into Market Darley. She did her hair with especial attention and even put on a little pale lipstick and powder and her best day dress, in case she had the chance to shake hands with one – or more – of her heroes, and had decided that she would do a little rooting around herself in some of the junk shops, in search of little presents for her acquaintances.

She packed her large handbag carefully with her knitting, just begun, as she would need something to occupy her as she digested her lunch at the old folks' centre, and set off for the bus stop just as the shops were opening. She was prepared for a long day on the off chance that she might rub shoulders with 'celebrities', and planned to husband her energy carefully. She wouldn't go haring off from one shop to another, as she might miss the filming crews at every visit. She would just mooch around in one or two that she knew had more interesting 'junk' in them until lunchtime, then try a different area of the town during the afternoon.

She began in The Shambles, a very untidy and overcrowded shop in an alleyway just off the Market Square, and became quite engrossed in rummaging through boxes and under tables. It really was a fun way to pass some time, and she made a pact with herself to carry on with this pastime after this particular day. Some of the items she came across brought back such memories for her, of her parents, grandparents, and even of her own childhood.

This interest in bygone things had been something that had only sprung up in the last few years, as her spry early old age had given way to a rather frailer second phase, and she had started doing the unthinkable: watching daytime television. It had opened up new worlds to her, however, as there seemed to be quite a lot of programmes on collectables and what she considered was just junk; like Clarice Cliff, which used to be sold in Woolworths – all gaudy colours and inept hand-painting, in her opinion. *Get One Over*, however, was her definite favourite, if only it hadn't been for that dreadful narrator.

By lunchtime she had made several inexpensive finds which would serve well as presents for her friends, and she headed for the old people's centre with quite an appetite. It turned out to be steak and kidney pie, one of her favourites, on the day's menu, and she cleared her plate in quite a short time. Then, it was time for a little rest with her knitting on her lap and, perhaps, a surreptitious nap in one of the wing-backed armchairs; it was more private in one of those, with its full sides that were made to support and keep draughts away from the head.

As she slept fitfully, her dreams were full of that voice that so irritated her and she woke up feeling quite disorientated and cross. It was in this mood that she shoved her knitting into her bag and set off again into the streets of Market Darley in search of the film crews. She knew there would be one for each location, because little treasures didn't just float into the air in front of one, and there was quite a bit of searching involved, playing to the camera the whole time. She had decided that she would head for another quarter of the town where she might have more luck, then, possibly, get a bus out to a table sale that had been advertised in the local paper as taking place that afternoon.

FOUR

Falconer and Carmichael had made a short foray out into the town without telling anyone what they were up to; it would have been too embarrassing to say that they were chasing the filming of a television programme. They struck lucky, however, at the first destination they tried. It was a small shop stuck between two discount shops on the main square, called 'Times Past'.

In front of the shop they saw a camera crew talking to a face they knew only too well, that of Charlie Huggins, amateur antique dealer and one of the series' stars. He was speaking to camera while another man helped out what looked like one of Carmichael's little dogs on the end of a stick, but which was, on closer inspection, a microphone. There seemed to be some sort of director there as well, who called 'Cut' and asked them to go again on the last piece, with a bit more 'thrill of the chase' attitude on the part of Huggins.

'I've visited this little gem of a shop on one or two occasions in the past,' he almost leered to camera, as if he were contemplating a night with a beautiful woman, 'and I'm certain I shall come up with a show-stopper within its walls.'

As the action was cut again, the leer disappeared to be replaced by a rather angry scowl. 'Can't we just get on with it?' he asked in a thoroughly fed-up voice. 'I could do with a large, stiff drink.'

'It's only five to twelve,' said the man who appeared to be running the action.

'I had to get up at half past four this morning to get down here, you know,' he replied, crossly.

'Yes, but you did have a driver all the way down, and he told me you snored like a drain the whole journey,' replied the offended man who wielded the clapperboard. And it'll soon be your turn to be replaced, he thought with a great wave of *schadenfreude*. Let's see how you fare when your face has been replaced by a newer and fresher one.

'I still need a drink. I can't stand these provincial little towns. I'm a celebrity now, you know, and I go to a lot of parties.'

'Which you will continue to get invited to if you start co-operating and stop going on like a damned diva.'

Falconer coughed from just along the street, then he and Carmichael waited while the scene was finished to the satisfaction of the fussy little director, then they stepped forward and Falconer was the first to speak. 'I'm sorry to interrupt you while you're working ...' He then went on to introduce them and ask if they'd like them to accompany them on their filming visits, in case there was any interference from an over-enthusiastic public.

Carmichael found himself incapable of speech, but nodded his head in agreement at everything Falconer said, then held out his notebook for an autograph from the nouveau celebrity. Their offer was accepted, as they were now drawing quite a crowd, and if there was one thing the director realised, it was how quickly these two new additions to their crew could call for uniformed back-up if anything got out of hand, which wasn't pushing things too far given the current popularity of the programme.

'You can't collect autographs in your official notebook,' Falconer informed the sergeant. 'They have to be filed away in case they're ever needed for evidence.'

'Blast,' replied the sergeant, rummaging through his pockets until he came up with a tiny notebook which he kept to note down anything that Kerry needed him to bring home. 'I'll have to use this. By the way, sir, are you still up for that pantomime in Carsfold over Christmas?'

'Yes,' sighed Falconer, in a resigned voice. He knew it was a treat for the Carmichael family, but he just wished he had a twin that he could send with them instead of going himself. He really felt uncomfortable in the company of children, and there were now three of them with another two on the way. Carmichael, meanwhile, had gone back for his second autograph, which was duly signed albeit with a sigh and much rolling of eyes by the author.

When the filming broke for lunch, the two detectives found themselves accompanying the little party off to a catering van that was parked just outside the town centre on the outskirts of a small industrial estate, where the other three new celebrities and other filming crews were filling their faces before things got underway again during the afternoon.

Even Peter Potter-Porter was there, looking very superior and condescending, and Falconer suddenly remembered that the man always did a piece to camera before the show was broadcast, the rest of his voice-over being recorded in some studio or other, the supercilious script written by him after he had been shown the first rushes. The inspector ignored him, being more anxious to speak to the assembled experts on one of his new interests, but Carmichael headed straight for the man himself, and held out his tiny notebook this time.

With almost a sneer of contempt, the narrator scrawled his name, then said something curt and dismissive to his admirer, but Carmichael was totally immune to his rudeness. He had actually told the man that he thought he was very funny and, although this had not been very well received, the sergeant was walking on air. Just wait until he got home and told Kerry that he had got the man's autograph and had actually had a conversation with him, if you could call being dismissed as having a conversation.

A few minutes later, it became evident that there was some sort of disagreement, as angry voices sounded clearly above the low level hubbub. 'Don't you dare speak to me like that,' shouted Charlie Huggins, his normally jovial face now bright red with temper, 'you jumped-up little voice-over man.'

'And you're what? An elderly lothario who drinks too much? Don't get ideas above your station. You'll be for the chop after this edition, whereas I shall sail on undisturbed. I'm permanent.'

'Don't be so sure of that, matey.' This last wasn't so loud, but it carried to the inspector's ears, and he watched Huggins stalk away in indignation. He stopped by Peter Derby, another of the show's experts, and they fell into conversation that seemed to be directed at the narrator, who pointedly ignored them.

After about forty-five minutes, the small crews formed again, and went their separate ways, Falconer and Carmichael sticking with the one that accompanied Charlie Huggins, Peter Potter-Porter, self-styled Golden Boy, with a slight curl of his upper lip, leaving with his own crew, evidently to film the introductory piece before he left the mundane work to others.

As the afternoon's rummage visit began at 'Junk 'n' Stuff', the two detectives noticed that the inside of the shop was already decorated for Christmas. They had noticed a few strings of coloured lights winking in the window, but inside sat a real pine tree which would probably last until it closed for the Bank Holidays, as central heating wasn't an option, given the fact that they had delicate wooden furniture that could dry out and fall apart.

On the tree were antique decorations that really gave it an air of times past. Some of the pieces were Victorian, others were from the early twentieth century. A set of lights, probably from the fifties and with only twelve bulbs, added to its sense of long ago, as did paper decorations suspended from and across the ceiling. Faux presents surrounded the bucket in which the tree was planted to add to the seasonal atmosphere.

As the crew entered the premises, Falconer and Carmichael also went inside for a little look around, Falconer keeping out of the way of the film crew, Carmichael bobbing up all over the place in the hope that he might get his mug on the telly. He had just appeared as if by magic, another large pink bubble obscuring half his face, behind Huggins who was doing a piece to camera about a piece of Mauchline ware he had just come across in a box of oddments, when a voice cut across the filming with a very sharp edge to it.

'Look, I don't know what the hell you think you're doing, but could you please keep out of camera shot. I know you're being very protective of us, but you're really not helping things. Perhaps you could be of more use outside. I notice there's quite a crowd gathering at the window.'

As he finished, Falconer grabbed his sergeant's arm to stop him mugging at the camera and led him out of the door. 'Come along now,' he said in his best police manner. 'Clear away and give people room to do their jobs. Nothing to see here.' Carmichael frowned at the crowd and looked menacing, when he was actually just rather cross about having been ejected from the inside of the shop and having his bubble gum confiscated once again, but the surrounding members of the public took the hint and moved further away from the premises.

'Aw, sir,' he complained when they were at last alone at the window, 'I could've been on the box.'

'I think if I hadn't taken you outside, that director would've had you removed *in* a box,' concluded Falconer, giving him a sardonic smile.

FIVE

Emily Jarvis had indigestion. The acid burned up from her stomach, making her feel unpleasantly ill. She had wandered the streets all morning and had not even had a glimpse of a film crew. She had left her antacid tablets at home in a kitchen drawer, and now she was suffering from aching feet as well. As her feeling of injustice mounted, she began to develop a headache, and life definitely seemed unfair today.

Ignoring the early signs of the Christmas season such as the lights strung across the Market Square, the tinsel and fairy lights decorating shop windows, with even the odd crib scene here and there – how very un-PC – she headed down one of the little lanes where she knew there were likely to be junk and second-hand shops, the owners of which now considered their premises as antique retail centres, given the popularity of such television shows as *Get One Over*. This should prove rich hunting ground, but again she had no luck, and her temper rose even further as the acid burned a trail from her stomach to her throat.

Suddenly, just around a corner into another narrow road, she saw a television camera ahead of her, and quickened her pace to see which of the celebrities was being filmed. She had no memory of a suitable shop down here, and was using it merely to cut across to another street. And there *he* was, just a few yards in front of her, his irritating voice grinding away at this piece to camera, his sneering tones belittling this season's experts who were using the show as a springboard into the trade as professionals. Why did he always have to look down on people so? He was such an unpleasant character whose intrusive and domineering narration was to the detriment of the overall production.

Why couldn't the narrator be changed each season, as were their amateur experts? Why did his whiny voice have to ruin every episode she watched? Surely he was losing them viewers, rather than picking them up? Her temper flared even higher as she grasped her handbag tightly and moved slightly forward.

The crew had finished now, but the superior sneer on Peter Potter-Porter's face had changed not a jot: this was evidently not a persona he put on for the cameras, but who he really was. One of her hands snaked unheeded into her handbag and rummaged around in there until it came across what she was subconsciously searching for. I'll give him a piece of my mind if it's the last thing I do, was her last coherent thought.

SIX

At about five o'clock, all natural light long gone, the filming was completed, and the crews met up in the Market Square, Falconer and Carmichael still clinging to their coat-tails. They stood there amidst a lot of technical chat about what they had achieved, and when and where they would meet again to film the objects being valued by their resident professional. This was agreed upon as next week, and the auction was to be two days later, so that they had time to edit the film and have it ready for screening on the twenty-third of the month.

As they began to drift away, a small group of children assembled under the Market Cross and began to sing Christmas carols and Falconer noticed that they were collecting for Help for Heroes, much to his approval. If anyone needed help, it was those maimed in fighting for their own country.

Eventually, all the technical staff had left, and they were left with just the experts, glowing in the light of their own temporary fame. They might as well, as it wouldn't last for much longer. Household names soon degenerated into has-beens in the inspector's opinion, once they had stopped appearing on the nation's screens regularly – and this programme went out five days a week and had a tight filming schedule to keep to.

Charlie Huggins was the most smug and self-satisfied, but then his bravado had probably been fuelled by the silver hip flask that kept appearing from one of his pockets, and he seemed to have forgotten his little disagreement with the narrator at lunchtime, whatever it had been about. Mairie McManus was the only woman in the team, and she was flirting and generally acting like one half her age, to match the way she dressed. Another of them who had been noted to slip into the pub before the end of filming, Peter Derby, was beginning to turn from sweetness and light to pure acid, and nudged Charlie Huggins until the latter offered him a pull at his hip flask.

The fourth member of the team, Johnathan Mull, stood slightly to one side. A very well-educated man, he found the self-congratulation and mutual admiration somewhat embarrassing, and began to suggest that maybe they should head for home. Peter Derby, however, completely disagreed and urged them towards The Cattle Market, a pub right on the Square. 'After all,' he said, 'this is our last treasure hunt for this year. We've only got the valuation and the auction to go now, and we're finished until the New Year, with all the other episodes in the can, and who can say whether they'll retain us in the light of going national?' So, he was harbouring hopes of retention.

This declaration seemed to do the trick, and the group was just turning towards the pub when Falconer's mobile rang. He answered it, Carmichael still by his side but looking longingly at the disappearing minor celebrities. As the phone call proceeded, the inspector's face became more and more serious and incredulous before he hung up and said to his sergeant, 'Do you want to go inside the pub?'

'Oh, yes please, sir,' replied Carmichael, a broad grin across his chops, at the thought of more basking in the company of celebrities, 'but why?'

'Because I've just had a phone call to say that a beat PC has found Peter Potter-Porter lying in one of the back streets, and he's dead.'

'That hilarious narrator chap I was talking to earlier, when I got his autograph?' Carmichael could hardly believe his ears.

'That's the one. The uniformed constable is going to stay on guard until they can get him pronounced dead and a SOCO team to photograph and record the scene, but I said we might as well take advantage of having all the show's "stars" together in one place, before they scatter to the four corners of the country. We'll just have to get someone to question the technical team later, but I assume they'll all live within easy reach of the studio, so they shouldn't be too geographically disparate.'

'How do we know it was one of them, sir?'

'Well, it seems a reasonable hypothesis. His wallet was undisturbed, he still had his mobile phone, and, as far as we know at the moment, he doesn't know anybody in the town and doesn't live nearby.'

'Were there any witnesses?' Carmichael suddenly thought that he might still get on the television, and puffed himself up with pride.

'Apparently, there were no pedestrians visible in any direction, and the body was still twitching when the PC discovered him. The only person he could find was a little old lady in a wool shop choosing a pattern for a matinee jacket, and she hadn't heard anything. Neither had the woman who owns the shop.'

'Was there a weapon on the scene?'

'Nothing at all,' replied Falconer as he directed his footsteps towards The Cattle Market's welcoming lights.

SEVEN

Inside the saloon bar, Charlie Huggins, Mairie McManus, Peter Derby, and Johnathan Mull sat round a table, all acting the life and soul of the party and glancing round them to see if they'd been recognised, but they were out of luck, and it was only the inspector and sergeant who headed over towards them. As Falconer asked Carmichael if he would like something, they all drained their glasses and raised them towards him, evidently assuming that he was getting a round in. The inspector sighed and took their glasses, two in each hand, and approached the bar.

When he returned to the table, he had two vodka and tonics, two gin and tonics, and two large coffees on a tray: he and Carmichael never drank on duty – in fact, they very rarely drank at all. He settled himself in a spare chair that his sergeant had rustled up and began to tune into the conversation. 'He was absolutely poisonous to me at lunchtime,' Charlie Huggins said without a trace of self-consciousness. 'Seemed to think I was some kind of drunken gigolo.'

'Good judge of character, then,' said Johnathan Mull, grinning at his colleague. 'He is always having a go at me about my public school accent, which I can't change even if I wanted to. He was a swine with how he talked about us during his narration, though, wasn't he?'

'An absolute pig,' chirped Mairie McManus, 'and he even called me something akin to mutton dressed as lamb, once. I could have cheerfully killed him, considering how much I spend on clothes and my hair, and how much time I spend in make-up.'

'He was really rotten to me recently, saying I couldn't spot a genuine antique if it jumped up and bit me: accused me of only buying obvious stuff and that I had no intuition,' interjected Peter Derby.

'He really is a nasty piece of work,' confirmed Mairie McManus, once again claiming the limelight.

Falconer cleared his throat, returning his cup to its saucer. 'I'm sorry to have to inform you that Peter Potter-Parker is dead,' he announced to the table at large.

'Good.'

'Serves him right.'

'Couldn't be happier for him.'

'Are you serious?' This last was Mairie again, her face screwed up in surprise, or at least, an approximation of it.

'Deadly serious, I'm afraid,' replied Falconer, as Carmichael drew out his official notebook. 'Now, I realise he wasn't a popular man, but can you please tell me what you know about him, and how he got on with the film crews?'

It had seemed that he'd upset quite a few of the technicians too, and was universally quite disliked, much to Carmichael's surprise. 'When did you last see him?' the inspector asked.

'I haven't seen him since lunchtime,' declared Charlie Huggins, his face growing worried and pale as he remembered the words they had had.

'I saw him then but didn't speak to him,' added Peter Derby.

'I spoke with him,' admitted Mairie McManus, 'but I think, underneath all the banter, he was rather sweet on me.' As she was at least twenty years older than him and obviously dyed her hair dark, this seemed more fantasy than fact, and Falconer didn't dig any deeper for now. The sourness about the mutton dressed as lamb comment could bide its time.

'I didn't even see him at lunch,' Johnathan Mull told them, his face a mask of innocence, 'but then, we don't get on very well. I simply don't like his attitude.'

That was not the first negative thing they had heard about the deceased, but the inspector leapt on it like a starving man on a fish and chip supper. 'Why didn't you get on, sir?' he asked.

'Because he was a supercilious, narcissistic twit,' came the answer. 'He was superior whilst actually being inferior. The ability to make the most appalling puns and poke fun at everybody else involved in the show is not exactly a talent that would have seen him go far,' Johnathan told them, a slight frown of distaste wrinkling his brow. 'And he was, I believe, jealous of my schooling.'

'Thank you for your honesty, sir,' said Falconer.

'But *I* thought he was very funny.'

'Do shut up, Carmichael, there's a good chap.'

'Sir?'

'Have you got a note of everything said so far?'

'Yes, sir.'

'Good. Did anyone else feel that his so-called humour was detrimental to the show?' he asked of the table at large, following his own thought processes for a moment.

'Well, we thought he was a huge show-off,' added Charlie Huggins, which really was the kettle calling the pot black.

'But we do need to attract a certain type of viewer,' explained Mairie McManus.

'And what sort of viewer is that?' asked the inspector.

'The more common sort, if you want to know. There are so many shows like ours these days that we needed a USP, if you know what I mean, and he was it.'

There were nods of reluctant agreement. 'But none of us enjoyed the way he talked about us on his voice-over,' said Peter Derby, draining his glass in one.

There were nods of agreement at this, and looks of disbelief as Falconer asked them to give their full names and contact details to his sergeant and make themselves available for questioning the next day. 'Maybe your production company will fund you to spend the night in Market Darley,' he finished, rising from the table. Leaving Carmichael behind to deal with their disapproval at this request, he went out into the cold, crisp air and listened to the children singing, plumes of breath rising like smoke from their young mouths, their voices sweet and innocent.

EIGHT

After the warmth of the pub, the cold outside was more noticeable, especially in the dark, and there would, no doubt, be a heavy frost tonight. It was turning into a cold winter and Falconer only hoped that they did not have the snowfall they had had the previous year. Unwelcome memories of the Great Dane, Mulligan, rose unbidden to his mind, and he gave a quick shudder inside his coat, which he then pulled tight around his neck.

Carmichael re-joined him and, as they were only a few minutes from the body, they headed in that direction and they found the PC there, guarding his crime scene and stamping his feet to keep warm. 'Doctor arriving in a minute, sir, and the SOCO team's on its way,' he informed his superior officer, and Falconer looked down at the earthly remains of Peter Potter-Porter.

'Any idea what happened?' he asked.

'Not much, but his coat is undone, and I had a quick peek under the sides. There seems to be a small amount of bleeding on his left front.'

'Possibly a stab wound, then,' replied Falconer, and looked, with relief, at the figure approaching from the other end of the road. Dr Philip Christmas – very seasonal name – was arriving and would soon relieve them of the need to hang around any longer in the icy temperatures. 'Oh, by the way, Constable, we were told there was an elderly woman in a wool shop present when the fatality took place. Do you have a note of her details?'

'Right here in my notebook, sir. I'll get them to you as soon as I get back to the station.'

'You could just give them to my sergeant now, and then we can get straight off and interview her after we've talked to the owner of the shop. On second thoughts, why don't you do that when the SOCO team arrives? We'll get straight off to this ... Miss Jarvis,' he concluded, squinting to read the handwriting in the PC's notebook, as he showed it to Carmichael.

Emily Jarvis' residence, for her, was quite a meandering bus ride away from the town centre but was, in fact, just a ten-minute drive in a car. As they pulled up at the door, they saw the bowed figure of a white-haired woman just inserting a key in the lock. They had nearly beaten her back home.

She turned, as they walked up the front path behind her, and looked closely with myopic eyes at the identification they offered, even breaking off and removing her spectacles carefully from her handbag to read them properly. 'Sorry about that,' she said, 'but we elderly people can't be too careful with people that come to our houses.'

'Quite right too, Miss Jarvis; couldn't agree more,' replied Falconer. 'We're calling about a death that occurred in the town earlier today – that of a man who was in the process of making a television programme, and the constable who stumbled across his body said that he found you in a wool shop nearby.'

'That nice young man in uniform?' she asked, with the merest twinkle in her eye. 'What a presentable lad he was. I didn't see anything, you know, and I heard nothing either. My ears are like my eyes – getting to the end of their useful life, now. And I'd walked round all morning hoping to catch a glimpse of my favourite antiques experts. Rub shoulders with celebrities before I fall off my perch, you know.'

Neither of the detectives knew what to say to this indication of mortality, so Falconer just put on his most polite smile and asked if they might come in for a few minutes. 'I'll just put my coat and bag in the under-stairs cupboard, if you don't mind,' she said, acting as she spoke, then directed them into her sitting room where she switched on a gas fire. 'That'll warm us up in a minute or two. Can I get you a cup of tea?'

'That's very kind of you, Miss Jarvis. We would be grateful, as it's so cold outside,' Falconer accepted on behalf of them both.

'Fancy me being so close to him and not even catching a glimpse,' twittered Miss Jarvis as she went out to the kitchen to boil the kettle.

Although Miss Jarvis offered them no information whatsoever on the death, they did chase the cold out of their bones, and hadn't chilled down too much when they got back to the station. The four 'celebrities' would be coming in to make formal statements the next day, and other officers would be seconded to visit the technical staff of the crews. Doc Christmas would, no doubt, carry out the post mortem as soon as possible, and they should be able to get this wrapped up very quickly – unless, of course, it was a disgruntled dealer who had previously been portrayed in a bad light, or a viewer who thought they had an axe to grind.

The death, now officially classed as suspicious, made the front page of the local paper, it was on the television news, and Doc Christmas confirmed that the man had been stabbed with an implement that was long and round, at about chest height, and puncturing the heart. To Falconer, this suggested quite a tall assailant, and he thought back to those he had met on the filming today, to see if he could recall anyone who was above average height.

Over the next few days, minute questioning of all those who could be involved produced no solid evidence. No one had seen anything or heard anything; in fact, each and every crew member who had done the filming had left with his own iPod plugged into his ears. It was finally agreed that none of the show's experts would have had time or opportunity to carry out the deed, and none of the other technical crews had been nearby.

After about ten days, it seemed that they would never solve the crime, the intense investigation was scaled down but the file was left open for any unexpected developments. These were unlikely now, though, in the proximity of the festive season, with everything closing down for the better part of a fortnight. The trail was well and truly cold, if not frozen, and there was nobody left to question.

Market Darley was, indeed, sorely in need of some CCTV cameras in its quiet back streets which, at the moment, it lacked.

NINE

On December 23rd, Emily Jarvis had her three bridge-playing friends round to lunch, so that they could all sit and watch the *Get One Over* Christmas edition that had featured Market Darley. She had got a better bottle of sherry in than she usually drank, and had bought some little cocktail biscuits for them to nibble as they watched. She was looking forward to it enormously.

The three visitors, Theodore Matthew, Camilla Smethurst, and Veronica Carlyle, were all crowded on the sofa next to each other while Emily Jarvis, their gracious hostess, sat in solitary state in the only armchair. The opening piece to camera came on, and Veronica squeaked like an hysterical mouse. 'Look! Look!' she said. 'They haven't used the piece to camera from that despicable man who got murdered. They must have recruited a new team member and got him to do it again.'

Emily sipped her sherry contentedly and thought, written out at last!

All eyes in the room were on the new figure, all ears concentrating, even though the volume was turned up, on his mellifluous and well-bred voice. 'Oh, how lovely!' sighed Emily. 'What a very good choice for a replacement.'

The new team member was neither sneering nor condescending about the programme's amateur experts, and spoke about the market town as a jewel of a place, the discovered objects as real finds, and the outcome of the auction as a terrific success. This was Johnathan Mull's fifth win of the season, and he donated the money raised by the auctions from the shows he had won to Help for Heroes, the charity for which the singers in Market Darley had been collecting.

Emily Jarvis poured them another glass of sherry as the closing credits ran, and a small smile of satisfaction settled over her face as she lifted her glass to her lips after turning off the television.

'Anyone for any more nibbles?' she asked after draining the measure, filling her glass for the third time, and raising it to a Merry Christmas and a very peaceful New Year, what with that terrible young man disposed of, or 'put down' as she preferred to look at it.

After all, it could be her last Christmas, and it was her own happiness that she needed to attend to. This was the perfect present. The knitting needle which she had wielded in sheer fury at Peter Potter-Porter was currently residing down the back of her armchair, suitably washed and rubbed over with a bleach solution to remove all trace of the event. She was fairly confident that she would pay no price for arranging things so much to her satisfaction and for her viewing pleasure and that, if the needle were ever found, it would be after her death, when it would just be another lost knitting needle ...

Harry Falconer watched the episode on its evening re-run, and it left him with the feeling that someone had, somehow, put something over on him, although he couldn't think what it could be, but it continued to nag at him for a while. The impending pantomime visit with the Carmichael family, however, soon took top priority in his uncomfortable thoughts.

Carmichael watched it with Kerry, and when the new narrator did his piece to camera, the gum bubble he was blowing burst, and had been so big, it stuck to the front of his hair. Kerry sighed, and leaned over her enormous bump to help him remove it and get him out of his predicament.

'I like this new narrator,' she commented, pulling sticky strands off his forehead.

'I don't,' replied Carmichael mournfully. 'He's not half as funny as the last one.'

THE END

Death of a Pantomime Cow

The town has recently opened it's new theatre and the Town's Women's Guild is to present it's first live performances the pantomime 'Jack and the Beanstalk' - over Christmas.

DI Harry Falconer has managed to duck two days spent over the festive season in the Carmichael household by pleading other commitments, but treating the whole family, himself included, to tickets to the first performance, on Boxing Day.

But he seems to be able to do nothing straight forward, and when tragedy strikes in the very first Act, he is catapulted back into his professional role with a vengeance: and on a Bank Holiday, too.

Christmas Eve – one thirty in the morning

All the participants in the forthcoming tale were asleep, all excitement and anticipation that had kept this state at bay, now calmed by regular breathing and bright, hopeful dreams of the morrow.

But, no, one figure is still not abed. There is one still up, and in the Carsfold Community Theatre. Incongruously dressed in the costume of a pantomime cow, she has deserted her partner so late, and made her way to this location, for a little extra rehearsal for one of her parts, to be premiered on Boxing Day. Kate Kerridge did many things fanatically, and her partner, realising this, had long since made his way to bed, and thus to sleep, unwilling to wait up for her return, which he expected to be very late indeed.

Outside, the night was crisp, with frost twinkling in the moonlight, turning each leaf and blade of glass into a precious jewel which could never be replicated by human hands. It was a peaceful night, cold but beautiful. In fact, all was calm, all was bright.

The sound of sleigh bells was not yet discernible, and there were no reindeer in sight up above, but it would not be long before there was plenty of creeping about, accompanied by the furtive stuffing of stockings and pillow cases, to keep the legend alive for yet another year.

25th December

33 Letsby Avenue, Market Darley

Detective Inspector Harry Falconer placed his knife and fork down side-by-side, perfectly parallel on his plate, and belched very discreetly, a hand covering his mouth for the sake of manners, even though his only company was his five cats. Not only had he managed not to be on duty over the two most important days of Christmas, but he had managed to arrange things so that he did not have to drag himself to someone else's house, someone else's celebrations, and fit in with whatever family traditions they wanted to re-enact, eating up his precious free time with pastimes that meant nothing to him.

Following a kind-hearted and well-meant invitation to join he and his kin for the two days of celebrations, he had managed to bamboozle his soft-hearted DS, Carmichael, by explaining how his mother had invited him to spend a family Christmas with her and his father, as it had been some time since he had managed to be with them at this time of year. *And* he had managed to fool his mother by explaining to her how much his DS wanted his boss to spend a family yuletide with his young family, with all the trappings of stockings and under-tree presents, crackers and paper hats that this involved.

In fact, both invitations had been issued, their only real function being as a tool to turn down the other, and he had eventually achieved what he had long aimed for – a quiet Christmas Day *on his own*.

In celebration of this unexpected victory, he raised his wine glass and drank a toast to the deliciousness of solitude when properly planned and executed. He remembered the chaos that had been Christmas the previous year, which was spent actually staying in the Carmichael household as a hostage of the fearsome weather, rather than making the two planned, far briefer, daily visits.

Earlier, Falconer had stuffed two guinea fowl with apricots and wild rice, and roasted them with mouth-sized pieces of parsnip, carrot, and potato. These, with a few mange tout and his favourite homemade bread sauce, had made a feast fit for a king, and a rather good lunch for the cats as well, who were developing quite sophisticated tastes, with his particular left-overs for titbits of an evening.

His stomach pleasantly full, he eyed up his sofa with longing. A stretch-out and nap on that would be most welcome, with no friends, relatives, or their children to whom he must be polite and social. He could be as lazy and selfish as he liked, with no one at all to criticise him or look askance at his lack of communication or mingling.

As he got himself comfortable to doze off, he was aware of a number of warm, furry bodies sliding themselves on to the sofa beside, and even on top, of him, and he smiled in gratitude that he had this undemanding company which always delighted him. Some had commented that five cats were far too many for one household with but a single occupant, but he couldn't disagree more. What could be pleasanter than stretching oneself out under a furry eiderdown that purred its pleasure and contentment, as it simultaneously lulled one off to sleep?

His descent into the arms of Morpheus was momentarily disturbed by what he had planned for the next day, but he did not allow it to delay him long.

The next day he would be seeing his festively-enthused DS, for part of his bribing Carmichael to accept that he and his brood could survive the twenty-fifth without his, Falconer's, company, had been to declare that he had purchased tickets for them all to the pantomime that was being performed in Carsfold. Its premiere of three performances was scheduled for Boxing Day, and that he would be accompanying the Carmichael clan as it was his seasonal treat.

Carmichael was, as expected, utterly enchanted with the idea, as two years earlier he and his wife, Kerry, had had a pantomime-themed wedding on New Year's Eve. Not only would it bring back a plethora of happy memories, it would also give him and his family the opportunity to spend some quality time with Falconer, who had become one of their favourite people, much to the inspector's surprise.

In fact, he was now officially godfather to all three Carmichael children: Dean and Kyle from Kerry's first marriage and whom Carmichael had officially adopted after he had married their mother, and Harriet, very much the baby of the three, whom Falconer had actually delivered safely into this world during the period of severe weather between Christmas and New Year the year before.

It had been a rash act to make the ticket purchases, but he reasoned that if he made this generous gesture, not only would he give the family a treat they might not normally have found easy to afford, but if he could have met them at the theatre, and driven home in his own car afterwards, without going to Castle Farthing for a home visit, he would have won. He could have appeared an open-handed benefactor without having to sacrifice too much of his precious down time on his own.

Unfortunately, his own inability to say 'no,' especially where the Carmichaels were concerned, had interfered with the arrangements, and he had found himself agreeing to call at Jasmine Cottage for them so that they could drive in tandem to the theatre, thus negating the necessity of searching for each other amongst the crowds of other ticket-holders.

He had also found himself agreeing to follow them home again after the performance, for a glass of seasonal sherry to toast the occasion. What a weak-willed fool he had proved! Still, nothing could be as bad as last year had proved to be. [1]

Gently, and in a refined manner, his polite snores blended perfectly with the chorus of purrs which rose from the sofa, in a miasma of contentment.

Carsfold Community Theatre – the auditorium

'I don't see why you had to schedule a ruddy run-through on Christmas afternoon. That's a bit over-the-top, even for you, Kate,' moaned Dani Greenaway, who was officially 'front-of-house' and, technically, not needed at all, on today of all days.

The auditorium of the Carsfold Community Theatre echoed with complaints, all directed at the director of the pantomime which would have its premiere performance the next day, and some about matters that had nothing whatsoever to do with the production.

'I've got my old mum over and we've had to leave her on her own,' grumbled Wendy Wainwright, who was scheduled to play the self-playing harp belonging to the giant in 'Jack and the Beanstalk.' Her main problem was that her teenaged son, Martin, was cast as the goose that laid the golden eggs, and her husband, Peter, a very tall man, was the giant.

'Thoughtless bitch never gives a thought for those imprisoned by her bloody hedge,' piped up a voice, changing the subject completely. 'You can barely see your hand in front of your face in my conservatory on dull days like today.'

'Never even offered a penny towards a new wing mirror, when it was clearly her fault,' chimed in another, with another complaint against the same individual.

Other voices muttered an even wider range of grudges, all apparently aimed at the pantomime's director, Kate Kerridge. And they had not even been granted the boon of having the heating on today, it being an official Bank Holiday, and the theatre not being officially open.

'If you'd all quit whining you could be home in no time. It's only a quick run-through to make sure there aren't any lurking Pooh-traps for us tomorrow,' bellowed Kate Kerridge, in a voice that would have done justice to the giant. She was the script-writer, director, casting, and player of two parts: the giant's wife, and Daisy the Pantomime Cow – this latter on her own, she might emphasize, for she was also the creator of the device that allowed her to do this without another person lodged up her backside. Being personally responsible for so many roles in the production, she was feeling enraged at such lack of enthusiasm on the part of the other members of the group.

When the idea of using the newly opened community theatre to put on a pantomime had first been mooted in the first September meeting of the Carsfold Women's Guild, there had been nothing but unbridled enthusiasm. In fact, so carried away were the members by the idea of appearing on stage in public that no one seemed to notice that the person who had suggested it – Kate Kerridge – had already written a script with such a run of performances in mind. They should have known better.

Slowly, Kate had revealed herself to be a control freak and a slave-driver, something that really should have been suspected beforehand by the other members, given the way she had joined the guild, and then taken over as both chairwoman and secretary, all within six months.

Less than twenty, however, made up the final team. The Wainwrights took three parts and Kate herself took two. This left only the eponymous Jack – Jennifer Bray, Kate's next-door neighbour and best friend at the time had taken on that role – and the bean seller, Simon Blackwood. All the other members were awarded positions on the technical team, thus Gemma Blackwood was given the role of prompt and, as has already been mentioned, persuaded to bring in her husband Simon for the part of bean seller – he could prove so useful if there were any hiccoughs in scene-shifting, being well-muscled and fit – and Christine Turner given lighting and sound (music, mainly).

Candy Taylor was, to her delight, asked to take responsibility for wardrobe, and half a dozen of the younger members were designated dancers in non-speaking parts for the market scene (when Jack goes off to sell Daisy) and for the general rejoicing when the beanstalk falls and the giant is killed.

The novelty of the idea of putting on a new pantomime went a long way to assuage the doubts of those who felt they had been dealt a bad hand, and an uneasy truce reigned until the beginning of December, when real life starts to take up so much more of one's otherwise free time. There are the carol concerts and nativity plays in which children or grandchildren are appearing, and which simply must be attended; the cards to write; the presents to shop for, wrap, and dispatch; the Christmas markets to visit and the extra catering to be planned. Extra rehearsals were just out of the question.

And yet, here they were, on Christmas Day afternoon, in the theatre, ordered, obedient little drones for General Kerridge! Why? How?

Jasmine Cottage, Castle Farthing

It would be too easy – and far too cheesy – to compare the Carmichael household with the Cratchits making merry on Christmas Day. Far better to say that their celebrations and outrageous sense of fun far outshone anything that the fictional Dickensian clerk, Bob, could have dreamt up or devised for his own household.

The ceiling was a sea of tinsel and glittering garlands, traversing it length and width with colourful abandon. Holly decorated the top of each picture frame on the walls, and a bunch of real mistletoe hung in the doorway to the kitchen, and had been the scene of many an ambush on Kerry by her husband.

Seasonal greeting cards hung down the walls in large loops from string which was attached to this uppermost perimeter, and gave the impression, almost, of Christmas wallpaper, and everything that could have fairy lights strewn round it boasted a string of twinkling colours, in the form of little lanterns, or icicles, or any other shape that could be reproduced in plastic and wired up in multiples.

The double living area with the fireplace in the middle was awash with seasonally decorated paper, casually discarded as it had been enthusiastically ripped from around presents. Bows and ribbon also casually festooned the furniture, hanging from chair-backs and draping from armchairs like exotic decorations devised by a mad interior designer.

Tins of sweets and boxes of chocolates lay open all over the room, proving that the inhabitants of this dwelling had Catholic tastes in sweetmeats. They also shared a boisterous nature, as evidenced by the amount of horseplay that was currently taking place within this large living space, with the participation of adults, children, and animals, the largest of which was a huge Great Dane who was staying for two days while his owners visited their daughter, who did not have sufficient living space to cope with such a large quadruped.

The quadruped in question, Mulligan, was having the time of his life, romping as gently as he could with the home dogs, Mistress Fang – Chihuahua – and Mr Knuckles – a Yorkshire terrier. Dean and Kyle, the sons of the household from their mother's first marriage, climbed on to the huge dog's back and their adoptive father, 'Davey' Carmichael, joined them all on the floor to sort out and pull apart the jumble of bodies. Even baby Harriet, just approaching her first birthday, crawled a little closer to the action and reached out to pull one of Mulligan's vast ears.

The noise was indescribable – but I shall do my best.

The miniature canines yipped with excitement, while the monstrous dog whined with pleasure. The two boys whooped with joy, while little Harriet burbled, 'Bababbaba,' in her approval of the uproar. Carols spilled from the CD player, overlaying everything else with a blanket of rich harmony.

A voice broke into this thoroughly good-natured chaos. 'Come on, you guys! We haven't even finished opening all the presents yet, and I say that all this Christmas paper has to be in black bags before we put even more all over the place.' As usual, it was Kerry Carmichael who was trying to produce order out of mayhem, and get their day back on schedule.

'First one with a full bag gets a sausage roll, and they're still warm; just out of the oven.' That created some movement – blatant blackmail always worked – and three male bodies suddenly thrust themselves upright, and disappeared into the kitchen in search of the aforementioned receptacles, gluttony being an obligatory part of today's proceedings. Thus, they left the three dogs and baby Harriet looking most surprised at this sudden desertion and the abandonment of their game, and the lady of the household triumphantly confident that the mess was not going to get out of hand after all.

As the three willing volunteers tore round the room, in a contest to see who could collect the most, the fastest, Kyle tried a joke to enliven the proceedings. 'Why are pirates called pirates?' he asked, with a cheeky grin.

'Don't know,' admitted his stepfather, as his brother shook his head.

'Because they "arrr",' replied the little comedian.

Daddy Davey stopped his bending and bag-stuffing, his face a mask of puzzlement, until Dean provided him with enlightenment. 'You're right!' he exclaimed suddenly. 'They do, don't they?'

26th December – morning
Carsfold Community Theatre

'I can't believe you got us in at nine o'clock for an extra run through, only to find out that it was Daisy's dance you wanted to spend most time on.'

'Quite right, Kate! You didn't really need any of us for that. That's just you.'

'Jack and the bean seller are on stage at the same time,' Kate Kerridge defended herself, indignantly.

'But they're just pretending to have a conversation. They're not actually a part of the action. That's all Daisy.'

'But I need opinions on how it looks from all angles. This is Daisy's big scene and it's very important.'

'This is *your* big scene, you mean. It's nothing to do with Daisy. You're just hoping that there's someone in for one of the three performances from the Market Darley AmDram Society who'll decide that they must have you amongst their ranks.'

'The thought never crossed my mind!' retorted Kate vehemently, but she couldn't stop the blush that rose up her cheeks and suffused her forehead. 'Anyway, the least you can do is to give me an opinion on it, now that you're all here. It won't take more than five minutes. I'll start right now.'

With grim determination, Kate Kerridge slipped efficiently into the one-person pantomime cow costume of her own devising. This had been essential, as she wanted the comedy dance routine of the cow's for herself, but didn't really want another actor huddled behind her, positioned just at her bottom. In any case, there had not been an overwhelming number of the Guild members who had volunteered to take a part in that particular position.

Those with technical roles had, in fairness, offered to cover for the back end of the cow, but Kate had stuck to her guns (and her distaste at the thought of someone's nose up her bottom) and had insisted that their presence, at the ready and in their particular roles at all times, was essential.

She had been quite inventive, really, using an old trolley for the back legs and feet. Once the stitching on the hooves had been undone to make holes for the wheels, the trolley could be easily pulled along behind one, with the addition of shafts. It only took a huge wad of padding, giving the body bulk, to complete the illusion of a fully-populated pantomime cow – but one that could do a whole range of tricks not available to one that actually had two people inside it.

Kate's choreography for Daisy – another little task she had undertaken herself – featured rather a lot of swinging round a metal lamp post that stood centrally at the back of the stage, and made an ideal prop for making the most of the cow's madcap capers. It should certainly get her noticed, and this *had* been one of her central motives for taking the part herself and writing the scene. She had ambitions, after all. Market Darley ADS was her eventual ambition, but she wanted to audition with a triumph under her belt and, surely, at least one of its members would be present at one of their three performances, to report back on how good she was?

And she had the part of the giant's wife with which to make an impression as herself! By hook or by crook she'd get herself noticed this Christmastide.

And how right she was in her prediction.

'I'm going home. I spent enough time here on Christmas Day.'

'Me too! Selfish bitch, calling us all out just to watch her caper around like a fool, in that damned silly costume of hers.'

'It makes me cross just to look at her, when I think how she acted with *my* Bob; well he was, at the time. Although not for long, once she got her claws into him.'

'Just snatched it out of my hands, she did, and said all was fair in the sales. I notice she had it on yesterday, flaunting it in front of me as if it were only last week it happened, and not nigh on a year ago. Well, I shan't forget. That should have been mine, by rights.'

Cutting through all this bad feeling and dislike, a voice as sharp as a razor sounded. 'Can someone tell Wardrobe I've ripped the giant's wife's frock? I forgot to mention it earlier.' That was typical of Kate; always trying to have the last word.

The rumbling of discontent and resentment continued, as the rest of the cast slunk sulkily out of the theatre and headed for their various homes, knowing that they would have to return to the building again that afternoon for their first performance.

Kate capered on in her ridiculous costume, totally unaffected, her head full of dreams of when she had become a leading light in the Market Darley ADS.

Jasmine Cottage, Castle Farthing

Boxing Day morning in Jasmine Cottage was proving to be as chaotic as Christmas Day had been, with new toys, games, and books scattered everywhere, and sweets left open, perilously attractive to the three doggy residents, who were on the prowl, as usual, for any treats available.

Two loops of Christmas cards had defied the piece of tape that separated them, and now dropped as one large loop, hanging over three wall-mounted advent calendars, their doors now all opened.

A tinsel garland, its tape similarly defeated from what was probably the sheer heat from so many enthusiastic residents, draped itself across the crib scene with which Kerry had decorated the sideboard. It had survived since her childhood, and she could not imagine Christmas without it being on display.

The family had breakfasted that morning, on eggs from their own chickens. These birds, along with their wooden and wire mesh house, had been a present from Carmichael to the whole family the previous December, and they had proved a popular addition to the household, providing not only food but much entertainment at their various antics.

That meal now cleared away, Kerry was like a whirling dervish, collecting up chocolate bars, closing packets, boxes of chocolates, and selection boxes, for she suspected that Mulligan was not beyond eating sweetmeats which were still inside their foil and paper wrappers.

Daddy Davey lay, a huge landslide of an obstruction, in the middle of the floor, putting together the rather lavish train set that his stepsons had received the day before from Uncle Harry. He may be the grown-up male in the household, but he was delighted with his superior's generosity and imagination, and planned to set up the whole layout eventually, in a dead space on the landing where the two originally separate cottages were now somewhat imperfectly joined.

How very perceptive of the inspector. If Carmichael had had to guess at what Falconer would buy his sons as a Christmas gift, he would have had a stab at book tokens or something similarly dry, but this choice of a rather super-duper train set had put him up several more notches in Carmichael's estimation. The man did have vision and imagination after all.

And they were all going to the pantomime this afternoon: he could hardly wait. How he loved the atmosphere, the costumes, the cheesy audience calls – 'He's behind you!' He must get their wedding photos out when he'd got this model railway together, and have another look at the imaginative costumes in which their guests had attended the occasion.

Kerry was now in the kitchen preparing the traditional meal of cold meats, mashed potatoes, pickles, and salad, and singing while she worked. Everyone in the household was in a sunny mood.

33 Letsby Avenue, Market Darley

Harry Falconer also awoke in cheerful form, after his deliciously peaceful day the day before, but it wasn't long before memory returned, and he recalled that he would have to make two visits to the Carmichael household before the day was out, although he could, at least, make the first one very short by turning up dead on time, meaning that he would not have any chance to linger.

He breakfasted off Christmas cake and mince pies, feeling like a naughty boy who had raided the pantry as he did so, and turned on the television; an unheard of action at this address during the daytime. It was a time of year that most people felt should belong to children, therefore he'd act like one, and look for some cartoons to watch.

He'd made the necessary call to his parents the day before, getting it over with early, and hinting that he needed to do so at such an hour, as Carmichael and family would be eagerly awaiting his arrival. He didn't lie outright; merely became a mite economical with the truth and didn't quiet tell all of it, so that he could give the right impression without giving offence at not wanting to spend the day with them.

He envisioned a lazy morning ahead of him, followed by a scratch lunch of cold meat and salad sandwiches, before he went off for what he hoped was not threatening to turn into a regular yuletide penance with his DS and family.

Carsfold Community Theatre – stage and backstage

The stage and backstage areas of the theatre were buzzing with activity, as both performing and technical staff hurried about their appointed duties.

Dani Greenaway was in the foyer welcoming the earliest arrivals for the audience, encouraging them to purchase programmes and, maybe, a little something from the refreshments' table, currently being (wo)manned by Gemma Blackwood who, as prompt, was only needed during the actual performances, when the concession would not be open. This had been a late appointment, as Kate Kerridge had completely forgotten that a fair amount of money could be made towards the cost of putting on the production from products purchased from this little money-spinner.

Gemma took her press-ganging well, outwardly, but inwardly seethed at such an incompetent omission, and the loss of the little bit of time she had free at the interval, as she would need to be present in the 'prompt' position for the whole of every performance.

Performers were all earnestly applying their stage make-up and putting on costumes, leaving the technical staff to help in setting the first scene, before applying themselves to their own particular sphere of expertise.

It was Christine Turner who jumped ship first, claiming that her responsibility, not only for the lighting, but for the sound –

especially for the music – meant she would have to spend as much time as possible checking her cues and getting her equipment set up.

Kate Kerridge helped no one. She was far too busy checking over Daisy's costume, making sure that the shafts were securely attached to the trolley, and that the wheels protruded sufficiently to allow them to revolve, so that she could perform her trickier comedy moves while wearing it. The dance routine for the pantomime cow meant so much more to her than any of the others could ever fully realise.

In the auditorium of the theatre, with the arrival of the first members of the audience, a pleasant buzz of excited conversation was discernible, and the atmosphere of live theatre began to build nicely, and would continue to as the place filled, for the tickets for all three shows were a sell-out. This was, after all, the first year of the theatre's existence, and the first time anyone had attempted to offer Carsfold its own pantomime in living memory, even though it boasted a few suitable halls within its borders.

26th December – afternoon
Jasmine Cottage, Castle Farthing

Pulling up outside the double residence, Harry Falconer shuddered as he was suddenly drenched in memories from the previous year, some of the embarrassing moments he had undergone under that thatched roof coming back to him vividly, in flashback – less serious than shellshock, but 'Carmichaelshock', all the same. Well, all he had to do now was get the family out and into the battered old Skoda that Carmichael still had the brass neck to drive about in, and they'd be on their way to the performance, then all he'd have to steel himself for was the glass of sherry on the way home.

His ring of the doorbell caused quite a ruckus: dogs yipped and barked and children crowed with delight at the announcement of the arrival of their beloved godfather, and Carmichael himself opened the door to their honoured guest.

It was Mulligan who managed to fight his way to the front of the greeting queue, having heard the voice of his best mate – with whom he had shared a bed during the arctic conditions of the previous year – and feeling the irresistible urge to be the first to say hello again, after such a long absence.

Two giant paws met round the back of the inspector's neck, and an enormous pink tongue, extremely rough in texture, obscured his vision, as the weight of the canine body leaning against him drove him down to the doormat. There he subsided in submission, knowing that when Mulligan had business with you, you didn't even consider thwarting him.

'Get off, yer great lump!' Carmichael's voice ordered, in vain. 'Let the poor man get to his feet.'

When Mulligan claimed something for his very own special possession, it took some exceedingly persistent persuasion to get him to give up ownership, and thus it proved with Falconer. It was a good ten minutes before they had the inspector sat on the settee, a hot, clean flannel at his face, and a hand mirror available, so that he could straighten his tie, collar, and hair.

'Sorry about that, sir,' apologised his DS. 'I forgot to mention that he was staying over the Bank Holidays, and he just sort of got away from me when the doorbell rang. Are you all right?'

'Just about. My face seems to have had a good scour, at any rate.' Falconer was feeling fatalistic about his unexpected meeting with the hound, and resigned to the fact that the vast heap of canine flesh would no doubt attempt to sit on his lap when he returned later for his Christmas drink. He was glad that he had not worn his best trousers, putting on some slightly older ones in anticipation of drips of ice-cream and other snacking disasters in the company of his godchildren.

'Come on, Carmichaels! Get yourselves in good order, or we'll be late and miss the start,' he called, sounding in very good spirits, but actually putting on an act worthy of the best that Market Darley ADS could offer, at the cheering thought that, in a few short hours, his ordeal with this crew would be over and done with for another year – bar unexpected invitations to birthday parties and picnics.

As he recovered from the shock of this unexpectedly enthusiastic greeting, he noticed, with a renewed sense of surprise, that his sergeant was wearing an outfit that looked, not only smart, but distinctly fashionable. He could only conclude that Carmichael's wife bought some of his clothes and, as today was a special day, Kerry had left out his garments for him, taking personal responsibility for his appearance at such an important event. Hurriedly, he closed his gaping mouth, before anyone could notice, and discern his thoughts.

All the time Carmichael had been a member of the CID department, he had earned a reputation for wearing the most outrageous clothes, and here he was, dressed like a real grown-up. It was something that rarely happened, and Falconer just sat back and appreciated the fact that, for once, when they were out together in public, the sergeant would not be a magnet for all eyes, barely able to believe what they were seeing.

Carsfold Community Theatre

Cars safely stowed in the car park, taking almost the last two spaces, the mass of Carmichaels plus one Falconer now stood at the refreshments table in the foyer, choosing various treats with which to enhance their enjoyment of the afternoon's performance.

Chocolate, toffees, popcorn, and violently-coloured fizzy drinks figured large in their choices, as they deliberated each individual purchase with the utmost care and deep consideration. They rarely went out *en famille* like this – as in with paid-for tickets – and such things were of the utmost importance to the two boys.

The auditorium was in the same condition as the car park; almost full to bursting point – and the noise level was high, as a host of children, already excited by the season of the year and all the presents of the day before, absorbed the excitement of a live performance of a pantomime in a real theatre.

When Falconer tipped down his seat as he took it, he had a brief flashback to the last time he had attended the opera; a provincial performance only, but not vastly inferior because of that. Davey Carmichael landed in his seat with a 'thunk', remembering with a whiff of nostalgia the one time he had been taken to a pantomime when he was a child in Market Darley, by his parents, who must have been going through a particularly flush period at the time.

Kerry had more pragmatic things to think about, as she tried to make herself comfortable. Baby Harriet had not had to have a separate ticket, being less than one year old, and would, therefore be spending the whole performance seated on her mother's lap. The latter only hoped that the little madam would take the opportunity to have an after luncheon nap for the sake of digestion.

Noise rarely disturbed her; she would sleep through anything, so the presence of several hundred strangers did not worry her at all, and the thought of her squirming and babbling away for the whole of the pantomime was a nightmare she didn't even want to contemplate.

Suddenly, loud recorded music started to issue from large speakers placed each side of the stage, and a figure in costume walked out in front of the curtain, raising its hands for silence, as the music faded. It was, of course, Kate Kerridge in her everyday clothes, from which she planned to do a quick change into Daisy's costume before the curtains rose on the first scene. She really trusted no one to do anything she could not do herself.

'Good afternoon, ladies and gentlemen, boys and girls. Have you all come here to have a good time?'

'Yes!' replied a loud unison voice, proving that the audience was already in pantomime mood.

'Do you all want to see the story of Jack and the Beanstalk?'

'Yes!'

'Well, you must remember to cheer when Jack comes on stage, and boo when the Giant appears. Let's just practise that.'

At the right side of the stage, Wendy Bray, in costume, made herself visible.

'Why, here's Jack now!' announced Kate, raising her hands to encourage the loud cheer that was already emanating from the auditorium.

Jack ducked back out of sight, and Peter Wainwright, also in costume and on the stilts, his proficiency on which was paramount in his being cast in this particular part, tottered out into view. Kate hardly had time to raise her hands at his appearance, as the booing from the audience was almost deafening.

Jack and the giant bobbed in and out of view one more time, to wind up the audience into a suitably enthusiastic mood, the music began, once more, to issue from the speakers, Kate vacated the platform, and the curtains began to move apart. The pantomime had begun.

Carsfold Community Theatre – out front

Falconer had been given what, in the eyes of the parents Carmichael, was the position of honour – between Dean and Kyle who were, as the first scene played out, goggling at the stage while juggling large bags of toffee popcorn and rather unstable plastic containers of a violently orange-coloured drink. The inspector could barely take his eyes off these phenomena long enough even to glance at the action on stage.

The story had reached the part where Jack has been sent off to market to sell Daisy the cow, but has had no luck so far in this enterprise – cue dancing girls for lively market scene. The eponymous star was now on the lonely road home at dusk, where the scene was lit by a single old-fashioned metal street lamp. On his way, he had met a strange man who was earnestly trying to do a deal with him in a corner of the stage, while Daisy's leash slipped out of his hand, and the animal wandered off on her own.

This was Kate's cue for her comedy dance routine, and little did she know how many of the cast and crew were crossing their fingers that she fell flat on her face. She had a particularly thick skin, and so had no inkling whatsoever just how unpopular she was. Off she trotted, trolley wheels wagging behind her, then she broke into a little skipping step while tossing her head, and titters began to rise from the audience. She was off.

Her finest and funniest bit was doing the can-can using the street lamp as a prop for her hands, slipped out of the costume for the express purpose of gaining extra balance on the lamp, but completely unseen by the members of the audience. She would end this section by grasping extra hard and jumping in the air, pushing out both legs to the side in a sort of off-the-ground front splits.

The introduction had gone well, her quick change, smoothly, so it was with supreme confidence that she approached the street lamp, the beginnings of laughter echoing triumphantly in her ears.

There! I knew it! thought Falconer. As a tremendous roar had started in the audience, there had been a significant spasm of movement from both boys, and one had tipped his day-glo orange drink over Uncle Harry's trousers as the other showered a sticky stream of popcorn over his legs.

'Careful!' he shouted, reaching for his handkerchief with one hand and brushing off toffee popcorn with the other, before realising that something untoward must have happened, as the whole audience, and not just Dean and Kyle, seemed to be in uproar. Whatever could have happened to cause such a reaction?

A microphone-enhanced voiced requested that, if there was a doctor in the house, would he or she please come to the stage area, as the curtains chugged unevenly closed, and a figure, instantly recognisable as Dr Philip Christmas, fought its way to an aisle, three rows in front.

Falconer and Carmichael also rose to their feet and began to make their way forwards. If what had happened wasn't criminal, the pantomime crew might still need some help in mustering the audience out of the hall and to their cars, if the performance couldn't continue. And re-enforcements they could also summon, should that be necessary.

After a plea to stay in their seats until more information was available, the members of the audience were well behaved, and the two detectives were only a few paces behind Philip Christmas, the area's forensic medical examiner, as they mounted the stage to hear more than one voice warning, 'Don't even try to touch her until we're absolutely sure the supply's disconnected.'

The scene that confronted them was bizarre. The cast stood in a mesmerised semi-circle around the prone figure of Daisy the Pantomime Cow, the body of which still twitched, and gave off a faint humming noise. From the front of the costume two all-too-human hands protruded, clutched tightly round the metal shaft of the lamp post, which was the obvious source of the trouble.

'Power's off,' a voice called from backstage, and the cow's body stilled in the sudden silence.

'Something must have gone wrong with the electrics. That thing must have been live,' stated a figure dressed as a human-sized goose.

'I never did anything wrong. Don't look at me. I was meticulous with the wiring,' defended a female figure identified as Christine Turner, responsible for lighting and sound and therefore, by default, for wiring, her hands on her hips and a defiant expression on her face. 'If anything was wrong with that lamp post, it was done maliciously.'

'No one's accusing you of anything, Chrissie,' soothed a woman dressed, bizarrely, as a harp.

Simultaneously, Doc Christmas leaned over to whisper in Falconer's ear. 'Stella and I brought the nieces and nephews to give their parents a bit of a break. Some break this is turning out to be for us, eh?'

'I've treated Carmichael's family to tickets,' replied Falconer, in explanation, before continuing, 'Don't you think we ought to identify ourselves, so that we can take over and create some sort of order out of this situation?'

Taking this cue, the doctor cleared his throat and identified himself as a medical man, asking the cast and crew to stand back so that he could examine the victim of the accident. He also took the opportunity to introduce the two representatives of Market Darley CID, suggesting that they take over the organisation of the rest of the proceedings, so that they ran as smoothly as possible, given the tragic circumstances.

Crouching by the costume of the cow, he hauled off the head half and examined its recent occupant, without positive result, for a pulse. 'No, definitely dead,' he confirmed, so that no one should foster false hope for the fate of the faux farm animal. 'We'll need some technical support to examine this lamp post prop,' he advised, and looked pointedly at the inspector, whom he expected, now, to take over.

'OK, everyone, I shall inform the authorities and arrange for the – er – body to be taken away. If you have a dressing room you could all assemble in backstage, I shall have to deal with the dispersal of the audience, first. All those people can't just be left out there without information, and the show, obviously, can't go on.

'Is there someone here who can give them notice of how to apply for refunds? We may end up with a stampede on our hands, if we don't handle this diplomatically.'

Dani Greenaway, representing front of house, moved in the opposite direction to the Guild members heading for the dressing room, and presented herself in front of the inspector with a quick query. 'Kate Kerridge, who was the cow,' – in more ways than one, she thought – 'was also secretary and chairwoman of the Carsfold Women's Guild. I obviously can't give *her* name as the person to contact. Should I use the name of the deputy chairwoman?'

'Absolutely!' agreed Falconer. 'Who is the deputy chairwoman, by the way?' A name would, at least, give him a starting point.

'Selina Slater. Oh! She was doing props!' She added this last as if it were a total surprise to her, and not a nice one at that. 'Not that I'm implying anything by that statement.'

'Of course not. Shall we be off to the other side of the curtain to break the bad news to the masses?' he asked, a sick smile on his face, at his anticipation of the reaction of so many people to the information that the party was over, and they all had to go home without being entertained.

Carsfold Community Theatre – in the seating area

Stella Christmas, with her years of experience as a doctor's wife, realised almost straight away that she would be driving their nieces and nephews home unsatisfied, and that Philip would get home as best as he could, when he had finished what it was his duty to do. She took the announcements by Dani Greenaway and Inspector Falconer, whom she knew, philosophically, and organised the putting on again of hats, coats, scarves, and gloves in order to face the elements outside the theatre once again.

Kerry Carmichael was also gaining in the experience of being married to someone in public service, and realised that it was up to her to get the children back to Castle Farthing, as her husband would obviously be seriously delayed. She had no doubts that Falconer would make sure that Davey got home safe and sound, and immediately set her mind to devising suitable substitute bribes for what should have been an afternoon of live theatre, as she fitted a sleeping Harriet back into the pushchair she had just unfolded in the aisle.

They had brought the really ancient one with them – the one that folded down almost as small as an umbrella – so that the aisle next to her seat would not be blocked by the bulk of the everyday vehicle. They really knew how to design things for practicality and convenience in the seventies, she thought.

It was lucky that her first husband had worked in a garage, and that she had learnt to drive during her years with Mike. At least she'd be able to get them all back home this afternoon and, once they could afford a second vehicle, you wouldn't see her for dust.

Kerry had plans.

Stella Christmas, three rows in front, turned round in her row of seats to assist with the sleeve of a coat, caught Kerry's eye, and waved at her, giving her a rueful smile of understanding. They were both in the same boat, after all.

Leaning over the intervening rows which had already been vacated, Stella called out, 'Why don't you all come back to ours for a couple of hours? The kids are about the same age, and it might take the sting out of the tail of the show being cancelled, having someone different to play with.'

'Great idea!' Kerry agreed. She didn't know the doctor's wife well, but this was an ideal opportunity, not only to get to know her better, but to divert the boys' disappointment using the novelty of making new friends in new surroundings. 'I'll follow your car, if you'll point it out to me in the car park.' There! It looked like the afternoon was sorted!

Carsfold Community Theatre – backstage

The hubbub from the small group of Women's Guild members (and a few partners) seemed to make more noise than the whole of the audience, or maybe it was just a trick of the acoustics of the large communal dressing room, and Falconer had to shout to make himself heard.

It was just him and Carmichael now, Doc Christmas having stayed with the body until support arrived. The audience had had to be allowed to disperse, as it seemed impossible that, if there had been any monkey business with the wiring, it could have been carried out by anyone seated that far away. An electrician was expected at any minute, and his diagnosis of the problem would determine whether what had happened this afternoon would be treated as just a tragic accident, or as cold-blooded murder.

As there would need to be witnesses called at the inquest, the two detectives passed the wait for the technician by making a note of each person's name and address, and their connection with the pantomime; information that would prove very useful when they came to question them, should that prove necessary later.

This task just completed, a man in overalls arrived and asked to be shown to the power supply, drawing all attention to him, and heading for the fuse box and the lamp post like the pied piper of Hamelin, with the whole company in his wake.

Carmichael took the opportunity of a couple of minutes of peace and quiet to ask Falconer which way his thoughts were leaning. His reply was not unexpected. 'I've heard a lot of negative comments flying round in the last couple of minutes about this Kerridge woman who's died, which has driven my thoughts to a definite conclusion. To paraphrase, "Fee-fi-fo-fum, I smell the blood of a murderous one."'

'Oh, sir!' groaned Carmichael.

'I'm sorry, Sergeant. Sometimes execrable jokes are just thrust upon one.'

Carsfold Community Theatre – still backstage

As expected, Mr Electric Overalls returned with a concerned expression on his face, to inform them that the wiring of the metal lamp post had been tampered with, and the prop turned into a death trap: so it was definitely a case of murder they were dealing with, unfortunately. And on Boxing Day, too – whatever had happened to peace and goodwill to all men? There was neither peace nor goodwill in electrocuting someone as they entertained children in a pantomime.

'You take the two families, the Wainwrights and the Blackwoods,' suggested Falconer to the waiting Carmichael, 'and I'll take all the stray names. The dancers we'll split between us. We'll maybe take a break later to compare notes; see if we're getting anywhere.'

The sergeant gathered his little group together and took them down to the far end of the dressing room, before suggesting that they might be more comfortable out of costume and in their own clothes. He was about to question a group that consisted of a huge goose, a human harp, a giant (fortunately now carrying his stilts, though he was still impressively tall), the bean seller and, somewhat more prosaically, the prompt.

Falconer, who started straight away with his questioning, had only one member of his group in costume. That was Jack, who was not wearing anything uncomfortable or bizarre, and could therefore remain as she was.

Jennifer Bray, who had the part of Jack, was very agitated, and seemed keen to get something off her chest. She pushed herself right in front of the inspector, eager to speak to him.

'My name's Jennifer Bray,' she began, 'and I'd like to be the first to point out that Kate Kerridge, that's the dead woman, was *not* the most popular member of the Guild. In fact, she was very unpopular with just about all of the members. I want to get that straight right from the start, so that you don't think we were all great buddies with her, and that there's some huge mystery about what happened to her, because there wasn't. In my opinion, one of us hated her just that little bit more than the others, and went far enough to do something about it.'

Falconer was shocked at this candid statement, and tried to take in the implications of it as he did his notes. This was a slow process, as he was used to Carmichael taking notes as they usually carried out interviews together.

'And did you have a particular beef with Ms Kerridge?' he asked, expecting an answer in the negative.

'Yes, I bloody well did!' she spat, unexpectedly. 'I had a very good thing going with my Bob, and Mata Hari Kerridge there just swans in and pinches him right out from under my nose. Best friends we were supposed to be. He's living with her, now – well, he was, at least – and I'm all on my tod, as they say. So, yes, I did have an axe to grind with her, sitting on my lonesome on Christmas morning opening a present from my mum and dad, and with no partner to treat me like a princess. I'll bet she got *loads* of pressies from him.

'I've no idea how she managed to nab him, either – she was a good seven or eight years older than him, although I suppose I was a bit on the chubby – well, shall we say voluptuous? – side, in comparison. Still, it's all water under the bridge, now. And, no, I didn't 'do' for her, and I know absolutely nothing about electricity. I can't even wire a plug.'

'Can you give me an account of your movements from the time you got up this morning?' asked Falconer, still scribbling furiously to keep up. 'I assume the lamp post was all right yesterday – that's if you were in here yesterday, highly unlikely, it being Christmas Day.'

'Oh, we were here all right. She made sure of that: just for "a bit of last-minute rehearsal", though it was really just an excuse for her to practise her silly dance routine in that ridiculous costume, with us as an audience. The lamp post was absolutely fine then. She was swinging round it as if she was expecting tenners to be slipped into her udder.'

This reference to a pole-dancing routine may have been in bad taste, but it made Falconer snigger, and he had to fight to suppress the sound of his appreciation of the comment. Getting a grip again on his professional side, he asked, 'Do you know of any other grudges against Ms Kerridge that existed within the Guild members involved with this production?'

'Well, I suppose I'm not telling tales out of school, as you're going to question everybody anyway. I know that Christine Turner wasn't her biggest fan. She lives directly next door to her, although it's a detached house, and Kate has these tall – and I mean absolutely *huge* – Leylandii hedges. Chrissie's started referring to her conservatory, which used to be fabulously sunny before Kate planted those rapidly-growing horrors, as the "Black Hole of Calcutta". The trees are on Kate's land, and even if Chrissie lops off the branches that stray over her side of the fence, she can't make any discernible difference to the light levels.

'Candy Taylor lives just over Kate's back fence and is fanatical about her laundry. She's got two young kids and has always got washing on the line. Unfortunately Kate gardens – oh, *gardened* – like she did everything else – fanatically – and so she had a small bonfire several times a week, just to keep up with getting rid of the weeds and cuttings – she was always very anti-compost heaps; finds them unacceptably untidy. As you can imagine, Candy's laundry suffered every time she had a fire. There wass no love lost there, when she has to take all the little clothes in and wash them all over again.'

'Now, don't think I can help you with any more, Inspector, but that should give you something to be going on with. I hope everyone else is as up-front as I have been. We don't want this hanging over us for months on end, blighting new membership and support for any other events we organise. We're going to be in the doghouse for long enough as it is, after having to cancel this pantomime after all the puff of publicity we've given it, – we were actually selling out on tickets. Maybe if you could get things cleared up quickly, we could reschedule it for January and really save our bacon. It should be easy enough to re-cast her parts, then we wouldn't have all the nausea of refunding all those charges.

'Gemma Blackwood's the prompt at the moment,' Jennifer continued, in thoughtful mood. 'She must know all the parts by now, and we should be able to replace her easily: after all, it's only sitting at the side of the stage with a copy of the script, to remind people of their lines. Yes, I think that would work admirably. All is not lost, Inspector.' Her face glowed, as she finished this little speech, and she seemed not at all perturbed that one of their number had lost her life that afternoon.

This hard-hearted, pragmatic attitude surprised Falconer, but then the toughness of some of the women he met in the course of his work never failed to astonish him.

Her account of what she had done that morning did not include an interlude when she rewired the street lamp to a lethal condition, and he let her go, feeling that she had been perfectly honest with him, and rather helpful when it came to information about some of the other members of the Guild, and their attitudes towards the deceased.

He asked for Candy Taylor to be sent to him next, having consulted the list of names he had made earlier, and hoping for confirmation of what Jennifer Bray had told him about the laundry situation and the bonfires. A mousy little woman just entering early middle-age scuttled over to the chair opposite him. 'I'm Candy Taylor,' she almost whispered at him, 'and I had nothing to do with what happened to poor Ms Kerridge,' turning her head from side to side, furtively.

'Can you tell me if there was any bad feeling between you and Ms Kerridge? Had you had any fallings-out or disagreements with her that hadn't been resolved?'

'I don't fall out with people,' she stated under her breath.

Falconer was just about to question this, when she added, 'But we didn't reach full agreement on her Daisy the Cow costume.' Mrs Taylor was wardrobe mistress for the production.

'In what way?' Falconer asked this, sitting as still as he could, so as not to disturb Candy's confidential mood.

'I disapproved strongly of the damage that was done to the back hooves of the costume when the stitching was unpicked to accommodate the wheels, and I thought the use of the trolley made the wheels a positive danger when cavorting on the stage.'

'And you had words about it?' he asked, still being very cautious not to alarm her.

'Not exactly,' she replied, and relapsed into silence again.

'What do you mean by 'not exactly'?' Falconer was completely in the dark.

Candy Taylor heaved a huge sigh and explained, 'It means I told her about my concerns, and she rubbished them and railroaded her way right through them. End of story as far as she was concerned.'

'Didn't that annoy you, somewhat?'

'There was no point in being annoyed. It was the way things always happened when Kate Kerridge was involved. My conscience was clear, however, as I'd warned her about the danger of the wheels and the possibility that there might be fines to pay to the costume hire company for the damage we'd done to the cow costume; not to mention the fact that the current arrangement may be the cause of an accident – not that I'd care. My duty, as I saw it, had been discharged.'

Selina Slater, who was in charge of props, was next, and of some interest as the lamp post was indeed a prop and under her jurisdiction.

'Of course I had a bone to pick with 'er. Who didn't?' she replied, to the inspector's direct question, and went on to explain. 'I live a few doors from 'er, and she was coming out of her drive one day as I was passing on my way home, when she swung too close to my car and gave the wing mirror an almighty knock – left it hanging on by a wire.

'Of course, there was no damage to 'ers, and she just drove straight on; never stopped and apologised, or offered to pay for repairs or give me her insurance details. I'm not all that flush at the moment as my Trev's gone and left me, so it was a real pain to have an extra unnecessary expense like that.

'It wouldn't have dented her pocket very much to have sorted it out for me, but, no, not even an *acknowledgement* of what had happened, let alone an apology and an offer of compensatory cash.'

Dani Greenaway, who was representing 'front of house', claimed to have no grudge against Kate Kerridge, but did admit to a huge 'clash of personalities'. They simply didn't get on, and this situation would never have changed, according to Miss Greenaway. They had literally hated each other's guts, and Dani was surprised that, with Kate being so unpopular, the pantomime preparation had been so successful.

Christine Turner was Falconer's last candidate for questioning before he turned to the three dancers that had fallen to his lot. If he remembered correctly, this woman had been responsible for lighting and sound. That, to his mind, meant the electricity supply and, by inference, the wiring. Was he about to speak to a killer?

Christine Turner was a decidedly tubby woman who positively wobbled towards him for her 'grilling', as she thought of it. Her buttocks hung down over each side of the small wooden chair upon which she shortly sat herself down.

'There was absolutely nothing wrong with that lamp post when I left the theatre yesterday afternoon,' she stated emphatically, before the inspector could open his mouth.

After a moment to let her calm a little, he asked, 'Could anyone have tampered with the prop after you left, or before everyone arrived today?'

'I don't see how. Yesterday was obviously a rather special day, given the date, and everyone except Kate was anxious to get back to their homes. I must have been about the last to leave. There was certainly no one left on stage when I went out, and I arrived pretty promptly this afternoon.'

Falconer felt he wasn't getting very far. He'd uncovered plenty of motives and ill-feeling, but no one who was obviously guilty, and the women weren't hurling accusations round the way he'd hoped they might. Oh well, he'd better deal with his three dancers, who had been dismissed early the day before, and arrived late and already in make-up and costume today to save changing space in the dressing room. He hoped that Carmichael's lot were being a lot less inhibited when it came to putting someone in the frame.

Carsfold Community Theatre – the other end of the stage

Carmichael, pleased to find that his notebook was still in his mackintosh pocket, sat down and prepared to question his three dancers first, having been informed that they had not spent as much time in the theatre as the other company members over the last two days, and not having their everyday clothes with them in which to change into. This accomplished without too much expense of time or trouble – or interest, if he was honest – he decided to speak to the Wainwright family first.

The harp – Wendy – the giant – Peter – and their son, the goose that laid the golden eggs – Martin – all pulled up wooden chairs gathered from various corners of backstage and gazed at him earnestly.

Wendy kicked off the proceedings. 'She wasn't very popular, you know. Although I'm truly shocked that it's ended in murder, there was obviously something about to kick off, she's fallen out with so many of us.'

'And does that include any of you?' asked the detective sergeant, pencil at the ready.

'I'm afraid it does,' she replied, drawing concerned looks from her husband and son, who had thought she would not mention what had happened. 'I have to say something,' she declared, turning to look at them. 'If I don't, somebody else will.' And with that, she turned back to Carmichael and began her tale.

'When Kate first joined the Guild, I was chairwoman and secretary, and had been happily in those positions for two years. Well, it was obvious from the very beginning that Kate had ambitions to play a leading role in our little society, and she wasted no time in trying to undermine my authority and standing.

'And it worked. She was as nice as pie but, within six months, she had the reins of the Guild in her hands; she was chief of all the Indians, and I was history.'

'Didn't you mind?' asked the sergeant, with a quizzical look.

'I was furious at first.'

'And so were both of us,' butted in her husband, Peter, 'but Wendy cooled down really quickly and seemed to be so much more carefree with less responsibility, that we had to cool down as well.'

'I hadn't realised how stressful the roles were, or how much of my time they were taking up. Within a very short time, I realised that she was welcome to be queen bee. I'd got back the life I hadn't even realised I'd lost.'

Finishing up with their movements the previous afternoon and since they had arrived at the theatre today, Carmichael thanked them for their time and co-operation, and waved Gemma and Simon Blackwood over to where he was sitting.

Prompt and the bean seller sat down before him, earnest expressions on their faces. 'How can we help you?' asked Simon, looking slightly ridiculous in his costume, as he had not bothered to take the opportunity to change.

'Well, it's been brought to my notice that Ms Kerridge wasn't the most popular member of the Guild, even if she was the one who officially headed it up.'

'You can say that again!' exclaimed Gemma. 'She was just such an infuriating and irritating person, and we should know. There're three of us Guild members live in a row, and we're on one end semi-detached with her. Her feller must be hard of hearing, and they have their music up so loud, and their TV of an evening, that we have to watch the same channel as them, or we can't hear a thing. It's enough to drive you bat-shit at times.'

'I have to listen to all my music on headphones, but it still gets through sometimes,' interjected young Martin Wainwright, who was still sitting within earshot, a little way away from his parents. He continued with a pained expression of teenaged disapproval on his face. 'I hope her feller has to move out, now she's dead. I'm sure it's him that's deaf.'

'Martin!' cried Wendy, in shock at her son's hard-hearted attitude.

There was little to be learnt from the rest of his questioning, and Carmichael soon let them go and ambled down to the other end of the stage to see if Falconer had finished his questioning.

He had, and was suffering from a severe lack of tea. 'We could do with pooling our information, and I don't want this lot to go just yet. They wouldn't be home yet if the performance had gone ahead. I'm going to see if there's the possibility of firing up an urn and making us all a cuppa, while you and I have a bit of a chinwag about what we think actually happened here earlier.'

Carsfold Community Theatre – foyer

The entrance to the theatre was now swarming with tea enthusiasts. The Guild's very own urn, which was brought to the building every time they used it, had been set up on the table from which the snacks were sold, and was dispensing a hot steaming liquid to all comers, as well as the snacks that had been its staple stock before.

Carmichael had managed to get served quite quickly – Falconer wondered if they still had any sugar left, as his sergeant took six spoonfuls per cup – leaving the inspector to join the queue of others who had not been so fleet of foot. He was aware of a buzz of conversation both before him and behind him, but was not aware of any particular subject being discussed, until he heard the voice of Gemma Blackwood, which was shrill, and unknown to him, as his sergeant had interviewed her.

'Hey, Jenny!' she called out, addressing her remarks to Jennifer Bray who was two ahead of her in the queue and, therefore, directly behind Falconer. 'Do you remember Kate announcing that she'd torn the giant's wife's dress yesterday, just as we were leaving?'

'Indeed I do! I thought it was typically thoughtless of her to leave telling anyone about it until just as we were going home, especially as it was Christmas Day, and not just any old day.'

'That's what I thought!' Gemma Blackwood's voice was thoughtful. 'But, do you know, when it was mentioned that we might have a stab at putting this thing on in January, and that I might take over her parts, I went to have a look at the costumes. And there was no new damage to the garment whatsoever. There had been some sort of tear, but it was beautifully mended. You could hardly see it at all.'

'How odd!' replied Jennifer. 'It must have been a coincidence. She may just have given it a huge tug and just thought it had torn. I can't think of any other explanation.'

'Neither can I. Still, at least it's a mending job off the agenda, eh?'

Falconer took the plastic cup of tea held out to him, looking enviously at those who had known about the urn and who had thought to bring a more substantial vessel from home, and wandered off to have a quiet think after what he had just heard, before having a quiet word with Carmichael.

He eventually found his sergeant at the sugar basin, as he had just obtained a second cup of tea. Carmichael was scraping round the bottom of the bowl at the dregs of the sweet powder. 'Only just got enough for this one,' he announced lugubriously to the inspector.

'I'm not surprised, the amount you take,' was all he got for answer. 'I've got a theory,' – these words riveted his attention on the senior officer – 'and I want to try it out on you,' and, with this statement of intention, the two men separated themselves from the crowd and went into a huddle by the doors to the auditorium.

After a few minutes, Carmichael slipped out of the theatre, a man on a mission, while Falconer made a round of those present, making a note of what time they had arrived home the previous day, after the extremely unpopular rehearsal.

Carsfold Community Theatre – backstage

The Guild members had reassembled backstage again when Carmichael returned, and Falconer called this new meeting to order, while his sergeant wandered off, seemingly aimlessly, to stand by the nearest exit.

'If I may have your attention, please, ladies and gentlemen,' he called. 'I want to describe a little scenario to you, which is what I think happened here yesterday afternoon.

'I believe that Ms Kerridge had genuinely forgotten that she had damaged her costume as giant's wife when she made her late announcement. I also believe that there was one amongst you who had every intention of staying on a little bit later than everyone else, in order to set a lethal trap for Ms Kerridge the next day.

'I suggest that this person did stay on after everyone had gone, maybe having secreted themselves in the folds of the heavy curtains to avoid detection, and that when that person emerged, they then tampered with the lighting of the metal lamp post, so that when it was switched on, it would become live and lethal.

'Their reasoning was that Ms Kerridge, in her Daisy the Cow costume, should be the next person to lay hands on it. Although this wasn't guaranteed, it was extremely likely and, in fact, proved the case, quite fortunately for this individual with such ill intent.

'This person then carried out a task that was absolutely irresistible to one of her nature. She mended the tear in the giant's wife's costume, because she was passionate about garments and their care; someone who suffered in her private life from having her children's freshly washed clothes ruined by the thoughtless and frequent bonfires in the Kerridge garden, and someone who was, without a doubt, ideal to be wardrobe mistress for this production of Jack and the Beanstalk.'

As he had been speaking, Carmichael had moved in on Candy Taylor, whose face now bore a hunted look. Moving over to make a trio, the inspector began the necessary announcement, 'Candy Taylor, I am arresting you on suspicion of the murder of Kate Kerridge ...'

'Candy Taylor, you're nicked,' intoned Carmichael, adding, out of the corner of his mouth, 'I've always wanted to say that phrase!'

Carsfold Community Theatre – the car park

Candy Taylor had been borne away in a police car by a pair of uniformed officers, and the two detectives now stood outside beside their cars, ready to head for home. 'Are you coming in for a Christmas drink like we planned, sir?' asked Carmichael.

'I rather think I'd better give it a miss. We've rather over-run on time, what with everything that's happened, then having to wait for the Uniforms,' replied Falconer, just as his sergeant's mobile rang.

Excusing himself for a couple of minutes to answer the call, he spoke just two words into the instrument – 'Will do' – and ended the call. 'That'll be fine, sir. That was Kerry,' the younger man informed him. 'Apparently she went back with Stella Christmas so that all the kids could play together, as some sort of compensation for not seeing the pantomime. I've been asked to drop in for a snifter before I go home.'

'All's well with the world, then,' replied Falconer, his pleasure of not having to run the gauntlet of Mulligan again outstripping any nose-putting-out-of-joint that his exclusion from the invitation might have conjured up. 'I'll see you back at the office then.'

'Sure thing, sir,' replied Carmichael, mentally running through the route to Fallow Fold, and Christmas Cottage, the historic family home of the doctor's family.

Falconer pulled out of the car park and turned towards Market Darley with only the tiniest twinge of sadness in his heart, at the last-minute change of plan, even though he had been party to it.

For all he knew, he might have turned out to have had real fun in Jasmine Cottage, with its eclectic mixture of residents, both human and animal. Maybe he had actually done himself out of a treat.

THE END

[1] See Christmas Mourning

Also by Andrea Frazer

The Belchester Chronicles
Strangeways To Oldham
White Christmas with a Wobbly Knee
Snowballs and Scotch Mist
Old Moorhen's Shredded Sporran
Caribbean Sunset with a Yellow Parrot

The Falconer Files - Brief Cases
Love Me to Death
A Sidecar Named Expire
Battered To Death
Toxic Gossip
Driven To It
All Hallows
Written Out
Death of a Pantomime Cow
The Complete Falconer Files Brief Cases Books 1 - 8

The Falconer Files Collections
The Falconer Files Murder Mysteries Books 1 - 3

The Falconer Files Murder Mysteries Books 4 - 6
The Falconer Files Murder Mysteries Books 7 - 9
The Falconer Files Murder Mysteries Books 10 - 14

The Falconer Files Murder Mysteries
Death of an Old Git
Choked Off
Inkier than the Sword
Pascal Passion
Murder at The Manse
Music to Die For
Strict and Peculiar
Christmas Mourning
Grave Stones
Death in High Circles
Glass House
Bells and Smells
Shadows and Sins
Nuptial Sacrifice

The Fine Line
High-Wired
Tight Rope

Standalone
Choral Mayhem
Down and Dirty in the Dordogne
The Curious Case of the Black Swan Song

A Fresh of Breath Air
God Rob Ye Merry Gentlemen
The Bookcase of Sherman Holmes

Milton Keynes UK
Ingram Content Group UK Ltd.
UKHW040641040923
428018UK00001B/134

9 798223 478461